"*NIGHT WOMAN* moves along briskly in the stylish manner fans of Price have come to expect, and it is highly recommended."

—*Library Journal*

"Price has the right ingredients for a suspense classic. . . . Don't even wait for the movie."

—*Kirkus Reviews*

"An interesting plot and Price handles it well . . . intriguing and well written."

—*Lincoln Star Journal*

"WELL WRITTEN AND ENGAGING . . . AN INTRIGUING SITUATION . . . THE BOOK PULLS ITS PUNCHES UNTIL THE VERY LAST CHAPTERS. . . . GRITTY, WRY CHARACTERIZATION, CHILLING IMAGES OF INSANITY, AND A LONG, ULTIMATELY SATISFYING TEASE . . . WILL KEEP READERS FLIPPING PAGES."

—*Publishers Weekly*

Books by Nancy Price

A Natural Death
An Accomplished Woman
Sleeping With the Enemy
Night Woman*

* Published by POCKET BOOKS

NIGHT WOMAN

NANCY PRICE

POCKET STAR BOOKS

New York   London   Toronto   Sydney   Tokyo   Singapore

This book is a work of fiction. Names, characters, places and incidents are either products of the author's imagination or are used fictitiously. Any resemblance to actual events or locales or persons, living or dead, is entirely coincidental.

 A Pocket Star Book published by
POCKET BOOKS, a division of Simon & Schuster Inc.
1230 Avenue of the Americas, New York, NY 10020

Copyright © 1992 by Nancy Price

ISBN: 0-671-74994-3

First Pocket Books paperback printing October 1993

10 9 8 7 6 5 4 3 2 1

POCKET STAR BOOKS and colophon are registered trademarks of Simon & Schuster Inc.

Cover art by Gregg Gulbronson

Printed in the U.S.A.

Gratitude is due
Catherine, David, John, Charlotte, and Derrick
as well as
Pam Bernstein, Michael James Carroll, Amy Lockard,
and Barbara Lounsberry.

— I —

MARY'S LAND

1

MARY ELIOT STOOD BESIDE RANDAL ELIOT. HOT LIGHTS were on them both, but the television cameras watched Randal, and so did crowds in evening dress, filling the Plaza Hotel with chatter.

Cameras recorded Randal Eliot speaking to the mayor of New York . . . Randal Eliot and a Nobel Prize winner . . . Randal Eliot and a movie starlet. They followed him to a head table with close-ups of the cut of his rented tuxedo and sweat beginning to glisten on his bald head.

The cameras were not interested in Randal Eliot's wife. Mary was left to enjoy the scent of her rose corsage. She finished her champagne and felt the secret slither of her best silk underwear against her skin. A famous writer on her left said nothing to Mary; he leaned across her to shake Randal's hand, and Mary was grateful for his cool shade. "So you're the writer who writes in a trance," he said to Randal.

Dinner was the constant appearance of small amounts of delicious food on large amounts of china. Mary had hardly finished her chocolate mousse when the voices of speaker after speaker bounced wall-to-wall on the public-address system, praising Randal Eliot's craft, Randal Eliot's imaginative gifts, Randal Eliot's genius.

Mary bowed her head crowned with dark braids and sipped her coffee. Cameras focused on the man to her right, then on the man to her left. She thought that she was glad no one was photographing her forty-seven-year-old face, or talking of her craft, her imaginative gifts, her genius.

Randal rose to accept the prize. They had heard of publish or perish, he said. "Twenty years ago I was a young university instructor, and I was perishing." He smiled at the great room's attentive faces. "I had a wife and four small children, and the head of my university department told me that I would lose my job unless I wrote something, published something. So . . ." Randal paused. "I committed myself for a third time to a mental hospital."

Mary watched Randal. He believed what he was saying. She had listened to this speech of his a dozen times, but never in such a place—never before an audience of New York's reviewers, publishers, editors, critics.

Randal was trembling a little, and his fingers twitched on the tablecloth. "And when I came from the mental hospital knowing I would lose my job, knowing no college or university would hire me, thinking I had never written anything . . ." Randal paused, and there was no sound but New York traffic on the streets below. "My wife told me that I had finished my first novel, *In the Quarters,* before I entered the hospital."

Randal spread his hands above the linen tablecloth as if a manuscript lay there. "I couldn't remember dictating a word to her, yet there it was: the book I'd had in my head. And my subsequent novels have all appeared this way." Randal smiled again. "Electroshock treatments. I recommend them as an effective cure for writer's block."

The audience chuckled.

"But," Randal said, his voice dropping into mock seriousness, "I mustn't forget to thank the Muse, that fickle woman who visits writers by night, by luck, in secret. One must not offend the Muse."

The audience clapped for Randal Eliot, and so did Mary. "Writer of the seventies," another speaker said. "The voice of his generation. The next winner of the Pulitzer Prize."

Mary stared at hundreds of clapping hands as if she didn't see or hear them. *"Pulitzer Prize?"* she whispered to Randal.

"Heard about it last month. There's a chance. But I only have four books out," Randal murmured, smiling and nodding at the waves of applause.

Suddenly Mary heard an amplified voice braying: "And now I would like to introduce Mary Eliot, Randal Eliot's wife—the woman behind the great writer we honor tonight!"

Mary stood up. The Pulitzer. She hardly saw hundreds of faces above white linen, black tuxedos, brilliant evening dresses. Television cameras were recording her trembling hands and the fury in her eyes.

"Let us applaud the wife who works at the side of Randal Eliot, taking down each word of his magnificent novels before they are lost!"

Mary Eliot bowed to the hundreds of dutifully clapping hands. Her lips were moving. Was she saying, "Thank you, thank you"? No one watched her closely enough to tell.

The cameras turned back to Randal Eliot. Mary Eliot sat down, still shaking.

Ten years later, a *New York Times* staff writer found a film clip of that evening, read Mary's lips, and wrote a famous article on what "Mary Eliot" said at the Plaza on August 5, 1977.

Randal was brilliant with the brilliance of the Plaza evening. The after-dinner crowd surrounded him with bursts of laughter and animated voices. Randal Eliot, writer of the seventies, was a dazzling talker on such public occasions—he had a genius for that.

Mary watched him finish his second drink, then found a chance to whisper to him that they had a plane to catch early in the morning.

Randal was tired; he willingly trailed his charm through

the crowd and out the door. He was silent in the elevator and silent in their room while they hung up their evening clothes, yawning.

Mary said nothing about the dinner, or the speech, or a Pulitzer. She crawled into her twin bed and shut her eyes, grateful for quiet that was as tranquil as a lake of still water.

Randal lay down, but in a few minutes he was on his feet again. Mary watched him between half-shut eyelids; she had learned not to sleep when he was awake.

New York's all-night glow lit the ceiling and shone on Randal's bald head as he walked to one wall, turned, turned again.

Pretending to sleep, Mary stayed awake with the memory of the dinner at the Plaza: Randal as the focus of hundreds of clapping hands, hot lights, television cameras, and herself one chair away from the center of attention . . . one step away from a Pulitzer Prize.

Mary, half asleep, dreamed herself cold and calm, her steady gaze moving from face to face across the crowded Plaza room. "You have heard Randal Eliot say he cannot remember writing four novels. The reason he cannot remember is that the four novels are mine. I wrote every word of them: Mary Quinn, the next winner of the Pulitzer Prize, the writer of the seventies, the voice of her generation."

Mary woke from her half doze: Randal had stopped his barefoot pacing to light his pipe. The faint chink and flare of his lighter brought Mary back from her dream of the Plaza crowd's astonished faces: they would have hung before her, a wall of shock, while television cameras homed in on her like one-eyed sharks.

And then there would have been the laughter, the embarrassment, the scramble to remove unfortunate Mary Quinn Eliot from public view.

But she had said nothing that anyone had heard. Mary gripped her bed sheet with cold, wet hands. Crowds and television cameras had left the Plaza long ago. Randal's pipe smoke hung above her bed.

Suddenly Randal grabbed Mary and shook her. "Wake

up!" He let her go, turned on a lamp, and rummaged in a desk for a handful of hotel stationery and a pen.

Mary sat on the edge of her bed, aching for sleep. "Take this down!" Randal cried, thrusting the wad of papers and pen at her. "An idea for another book!"

Mary began to record Randal's neatly wound-up plot, and then the characters to fit it. Randal insisted that she read "the theme" back to him over and over again while he changed a word here or there.

Half asleep, covering page after page with her neat writing, Mary laughed to herself to keep the bitterness away. Plot? Characters? Theme? Randal wanted them down on paper as if they would somehow become a novel, as if a book could be born that way. Poor Randal; he had never written a book.

Mary was cold. She pulled her blanket around her and kept on writing. Somewhere on the pages that littered her bed she would find what she could use . . . something that would make Randal think the work was his.

Randal paced the room in silence now. Mary waited awhile, then turned off the light and lay down. Randal padded back and forth, back and forth.

When dawn came, he sat on his bed, shoulders hunched, pipe out.

Mary could not kiss him, hold him, comfort him. He did not want to be touched.

Randal lay down. His breathing slowed and deepened. Mary closed her eyes and slept.

2

"Paris! London! Rome!" Randal shoved himself back in his old plastic-covered recliner and grinned at Mary, who was washing his study window. "We're all going—the five of us! September until Christmas!"

Mary stopped wiping the glass dry. "What?"

"I've planned it."

"You aren't going to teach?" Mary stared at him.

"I asked for unpaid leave for the fall semester, so no classes for me until January. We're going!"

Mary turned back to the window. The old Nebraska house had expanses of plate glass, and this one reflected Randal's sunlit desk, multicolored editions of his novels above a worn rug, and Mary, squinting against the light. "If you aren't getting a salary, what will we live on?"

"You haven't seen the letter," Randal said. He was still smiling.

"What letter?"

Randal settled deeper in his battered chair. "My *Net Worth*'s going into paperback."

"Paperback?" Mary's voice sounded stupid in her ears, repeating after him.

"Take a look." Randal held out a piece of paper. Mary took it: a check for thousands of dollars, made out to Randal Eliot.

Mary looked down into Randal's green-gray, glittering eyes. They shifted from her to the row of books on his study shelf—books with his name on them. The check was made out to him. "When did this come?" she said, giving it back.

Randal laughed. "The day we flew from New York. But I've known for a couple of months."

Mary sat on the arm of his chair, her face reddening under its crown of silver-streaked braids. She looked at the old Nebraska house around her without seeing it. Then she gave a small, breathless laugh and pressed her hands to her cheeks.

"Thousands of dollars," Randal said to her. "Wouldn't you like to get your hands on it?"

Mary didn't seem to hear him. "Paperback!" she said. "Think of the people who'll read the book now!"

"Success! Not just good reviews of my novels—success!" Randal cried. Mary opened her eyes to look at the check again . . . put her hand out to touch it . . .

Randal jerked it out of her reach. "We'll take the children and go!"

"'The children'? We're all in our *twenties* now!" Beth came from the kitchen. She was flushed with summer heat that made her bright brown eyes brighter still. "Go where?"

He waved the check at her. "My *Net Worth*'s going into paperback! Money-money-money! We'll all travel overseas —why not? Paris! London! Rome! Athens!"

Beth didn't look at her mother; she didn't need to. She said she'd never seen a check for that much. "It's *wonderful—*"

"What's wonderful?" Jay came in and Don followed: two blond-haired, shirtless young men in baggy jeans, their pockets sagging with wrenches, clasp knives, chisels.

"Look at this," Beth said.

Mary saw Jay's quick, careful look that had been in Beth's eyes, too. "Something's happened?"

"Your unrewarded father!" Randal cried. "He's finally getting *money* for his books—my *Net Worth*'s going into paperback. What does this look like?" He held the check out to Jay and Don.

"Money," Don said.

"No, stupid!" Randal yelled. "It's London! Paris! Rome! Athens! For all of us! The whole fall semester over there! We live in this old dump, but by God, we can travel!"

They all began to talk at once, except for Mary.

Mary went into the kitchen and began peeling potatoes for supper; the children's triumphant, proud voices came to her from the study.

"Lots of excitement here," Don said in a few minutes, coming to take the knife from Mary to finish the potatoes. He'd grown a thick beard since May. Now the handsome boy was a man whose straight nose and green eyes Mary still recognized most of the time.

Mary watched the thin strips of peel fall.

"Dad's got all that money," Don whispered.

"He's high," Mary mouthed at him.

Beth came in. "Are we going?" she whispered to Mary.

Mary shrugged. When Jay came in, he said, "How about it?" in a low voice.

"We don't know," Beth whispered.

Mary sighed and went to help Beth sear pork chops at the stove. Jay said, "How about brussels sprouts?" and started to pick them over at the sink.

Suddenly Randal stood at the kitchen door. "We're going overseas, stupid ass!" he shouted at Mary. "Either that, or I go by myself—or the kids will be happy enough to go with me. You can stay home."

"It's not that I don't want to go." Mary didn't look at Randal's green eyes sparkling with anger.

"It's thanks to me we've got the money!" Randal yelled. "You think I won't take this chance to work in libraries over there? The rest of you do what you want—I'm going!"

The three of them heard Randal slam the screen door. He

would bicycle a mile or two; he bicycled every day he could, and went bowling, but he was growing fatter with each year.

"What'll we do?" Beth asked.

"I'll call Dr. Parker while Randal's gone." Mary closed the kitchen door and stood by the telephone a moment, feeling her home around her: family voices, family clutter, the fragrance of supper cooking.

She had to wait before Dr. Parker came on the line. "I'm sorry to bother you," she told him, "but I'm worried about Randal. He'll be talking to you tomorrow—he's determined to go overseas from September first until almost Christmas, and he'll fly over by himself if the rest of us won't go with him, he says."

Dr. Parker's reserved voice was more reserved than ever at the length of the telephone lines. "Can you get away?"

"I could. And the children might take time off—"

"I think you ought to consider it," Dr. Parker said.

"Take him thousands of miles away?" Mary said.

"The trip would do him good," Dr. Parker said in his cool, dispassionate voice.

"But what if it upsets him, going back there? Can he stand being in a mental ward a *seventh* time? He might lose his job—"

"Randal's pretty secure at the university, I imagine," Dr. Parker said. "With his reputation. I'd suggest you let him do what he wants. I'll give you the name of a good doctor in England."

"But what if Randal—"

"You can't be your husband's psychiatrist," Dr. Parker said crisply.

Mary bit her lip. "Oh, can't I?" she cried. "Then who will? Are *you* going overseas with him to watch him and get him to the hospital in a foreign country?"

"Sometimes chances have to be taken." Dr. Parker's calm voice was more distant than ever.

When he said good-bye, Mary put down the telephone, her hands shaking. Supper simmered on the stove. The children were waiting in her small study upstairs where a fan stirred papers on the desk.

"Are we going?" Jay said when Mary came in. He ran a hand through his curled-tight blond hair; he was tall and skinny and strong.

"Randal says so. It's his money," Mary said. "But what about graduate-school tuition for you and Beth, and capital for Don's business?"

"We'd see London and Italy and Greece!" Beth said.

"But I want to start the new store . . ." Don said. "And Carla—I'd have to go without her . . ."

"Love, love, love," Beth teased Don.

"Go before marriage gets you!" Jay said to Don.

"Carla could house-sit," Don said. "If Mike hadn't got that grant, maybe he could have gone with us."

Mary leaned back in her desk chair, thinking of Michael, the missing child, the eldest. "Mike's the happy anthropologist with the chance of a lifetime—he wouldn't want to trade three years in Africa for this."

"You talked to the doctor?" Beth said.

"Just now. He doesn't think there's any danger," Mary said. "Randal sees him tomorrow."

"If Dad got out of that chair of his—out of his rut—maybe it would help," Jay said. "He's getting fatter than ever, and he's not interested in anything."

"He doesn't even go out in the garden. He used to wander around and ask what Jay and I were planting," Beth said.

"He never could remember plant names," Jay said.

"He's writing," Mary said.

"Scribbling on the backs of used envelopes," Jay said.

The children glanced at each other. Mary went downstairs to finish making supper. After a while she heard Randal return.

"Come and eat!" Mary called to Randal in his study. She was sitting at the table with the children when Randal flung open his door.

"There's five dollars missing from my billfold!" he shouted.

Blank looks settled on the faces around the table.

"You said I could take it to buy another paintbrush," Don said.

"And you haven't even *started* painting the porch floor!" Randal's green eyes glittered.

Nobody answered. They waited quietly. "I don't want any supper—throw it out," Randal said, and went back into his study, slamming the door.

Don and Jay ate their own suppers, and Randal's, then went down to the basement with a thump of big feet. Mary was clearing the table when Randal opened his study door and advanced on her. "You've raised your children to break promises! Don promised to do the painting. Is he doing it? No!" He was so close that Mary could smell the wine. Spit hit her face: he was drunk enough to slur his words. "Smartass! Bitch who thinks she's so smart! Piece of shit!" He slammed the study door behind him.

Mary went to the kitchen. Beth was shaking food scraps from the sink drain into a trash sack; she looked at Mary and rolled her eyes at the ceiling.

Mary laughed and let anger go. She went through the garage's useful clutter to sit on the patio bench and stretch her tired legs.

High above her the old Nebraska house stood against stars: high gables, lighted windows. Don and Jay were working on Jay's motorcycle; their hammering joined insect sounds in the summer night. Children shouted in the park across the street.

There was a rustle in the side-porch grapevine: a sparrow had her nest there, and was settling for the night. Then the kitchen's screen door slammed deep in the garage, and Beth's white shirt glimmered as she came toward Mary.

"What've you got?" Mary said.

"Hot cat," Beth said, putting the old tom Waldo down in the grass. She joined Mary, and they sat for a while in the faint radiance of the park light.

"I love it here in the dark," Beth said, scooping up Waldo. She sighed. "What about going overseas?"

Mary's eyes were on Randal in his study window. His bald head shone in the lamplight. "I think about graduate-school expenses for you and Jay, and money for Don's new shop . . . and whether Randal will keep well over there."

"If only Mike were going too . . ." Beth sighed. "He was so far away when he was only teaching at Yale—now we can't even *phone* him. Letters take *weeks.*"

"He won't know we've gone, not for a long time."

"A remote village in the middle of all that Africa—I find it on the map and try to believe Mike's there, but I can't. I write and write and don't even know if he's getting the letters."

The two sat quietly in the dark, thinking of Michael.

Finally Mary said, "It scares me to think of Randal going back where we had a perfect honeymoon—where we were both such different people."

"Maybe he'll remember and be happy," Beth said. "He'll think he's come *so far* since the honeymoon—all his novels—he's famous! The prizes, and now the paperback!"

"Yes." Mary's voice sounded dry and flat. "He has all that."

When Beth and Mary went into the house, it still smelled like supper. They went upstairs to bed, taking the narrow flight of stairs in the dim light from Randal's study.

Mary found Don almost asleep. "G'night," she said, patting his warm, sheet-wrapped shape on the bed. He grunted, and she picked her way back to his door through stacks of magazines and shop floor plans and photographs. Once he'd shared the room with his big brother, but Michael's bed was gone now, and Don had let Jay build the big light tables for orchids along his walls.

Beth sat next door in her lamp's hot circle of light, typing a card catalog of her dearest possessions: the books she owned. Beside her typewriter was a stack of them she had read that summer: the assigned readings for her graduate studies in the fall.

When Mary went into Jay's room, it vibrated with the big floor fan. "G'night," he said, seeing her in his doorway.

Mary said good night and left Jay in his useful zoologist's clutter of forceps, glassine envelopes, bottles, labels, insect carcasses, pressed flowers, seed packets, knives from her kitchen, sticky spoons.

The big fans hummed. Mary stripped in the bathroom and stood under the shower's cascade of cool water, then toweled herself dry, put on a nightgown, and stepped into the hall.

She caught a spoiled-raisin smell of wine and sweat: Randal must be in bed already. Every room was dark now, inhabited by the steady pulsing of fans through open bedroom doors—the sound of years when Randal had waited for her in their bed, impatient, his hands on her bare skin before she slid into his arms, laughing, kissing. Their bedroom door had no lock, so they'd wedged a table in front of it to keep the children out . . .

Mary crept downstairs. The broad steps squeaked in certain places and creaked in others, but no one would hear her through the thick hum of the fans. She took the narrow, shallow last steps, her feet sidewise, her hands sure on the woodwork and balustrade.

Moonlight threw slanting carpets through the big rooms downstairs, and doors stood open to rustling trees and the singing of night insects. A light in the park across the street cast shadows of swings like a spider's legs.

A ray of moonlight quivering with shadows of maple leaves lanced Randal's study. Randal was not in his chair; Mary could take the novels with his name on them from his study shelf and hold their solid, heavy shapes in her hands.

On a lower shelf were scrapbooks. Now and then Randal said, "Here—paste these in the scrapbooks," and handed Mary a sheaf of clippings. Only then did she discover that her books had won prizes . . . had been attacked, analyzed, praised.

Now Randal's face smiled at her from a scrapbook page. Mary could read it by the bright moonlight: "More than any contemporary writer, Randal Eliot captures what a twentieth-century man may feel but does not say. Many modern novelists recognize Eliot's genius. None can approach it."

Mary put the scrapbook back on the moonlit shelf.

The check for thousands of dollars lay on Randal's desk. *"Wouldn't you like to get your hands on it?"*

Mary picked up the check. Her own check. Now every word she had written in her last book was bringing in a dollar—every "the." Every "a."

She put the check down, listening for any sound in the house, and heard nothing but insects, rustling leaves, a car passing.

Mary climbed on a chair beside a wall of kitchen cupboards. No one ever opened the top door in the corner: its handle was missing. She hooked a fingernail under its edge and brought a notebook down.

"I'm just writing in my journal," she'd say if anyone caught her at work.

In a few minutes, hunched under a living-room lamp, she was lost in her almost-finished book. The last chapters of Randal Eliot's next novel grew beneath her faintly scratching pen.

Yellow leaves blew across the lawns of town. Children went back to school in hot morning sun. Mary helped pack suitcases, found a neighbor to feed Waldo the cat, stopped newspaper deliveries, and brought everyday life to a halt before five airplane tickets that lay on Randal's desk.

"I'm scared," she told Nora Gilden. She had gone for lunch at Nora's house every month for years; they chattered over their salads and wine like the two old friends they were. Nora had been a poor North Carolina girl "who married for love and got hell," she always said. So she divorced her "hell" and married money. Now Nora was a rich widow with a redbrick house full of antiques. She taught at the university "for fun."

"Afraid of Randal getting sick over there?" Nora said.

"It's a shame Michael's in Africa—but your other three children are just as much help, so steady . . ."

"Randal swore he'd go alone if we didn't go with him." Mary paused. Then she cried, "If he'd just tell me what's happening! Awards . . . letters from famous people . . . this talk about a Pulitzer Prize . . . his asking *last June* for an unpaid leave—he never tells me!"

Nora shrugged. "He's a celebrity." They looked at each other, then Mary smiled at Nora, whose body was round and whose mind was rounder; it was an immense circular file of vital statistics about more people than Mary had heard of—a file that Mary could open with a single question.

"When Randal's father sent us over there on our honeymoon, we were so happy." Suddenly Mary's eyes filled with tears.

Randal's father sat in the kitchen of his sister's house on the edge of town. He looked at Mary and Beth as if they were strangers.

"The five of us leave tomorrow for Europe," Mary said to D.L. The kitchen was cool. Aunt Viola's kitchen windows showed the hot world beyond.

"She's Mary, your daughter-in-law," Viola said in her quavery voice, bending over D.L. the way she always did, her hands brushing his shirt or smoothing the few hairs on his head as if she could bring back his memory that way. "You remember her."

"And I'm your granddaughter," Beth said.

D.L. didn't answer. He wore a gravy spot like a brown heart on the lapel of his sport jacket. Mary and Beth sat on either side of him, but his watery ninety-year-old eyes avoided them and wandered around the kitchen.

"Your son, Randal," Mary said. "My husband. The doctor says it might do Randal good to go abroad—that's why we're all going. He's your son, remember? Remember Randal? Remember you gave Randal and me our wonderful honeymoon in Europe?"

Beth said, "Dad's been sick so many times! We've *got* to get him out of his rut. And he's the one who wants us all to go overseas."

D.L.'s eyes in their wrinkled sockets watched the lights of a school across Aunt Viola's garden. "Legislature's working late," D.L. said. He thought he was living across from the Capitol building.

"Randal couldn't come to see you—he had so many things to do before we leave," Mary lied, knowing D.L. had forgotten that Randal never visited him, would not go, had not seen his father for years.

D.L.'s eyes made their slow way from the school's lighted windows to his hand on the table.

Mary said, "Aunt Viola takes such good care of you—we won't worry a bit. She knows where to reach us if you should want us." She smiled at Viola, who smiled tremulously back.

"We wish you could come, too, Grandpa," Beth said.

"We'll have to be leaving now, because you're going to have supper, but we'll come again when our trip is over." Mary kissed the top of D.L.'s bald head.

"Good-bye, Grandpa," Beth said.

D.L.'s eyes were on the lights of the school again. "The legislature's working late," he said.

3

THE CHARTERED DC-8 ROSE FROM THE RUNWAY, BANKED over Chicago, and turned east.

"All five of us over that ocean—it scares me," Mary whispered to Randal.

Randal didn't answer; he sat beside Mary, his eyes closed. Mary hardly breathed until clouds wiped out the earth below them, and stewardesses offered them commonplaces for comfort: magazines, newspapers, a cold drink.

"You pull the little tables down," Beth said, unhooking the one in front of Randal.

"Push this button for light," Jay said.

"And this one's for air," Don said. "Blasts of it."

At sunset, the sky turned into something like Dante's hell: caverns and landscapes of cloud stretching away forever, floored with cobblestones of mist. That vastness darkened and darkened like hope abandoned, while the sun died in a scarlet hole, spouting blood. They watched the inferno sink for an hour into blackness; it turned to a red streak, and went out.

Now the plane was a shell filled with lighted spaces where people read or slept or had drinks by blind portholes. The five Eliots flew through the night eating dinner from little plastic platters over an invisible ocean. They walked the aisles, read, talked: a family with no possessions but their coats and five shoulder bags at their feet. When Mary's eyes met the children's, she saw they were all too bewitched to sleep in this adventure that droned like a monster hive of bees, hour after hour. Randal slept.

Then the sun dawned. "What's morning coming in the middle of the night for?" Beth said in a cross, sleepy voice. Her head had fallen on Mary's shoulder; her cheek was creased and pink. Sunlight streamed over lumps of slumbering people, row after row.

Down the plane sank to the brown crust of Iceland. "It looks like a burned cookie," Jay said. The five Eliots, blinking and yawning, wandered the aisles of the airport's duty-free store, then climbed into their seats again.

"Where did the night go?" Don said when they stood in the Luxembourg airport at last, looking through windows at the sunny afternoon. It was the first foreign country Beth, Jay, and Don had seen, and they stared.

"They look just like Americans," Beth said, waiting at customs.

"They don't sound like us," Jay said.

Randal followed the four of them to get money at the airport bank. "Money?" Don said, looking at pieces of fancy paper. Neatly lettered signs on the bus they caught made no sense.

Now, walking to their hotel, they began to believe the thousands of miles they had come. "Look! Did you see that?" they cried. "What's that for?" "What does this say?" Randal's heavy-soled shoes seemed too big for him; he shuffled slightly as he tried to keep up. How stooped and fat he was, Mary thought, looking back at him along Luxembourg streets.

The hotel rooms were cool and clean. They put down their five shoulder bags. "Groceries for supper and for our train ride to Paris!" Beth cried.

"Come on!" Don said. "Let's the three of us go find some."

Off they went, and Mary, washing her face, was thankful for the energy in three young bodies: it was like traveling on a cushion of air. Randal sat by a window in their room and filled his pipe.

Mary pulled window curtains aside. She was used to talking to herself when someone called "Randal" was there. "Tomorrow we go to Paris. You and I haven't seen Paris together since our honeymoon. Remember how it rained?"

Randal said nothing. "Remember?" Mary said, as if he were the Randal who would remember, who would turn to her and smile and say: *Remember the rain outside the little pâtisserie where we had cakes? Remember we made love most of the night in Paris?*

"This hotel's going to cost us sixty dollars for one night," Randal said. "We can't afford that. This whole trip is going to cost twice as much as I thought. We'll have to go home in November, if we last that long. And how will the children find the hotel again? Did you ever think about that?"

"The kids can remember the hotel's name, and they've got a good sense of direction—not like me. Don took us all over Denver, remember?" Talking to herself again, Mary said, "Look at these beds—they haven't changed since we were here last. You've got two choices: sleep under just the sheet and freeze, or sleep under this short feather-bed kind of thing and cook. If it's the feathers, you've got two more choices: whether to let your shoulders turn to ice, or your feet."

"This was your idea," Randal said. "The whole thing was your idea. You're out of your mind. Sixty dollars for one night, and that doesn't cover any food but breakfast."

There had been a baby crying, Mary remembered. When she'd been with Randal their last night in Europe, a baby cried all night somewhere. She pulled the curtains aside again. The window was open. All she could hear was traffic, and children calling to each other as they played under the still-green trees.

Don and Jay carried the picnic lunch when they boarded the train for Paris. How clever the Eliots thought they were to find seats on the crowded train. How were they to know that they were in a first-class compartment? Randal had to pay the conductor thirty dollars' worth of francs.

"At least we get to eat our picnic sitting down," Beth said. "The second-class coaches are full of people standing up." Randal scowled out the dirty train window.

Paris! Mary and Don studied their metro map. "How do you know which color of line to take?" Beth said, looking over their shoulders.

"The end of the line is the name of it," Don said. "Come on." Randal followed them up and down stairs and on subway cars to the Louvre stop.

Traffic hooted and roared along the rue de Rivoli, and there was the Hotel St. Ignace and rooms Mary had booked. "Remember when our ceiling leaked on our bed here, and we couldn't make the man at the desk understand? So we brought him upstairs and he took one look and yelled, *'Mon dieu!' "* Mary asked Randal.

The children laughed as they pushed the glass doors open and went to the desk, but Mary had gone on to remember Randal making love to her in that hotel almost thirty years before. Curtains had billowed at their balcony windows. In the morning a maid had burst through the door with a breakfast tray to find them still asleep in each other's arms.

This time the children's room was huge and airy, curtains stirring before the view over Paris. Randal and Mary's room had no windows at all: it was dark as a closet, with a closet-sized bath.

"Ugh!" Mary said. "It's nothing but a dark hole!" Then she saw double doors on one wall. She opened them. A wrought-iron railing barred away a small air well with a few plants in it. Pearly radiance from a sky she couldn't see fell on pillows and quilts, their shoulder bags, and Randal's bald head.

When they went into the streets, the last sunlight touched Paris like an impressionist's brush, gilding a spray of leaves, a passing child's hair, a stone tower.

"Paris!" Mary cried when they entered the Tuileries gardens.

Randal stopped with the Louvre to his left, the Arc de Triomphe to his right. "The children will get lost. I told them to stay with us," he said. Then Don and Jay and Beth caught up, and the family stood together in their uniforms of dark pants and jackets: a sober spot at the heart of long green and white vistas from the Louvre through the gardens, across the Place de la Concorde, up the avenue des Champs-Elysées to the far-off, misty Arc de Triomphe.

"What I wanted for us!" Mary cried. "The Voie Triomphale." No one was near. It might have belonged to them. Soft wind blew Beth's long, light hair against the Triumphal Way.

They walked along the Seine to Notre Dame. "You thought you'd never see Notre Dame again," Don said to Mary.

"What are you going to do about our meals tomorrow?" Randal said. "We can't afford—"

"We'll go out after breakfast and get picnic stuff—there are dozens of shops around our hotel," Don said.

"I brought instant coffee and sugar and creamer, and hot chocolate mix," Mary said.

Light was blue now on the Seine, the strolling people, the cathedral's face.

Randal said he was tired. When they walked back to the hotel, he went to bed while Beth and Don and Jay came with their towels to use the shower, sitting on Mary's bed to wait their turn. The excitement of newness and strangeness shone in their eyes.

When they were gone, Mary took her shower, and dried herself. Soft sounds of chinking china and silver came across the air shaft to their open window.

The Hotel St. Ignace was old and had descended in the world, Mary thought, crawling into bed. Perhaps the room she'd shared with Randal had been divided into two or three by now. As she drifted into sleep, she saw the long-ago room that had been scattered with swiftly discarded clothes . . .

"Dad didn't have any wine today," the children whispered each night.

Randal followed them to the sound-and-light show at Notre Dame. They went to the Louvre, the botanical gardens, a Renaissance concert at Sainte-Chapelle, a boat trip on the Seine, the Jeu de Paume. "Dad isn't an alcoholic," Jay said at the Cluny. "He hasn't had a drink in nine days."

And they went to Chartres, of course, on a cloudy morning. There was Chartres' rose-window face around a bend in a road. "Oh, look! Look!" Mary cried. Great stone figures on the facade watched them come.

When they stepped into the cathedral's cave, rose windows hovered overhead, shifting their fires at each step Mary took.

The cathedral hushed their voices. "Where's our Christmas window—*La Belle Verrière?*" Beth whispered. They stepped softly, looking for the madonna and child Mary had copied in transparent paints on plastic. Each Christmas she taped it to a side window of their front door.

"There it is!" Jay said. "Just the way you copied it! Way up there! Look!"

They stood in a scatter of light on the stone floor, craning their necks, their faces solemn. Only the heads of the mother and child were familiar to them. Now they stood far below the madonna's great body that was the center of topaz and emerald, sapphire and ruby, glowing deeper than any jewel.

"Our window," Beth said. And the twelfth-century faces of mother and child, crowned and austere, looked down with familiar, piercing eyes at the Eliots and were, indeed, theirs. Mary looked back as she walked away, and saw the children, too, turning to see that immense fire of colors once more.

When they came from the dimness at last, five tired people blinked at each other and whispered that they were hungry. There were tables in a small garden; they sat under gray skies to eat their picnic lunch, and Jay pried off the tops of their pop bottles on the edge of a trash bin.

Now the rain began. In the women's toilet across the road Mary washed her hands under a faucet in a wall, and rain fell on her.

They went down to the dark, cold cathedral crypt, where a man with a German accent wailed through the guide's French and would not be comforted. "The kneeling angels!" he cried. "Where are the kneeling angels!"

The guide brought a book. The man said, "Yes—yes, there they are, see, see?" he asked anyone, everyone, holding the book out as if it were a small corpse. "That's the way they were! To wipe them out, the beautiful angels, because the paintings beneath are *older,* that is all! The older ones aren't beautiful! The older ones aren't angels!" He sat with the book on his lap. The guide's precise French pattered on his bowed head.

Cold rain blotted their last view of Notre Dame. They took refuge in the warm station buffet, glad to be warm, and counted their blessings as they drank hot chocolate. Randal counted his change, shaking his head.

Too much, Randal said. It was all costing too much.

Their last night in Paris was a warm, caressing evening. They walked down the avenue des Champs-Elysées to the Arc de Triomphe. Randal stayed five or ten feet behind them, shuffling his heavy shoes. It was Jay and Don who walked beside Mary, two blond young men where there had been one beside her twenty-nine years before.

Beth looked back and smiled at her mother. Neon colors played over them. Tomorrow they would be in London. Far ahead floodlights spotlit the Arc de Triomphe's huge door open to nothing but night.

The unknown soldier was buried in the ground; they soon saw that. His superiors were above him: walls of officers' names. The top of the Arc was engraved with famous battles.

Mary put her arm around Beth, looking at stars through the triumphal arch. "When are we ever going to see a woman's Arch of Triumph?" Beth said. "Maybe a huge circle or egg shape with women's names, and fine things they did that weren't killing, and the names of their famous children?"

They walked away from the triumphal arch in the glitter of a great city: two handsome young men, a beautiful young girl, and Mary. Mary looked back to the Arc de Triomphe, aware that someone was shuffling behind the four of them: a man she hardly recognized, a dogged shape against the brilliance of Paris.

4

THE MONTROY PRIVATE HOTEL IN LONDON WAS JUST AS
Mary remembered it: hot showers, and breakfasts of a
thimbleful of canned orange juice, fried eggs, fried tomatoes, corn flakes, and cold toast in racks.

"Unmelted butter on cold toast!" Beth said the first
morning. "They don't do it on purpose, do they?"

"Dirty clothes, everybody," Don said when they were
back in their rooms. "I'll make a trip to the Laundromat."
He came home at suppertime with clean clothes and said,
"I've been thinking—maybe we should go to Scotland
before we rent a flat."

"We wouldn't be paying for hotels in Scotland and rent in
London at the same time," Beth said.

"We can go to Edinburgh from London on the train—
there's an express," Mary said. She looked at Randal. "Shall
we?"

"We're Scottish," Jay said. "We ought to go."

"Before it gets any colder," Don said.

"Should we?" Mary asked Randal. He wouldn't answer.
He smoked his pipe and watched them pack the five
shoulder bags.

They were off the next morning.

Mary watched Randal on the fast train to Scotland. He looked out the window with a blank gaze, showing no more interest in scenery or his fellow passengers than the window shade jiggling above his head.

Randal followed them to the tourist bureau in Edinburgh, and waited while they tried to find the cheapest bed-and-breakfast.

Their bus traveled a street that changed its name eight times. Finally it led them to what they wanted: a bed for the night.

"What a barn!" Beth said when the bed-and-breakfast landlady left. There were six beds in what had once been a huge front parlor. In one corner was a sink, in the other a shower. Walls, carpet, and curtains vibrated with immense and clashing patterns of purple, red, and green, so that the ceiling seemed plain—it had only an intricate plaster design and a chandelier icy with prisms.

They all had showers, then five tired people lay in darkness and talked. "When we're together like this, it reminds me of our camping trips with all of us in one tent," Beth said, her voice surrounded by the immensity of the room.

"No skunks—or Mom and Dad's camper breaking down and dumping them in the dirt at two A.M.," Jay said.

Mary, half asleep, saw Randal pitching tents, bringing water, helping to blow up sleeping bags. He had loved, above anything, to build a fire. But shock treatments and drugs, year after year, had brought vacations to an end . . . Mary could not even remember which camping trip had been the last.

Beth laughed. "Remember all of us trying to sleep in one car in the rain because our tents were blowing away?"

Jay sounded sleepy. "Ditching the tents in snow at the Tetons. In July."

"Randal—remember how hard we worked getting those tents up when the kids were too small to help?" Mary said.

There was no answer.

Mary pulled her blanket up to her chin, snug. The five of them were together, safe in the dark. One by one they fell asleep in Scotland.

The weather turned cold. Winter was coming.

"Randal?" Sometimes Mary said his name, wanting him to enjoy this, notice that. Was it because someone with his name had been with her in Edinburgh once and made love and laughed and planned, and even caught cold with her, so that their hospitable Scottish landlady had made them hot soup and oatmeal?

"Look at these aerial photographs!" she said in a dusty Edinburgh museum, pulling the man called Randal by the arm. He came to see patterns of Roman forts hidden beneath English farm fields. "No one guessed the forts had ever been there—you couldn't see anything at all from the ground," Mary said, watching Randal's bleak face, his opaque eyes. He was a "famous writer." Could he feel the mystery of ground packed so hard by Roman soldiers that, eighteen centuries later, grass still grew less green where they had walked?

Randal wandered off. Mary stood alone again looking at scars that had never really healed. The shadow of Rome lay like a ghost under English grass.

Certainly Randal would want to see Stratford-on-Avon again, and a Shakespeare play, they said to each other. But were they losing heart? Mary thought they were.

They took a bus to Stratford.

"Mom?" Jay whispered on the bus, "have you heard what's going on?"

Mary stopped talking to Beth and listened.

"No! No!" a passenger said to the bus driver, "you turn that way . . . around the corner . . . that's right!"

The bus turned around, went that way and around the corner.

"Now you take the lane there, and then the main road to the left," somebody else said.

"The bus driver doesn't know where he's going," Beth whispered.

Mary looked at lovely British countryside rolling past. Signs on the bus seemed to be calm, logical: First Aid Kit. Used Tickets Here. Please Keep the Platform Clear Do Not Distract the Driver's Attention Whilst Vehicle Is in Motion. But a reasonable world seemed suddenly like a necklace of beads from which the string had been pulled. "Left!" a passenger called. "Go left just here!"

Mile by mile they worked their way past green fields in sunset light. Bus riders told the driver where to stop, and then got off the bus in old, stony villages.

"It was my first trip," said the driver unnecessarily as he watched his last passengers climb out at Stratford. Randal came down the bus steps one at a time, like an old man.

Randal saw Stratford. He paid seven pounds so that the five of them could stand through a performance of *As You Like It*. Mary stood where she could lean against a theater railing. Actors' voices ran up and down, playing the scenes like a song.

Closing her eyes, Mary felt the great theater around her, and Shakespeare's hometown that drew a world of visitors because of one native son. Yet no one was sure he had written the sonnets, or the comedies and tragedies that were playing every minute somewhere on the earth . . .

Once they were back in London, Mary and Randal went to look for flats. The first was in the suburb of Maida Vale: a basement flat. Randal smoked his pipe and said nothing at all; Mary asked questions of the man, thanked the man, said it wasn't quite what they had in mind, and felt like the cartoon wife who yammers away so that her husband can't speak.

The second flat was on the ground floor. Kensington

Church Street ran along its wall until the wall turned a corner to quiet Haverford Gardens. There was a small front yard, and an even smaller terrace at the back door; Mary stepped out beside a neighbor's small greenhouse to find cars and double-deck buses rushing past, just over the wall.

Dark red carpeting, white walls, orange or turquoise curtains—it was cheerful. The hall had a single cot in an alcove; there was one bedroom with twin beds, a living room with a kitchenette, and a bath. Beds for the boys nested beneath shelves in the living room; Beth could have the hall for herself. "Shall we take it?" Mary asked. "We can move in today."

Randal didn't answer. Mary and the landlady waited. At last Mary said, "Well, I believe we like this one." Randal said nothing, but followed her out the door while she arranged to come back with the down payment in cash and said good-bye to the landlady. He might have been a ghost, Mary thought, except that when she took his arm, there was a man solidly beside her, pipe in mouth.

"A flat!" the children said. Randal said it was going to be terribly expensive.

Beth and Randal went to American Express to bring back more than five hundred pounds—six weeks' rent. The children went to the Montroy Private Hotel to check out and pack up. By suppertime the luggage stood in the middle of the living room, and their kitchenette work space was crowded with cardboard boxes of groceries.

"Furnished in Early Battered," Beth said, "but really not bad."

"Late Dingy," Jay said.

"It takes *dollars* to get us anyplace and back on the underground," Randal said.

He sat in a corner and smoked his pipe while they explored a pay telephone in the closet with the water heater, and a bathroom towel bar that plugged in to heat towels. "We'll have hot towels and a cold bathroom—no heat at all in there," Don announced.

The children groaned, but after so many rootless days they unpacked with contentment, allotted drawers and shelves to the groceries, and explored. "The supermarket's at Notting Hill Gate, and there's a little place even closer," Don said.

"Post office down there," Jay said. "And the tube station."

"Movie theater," Beth said. "Lots of shops, and bookstores."

Nobody mentioned the wine shop they could see from their front windows, waiting across the street. While they were getting supper Randal went out and came back with bottles.

"You're going to have to stop smoking in here," Jay said, looking at Randal, looking at the bottles. "Who wants to eat smelling that? And we've got to sleep in here."

"Don't do it in my hall," Beth said, scowling at Randal.

"Or the bedroom," Mary said. They didn't mention the wine Randal was pouring into a juice glass.

It was growing dark on their little terrace off the living room. Mary and Beth went out to stand by the greenhouse that formed one wall of it. "We're so mean to Randal," Mary said.

"It's because we can't stop him," Beth said. "He'll drink and send himself to the hospital, and we can't stop him, so we're mad and mean."

"It's so easy to think, 'If he'd just *try.*' But the fact is that he can't try," Mary said.

Cars and taxis and big red buses passed their small terrace in the twilight. Beyond the traffic, Kensington Church Street's antiques stores gleamed like polished breakfronts, their treasures shut behind glass.

Mary and Beth stepped back into the flat, where a lamp poured yellow light over a plastic tablecloth. The room smelled of canned beef stew. What a pleasure to lay out silverware, pour milk, break up lettuce. Jay and Don brought the stew all steaming to the bright table. Even

Randal was touched by the yellow lamplight and came to eat with the rest.

"Now we're all together in our own home," Mary said.

"You can put your elbows on the table," Don said.

"Just don't get up in the night—I'm in the hall, remember?" Beth said. "The bathroom door squeaks. And why is there a tiny window beside my bed—did you see it? It's only about knee-high and has sliding shutters, thank goodness, because I see people walking by on Kensington Church Street from it, and buses, and everything."

"You can stay up all night and write Pete," Mary told Beth. "Won't bother anybody."

"And the hotel owner won't shut off the light on you, like the man did in Paris when you sat out in the hall scribbling," Don said.

"It's really my journal," Beth said. "I send it to Pete. Mom keeps her journal. You lose a whole trip if you don't write down what's happened right away."

"Photos are my journal," Don said.

"How about a few snapshots of us in our new flat?" Mary said.

"He photographs *abstracts*," Jay said. "Torn wallpaper. Orange peels on the sidewalk."

"Some of it's fascinating," Mary said.

"Well, it's not *us*," Jay said. "We won't have a single picture of us, want to bet? Any more stew, anybody?"

"Split it with you," Don said.

"Cut the cake while you're up, will you?" Mary said to Beth.

"I've got to get to the libraries tomorrow," Randal said.

"I've got subway maps for you," Don said. "I'm going to see films all day every day."

"We picked up enough maps for everybody," Jay said.

"We can rent a TV to see what kinds of shows the British watch," Beth said.

"We ought to," Mary said. "For the news. And there'll be plays and ballets on it, almost free."

"Oh, boy, no dishwasher," Jay said. "Dishpan hands, everybody. Whose turn is it, and who remembers?"

"We did the shopping," Beth said.

"I'll do the dishes—I want to soap things down anyway," Mary said.

She craved work with her hands. The kitchen was complete with dishrags and tea towels and sponges. It was a pleasure to wash strange new plates and glasses and cups and saucers and pans. She soaped down the work space and little stove and the top of the bar that divided the kitchenette from the living room. Slatted shades pulled down to close it off completely.

Traffic rumbled and whined and ground gears just beyond their wall. Mary unpacked, hanging her clothes in the big walk-in closet off the bedroom. The flat had closets and cupboards and dressers, but the five of them had so little to put away.

In and out of bathroom and hall and living room and bedroom she went, enjoying the quiet of them all together, reading, writing, looking at maps. Jay came to tinker with the water heater, finding out how it worked. "We have to shut it off when we don't need it," he said after a while. "And the radiators store heat at night when the rates are low, and give it off in the daytime."

Mary sat by the bedroom window and took her long hair down from its heavy braid. "We're all missing Michael. I can feel it. There's a Michael-sized hole in all this."

Suddenly a double-deck bus went by. Two tiers of bus passengers looked at Mary unbraiding her hair. "They can see right in!" Mary cried. Another red double-decker followed, and then another. She jumped up to pull drapes shut on that side.

Jay was down on his knees looking at the radiator now. The children always wanted to know how things worked; Mary was more apt to wonder how it felt when things worked, or didn't. "People ride by and see this moment of our lives," she said. "Do they try to guess if we're saints? Murderers? A bored family full of supper . . ."

"Anybody for bed?" Don said, lounging in the doorway. "I hate to say this, but it's nylon again."

"No!" Beth wailed from the hall.

"Nice, short, slippery, fuzz-ball nylon sheets and cases, no bed pads, and granite pillows," Mary said. "I didn't tell you when I found out. Thought it would spoil supper."

"Well, I'm going to bed anyway," Jay said, and went to knock on the bathroom door. Randal sat on the stool lid smoking, his wineglass on the bathtub edge. "Bedtime, Dad. You'll have to smoke up the living room for a while."

"Don't let smoke out into the hall," Beth said.

Jay shut the bathroom door behind him, and Randal went into the living room and sat in a chair, his unlit pipe in one hand, glass of wine in the other.

Mary washed her face at the kitchen sink and crawled half asleep into her twin bed. She was surrounded by her family; she smiled and curled her toes and thought of the sparrow folding her nestlings under her feathers in the grapevine at home.

She would see Italy again. Greece waited for her: great golden stone limbs and broken faces . . . sunlight and Greece!

Randal came into the bedroom and sat in one of the chairs in the dark.

Mary smelled smoke and wine. A pipe glowed.

"How do you like it, now that we're moved in?" she asked in a low voice after a while.

"Fine," Randal said.

"We'll see Italy in November. And Greece. Think of it!" She heard Randal take a sip of wine.

"I think Beth misses Michael the most, but I heard the boys talking about him today. Don't you wish he could be here with us, not somewhere in Africa?"

"Um-hum," Randal said.

"Oh, well." Mary sighed. "He's got his grant and his leave and his project—he's happy. And the rest of the family's going to scatter in all directions—what a chance for them—museums and zoos and arboretums. Films. Concerts."

Randal didn't answer. Beyond the sound of traffic on the street outside was the dense, dim roar of miles of London in all directions, moving, murmuring, breathing, surrounding this small cell where the children slept and Mary lay watching a burning coal, a shape sitting in shadow.

5

MARY CALLED RANDAL'S AGENT IN NEW YORK, REVERSING the charges. "We're settled here in London," she told him.

"How is he?" George Blumberg said. He knew she was calling when Randal wasn't there. How many conversations like this had she had with George over the years?

"We're working on the new book," Mary said. "Any more to report about *Net Worth?*"

"Paperback'll be out before long," George said. "What's he calling the next one?"

"He's not sure. Maybe *The Host.*"

"Okay—I can work with that, maybe get it sold before he finishes it. Send me the first part."

"He doesn't like to do that."

"Work on him," George said. "He's so good, tell him that. Encourage him." Mary felt words like roses thrown past their mark to fall at Randal's feet. She sighed. The blame missed her, too—the nasty reviews, prying questions, the envy of would-be writers.

"And have yourself some fun," George said to the writer's wife, the one with the secretary's pencil and the typewriter. Mary imagined George in his agency's tall building in New

York. Her words had passed over his desk and between the covers of books, and those books were on library shelves this morning, neatly labeled with their "E" for "Eliot." They lay on coffee tables, were stuffed in purses and overcoat pockets and suitcases, waited in bookstores to be carried away and read—books that had kept Randal's job that fed and clothed the family, housed them all, would put Beth and Jay through their graduate work and set Don up in business— Randal Eliot's books.

Randal went to libraries once in a while, and to the liquor store, but when the others came home, tired and hungry, they usually found him in the flat with his pipe and his glass of wine and his tablet of paper. He was working, he said.

Jay and Beth went to Kew Gardens twice in one week: September was almost gone. Jay walked all the way to Westminster Abbey and back. " 'What is a painting?' " Beth asked as they got ready for bed one night. "That's what the lecturer said today at the Tate. Is it a window on the world, or a surface with paint on it?"

When they asked him, Randal said he was getting some work done. This wasn't a holiday for him, he said: he'd have to have something to show for it.

"But you don't have to *do* anything if you're on unpaid leave, do you? The university isn't paying you to come here," Mary said. She had looked at his tablet pages, covered with the scribbling she recognized: an aimless child's scrawl signifying nothing but his need to write, to be a writer.

Randal didn't answer. He looked out at the linden by their front wall that dropped its leaves slowly. London's September wind was growing colder. They were watching a television news program which informed them that "the bones of John Peel, Cumbria's famous huntsman, were dug up today and thrown into a cesspit. The grave was dug to a depth of about three feet and a fox's head and a note in the form of a poem were placed in it, conveying that it was an act of

revenge on behalf of all the foxes that had been killed—"
Randal turned the set off. It had always been his habit to
turn the television set off while they were watching it.
Sometimes he stood in front of the screen. No matter how
any of them pleaded, they would not be allowed to watch the
rest of the play, the concert, the lecture. No one knew why. It
was only something Randal liked to do.

Don found a London store that specialized in jeans and
tooled leather boots and western hats. Just the kind of
business he wanted to start, he said at the dinner table the
next night. "I'd like to go back home," he told them.

"Lonesome for Carla?" Mary asked. "And a whole house
to share with her till we come home?"

"You're crazy," Beth said.

"Not see Italy and Greece?" Jay said.

"Love, love, love," Beth said.

Mary felt such sadness. "You ought to go home if you
want to start your new business and be with Carla. We all
understand," she said, but she felt as she had felt when
Michael went to Africa: the family seemed to crack like a
china plate, like the fragile circle it had always been, after
all. Randal didn't seem to hear the conversation.

Don left the next week. Coming home from a play, Mary
and Jay and Beth met him at twilight on a rain-slick
Kensington Church Street; he was on his way to the train,
the channel, Luxembourg. "Did Randal give you enough
money?" Mary asked.

"Yes, but I don't think he knows I'm leaving," Don said.

"Be careful. Give Carla our love."

"I'm okay. We'll have Christmas ready for you—the
Chartres madonna on the front-door window—everything," Don said, and kissed her in the rain, squeezed Beth,
clapped Jay on the back, and was gone.

They walked home single file on narrow, slippery
sidewalks . . . three of them where there had been four.

Nobody spoke. The wind blew mist before them. Waiting

to cross the street, Mary looked up to see a dozen black button eyes watching her from gray faces.

She had seen them before: a crowd of old stuffed toys jammed between outer and inner windows of a house on Kensington Church Street. Colorless teddy bears and ducks and puppies were abandoned lumps behind the glass. What child had left them, and why were they still packed in a front window in plain sight of anyone on the street? They had not been moved since Mary and the children first saw them; they were faded, as if years of sun had bleached them.

Crossing the street, Mary looked back. Rain on the window glittered like tears across the patient gaze of the toys.

Did Randal notice Don was gone? He stayed in their flat day after day, smoking in the bathroom, looking at the wall.

"You've got to get out, Dad," Jay said. They persuaded Randal to go to Greenwich, and he went in a kind of dream, Mary thought. Was he seeing miles of London docks, or the *Cutty Sark*'s witch figurehead, staring back at him from the bow high above?

Randal was far behind them as they descended to the *Cutty Sark*'s hold, smelling her fusty odors of age and the sea. "Dad's not so good," Jay said. "I thought he'd be better if he got out in the world, away from his chair and the wine."

Mary couldn't answer. She looked instead at a double row of great figureheads from vanished ships: they lined the walls, a gauntlet of more than life-sized faces, slick with bright paint. She bent to read a label under a wooden Abraham Lincoln's glossy gaze: "This figurehead is from an unknown ship and was found at Black Gang Chine, Isle of Wight."

"Dad sits in the bathroom all day. Doesn't even go to the library any more," Beth said.

"In the middle of London!" Jay's voice went up, incredulous. "For weeks we've gone to the Tate and the National Gallery and Albert Hall for concerts, and to plays, and

Covent Garden, and on those walking tours, seen the Abbey—he just sits and scribbles."

"He's got his new book almost done," Mary said. "I'll have to type it when we get home."

"Well, good!" Beth said.

Jay said, "That's something."

"*Diana*," Mary read to herself. "Figurehead of a ship built in 1799. She went to the Arctic to search for Sir John Franklin's Northwest Passage expedition, and sank . . ."

"We got him out today," Beth said, and looked at Randal, who was coming down rows of lost ships.

"*Maude*," Mary read to herself. "A barque of 1,108 tons, built in 1878, she eventually became an isolation hulk at Plymouth."

Randal walked between rows of great wooden faces, not reading labels, looking past them at something else.

"*Gravesend*. From a schooner of one hundred and thirty tons and built in 1867 at Salcombe. She was originally named *Spring* and was one of the fast 'fine-lined' Salcombe fruiters that were built for the West Indian fruit trade. She changed hands twice and was renamed *Gravesend*."

6

It looks like Dad's growing a beard," Beth said at lunch on a Saturday afternoon. For the last week they hadn't expected Randal to notice what they were saying, not even if they talked about him. He didn't notice now. He sat across from Mary and poked at his salad while Beth went into the bathroom to wash her hands.

"Are you?" Jay touched Randal's arm.

"Of course I am," Randal said, surprising them. He glared at Jay. "Haven't you been reading the papers?"

"The papers?" Jay said.

"Atomic war, stupid," Randal said. "You don't read the papers."

Beth hurried back to the table. "The bathroom window's broken!" she said.

"What could have happened?" Mary said, getting up. The three of them all went to look; Randal sat where he was. Cold air poured through broken glass in the window's lowest pane.

Jay went out to the small patio. "Mom," he said, coming back with Randal's razor and a package of blades in his hand. "He threw these through the window."

The three of them went into the bedroom and shut the door. "He's sick," Mary said. "We can't go to Greece day after tomorrow."

"We've got our tickets!" Jay said. "All that money—can we get it back?"

Randal opened the door. His mouth was full of salad. He yelled, "Atomic war, and all you want to do is eat!" Bits of food flew from his mouth. He slammed the door.

"I'll have to get him to a doctor," Mary said. "You can go to Italy and Greece. You can do it together, and have a good time."

"Without you?" Beth said.

"That won't be any fun!" Jay sat down beside Mary on the bed.

"Sure it will. No old folks dragging along behind you."

"Maybe he isn't so bad. Maybe he'll be better tomorrow," Beth said.

"He was up most of last night watching the traffic," Mary said. "If a light-colored car went by, that meant the atomic bomb wouldn't fall. If a dark-colored car went by, the world was going to blow up in twenty minutes."

"Oh, *Mom!*" Beth said.

"I've got the name of the psychiatrist Dr. Parker recommended," Mary said in a shaky voice. For weeks she had tried not to see what was coming, but there it was, and she recognized it by the lump in her throat, her wet hands.

"Call him then," Beth said. "Maybe if he can see Dad tomorrow, he can give him drugs and we can all go after all."

"I don't think any doctor will see him on Sunday," Mary said.

"Go ahead and call. I'll shut the door and talk to Dad so he won't hear," Jay said.

Mary's hands shook, dialing the number on their pay telephone in the hall closet. Beth stood by, feeding coins into the slot.

Mary stared at the queen's quiet profile on coins, and told a detached English voice that she and her family were Americans from Nebraska visiting England. "My husband has been committed to mental hospitals in the States," Mary said, noticing that her voice was trembling. "He seems to be sick again. His psychiatrist, Dr. Edward Parker, recommended Dr. Boone."

The voice cared no more than the queen's quiet profile on a coin that Mary's hands were shaking and her mouth was dry and Randal sat all night watching traffic for messages. It said that Dr. Boone could not see Randal until Monday morning at eleven. No, he didn't see new patients on Sundays. No, she didn't know of any doctors who would.

Jay came back from talking at Randal in the bathroom. "We see the doctor at eleven Monday morning," Mary told Jay. "Look—I'll start putting down everything I can tell you about the trip—where to stay, what to see, how to pick up mail and send messages. We may lose hundreds of dollars in airfare as it is: you two can go, at least—"

"Oh, Mom!" Beth wailed.

"It won't be the same without you!" Jay said.

"Next time," Mary said. "I'll go with you next time. Now I've got to telephone our landlord and see if Randal and I can stay here until mid-December."

Mary made one more call that divided her from Beth and Jay. Yes, their landlord said, they could have the flat until December fifteenth.

Mary rubbed her aching forehead. "That was *so lucky!* Where would we have gone otherwise?"

The three of them sat hunched on twin beds looking at each other. "Money," Mary said. "All our money is in traveler's checks. I've got some that I can sign, but I'll have to keep those. Randal has to sign the others—we'll have to change them to dollars."

"But we'll have to carry all that cash."

"Nothing else to do," Mary said. "We've got to take Randal to Heathrow—the bank's open there on Sunday for people flying in and out. You can buy Amex checks in Athens."

Randal rode with them, station by station, to Heathrow. He signed the traveler's checks one by one. What did he think he was doing? Mary wondered. The children watched him. They had twenty-four hundred dollars in cash now. Beth and Jay each had twelve hundred dollars in secret pockets of their jackets. As they rode home, Randal watched the back gardens of suburban row houses, each walled away from its neighbor, and from any light but high noon sun. At night he watched the street from their bedroom window, writing down how many cars were black, how many cars were white. He pawed through the mounds of papers that were his next novel: piles of scribbles. Mary would have to start typing, he said.

Mary must have slept, for Randal woke her, crying. "Two pushcart lights! Two pushcart lights!" His arms gripped her, hurting her.

"It's only the usual traffic," she said, running her hands over his bald head, rubbing his back.

"Going *down* the street!"

"It's a London street," Mary whispered, hoping the children wouldn't wake. How strange it felt to have her arms around Randal, and to have his arms around her. "That's all it is—just ordinary traffic. It's been going by our house ever since we moved in."

"And two lights of a plane." Randal was trembling and hot; his face was wet.

"Listen," Mary whispered, pushing back her sheet and blanket, trying to get Randal to crawl in her narrow bed beside her. "Do you remember we've always agreed that when your head isn't working quite right and you're afraid, you use *my* head until you're well again? Remember?"

"The world's going to die!" Randal's feet were caught in the covers; he wouldn't loosen his grip enough so that she could help him.

"Remember?" Mary whispered, holding him tight, struggling with blankets. At last he was under them, and she was locked in his arms as if they were lovers.

"Yes," Randal said, his voice muffled against her shoulder.

"Then you can take my word for it: those lights are just

lights. They don't mean anything. They're only lights of cars or planes or carts—they're people going to work or flying out of London. That's all."

Little by little Randal's grip slackened. He mumbled, "How's the novel coming?" and she said it was fine . . . it was almost done . . . it was going to be the finest yet. She knew what to say. His breath, still sweetish with wine, evened and slowed. She sat with her arms around him until she was sure he was asleep, then crept into his bed and tried to get warm. Her eyes wouldn't close. She listened to cars and trucks go by, faintly shaking the room.

When two alarms went off, Randal turned over but never waked. Mary got breakfast while a sleepy Beth and Jay dressed. They zipped their shoulder bags shut, one by one: the sound of the last minutes before good-byes. It made loneliness wash over Mary while lamplight still shone on Beth's long hair and Jay's curly head. The three ate breakfast without much talk, listening to silence from the bedroom.

"Good-bye," Beth whispered at the door. "Can't you come later?"

"Can't you meet us somewhere?" Jay asked.

Mary wasn't crying. She shook her head and kissed them both and followed them into darkness before dawn. Kensington Church Street lay still under streetlights; there was no sound from the flat behind her. She watched a young man and woman with shoulder bags dangling beside them go through their gate and pass the liquor store. They grew smaller and smaller, waving to her, and then the street's curve hid them.

Mary shut the door and stood in the flat's silent hall, but the thought of the children pulled like a taut rope. The rope tried to drag her to where they still walked down Kensington Church Street, so close yet, so close.

She trembled, feeling that strong, steady pull.

It wasn't too late to catch them. The hands of her watch

moved too slowly to be seen. Beth and Jay were on Kensington Church Street still—she could grab clothes from the closet, jam them in her shoulder bag with her air ticket from London to Athens, her train ticket through Italy and plane ticket to Luxembourg and home. She could still go. She quivered with the pull of that desire.

Her watch's hands weren't moving, were they? The tick of the children's alarm clock was gone from the living room. Her body crouched on a chair, ready to pack, to run.

The watch hands crept, and after a while she couldn't pretend: the children were off to the airport. But she could catch a taxi and be gone to see the Parthenon, the Acropolis, Rome, Florence! It hadn't been long. Milk was still beaded on the lip of Jay's glass.

A truck thundered down Kensington Church Street just outside the wall.

The hands of her watch crept. The massive cable drew her. Mary sat in her chair and held on. Sometimes she shook while a ghost woman ran from closet to dresser to bathroom, pulling on her clothes. She left a man asleep in a bed and ran down an almost empty street. Beth. Jay. Rome. Florence. Athens . . .

Mary never took her eyes from her watch. She held on.

After a long, long while, faint light showed the boys' beds that had been neatly made and pushed under their shelves. The living room looked almost as it had when she first saw it, except for dishes on the table where she had eaten with Beth and Jay. Beth's bed in the hall was smooth. There was nothing on the shelf above it now but a pile of London maps and magazines.

Mary didn't need to turn on a bathroom light. She crouched on the stool and looked at a broken window with newspaper stuffed in it. Hurry! her tensed muscles still told her—you can pack—you can go.

She crawled into Randal's bed and hung on to the head of it. Randal snored in her bed, turned over, began to snore again.

Finally a sun ray turned a dresser's wood taffy-brown and streaked a wall.

The clock said Beth and Jay's plane was in the sky now.

Mary loosened one of her cramped hands from the head of the bed, and then the second. She was nested in shadows of Kensington Church Street where walls shook with passing trucks.

The children were mounting the sky, flying east into light.

— **II** —

7

R ANDAL ATE A LITTLE BREAKFAST AND DRESSED IN THE dream he inhabited; he seemed to understand that they were going to a doctor who would help him to sleep. His new beard was a thin grizzle on his face.

"We'll take a taxi to the doctor's," Mary said. "Let me have some of our money, and I'll pay."

Randal took out his billfold. It gaped wide and empty.

"Where's all the money you had yesterday?" Mary asked.

"I mailed it home," Randal said.

"When?" Mary cried. "Where?"

"I don't remember." Randal scowled. "At the airport."

"Then we haven't got enough money for a taxi!" Mary cried. "I've only got enough to go on the underground."

"In one of those red mailboxes," Randal said.

Mary said, "We'll have to hurry." They left the flat and walked through ordinary shoppers to Notting Hill Gate. The underground blew its gritty breath in their faces as they went downstairs.

Randal said nothing as they waited for the right train, changed trains, walked up and down stairs, took escalators.

At Oxford Circus a tunnel resounded with a guitar player and "Mrs. Robinson." As they passed the man's red-lined guitar case Randal threw his tube ticket in it. The crowd pushed them on. "Hey, your ticket!" the guitar player yelled.

Mary grabbed Randal's arm and started to inch back along a wall of white tile and advertisements, pushing against the crowd. She worked her way with Randal along a huge underground poster of a father looking with amazement at a nurse holding newborn twins. *The Most Surprising Things Happen,* the advertisement said in six-inch letters.

The guitar player was singing that heaven loved Mrs. Robinson more than she would ever know when they got back to his littered corner. He crouched beside his open guitar case, a young man with a long billy-goat beard.

"I didn't have any change!" Randal said while the crowd pushed against him on one side and Mary held his arm fast on the other. They would be late, Mary thought, finding his ticket among coins.

Crowds carried them down the tunnel and into a subway train.

Mary found an empty seat for them in the clattering underground car, sat beside Randal and got her breath back. A dark tunnel rushing by turned the car windows to mirrors: she saw herself beside Randal, reflected on still glass and rushing underground walls like all the others, a couple in a subway seat.

They changed to another line and went down stairways and through tunnels. They waited as minute after minute ticked away on overhead clocks. Randal's mother had thrown herself in front of a train once; a stranger had jumped after her and pulled her away in time. Mary stood between Randal and the rails.

A woman came down steps and began to go from person to person on the platform, chanting something about British veterans. Her face was kind and wrinkled above her bunch of paper poppies. Mary tried to block Randal's view of the woman, who didn't know she was dispensing omens and portents and messages from Armageddon.

Randal heard her mention war. He elbowed Mary aside and listened to the woman's speech about veterans. His face was white above the grizzled stubble on his chin. He got a shilling from Mary and bought a poppy. "Bless you!" the woman said.

"Our whole world will be blown up," Randal said to a man reading a newspaper next to him. The man nodded and then moved away.

"We are all doomed by atomic warfare," Randal told a woman with two large shopping bags propped against her feet.

The train's thunder grew down the tunnel; it pushed the usual gale before it, rattling newspapers, standing hair on end, skidding dust and cigarette wrappers against people's feet. Mary braced herself, holding Randal's arm, but he didn't try to leap past her to fall on the rails. They crowded into a car.

Now calm commuter faces surrounded Mary; Randal stood across the aisle. There was nothing to connect her to him, and so she pretended she had never seen the plump, bald, white-faced man in a dark overcoat, stubble on his chin. She rested a little, gripping a pole where other hands were, feeling the slight brushing of other bodies, ordinary bodies. She jiggled in rhythm with them, watching to be sure Randal stayed in the car.

Mary glanced at sane, everyday passengers who couldn't know what they were doing as they read their newspapers with the headlines in plain sight—how could they know that the man with the white face was reading signals wildly? His whole world depended on what headlines or underground ads or scraps of old newspapers would tell him before it was too late.

"Hiroshima was the axis and turning point of universal history," the white-faced man told a teenager with pimples and a long scarf. Mary observed them both with a calm face, as if she were a stranger.

"Everyone everywhere is coming to understand this axis and turning point of history," Randal said in a loud voice.

People were watching him out of the corners of their eyes. "Does anyone have a pin?"

The underground riders were city folk; they had seen such things before, their withdrawn looks said. How white his face was. Did they have a pin?

Some woman had a pin in her purse. They watched as the man with the white face pinned the paper poppy on the back of his left hand.

He looked surprised when the hand bled. People avoided the eyes in his white face.

Then the man whose hand was bleeding missed Mary. He looked for her, pushed and shoved his way to her, put his arms around her as he never did in public.

Was he molesting her? Mary could see the question in people's eyes. She put her arms around Randal. The glances turned politely elsewhere, and Mary couldn't pretend she was like the others any more.

Randal was shaking. She kept her eyes on his dark coat and tried to look at ease, as if men often pinned paper flowers to their flesh.

"We have to get off here," she told him at the next stop. Randal wouldn't let go of her, so they spilled out of the car awkwardly, a lump.

Mary stood with Randal on another platform with its clock and its drifting litter. Waiting for the train, Mary kept herself between Randal and the rails, and saw the sign with the new father of twins on it. The father's astonished face had blinked at her between underground cars and down tunnels. Sometimes all she saw was *The Most Surprising.* Sometimes it was *Things Happen.*

The train did not come, not for fifteen minutes. Twenty. Twenty-five. Randal's hand had stopped bleeding. He held the hand and the poppy pinned on it in front of a black man standing beside him. "I'll do what I can for you," he said.

The black man looked at Randal and then the poppy. His long coat streamed out in the blast from an approaching train; the train's noise let him escape answering.

Randal's arms and legs were rigid; Mary could feel them

against her when they stood together in a crowded car. She counted stations off as the car stopped and started, afraid she would forget and they would be lost in the dark under a strange town in a strange country.

Then Randal, with no warning, leaped off the car at a station. "Find a smoking car!" he cried to Mary. "We can't stay on a nonsmoking car!" His wild eyes said he was guilty of smoking: his mother had begged him to stop.

Mary fought her way out of the car to follow him. She had lost him once in Nebraska, and had driven with the police down street after street.

"Wait!" Mary cried, as if Randal could hear her, or would stop and turn back if he did. Crowds pressed against her, all going the other way.

Then she saw him disappear into a car. Shoving and thrusting, a crazy woman in an orderly British crowd, she managed to get into Randal's car just before the rubber-edged doors snapped shut behind her.

What if she had lost him? Where would he go? Mary, panting, clung to an overhead strap and felt so much of the old, familiar, naked anger that she thought she must give off smoke, like smokers in the car. She glared at Randal, a white-faced, grown man who could not be reasoned with, who would not listen, who cared for no one and nothing but delusions.

Mary was gripping the subway car strap so tightly her hand hurt. Randal might jump off the train again. Dollis Green was their destination, and seemed farther and farther away, a Doll's Green: Mary kept her eyes on white-faced Randal and saw two dolls walking in a meadow, the girl doll leading a boy doll with a poppy pinned to his hand.

But at last, there Dollis Green station was. They walked with the crowd along the platform and up the stairs. Mary took a deep breath: she had found the place where Randal would be safe.

But they could only go through a turnstile one at a time; Randal wanted her to go first. She pushed through and turned to find a stranger following her, not Randal.

Randal stood on the other side of the turnstile from Mary and would not go through. Mary waited in the rush of air from the open station lobby. A high fence and the turnstile blocked her way back to Randal. He could vanish in the subway, get in any car, be lost. "Come on through," Mary called to him in what she hoped was a calm, ordinary tone.

Escalators rumbled behind Randal. They led to shining tracks waiting below platforms. A desperate man could jump as a train rushed down on him. "We'll be late if you don't come," Mary called.

People went around Randal, pushed past him. She hoped he was only waiting for everyone else to pass through. Turnstiles clanged. Escalators rumbled and ticked. Damp, cold air breathed from below.

Randal would not look at her. He would not go ahead of anyone. "Randal," Mary called. He waved each person through the turnstile with his bloody, poppy-pinned hand.

The black man in his long overcoat was last. Randal waved him along.

"He would not go ahead of me!" the black man said to Mary as he passed her. His amazed eyes showed their whites.

And then, finally, Randal came through. Mary grabbed his arm, her heart beating in her ears. The father of twins on the poster watched them leave, his face wide-eyed with astonishment, and the nurse beside him beamed above two little pink doll faces.

8

"WE'VE GOT TO TAKE THE DOCTOR AN EGG." RANDAL scowled at Mary as they left the Dollis Green station.

"I'm sure he has eggs," Mary said.

"Eggs are zeros," Randal said.

"Maybe we can buy half a dozen," Mary said. "We have to find a taxi to take us to the doctor. We'll be late."

"One egg," Randal said. "We have to buy just one." He would not pass a single shop that lined the street by the subway station. He went into a shoe-repair shop and asked, his face very pale, "Will you sell me one egg?"

The man behind the counter had a leather apron on and one hand in a boot. "Greengrocer's at the top of the street," he said around the cigarette in his mouth.

A clerk in a chemist's shop asked if she could help the white-faced man and his middle-aged wife. "Will you sell us one egg?" Randal asked. He pronounced each word distinctly and slowly, as if each had its own significance.

The clerk smiled at Americans who knew so little about London. "You'll find a food shop at the top of High Street," she said, and Mary thanked her.

Perhaps they'd become a story that merchants here would

tell and retell, Mary thought, following Randal into a hardware store: they would be The American Couple Who Wanted to Buy One Egg. "No food here," the old man behind the counter said, and turned his back on Randal.

"We sell them by the half dozen," a grocery clerk said.

Randal stared at him. "We have to buy just one."

It was like a bizarre scavenger hunt, Mary thought, watching Randal ask a man at a magazine stand: "Will you sell us one egg?" in a voice that said the egg was sacred, significant. Mary met the man's eyes as calmly as she could, pretending there was a rational reason for what Randal said. All that mattered was getting to the doctor.

Randal trudged from store to store in his heavy shoes. They tried china stores, even a cleaner's. "Will you sell us a single egg?" Randal said, pale-faced and earnest, a stubble of beard on his chin.

An Indian woman at a street cart finally sold them their one egg. She never looked at them, and would not keep the change Randal wanted her to have.

Randal cupped the egg in his hand inside his coat pocket, and they stood on a curb in the cold wind. Mary saw a taxi stop in the next block: a passenger was paying the cabbie. Mary left Randal and ran to catch the taxi before it pulled away. She got in, and they went back for Randal, who had not stirred from where he was.

The taxi turned corners, went around blocks—Mary tried to remember the route. It deposited them on a street of row houses, Mary paid the fare, and they rang a bell at 101 Golder's Court.

The house was only one among other fairly new "detached" suburban houses, each with its own tiny front and back yard walled away. A young woman opened the door; Mary said, "Is this Fairlawn? We're the Eliots."

The young woman smiled and said, "Yes. Of course," with an accent, and ushered them into a small living room. They sat down on shabby upholstered chairs as if they were guests and one of them did not have a paper poppy pinned to his hand.

A young girl came in with a big red Irish setter. "Hello," she said. "I'm Peggy."

Mary waited, but Randal didn't answer. "How do you do," she said. "We're Mary and Randal Eliot." The girl laid her cheek on the dog's back, and her blond hair hid her face.

The woman who had opened the door came in with a young man. They were Jeanne and Rob, she said. They lived in the house and were psychologists and kept the place running, and would Mary and Randal like some coffee? Randal would not answer, though they asked him several times.

Finally Mary said, "Yes. Coffee would be very nice." She listened to her voice making friendly sounds, banal sounds. She said she and Randal liked cream and sugar, thanks.

When she ran out of things to say, Mary was glad to be shown to a toilet upstairs: the usual English toilet crouching alone in its little closet that was so small your knees almost touched the door if you sat down. Mary would have liked to sit there for hours looking at a friendly black doorknob, but out in the hall Randal waited to use the toilet next, his eyes never looking at anything but his heavy shoes.

When Mary went downstairs with Randal, Dr. Boone had arrived: a middle-aged man with a pipe jutting from his shaggy beard. He seemed to find the damp, chilly house, the living room, and the people in it to be as they should be. Randal crept on all fours to kneel before Dr. Boone, holding up his egg in his poppy-pinned hand.

Six people and a large dog crowded the small living room. Randal knelt before each person in turn.

"We do not use drugs or restraints to treat mental illness," Dr. Boone explained to Mary, who was listening, and Randal, who was on his knees by the dog. Others in the room looked as if they did not find it odd to see one member of a couple kneeling in the middle of a living-room floor with his head bowed and a paper flower pinned to his hand. Mary kept her eyes on a gum wrapper stuck to Randal's shoe sole.

"Randal will live here with Rob and Jeanne and Peggy, and help with meals and housekeeping. It may be a month before Randal feels well again. There will be group sessions, and Jeanne will be Mary's psychologist for scheduled visits," Dr. Boone said.

Randal didn't answer. The Irish setter stared at him, then curled up on the rug with a clink of his collar tags.

"Perhaps you would like to go home now and pack Randal's clothes," Dr. Boone said to Mary. "You can bring them tomorrow. Jeanne will find pajamas and toilet articles for Randal to use until he has his own." He turned to Jeanne. "Will you have a scheduled session with Mary tomorrow at one?"

"Yes," Jeanne said.

Dr. Boone rose. Mary saw that she could go. She could turn her back on Randal. She could leave him kneeling on a strange rug, safe in a strange living room in London.

So she said good-bye to Randal, who didn't answer, and to the rest. A kitchen table through a doorway was piled with dirty dishes; she skirted bags of old newspapers in the hall. Then the door of Fairlawn shut behind her.

Going down the walk, Mary was able to think of nothing but the fact that there was no lawn visible at Fairlawn. Empty pint milk bottles sat on front-yard paving stones. She walked two blocks and then, out of sight of the house, she stopped. She was alone. She had left Randal. London and its suburbs spread miles and miles on every side of her, and she had hardly noticed how they had come to Fairlawn. All that had been in her mind was "101 Golder's Court," a place Randal had to go.

Her hands were shaking. She took her notebook and pen from her coat pocket. Slowly, block by block, she wrote down every cross street, every landmark, asking the route back to the subway station from passersby. She worked her way across a busy highway, along the walls of warehouses, past a church, into a street of shops, and back to the underground station. When she put the map in her pocket again, it was a talisman, a key.

"You can take the tube if you like," a man at the ticket

counter said behind his grating. "But you can ride right down Kensington Church Street on the fifty-two bus."

He told her where a bus stop was, and Mary stood in a queue of black and white Londoners at Dollis Green. She had a scarf over her head against the wind, and so did many of the women.

Suddenly she took a deep breath of fresh, cold air. She was alone. She was safe among ordinary people. She stood in a line of black and white Londoners who were as calm and unremarkable as she was.

A fifty-two bus came. Mary rode quietly with people like herself, watching them read books and newspapers, look out windows, talk with each other, pay the bus driver for their tickets. Randal was taken care of: there were places for people like him. London names were beautiful to her now: Kensal Rise was like a lark singing at heaven's gate, and Ladbroke Grove held echoes of Housman's lightfoot lads who slept by brooks too broad for leaping. Her stomach unknotted. Her hands were dry. She sat and looked at the ordinary world and felt her muscles loosen one by one.

Finally a last unfamiliar street led to her own Notting Hill Gate, and she could remember that it was really "Nutting Hill," where nut trees had grown long ago. Now she recognized shops where Jay and Beth had shopped the day before. Kensington Church Street. She got off at her stop.

Don had said good-bye on that street almost two weeks before. Beth and Jay had walked away on it that morning. Now only Mary was there to pass the liquor store and go through their gate, bracing herself against loneliness. Their flat would look almost as bare as it had the first time she saw it. She would stand in echoes and emptiness where she had thought there would always be young bodies and bright voices.

But when she turned the key in the lock and opened the door, the rooms weren't empty: they were filled with peacefulness and afternoon sun. The refrigerator hummed.

Mary walked from room to room.

That peacefulness lay on smooth beds; it hovered about her in sunlit air.

Mary listened to quietness, and felt sun warm on her back. No one would speak to her. No one would have to be fed there but herself. Randal was gone with his white face and his sticky wineglasses and his bloody hand. He couldn't find his way home along her map of streets, or take the bus she had taken.

She ran from a little kitchen full of good food to a bedroom window where London buses were passing on a late, sunny afternoon. Her bedroom.

Her London.

Her flat in London.

Weeks in London: weeks and weeks in a city she could never get enough of—weeks alone.

Alone. With money.

Out she went again, locking her flat behind her. She got cash at a bank, then wandered around a supermarket at Notting Hill Gate, her mesh shopping bag dangling from her hand, and smiled to see only six kinds of cereal and two kinds of laundry soap, but shelves and shelves of tea and candy.

Lovely, ordinary things . . . she looked at beets in the fresh vegetable case. They were already cooked and peeled. She had never found milk sold in a container larger than a pint. Frozen foods came in tiny boxes. She bought a steak. She bought frozen potatoes topped with cheese, and a chocolate cake, and a bottle of cream sherry.

As darkness came, steak browned on the small grill of her very small stove. Potatoes filled the flat with the fragrance of onions and cheese. She poured herself a glass of sherry. She made herself a tossed salad. She set the table for one.

Yellow lamplight filled her living room. Evening traffic rumbled along her walls. She dished up a fine supper and sat down in the quietness of herself, the sound of one knife and fork on a plate. When had she last eaten alone?

The steak was delicious. After a few bites, she laughed and stretched her arms out in that tranquil place.

But the next day she would have to rent a typewriter. Her new novel, *The Host,* would be ready when Randal came to himself again; she had brought it with her in her "journal." When they went home, no one at the university would care if Randal Eliot had been "sick" in England—if they ever found out. He'd have *Net Worth* in paperback on the bookstore shelves and a new book ready, a book better than anything he'd done before . . .

"You bastard!" she said to that afternoon's Randal, who had knelt on the carpet with a gum wrapper stuck to his shoe.

Her steak oozed slightly red juice under her knife. "You spoiler of good times!" she shouted. Heat was coming from the radiators. She could enjoy television whenever she pleased; no one would block her view, or turn it off while she watched.

"To hell with you," Mary said. Her potatoes were golden with real cheddar cheese, and bright with little pockets of butter. "You son of a bitch."

She found her "journals" and opened them before her on the table. In the back of one were copies of book reviews—praise for a writer everyone thought they knew.

"Randal Eliot: Master Storyteller" . . . "Randal Eliot's Perception and Power" . . . "The Writer Who Knows Women." She always smiled, reading that last headline.

"Eliot is able, by the smallest touches, the least detail, to suggest in the reader's mind what the writer never says."

"And that," Mary said aloud, "is hard work."

Randal Eliot *represents.* Our ordinary writers are content to tell us that their characters are sad, happy, infatuated, suicidal—how easy that is. But Randal Eliot will describe rain soaking the side of a barn, and sadness breathes from it, never named. A woman watches the bright dance of bees in sunlight, and we know she is happy. If she wipes a spot of gravy from a plate, or lifts her arms to pirouette in a midnight room, we feel her infatuation—it is *there.* And when a man slides his hands across a desk and grips the opposite edge with white-knuckled hands, we do not have to be told that he thinks of suicide.

Mary jumped to her feet, her fists clenched. "Randal Eliot? Who's Randal Eliot? Somebody who calls me 'stupid' and 'piece of shit'!"

But she sat down again and put her face in her hands. Not all the reviews had been so kind. When she'd read the nasty criticisms, she'd felt how safe a clever fox must feel, hidden in her secret burrow while dogs as cruel as critics race over, and hunters as smart as famous novelists ride by on a false scent.

She sat up and sighed. Randal would have her new book out with his name on it. He'd be a constantly published novelist. If he made no sense in his university lectures, he'd be "quixotic," "brilliant," "a little mad." Novelists could be like that, afflicted with whatever the newest name for it was—"schizophrenia," "manic depression." He'd still have his job; the children would have money for graduate degrees, for Don's start in business.

Mary went to the window and looked at dark Kensington Church Street for a long while.

"But you're in London!" she said aloud, turning back to the bright room. "Browse in used-book stores! The museums! Half-price play tickets at Leicester Square! Good dinners!" She sat at the table again and had two small pieces of chocolate cake, not one.

Randal's pile of notebook pages lay on their dresser. His scribbles pierced the paper here and there: he had ground pencil lead in until the lead broke. The children said they couldn't read his writing—how could she?

"I can read anything he writes," she told them. "And he dictates when he's in his 'trance.'"

Mary did her dishes, then yearned for a hot bath. It was easy to take one when no one was there but her. First she stood on linoleum in her warm kitchen and soaped herself from head to foot. Then she ran for the tub in an icy bathroom and sank in hot water to her chin. It was delicious . . . Mary closed her eyes and thought of Randal's weeks of shock treatments, strapped on a table, until he could not remember, ever again, that he had run from his doctor to dark city streets, or that Mary had ridden with the police to find him crouched in an alley, hiding from doctors and hospital wards. And he believed he had written books. How proudly he said, "My book . . . my agent . . . my editor."

Remembering that, Mary smiled tenderly to herself; he had been so happy. His job was safe.

She stretched languidly in the tub. She had taped cardboard across the broken bathroom window.

Clean towels on the hot towel rack were all hers. Brahms from the radio filled her rooms now. "Ah," Mary said to nobody but her companionable self, and soaked in hot water until it seemed to her that she might—in time—be able to bear the memory of one egg . . . an astonished father of twins . . . even a red poppy . . .

When the water cooled, she wrapped herself in a hot towel and ran back to her kitchen. After all, she had lived through the day, and Randal was safe, and she was by herself, free! She did a little dance around her living-room table in nothing but her skin and the clashing cymbals of Rimsky-Korsakov's *Scheherazade*.

But it was night in London. Traffic of a great city echoed in her rooms. The refrigerator shut off. A truck shook the walls going by.

No children were there. They had taped museum schedules on the refrigerator and left a vase of daisies. Prints of their mouths were still on dirty cups in the sink when she washed dishes and put them away.

She was too tired to stay awake any longer. She peered through a crack in a living-room curtain to see shuttered shops along dark Kensington Church Street. Leaves fell from the linden tree.

There were five beds. She went from one to another. She didn't want Randal's, or her own. The children had made theirs so neatly, like small love letters left to say that they did not want to cause her any work, any pain. She thought of Michael and yearned for him—her eldest: tall, dark-haired like her, smiling . . . and so far away.

Beth's pillow smelled like Beth—Beth had slipped from her bed that very morning and left the scent of her hair.

Mary crawled into Beth's bed and lay cold and rigid, listening to London on the other side of the wall. Kensington Church Street traffic was only ten feet away. Doors were locked. She had a flashlight. She had a telephone.

She shivered for a while. The bed grew warm around her at last. Beth's scent breathed from it. Where were her four children sleeping tonight, all over the world?

She pressed her face into Beth's pillow and cried to think of Randal's white face and a paper poppy pinned to his hand.

9

LONDON TRAFFIC AND SUNSHINE WOKE MARY: SHE SAT UP
and found herself in Beth's bed. Doors of the flat stood open
around her in the hall. Quietness said she was alone.
"Randal!" she cried.

But familiar objects were there to tell her what had
happened, faithful when everyone else had gone. She followed old habits, one by one, and they were faithful, too:
washing her face, getting breakfast, brushing her teeth,
making her bed, dressing, doing dishes.

Randal was safe. She knew how to find him. She caught a
bus and went to find a rented typewriter.

The rental shop was small and dusty. Mary waited her
turn patiently and watched wreckers demolish a building
across the street. Old rooms with their pastel plasterwork of
flowers and fruit stood naked above traffic, like underwear
or intimate conversations violently exposed to strangers.

Mary brought the small portable home, packed Randal's
shoulder bag, and followed her map, street by street, to
Fairlawn.

There was the house. It had kept Randal safe all night
while she slept.

67

Empty milk bottles still waited beside the door.

Jeanne answered the bell. "You've brought Randal's clothes," she said, smiling. Her long, straight, dark hair curled a little at the ends; she wore no makeup. "You and I will talk a while," she said with her French accent, and led the way to a living-room sofa whose high back and arms made it seem like a room by itself. They sat each in a sofa's corner, their feet under them.

"You slept well?" Jeanne asked.

"Yes," Mary said. "I knew Randal was safe. Did he have a good night?"

"Not very. At two this afternoon we will meet all together with Dr. Boone and Randal. I understand that Randal is a famous writer in the United States?"

"Not famous," Mary said. "He's been well reviewed, and won quite a few awards. Can I see him?"

"He is not here just now," Jeanne said. "He has gone out in his pajamas to find a church. Would you care for some coffee?"

"By himself?" Mary said.

"It is difficult, I know," Jeanne said, "but we try to give people here their freedom to understand themselves by their actions. They act out what their problem is, do you see? Peggy is suicidal, and we have to watch her, but still she has freedom to find out who she is."

"Is Randal suicidal?"

"Somewhat," Jeanne said. "We think. Would you like coffee? Tea?"

"Coffee, please," Mary said, and heard the front door open and shut: Randal stood in the hall looking at her. He came to her in his pajamas, which were too small for him, and gave her his eyeglasses. The heavy black frames were twisted almost in two.

"Did you find St. David's?" Jeanne asked him, coming back with cups of coffee.

Randal said nothing. Mary took the glasses. "These will have to be fixed," she said. Randal's feet were bare and looked blue with cold.

"Rob loaned Randal his reading glasses until those can be repaired," Jeanne said, handing a cup to Mary.

"I left Rob's glasses on the floor in front of the altar," Randal said.

Rob, who was pudgy and owlish, came into the living room. "Randal left your glasses in front of the altar at St. David's," Jeanne told him.

"I'll call the church office," Rob said, going out.

"Aren't you cold?" Mary asked Randal. She said to Jeanne, "I brought him pajamas and a robe and slippers—should I go upstairs with him and help him put them on?"

"That would be fine, wouldn't it, Randal?" Jeanne said.

Randal went upstairs with Mary, and she opened his shoulder bag on his bed. Harsh wind blew through an open window, but Randal would not let her close it. He let her take his borrowed pair of pajamas off; he stuck his trembling legs and arms in the ones she had brought, allowing himself to be dressed like a shivering child. She put slippers on his feet, held his robe for him, and tied the belt. He had a bandage on his hand where the paper poppy had been pinned. "Do you want to go down with me?" Mary said.

Randal would not answer; he would not get off the bed when she took his hand. She left him there in his cold room and descended narrow stairs to a narrow hall that smelled of cigarette smoke and dog.

Jeanne waited for her on the couch with their cups of coffee. Mary sat down, her hands cold and wet around a hot cup, her stomach in a knot because Randal wasn't safe after all, and because she didn't think she cared, but only wanted to leave and never come back. This room smelled like urine; there were crumbs on the couch arm and a pile of wet magazines and notebooks in the middle of the carpet.

"Tell me about yourself," Jeanne said. "You are having to take care of Randal, and you are important to us as we try to understand him."

"Tell me about yourself first, won't you?" Mary said. "You have an accent. Have you been in England long?" Her voice was level and cool. She did not belong in this house.

"I am from *Paris,*" Jeanne said, accentuating the word with a dip of her head, so that her long hair swung forward. "I studied in France and then went on to get my degree here."

"And I'm from *Nebraska,*" Mary said, dipping her head a little like Jeanne and smiling as if this were the usual social occasion.

"I have been married and divorced, and I do not have any children," Jeanne said. "But you have four, I think?"

"Yes. They are all in their twenties." Randal was upstairs on his bed in the cold, and the normal woman who was his wife was sharing a quiet exchange of talk.

"My mother is here with me," Jeanne said. "She is very lonely for France."

"My parents are dead. I miss them." Mary saw their faces, and was their child thousands of miles and years away, responsible for someone else's insane child.

"Tell me about them," Jeanne said.

Mary leaned her head on the couch back, closed her eyes. Of course she would be expected to talk. Randal's sickness always exposed her to strangers.

"I had a happy childhood," Mary said. A past of a thousand smells and sounds and tastes, sights and feelings surrounded her: long stockings pulled over long underwear on a cold winter morning . . . tapioca pudding . . . the stems of dandelions splitting against her tongue . . .

"My father taught high-school English classes," Mary said, and remembered her cat stepping through a window, his fur smelling of snow, and the bell of the ice-cream man on a hot afternoon . . . the horn of the ragman along the alley. Her father had given her a small black notebook to put her typed poems in. Her book. Slowly she had been able to write at the bottom of almost every page: "This poem printed in—."

"My mother taught for a while in a high school, too," Mary said, "so I was raised in a teaching family. An only child." She remembered the coarse pink net of her first "formal." Her first silk stockings had made her ankles feel naked and cold. "We had good times—played card games and ate Sunday-night suppers on trays while we listened to *Amos 'n' Andy*—a radio show. We went to movies, and out to dinner. My father loved to garden." Her father's blunt fingers breaking clods open, spreading earth smooth. A small girl shaking water over seedlings in wooden flats. She had not imagined families where people shouted and fought and hit each other.

"My mother loved people and entertaining," Mary said. "She didn't understand a daughter who wanted to stay in and read and write poems and stories." Books from the library, waiting while Mary pounded slices of white bread flat, spread them with butter and sugar and cinnamon, rolled them up, hooked her heels on the cording of upholstered chairs, and nibbled the sticky-sweet wads, hour after hour after hour, a book against her drawn-up knees. "They were kind parents," Mary said.

"You miss them," Jeanne said. The voices of the two women, closed in by high couch walls, were as ordinary as afternoon light falling on their faces, their hair, their coffee cups. "You married young?"

"I was nineteen. Randal was in the army in the Second World War. We married in 1948." White sheets were spread in a church's small room; Mary's borrowed wedding veil, misty, billowed around her.

"Randal fought in Italy." Mary looked at Jeanne and shrugged. "He's been through so much."

Jeanne said nothing. Mary smelled urine. The fireplace nearby was full of cardboard and paper bits. Someone ran water in the kitchen.

Randal's money from her paperback of *Net Worth* would pay for Jeanne's time. It would pay for Fairlawn, and for the bandage on Randal's hand.

"And you came over here after the war?" Jeanne asked.

"For our honeymoon, and to collect notes for his Ph.D. thesis." Mary remembered the London winter: their breath had showed in the cold corners of their Hampstead flat, but the top of an electric "fire" kept hot chocolate warm, and warmed the rug where they made love.

"He got his Ph.D.?" Jeanne asked.

"Yes. He found a job, and we bought a big old house in our hometown." Where had the For Sale sign been on the lawn she knew so well? Mary tried to remember, and saw their front porch: the pillars she had patched and painted above a neat gray floor . . .

When she opened her eyes, she was in a small living room in a London suburb called Dollis Green. A young woman named Jeanne was sipping coffee at the other end of an old couch, and Dr. Boone was coming into the living room. Peggy followed him with her red setter. Rob brought Randal in robe and slippers. Mary could not bear to look at Randal: she was there because of him, holding a coffee cup as empty as she was.

10

"WHAT SHALL WE TALK ABOUT, RANDAL?" DR. BOONE SAID.
Perhaps it was pleasant to be the center of such attention,
Mary thought. Maybe that was why people stuck poppies on
their hands with pins.

"About violence," Randal said.

"Randal urinated on a few books and magazines here,"
Dr. Boone said to Mary in a friendly tone, as if Randal had,
perhaps, helpfully watered houseplants. "He wants you to
buy new notebooks and crayons for Peggy. Hers got wet."

"Write all of this down," Randal cried, leaping from his
chair to grab a notebook from the pile on the floor. "Has
somebody got something to write with?"

The notebook in Mary's hand was wet and smelled. "Here
you are," Rob said, giving Randal a pen. Randal's hands
were shaking as he gave the pen to Mary.

Peggy told Mary what kind of paper and crayons she
needed, and Mary made a list. "Put the time down," Randal
said. "Down to the minute and the second." He gave her his
watch. "It's two-seventeen and twenty-nine seconds. Put
that down."

Mary kept one hand between the wet notebook and her

pants. She was to be some kind of secretary, evidently, as they discussed violence. She could have been in Greece, walking in the sunlight with Jay and Beth. "Put everything down," Randal said.

The doctor asked what kind of violence it was to urinate on books. Mary, constantly checking the time, writing what each person said, would never see Greece now because this Randal Eliot, this English professor, wanted to pee in a parlor instead.

Randal hung over Mary, watching her write on the wet paper. He was as particular about each word she used as if he had never given her a box of scribbled-on envelopes and told her to type his novel.

Dr. Boone, Jeanne, Rob, and Randal discussed violence. Randal wanted to talk about atomic war: they would all die soon, he said. *You die if you want to,* Mary said to herself. *I'll go to Greece.* Randal jumped up constantly to be sure she had the time down in the wet notebook. She must reword this sentence. She must copy that one over.

The notebook stank in her lap, and the pen skipped on wet yellow spots. Randal had a Ph.D., and had taunted her: *You've just got a high-school diploma. You don't know what real scholarship is. You'll never write anything—you're too lazy.*

At last Randal ripped out the shopping list for Mary to keep, and took his watch and the precious and smelly record upstairs.

Mary followed Dr. Boone into a small back room filled with books. She shut the door. "Isn't Randal in danger when he goes out by himself?"

Dr. Boone said, "Yes, but what's the alternative? If we want him to get well, should we fill him full of drugs and lock him in his bedroom? What's been done to him before?"

"He's been drugged and locked up," Mary said.

"We do things differently," Dr. Boone said. "I admit there's an element of danger, but we'll search for him if he's gone very long, and he's conformed to the rules so far and told us where he's going."

Mary turned away and sat in a chair, remembering how many times she had signed papers for commitment and papers for shock treatments. "I've always thought I should take his doctors' recommendations," she said. "What else can I do?"

Dr. Boone quickly went over his training, his degrees, his experience, as if this would keep Randal safe on a London street. Mary hardly listened: she was imagining taking Randal out of Fairlawn, the long trip home, the flat where she could not leave him, more calls to other doctors, another trip with Randal to another "Fairlawn" . . .

"We'll try to follow your husband, if that will put you more at ease," Dr. Boone said.

"It would make me feel *much* better."

"He is a writer, he says."

"He's published four novels," Mary said.

"Ah," Dr. Boone said, and then, as if the question logically followed: "Now, what shall we do about payment?"

"We have insurance in the States," Mary said. "Perhaps I should call our university." She looked at her watch. "It's after nine in the morning at home."

"You can call from here," Dr. Boone said, pushing a telephone toward her. Mary took out her address book, placed the call, and talked to a friendly Nebraska voice. She spoke to it quietly and firmly, as befitted a woman in charge, a woman at home abroad. She had taken dictation on a urine-soaked notebook, perhaps, but she made arrangements to pay Randal's expenses calmly; it was Dr. Boone who was at a disadvantage with his anxiety about being paid. He kept at it. Could she pay a few hundred dollars right away? She said she could, gave him traveler's checks, washed her hands at the kitchen sink, and left Randal behind her again at Fairlawn.

No one knew where she was going. She didn't know where she was going, not yet. No one would wait for her to come home, or care if she went to bed at all.

That had never happened to her. Mary found a seat on a bus and watched billboards and shop windows and Londoners waiting patiently in bus queues. It had never happened once, not once in forty-seven years.

So she took her bus map from the pocket under her arm and opened it only halfway, politely, not obscuring her seatmate's view. Passing Notting Hill Gate ... Knightsbridge ... Hyde Park Corner ... she remembered that her parents had expected to be told where she would be every hour of the day, even when she was a high-school graduate with a job. After that there had always been Randal wanting to know where she was going ... what time she'd be home ...

She took the tube to Leicester Square and climbed flights of stairs to daylight and Charing Cross Road. She strolled with the crowds by ticket agencies and souvenir shops and film theaters blasting modern music. She knew the quickest route to a ticket kiosk under trees in the square; her money was inside her coat in a secret pocket under her arm; she had no purse to snatch. She stood in line and read the chalked-up names of shows she could see that night.

Tales of Hoffman. Music and dancing. She put her ticket in her underarm pocket and cut through crowds to an Athena store where prints of famous artworks were crammed floor to ceiling. She had plenty of time. She bought Monet's lovely tree by the water, and Renoir's couple who danced in such light, such color, yet had cigarette butts and a dying bunch of violets at their feet.

Swiss Centre's menus were posted under lights; she held her rolled-up, wrapped prints under her arm and read names of delectable dishes, then descended to the three restaurants and the ladies' room.

There was no one in the ladies' room but an attendant at a table. She was reading a book, but she leapt up at sight of Mary.

"What are you reading?" Mary said, and smiled, and saw it was Neruda's poetry. "Neruda," she said to the woman. "And you can read him in Spanish?"

"My English it is not good," the woman said, wiping off a toilet seat and holding the stall door open for Mary.

Mary smiled and shut the stall door. When she came out, she looked for handles on sink faucets, but there were none.

"You push your foot, see?" the woman said, and pushed a cap in the floor. It hooted, and water gushed.

"Thanks," Mary said.

The woman watched Mary dry her hands. Mary carried a very small plastic brush and compact and lipstick in her coat pocket; she used them in front of mirrors. "Have you come from Spain?" she asked.

"No windows here," the woman said. "It is bad. The sun in Spain I miss."

"Yes," Mary said. "I am far from America, and from my children."

"Children?" The woman's face lit with happiness. "You have children? I have children!"

"Soon we will see our children again."

"Yes," the woman said, still lit with her happiness as Mary put fifty pence in the woman's saucer and said good-bye. She went out to be served a glass of wine at a small, softly lit table that was not very far and yet very far from a woman with children in the ladies' room.

The wine tasted of that distance; a waiter bowed to that distance, taking Mary's order. But both women had been happy when they talked of their children. Mary sipped from her glass, and her eyes glowed like the candlelit wine and the Spanish woman's eyes.

11

MARY WOKE WHEN SHE PLEASED THE NEXT MORNING. Randal's twin bed lay smooth and quiet beside hers. She stretched her arms and legs and yawned, and looked around her bedroom, and remembered *Tales of Hoffman:* costumes, music, rows of faces around her in the dark. No one had cared if she came home late or came home at all. She laughed aloud.

Her clean bathroom and kitchen and living room waited in light from a cloudy sky. Somebody else was feeding Randal. She could dress, and eat her good breakfast to music from the radio, and be the Artist in her London Flat.

She washed her few dishes and walked through the first rooms she'd ever had where every object would stay in its place until she chose to move it. Mary stopped in her bedroom doorway to think that perhaps she was an orderly person. "I may be," she said aloud.

Suddenly she laughed, grabbing the door frame in both hands. She would have houseplants for herself, and cut flowers, too. She would buy one beautiful, fragile antique wineglass at Portobello Road . . . no . . . something more . . . an exquisite china plate, and a saucer and cup.

Then she thought of her prints, and unwr̶
unrolled them on her clear living-room table in the sunshine: Renoir's *Dance at Bougival* and Monet's *Antibes.*

The Renoir was a lily-and-blood explosion, sexual and sad
and fiery. It turned her hand pink as she held it flat on the
table. She taped it to her bedroom wall.

Monet's tree by the water was another matter. She had
been with Randal at Antibes. She fastened the print above
her living-room table where her journal lay open to the new
novel's last chapter, then stared at her book.

She could write in the morning now, when she was fresh
and full of energy. No one would see her. No one would
interrupt. She could spread pages over the rug—tape
notes to herself on the wall—read her words aloud for
their cadence, their tension—for the sheer pleasure of the
sound.

Mary sat down and looked at her neat, double-spaced
writing, the corrections written between the lines. Every
word had come from her head.

She picked the journal up, held it tight. When her babies
had been born, she'd had every right to expect that they
would be babies. Her uterus would make sure of that. But
her head had no such program: it might very well discharge
her months of work as only half-formed body parts of a
novel: gobbets of words. And she, poor fool, would put
Randal's name on it and love it like a mother.

If she put Randal's name on it.

Mary's eyes widened, remembering last night's intermission at the London Coliseum. Animated chatter had surrounded her as Londoners ate ice cream from little wooden
paddle-spoons or gossiped in the aisles. She had sat in the
great theater, rich music still echoing in the air, and
suddenly thought: *Divorce. I could be free.*

Mary turned over the pages of her new book, her best
book. Its cover could read: *"The Host,* a novel by Mary
Quinn" . . . if she were free.

Randal was safe now. If he went into the mental ward
time after time, he would still be kept as a full professor. He

writer. If he never wrote another book, he
_____ ____ until he retired. The children were grown.

But she had no Ph.D., no job, and would there be
alimony? Money from her writing could be a feast, then
famine, and always a matter of luck.

She sighed, and heard people talking on the sidewalk
beyond her wall. She stared at Monet's tree at Antibes. The
tree was twisted almost off its foot, and its foot was almost
in the sea—yet it was green, and the sea was tenderly blue
under dappled miles of air.

There was a rustle at her front door. She found a letter
from Beth slipped beneath it:

October 17

Dear Sweetie,
    How is Dad? And are you all right? We hope all is
well. Jay and I arrived (with two hours' difference) in
Greece. Our plane landed at 3:15 Greek time, and I had
to laugh at the terminal—the stairs were all white
marble and the floors were black marble, we were really
in Greece! We saw olive trees, and then there was the
Parthenon, basking in the sun . . .

The Parthenon . . . only a short air trip away . . . Mary
picked at crumbs on her plate.

She saved the rest of the letter to read later, made her bed,
and called Fairlawn. She wouldn't be able to come to
Fairlawn that day, she told Rob; how was Randal?

"He slept a few hours last night," Rob said.

"That's good," Mary said. "I don't have an appointment
with Jeanne today. Will you tell him I called, and that I'm
going to take his eyeglasses to be fixed, and I'll be there
tomorrow with the new notebooks and crayons?" Rob said
he would, and she thanked him and hung up, and would not
have to do anything she did not want to—not for a whole
long day and evening—and Randal could stay at Fairlawn
and pee anywhere he liked. She locked the door of her flat

and was on Kensington Church Street, money and maps in her pockets, London all around her.

She remembered a shop with eyeglasses in the window at Notting Hill Gate. Bells rang when she pushed the door open.

"My husband's glasses need new frames," she told the tall, skinny man behind the counter.

The optician took Randal's glasses and stared at them. "What did the gentleman *do* to these?"

"I think he didn't want to look at the world anymore," Mary said.

"Ah," the man said, a question in his tone. He turned the skewed eyeglasses this way and that.

"How soon will you have them ready?"

The optician said, "You may call for them in two weeks."

Mary thanked him, went down the subway stairs to coin machines, bought her ticket to Tottenham Court Road as deftly as a Londoner, and thought of the Parthenon basking in that morning's Greek sun.

Lon̄ ˍˍˍˍ were going to work. Mary sat among rattling new ˍˍˍˍ ˍˍˍurled her toes at the thought of her luck, to be ˍˍˍ ˍˍ Great Russell Street and go under the g ˍˍˍ ˍˍ the British Museum.

ˍˍˍ ˍˍˍ walked in its fresh morning air in her se ˍˍ ˍˍ . No one knew where she was.

And she ˍ ˍˍ ˍˍ this forever.

Don't be silṉ, ˍˍ ˍˍ ˍrself, strolling from one big room in the museuṉ ˍ ˍ ˍandal wouldn't pay you alimony. You've only go ˍ ˍ ˍol diploma. You'd have to find a full-time job as a wa ˍ ˍ r clerk. When would you have time to write then?

People were bending over glass cases—what were they looking at with such concentration?

There were letters lying under the glass: letters written hundreds of years ago, black ink on fragile paper, struck over and scribbled sidewise in human passion. Mary went from case to case, reading old, yellowed sorrows: King

James I in 1623 asking his son to leave his mistress and come home; Margaret Tudor, a thirteen-year-old bride, wishing she were back with her father in 1503. There was no sound in the room but a floor-creak, a cough, the muffled sound of traffic. Under the glass before Mary, quiet penstrokes on an old page bore witness to the beheading of Mary, Queen of Scots, describing how her little dog stood guard over her corpse.

In another case was Swinburne's single blue page, an early draft scrawled and rescrawled, hardly readable: "For winter's rains and ruins are over/And all the season of storms and sins . . ." Mary found, all at once, that she couldn't read the words that were swimming before her eyes. She turned her back on the glass cases and blew her nose beside a ladder that climbed above her to shelves and shelves of books.

The voices of scrawled lines gathered around her. She took a deep breath, as she had in a bus queue at Dollis Green.

After a while she went to find the heart of Athens in London. Beyond a pair of big glass doors were the Elgin Marbles, the Parthenon's treasure.

Mary walked slowly in the immense room. Young Greek bodies and prancing horses carved in marble—beautiful, alive, perfect—came and went in glimmering bits, like a garden glimpsed through stone intervals where an idiot with an ax had been. Where the ax had missed, there was a laughing face . . . a hand looped with reins . . . a horse's head lifted as it neighed, perfect after twenty-two centuries. Then insane years had struck the stone again, and left nothing but yellow ruin.

12

PERHAPS WE ALL HAVE THE SAME QUESTION FOR YOU, NOW that we have come to know Randal a little," Jeanne said to Mary. "We would like to know why you stayed all these years with him, after he became so ill."

Mary shrugged. "I couldn't support myself—never mind four children. I never went to college. And in those days, divorce was still quite rare, and it was a disgrace." Sun fell on the big couch and the two women talking there.

"You couldn't go home to your family?"

Mary's eyes were bleak as she looked around the room. "My parents told me when I married Randal that I was always welcome in their home with Randal, but I should never come there without him."

"That was cruel," Jeanne said.

"That was the way it was where I lived. And Randal supported the family," Mary said, looking into her coffee cup, then into Jeanne's attentive eyes. "All those years he brought home his paycheck, didn't spend it first or give it to another woman. There's never been another woman, I don't think. Sometimes I wished he'd find one."

"Why?"

"If your husband had a mistress and you could talk with her, wouldn't it be a help and a comfort? Think how harems must compare notes."

Jeanne smiled. "All the women have the same husband."

"So maybe they tell each other: 'Be careful tonight—he's in a bad mood.' Or they say, 'Why does he tell that same joke over and over?' Or they ask, 'Does he say anything at all to you, or go through the whole thing without a word, like the Great Stone Face?' "

Now Jeanne laughed. Mary said, "In harems you'd have your own children and lots of baby-sitters, and you could share the man and the trouble."

"Did you have baby-sitters for your children?" Jeanne asked.

"No. Our parents were older people, and Randal never liked going out much, or entertaining." Mary turned her rings around on her hand. "I wasn't a very good mother— the children seemed to squabble all the time—I felt like nothing but a referee. I couldn't get away from them. I spanked them and screamed at them when I was terribly tired and worried . . . I could see how people could be driven to hurt their children . . ." Mary's voice trailed off.

"And when did he start becoming mentally ill?"

"The year our daughter was born—1955."

"Did he like being a father?"

"I don't know," Mary said. "He gave our first child, Michael, his late-night feeding so I could sleep, I remember. But he never helped much after that—he never gave a child a bath, or read to them at bedtime, or talked to their teachers at school conferences, or spent much time with them at all."

"So you did almost everything for them? No nurse-maids?"

"I had a cleaning woman once a week," Mary said slowly, thinking. "But I always told myself that for someone who wants to create things, to be an artist, it's an advantage to do it all—breast-feed the babies and change them and wash them and boil their diapers and spoon their food and clean up their vomit and bowel movements and nurse them and make their clothes and settle their fights."

"You wanted to create, to be an artist?"

Mary swallowed a mouthful of hot coffee quickly. "I always dreamed of it, but I haven't got the gift," she said, and shrugged. "I can write down what Randal dictates, that's all."

"But you've done what women have done from the beginning?"

"Yes—shared those elemental experiences. I felt the same way about the times we went camping as a family with a tent and a camp stove and a lantern. Once you make a home on bare ground, or raise a child, you have all kinds of important, bedrock understandings."

Mary sipped hot coffee in silence, listening to a car go by on the street outside. Randal was asleep upstairs. After a while she said, "I was sheltered, you see. With my children. There was our big old house. The four children had a normal life."

Mary shut her eyes and did not say: *But Randal began to pick on Don . . . he made Don cry every night at supper. He'd find something—maybe Don had left his wagon on the sidewalk, or hadn't washed his hands well enough— anything. The other three children could see it wasn't fair: Randal didn't pick on them. Pretty soon Michael and Jay and Beth wouldn't tattle on Don to Randal. Little children like to "tell on" each other, but they didn't tell on Don. I noticed that so early: they didn't do it.*

"You had a normal life?" Jeanne said.

Mary remembered tears running down Don's face into his food, and wanted to say: *If it was normal for me to split the family. I left the supper table with the children, sided with Don, fought for him, lied and sneaked behind Randal's back. But a man can take care of himself; children are weak.*

"A somewhat normal life," Mary said, thinking of her fear that Michael and Don and Jay, grown bigger and stronger than their father, would beat him up when he mistreated her.

"You are close to your children?"

"Yes," Mary said, and thought to herself: *We lie for each other and plan behind his back, and it's contemptible, and they've learned it from me.* "Yes," she said. "We're good friends."

"And so you never thought of leaving Randal?"

When he was making Don cry? When he says I'm lazy, and I'll never write anything? Mary kept her eyes on her coffee cup. "I'd never known a wife who left her husband—that sounds strange nowadays, but that's the way it was where I grew up. And I didn't have any way to make a living—I don't now. I couldn't go home. The only home I could have with my children was with Randal."

"How awful," Jeanne said. "How hard for you."

Mary, looking at Jeanne, thought that it was probably part of some treatment or other: to console the "patient." "Randal and I thought we'd have a wonderful life together. I don't know how much of Randal's sickness is my fault. It's as if I've been left with men who said they were Randal, but my husband has never come back." Mary was wet with sweat now under her polyester, and she did not say to Jeanne: *And I'm so sorry for him. And I hate him.*

"Don't," Dr. Boone said in the hall. He was talking to Randal, who was coming downstairs with a glass ashtray in his hand. "Please don't throw it," the doctor said.

Randal looked at Mary. He gave no sign that he had seen her, but he lowered the ashtray, then threw it on the living-room carpet.

Rob and Jeanne and Peggy came to sit with Mary on chairs and couch. Peggy's red setter lay beside her, his head on his paws.

"Sit down, Randal," Dr. Boone said in a conversational tone, but Randal would not sit down. He stood in the middle of the rug in his pajamas and robe, glaring at them all.

"Would you like to tell us what's on your mind?" the doctor asked Randal.

"I haven't slept much," Randal said. He went from one

person to the next, scowling. "I can't sleep. I've dedicated my whole life to peace, but I fought in a war. My father fought in a war."

Mary listened to Randal, but she saw herself with a handsome new husband—women had watched Randal when he was young. "We killed people. I'm not proud of that." Randal scowled at her.

He had never made Mary happy, he said. He hadn't been the right kind of father. The children never talked to him; they went to Mary.

Mary kept her eyes down and listened to their life being exposed in Randal's loud voice—private rooms of a marriage smashed open by a wrecker's ball. "Sex was good. It's not her fault it stopped—it's mine." When Mary looked up, some of the eyes watched her and some watched Randal. Only the dog had kindly gone to sleep.

"I've yelled 'Help!' out the door," Randal said.

"Why did you do that?" Dr. Boone asked.

"Because the world is going to blow up," Randal said. "Wait!" He pawed through a bookshelf to find the urine-stained notebook. "Write this all down!" Randal told Mary. "With the hour and the minute!"

The notebook was dry now, but it smelled; Mary opened it to a blank page and Jeanne gave her a pen. "Here's my watch!" Randal cried, handing it to Mary. She wrote "12:15" and waited. "Write down about the war," Randal said. "And our life together—everything. Put it all down."

At least it gave Mary work to do, decisions to make. On Tuesday she had chosen to write in third person and past tense, as if it were a story. Now she wrote: "Randal said that he had not slept much, and that he had dedicated his whole life to peace . . ." She could keep busy putting down time as it passed, deciding where to give direct conversation and where to use description, taking pride in her even, graceful handwriting, while the others had nothing to do but sit. She did not have to look at them.

"Were you close to your mother?" Dr. Boone asked. *Dr. Boone asked Randal: "Were you close to your mother?"*

"Yes. I had a sister, but she died when I was in my teens. I had polio when I was small, so I was a sickly child. Mother always thought I would be a famous writer. My father wanted me in his business, but she saw to it that I went to the University of California at Berkeley and got my doctorate."

"And coming to England brings memories back to you?"

"Memories of being here with Mary and doing all the work on my dissertation."

The circle of people watched Randal pace back and forth. "Mary helps me—she types my novels. I write them all at once—usually when I'm pretty upset—and she types them," Randal said. Mary, writing carefully on the spotted page, remembered how she had been trained to be the helpmate, the good wife who took her husband's dictation and typed his work. Now she wrote on urine-stained paper, taking dictation in a London suburb, her handwriting neat, her face expressionless.

"Mary encourages me—keeps my spirits up," Randal said.

Mary wrote: *Randal said that Mary encouraged him,* and thought that Randal had never encouraged her, or comforted her when her poetry wasn't published. After she didn't win the Mildner Poetry Prize, and was too old ever to try again, he called her "the Hotshot Mildner Prize winner."

"I don't need you, you bastard," Mary said to herself, writing, *She keeps his spirits up.* "I've learned to do without your encouragement and your lovemaking, and there's plenty left, thank God."

Dr. Boone said, "How about your father?"

Randal didn't answer. He had been pacing in a broken circle, stopping each time at a small coffee table. Dr. Boone's new hardback book lay on it: Boone's picture grinned up at Randal from the book's glossy dust jacket. It was a book about mental illness.

"Did you love your father?"

Randal said nothing. He circled, stopped by Boone's new book, circled again. He picked up the heavy glass ashtray and glared at the doctor.

"Please don't throw that," Dr. Boone said politely. He probably didn't know that Randal loved the smash of glass. Randal had thrown a paperweight through his study window at home, and his razor through the bathroom window in London. He'd thrown a tumbler of water the length of his classroom at the university. Once he'd leapt to kick out a restaurant's plate-glass door.

But now Randal was glaring at Dr. Boone. His hand shook, lifting the ashtray.

Mary felt that everyone was holding their breath.

Finally Randal put the ashtray down.

"Was your father a good father?"

Randal was circling in a few square feet of rug again, just missing outstretched shoes and the setter's front paws. He looked only at the doctor now, glaring at him constantly, circling, circling. *"Was your father a good father?"* Mary wrote on a yellowed page.

"Did your father love you?"

Randal stopped at the table. He stood there for silent minutes. Mary saw his bandaged hand twitch: the hand that had caressed her long ago . . .

Suddenly Randal snatched up the doctor's new book and began to tear it apart, page by page. He crumpled each page and threw it before Dr. Boone, who sat calmly and watched.

It took quite a while to rip a whole book from its binding. Every tear was as angry as if it had been an obscene word. Nobody moved or spoke.

Paper tore and crackled. A heap of pages grew on the rug. Randal ripped with shaking hands. His face was white, and sweat glistened on his bald head.

Sun came out as he finished gutting the new book; yellow light slanted across the rug and the crumpled pages.

Now Randal had tears on his face. The book's jacket lay at his feet, a picture of Dr. Boone smiling at him from the back of it.

Slowly, methodically, Randal tore the book jacket and Dr. Boone's grin to very small pieces. He threw them down before the doctor. He knelt before him and sobbed.

Five other people sat quietly for a while. At last Randal began to gather crumpled pages awkwardly, bundling them together as best he could. He got them packed into the covers at last, and stood, a big man with his head bowed, surrounded by watching eyes, as quiet as if he were alone with guilt, sorrow, regret.

"Will you autograph your book for me?" he asked Dr. Boone.

"Of course," Dr. Boone said, and smiled at Randal. He took a pen from his jacket pocket.

The pages were out of order: a crumpled pack. Dr. Boone turned them over, then signed inside the front cover for Randal.

"There you are," he said.

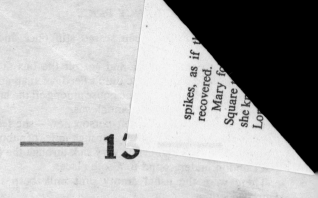

13

October 19
Delphi, Greece

Dear Mom and Dad,

We are now completing the first day of a five-day tour
of Greece. We got here at about 1 P.M. and will be here
until tomorrow morning. We have a very good guide
who has given us a good tour of the museum and the
famous site, which was at its height between 800 and
200 B.C. and was, of course, immortalized by Sophocles
in two of his plays.

Mary stopped rereading Jay's letter to look out the bus
window at Chelsea; she was on her way to Fairlawn. "Was,
of course, immortalized by Sophocles . . ." What fun to
have Jay dutifully, pedantically taking notes for those who
were absent. "Famous site, which was at its height . . ."
Suddenly loneliness washed over her.

But she was in London. King's Road shops glittered in the
morning sunlight. Mary's bus stopped and started in Chelsea traffic, and passed young men with hair in foot-long

ey had been scared stiff once and never

ided Jay's letter and got off the bus at Sloane
o take the tube. She didn't need her map anymore;
ew the route to that one house among all the houses in
don: the house where Randal was.

She was a slightly different person now—she felt it—a
person who could find her way through miles of suburbs in a
foreign city, or take someone very sick through the maze of
the London underground to a safe place.

There were the usual empty pint milk bottles beside
Fairlawn's door.

"Sit down," Jeanne said, meeting Mary in the hall.
"Randal's taking a nap." They took their usual places on the
high-backed, high-armed couch, and sipped their hot coffee.
"How have you been feeling?"

*Full of hate. I can't forgive Randal for not being a good
father, for not wanting to make love any more . . .* Mary gave
a dry laugh and said, "I can't forgive Randal for doing what
he can't help doing."

"Of course," Jeanne said.

"I've thought and thought about his tearing Dr. Boone's
book yesterday—tearing his picture up, crying, asking him
to autograph the mess he'd made."

"What are your thoughts?"

Mary tried to press the crease back at the knee of her
slacks. "The doctor was asking about Randal's father.
Randal kept coming back to Dr. Boone's book. When he
grabbed it and started tearing, it was violent; I felt as if he
were murdering someone."

"Yes," Jeanne said.

"Once Randal took our second son to the cemetery and
made him tear up pictures of Randal's father. Then he made
Don dig a hole and bury the pieces on Randal's mother's
grave."

"I see."

"And Randal ripped Dr. Boone's picture into *very* small

pieces, taking particular trouble with it," Mary said. "It was almost like a play—like a pantomime. And then he knelt down, as if he wanted forgiveness. He tried to put the book together again, and asked if Dr. Boone would autograph it for him. Dr. Boone signed it, and said, 'There you are.' I wondered if the doctor was seeing what I saw: that Randal might be angry at his father, who never shared anything with him."

"Do you think it is his father?"

"You know what I want to think," Mary said.

"But I'm sure you see what we see now?" Jeanne said. "That he has acted it out? That it is his father? You should feel much better—that it is his father."

Peggy and her red setter came downstairs in a rush; Peggy had a big towel, the setter was soaking wet. "I got him in the bathtub!" Peggy said triumphantly. "He's clean!" She started to rub the dog dry in front of a small electric fire.

"You think it is his father," Jeanne said. "That is what we think, too. I will bring more coffee." Jeanne went to the kitchen.

Mary, watching Peggy rub the red setter, tried to warm her hands by sitting on them. When she talked to Jeanne, horrors and terrors from the past turned her to ice.

But now, if Randal's father was the one who haunted him . . . Mary sat on her hands and took a deep breath.

Randal burst into the room from the hall. He was stark naked and staring.

Peggy gave him one horrified look and fled with her dog in a rush of bare feet and wet fur. Mary was left to hold a naked man as well as she could—Randal sprawled in her arms on the couch as if he were trying to curl in her lap, a baby again.

"I've attacked two women here!" he yelled against her shoulder, his bare, hairy legs under her chin.

Plump Rob, his glasses safely on his nose now, came calmly in Randal's wake, carrying Randal's clothes like a clerk in a men's store.

Mary, pinned beneath a naked man, tried to put her arms around Randal and, at the same time, make believe she was far away from a middle-aged body she did not want near her, did not want anyone ever to think had anything to do with her. But she could see that Rob thought Randal was hers: a fat, bare, trembling man she ought to recognize, if anyone could.

Rob stood over Randal and Mary. "Let's get your clothes back on," he said to Randal.

Mary had to help Rob get Randal's shirt on, pushing Randal's cold, grasping arms away from her to get them in the sleeves. She smelled Randal's sweat: he hadn't taken a bath for weeks. He wouldn't help them get his feet into his underpants.

From her cool, faraway corner Mary watched a middle-aged woman and a young man try to get another man's shanks covered, and hated herself for her detachment, her writer's cold eye that saw a scene in a book.

Randal would not help. When he was half dressed, he suddenly leapt from the couch, white-faced, dragging his pants up, fumbling for matches in his shirt pocket. He lit one, holding his pants and the box in one shaking hand.

"Randal," Mary said. He didn't answer, but ran to one of the windows. He held his match to the curtain until it began to smoke, then ran to the next, lighting match after match, waiting at each one until streams of smoke began to rise.

Rob calmly followed Randal, smothering the fires with a small fireplace rug.

"Help!" Randal yelled, and ran to throw open the front door. A woman walking past on the sidewalk stared at a man yelling for help, his pants half on, his eyes wild.

Dr. Boone came from the kitchen to push the front door shut and lead Randal into the living room again. Randal had said he'd attacked two women. Jeanne seemed calm as she came back into the room with Rob; she had said nothing about an attack. Peggy, returning with her dog and towel, seemed her usual pale self; she settled before the electric fire again and rubbed the red setter, watching Randal fumble through magazines on the coffee table with his free hand to find the notebook Mary must write in.

No one spoke until at last Mary was provided with the strong-smelling notebook, a pen, Randal's watch. Randal sat on a low stool, holding his pants together in front.

Dr. Boone cleared his throat. "Why not tell us about your family?" he said to Randal.

The doctor got no answer. Mary kept busy writing down the time and the question.

"Was your family a happy one?" Dr. Boone asked Randal.

Mary remembered D.L.'s angry eyes across a dining-room table. The children were small and put to bed, and she had given D.L. coffee and cake after he'd taken Randal to the psychiatric ward—again. "I just about had to marry Gertrude," her father-in-law had said. "If you so much as took a girl out for a buggy ride in those days, you were engaged. When I came back from World War I, there she was, waiting. I never should have married her."

Sadness made Mary sigh. *Dr. Boone asked Randal if his family had been a happy one,* she wrote in the yellowed notebook, and wished she had hugged Randal's mother whenever she could—held her stiffness in her arms and kissed her.

"Did you have a happy childhood?" Dr. Boone asked. *A happy childhood?* Mary wrote. Gertrude had been the perfect mother-in-law: not once had she criticized Mary, not even with a raised eyebrow or a look.

D.L. had shouted at his dining-room table when Mary was a visitor there: his son's fiancée. Randal had shouted, too. The father and son were fighting about politics, but their hatred and scorn and fear were as sharp-edged as the crystal chandelier and its reflections on china and silver.

"Yes," Randal said. "My family was happy. My father had a business of his own—a company that manufactured rotary pumps—and he was very successful, and made money."

And he was very successful, Mary wrote. After Gertrude died, Mary had sorted through Gertrude's keepsakes and discovered that young Gertrude had been called "the laughing one" by her friends. Mary wished she had held what was left of "the laughing one" in her arms, stiff as she was, silent as she had become. When Gertrude had laughed, it was a kind of bark, harsh, as if it surprised even her. Mary had never felt she should touch her.

"I was in the high-school orchestra, and I was editor of the high-school paper," Randal said. "I had the top grades, but I had to beg and beg before my father would let me go to the University of California. He had wanted me to stay in the east with him and my mother. I had to beg for everything, and connive with my mother to get it behind his back."

Randal began to fumble with his trousers, zipping them up, buckling the belt, going through the pockets.

I had to beg for everything, and connive with my mother to get it behind—Mary stopped writing as Randal yelled, "I hated him!" and jumped up to run to Mary, his hands full of what looked like pieces of paper.

"I hated him! Hated him! He never bought my mother anything nice!" Randal's hands leaked paper bits, and only when they fell over her in a shower did Mary see that they were bits of money.

Randal cried, "He could have bought her a new car, new house, new clothes!" Pieces fell over Mary's hands: George Washington's calm eyes, ripped from his face, looked sidewise at her.

Mary began to gather the bits in her hand: Hamilton's chin, the number ten, a staring eye in a triangle, some pillars of the White House, letters, leaves.

In a little while Dr. Boone said in his professionally tranquil voice, "I believe there are about a hundred dollars there." He was looking at Mary. "If you piece them together and take them to a bank, I think they'll replace them for you."

The secretary with the urine-smelling notebook made an envelope from one of the notebook pages; she gathered up torn bits of paper. Randal would not answer any more questions. They sat watching Mary put away small green pieces of American money.

14

A HUNDRED DOLLARS. MARY SPENT THAT EVENING TAPING bits of money together, her back against a radiator to keep herself from shivering. She wrapped a blanket around her legs and listened to wind whistling along Kensington Church Street.

The sun was out Monday morning, and warmed her as she walked to Notting Hill Gate. "I have some American money here," she said, smiling at a teller in Barclays Bank. "I'm afraid it's in bad shape, and I don't know what to do." She spread the humped, shapeless, taped-together dollars on the shelf before his till. "We had a small child visiting us last night. He got into my husband's wallet and had a fine time tearing up dollar bills."

"I see." The man smiled slightly. "He did a good job."

"I'm afraid so," Mary said, smiling with him at the mischievous child who had made so much trouble for grown-ups. "Is there any way we can replace these bills? There are ninety-five dollars."

"The little scamp did a *very* good job," the man said, looking at each bill.

"I hated to make his parents paste them together and bring the money in. They were our guests," Mary said, listening to her logical, whimsical lies prancing on and on. She could smile in this normal world of destructive children and responsible adults.

"They should have kept their eyes on him," the man said, still examining each bill.

"Children," Mary said. "I imagine you have some of your own." She watched him stack the bills as well as he could. "Will I owe you something for your trouble?"

"No trouble," the man said, bringing crisp dollars in rubber bands from a drawer. He counted out ninety-five dollars, then counted them again and passed them through to Mary. "There you are."

"Thank you very much," Mary said.

"Watch the little nippers," the man said.

Mary left, smiling at a child's naughtiness that was as real, for a little while, as the crisp bills, and as comforting, until she said to herself, waiting for the bus: *Lies, lies, lies.*

The telephone was ringing when she got home to the flat. "I never call unless I have good news," George Blumberg said. "And I've got good news about *Net Worth.* We're working on a movie deal. Nothing definite yet. How's Randal?"

"He's sick," Mary said. "He's in a psychiatric center here."

"He is?"

"Don has gone back to the States. I sent Beth and Jay on to Greece and Italy—there wasn't any reason why they shouldn't go where we'd all planned to go."

"I'm sorry," George said, then added cautiously, "I don't suppose he had any time to write . . ." he paused. "In that 'trance' he always says he gets into—"

"I'm not sure," Mary said.

"Oh," George said.

Mary smiled a little at the disappointment in his voice.

He thought of her as Randal's secretary. He had never asked what she thought of the books she had typed. Once when she had been rash enough to make suggestions about the second novel, George hadn't objected. He hadn't even heard her, it seemed. He went on talking to Randal, telling him the book was going to sell, Randal would be a rich man—his voice had flowed over Mary's words like syrup over a crumb.

"Listen," George said. "When he's feeling better, tell him to think about that new book. I'll sell it on the coattails of *Net Worth* and that will be *money*. All I need from him is a third of the book and an outline of the rest, and I'll get him enough to pay for graduate schools for the kids, a new house—"

"Yes," Mary said faintly, her eyes on Randal's new book shut away in her journal.

"Tell him there's interest in making a film of *Net Worth*," George said. "That'll cheer him up."

Freedom . . . solitude . . . Mary spent her hours like money she never expected to have again. She could write in broad daylight when she was rested and alert, revising, revising, finding new ways to show, taking out the places where she had explained.

A pile of fresh new black-and-white pages grew beside her typewriter, and sometimes she danced in her London flat, her eyes wide open, laughing, around and around the table with the manuscript on it.

At last she had typed the novel through to the end. She lifted the pile of neat pages in both hands. The title page had no author's name on it. For the first time, not one page had Randal's name on it.

And so she said aloud: "Divorce."

"Divorce," she said again. "My own books. My own agent calling from New York, saying, 'I'll sell it . . . it'll make you a fortune.' Find a room somewhere, until that first advance. Days like these, free to write."

Mary sat down at the table, gritted her teeth and spoke to

the London flat: "I'm 'Mom' to the children—the house-keeper, stenographer. It's *Randal* they're proud of."

Mary put her hands on the manuscript of her new novel, her best novel, then put her head on her hands.

Randal woke up one morning and said he was blind.

"This happens sometimes," Dr. Boone told Mary. "He really *is* blind—he can't see because he's under so much stress. He's told us that he won't ever write again. He thinks *Net Worth* is his last book. He'll lose his job, he says, if he doesn't publish."

Randal had to be led everywhere. His eyes stared straight ahead, no matter what moved before them.

"Take him home to your flat," Dr. Boone told Mary one morning. "Sometimes a change of scene can bring sight back. Randal can stay overnight with you and come back to Fairlawn for lunch tomorrow."

"He's been in hell for weeks, thinking atomic war will begin any minute," Mary said. "I've never seen how he suffers. He's always been locked away, shocked, drugged."

Mary packed what Randal needed for the night in his shoulder bag. Randal said nothing in the taxi all the way to Kensington Church Street.

Mary led him into their hall and shut the door. Randal put a hand out and found a door frame. "I don't remember this place," he said.

She told him he was home in their flat. She took his coat and hung it up, then led him to a chair in the living room. "Would you like some coffee?" she asked.

Randal didn't answer. He sat on the edge of the chair, staring ahead.

He sat there, unmoving, until lunchtime.

"I'll have to feed you, I guess," Mary said. "Open your mouth." She gave him a spoonful of spaghetti.

"You take care of me," Randal said. "You always have to take care of me. But you won't have to do it much longer." Some spaghetti fell on his chin.

Mary wiped it off. Randal's eyes were blank, though he looked at her. "You're just discouraged," Mary said. "You'll feel better in a few days, and we'll go home."

"What if I had to take care of *you?*" Randal said. "How would *you* feel?" He was wringing his hands in his lap. "I'd do it. I'd be glad to do it. But why would you want to go on that way?"

Mary touched his mouth with another spoonful of spaghetti. "We have to take care of each other," she said. There were tears at the corners of her eyes.

Randal didn't want much lunch. He sat in a chair without a word until supper, except when Mary took him to the bathroom now and then. After supper he sat in the dark, not moving. Once he said, "I'll never write again. And who am I if I'm not a writer?"

Traffic rumbled along Kensington Church Street beyond the wall. After a while Randal said, "The Pulitzer Prize." He sounded as if he were crying.

Mary put her arms around him and kissed him. He was as responsive as a large doll.

"I'll be nobody," he said after a while. "I'll be just another professor. Not even a good professor. My books are what they keep me for, and what if there's never another book? How long will they remember how good I was?"

"You're so unhappy," Mary said to him, a tremor in her voice. "You've been through so much, and you're so unhappy."

Randal said nothing.

Tears began to shine on Mary's cheeks. "You are my dear husband," she said. "I love you. I'd do anything to help you. You know I would."

Some people went by on the street beyond the wall of the flat, and their animated conversation seeped into the dark room as a few bright voice-notes.

"Remember when we first saw each other? I was in a canoe with Gwen Joplin, and you and Bob Fitch were on a dock?" Mary asked softly. "You men called to us and asked for a date. Gwen and Bob sat in the front seat and necked, and we sat in the back seat and quoted Robert Frost to each other and ate popcorn, and they thought we were crazy?"

Their past sounded strange to Mary: her words echoed a little in a living room in London where two middle-aged people sat across from each other in the dark.

Images, sights, sounds, smells came to Mary; she was as blind to the room around her as Randal was. "Our honeymoon in Europe . . . remember how we talked and talked about the book you wanted to write? The pink wallpaper we put up in our first apartment? Remember when we moved into our own house?" Mary's voice trembled, and now she gave a sob.

Randal said nothing.

Mary rubbed her wet eyes and tried to keep the quavers out of her voice. "You wrote your first book, *In the Quarters,* remember? And then came *The Strange Girl,* and then *For Better or Worse,* and *Net Worth.*"

"My books," Randal said. "My books. I won't write any more."

"You will!" Mary cried.

"No more," Randal said. "No more books. No more money."

"Even if you don't write, you'll enjoy teaching. You know how you enjoy teaching."

"Enjoy it when the whole department is laughing at me? They'll say, 'There goes the has-been author, the no-Pulitzer prof, the head that's dead.'"

Mary was crying now, and rubbing her wet eyes with both hands.

"It's very simple, you see," Randal said in his usual voice: calm, quiet. "When you aren't proud of yourself anymore, you don't want to live. You don't have to live."

"Oh, my dear, my dear!" Mary cried, kneeling in front of him, putting her arms around his waist. "Don't ever say that!" So close to his tortured face, she was crying, then she began to shake him by his shoulders wildly.

Randal let her shake him like a stiff doll. "You've got a new book!" Mary cried in a strangled voice. "Don't you remember? You've just finished a new book while you've been sick! Don't you remember writing it, week after week—piles and piles of notes that I've been typing?"

She jumped up to turn on a lamp. How pale Randal was, and how old. His empty eyes were blank with despair. "Let me show you!" Mary cried, and went to rummage in their bedroom closet. She came to put a crisp, clean manuscript on the little table beside him with trembling hands.

"The Host," she said. "You called it *The Host.*"

She took his hand so he could touch the thick manuscript. "Mine?" he asked. "My . . . new book?"

"Yes," Mary said.

"I wondered," Randal said. "I was afraid to ask . . ."

"Yes."

"I couldn't remember whether I'd written a single word."

"You did," Mary said.

"And you could read my notes for it?" Randal asked. "And I dictated it?"

"Yes. The same as always," Mary said. "I'll get some coffee."

Suddenly Randal jerked violently, then leapt to his feet. "I can see!" he cried. "I can see! I'm not blind!" He ran around the room, touching a wall, a kitchen counter, the table. "I'm not blind anymore!"

"Of course you aren't," Mary said, following him, putting her arms around him. "You're not blind. You never were. You were just worried about the new book."

Randal shook her off and sat down beside the manuscript. He drank his coffee without noticing it. He was reading his new novel. *"The Host.* I don't remember it," he kept saying. "I don't remember it at all. I never do."

"I think it's very fine," Mary said. "The best you've written."

Mary went into the kitchen to keep her hands busy, to do some dishes, to clean the small refrigerator. He hadn't had shock treatments. Would he believe he'd written a book . . .

Randal began to scribble with a pencil on the manuscript. Mary pretended to read a magazine, watching Randal turn page after page. Of course he'd believe it was his. Mary shut her eyes. *He can't bear to think it's not his. He has to be that blind always, book after book after book.*

Randal tried to smoke his pipe, but forgot it was there, and the tobacco burned away, the pipe cooled.

He might tear up the manuscript—he had done that more than once. Mary had made a carbon, and there was her journal copy, corrected and clear and locked.

Mary finally said good night. Randal jumped up to hug her hard, kiss her hard, tell her she was the most wonderful woman in the world—how could he have written any books without her to dictate to? "So wonderful," he told her. "Beautiful . . ." His eyes went past her face to the manuscript under the lamp's golden light.

Mary crawled into bed and only dozed. Randal might rush into the street at any moment, or set fires, or smash glass.

The now-and-then rustle of paper reassured her, and his voice as he talked to himself, or read the book aloud. He laughed. He said, "Ah-hmmmm. Yes." Somewhere in his mind that gave him such pain was a cold, perceptive critic. She felt warm, hearing those "Ah-hmmmm's" and "Yes's." She curled her toes in the dark.

Love scenes in her novel were unexpected and graphic. Long after midnight Randal must have read one, for Mary woke under his weight; he was trying to get his clothes off and kiss her at the same time. They struggled in the narrow bed full of two bodies, a nightgown, shirt and pair of pants, underpants, socks and shoes and kisses.

By the time they were only two naked bodies in bed, Mary was awake to the past behind them, the future ahead, and the London flat around them. She held Randal tight and kissed him back and felt the old sensations of close-fitted mouths and bodies, but he said, "The book's *good!* The book's *good!*" to the rhythm of his lovemaking, and she was a middle-aged woman with her eyes full of tears.

The minute he was through, Randal leaped off her and ran to the table and his manuscript in the next room.

Mary gathered up his flung clothes and shoes. "Get dressed—you'll catch cold," she said, holding out his flannel shirt. She had nothing on but her long black-and-silver hair. He stuck his arms in the sleeves of the shirt, pulled on pants, sat down at the table again. Their small travel alarm clock said it was four in the morning.

She pulled on her robe, made more coffee for him, and left a cup of it beside the manuscript. The page margins were scribbled over in pencil, but he hadn't put any marks between lines.

Mary got into bed again, shivering. Her book was gone. Her best book was gone.

She was trembling, but her family was safe. Randal was safe, and so was his job. She was safe to write her books in secret.

And they had made love, after the years without. As a young wife, she'd felt vital and alive afterward—she was a woman like other women in dark houses who were lying in a man's arms after love.

Cars were beginning to pass beyond the wall on Kensington Church Street. Mary shivered in her narrow bed.

She woke to sunlight and the smell of coffee—woke wild-eyed, afraid that Randal was not there—

"I make the coffee every morning at Fairlawn," he said proudly when she ran out to the kitchen. "Get back in bed and keep warm. I'll bring you some."

Mary crept under the covers again in morning light, and Randal brought a tray. Had he ever brought a tray to her? She didn't ask for cream or sugar, but drank the coffee bitter and black while Randal talked of changes in the novel. "It will take so much work," he said, striding back and forth in the bedroom. He had no shoes or stockings on.

"Aren't your feet cold?" Mary asked.

Randal didn't hear her. He mixed quotes from the novel with bits of his own life, bits of talk from Fairlawn, lines from his atomic-war statement he had pinned or taped on walls at Fairlawn. "This novel will take so much work,"

Randal said proudly. He always said that; it didn't mean anything. "But my voice, my real voice is there, better than ever."

"A lot of work?" Mary said, looking at the grounds in her cup. "Where? You don't want to spoil that 'first fine, careless rapture.'"

"Can't *believe* it!" Randal crowed. "I can't even remember it, but here it is! What if you hadn't been here to write it down?" He stared at her, came to grab her and kiss her hard, so hard that her teeth cut her lip. "You've got to have some roses."

Randal bought a bunch of roses at a street cart on the way back to Fairlawn. He insisted that she carry the big bouquet all the way on the bus, and he held her hand. A few people smiled at the demonstrative middle-aged couple.

"No, no!" Randal said when she suggested she leave the roses at Fairlawn where many people could enjoy them. "They're *yours!*" he said. Mary carried them back home to the empty flat and put them in a pickle jar.

Randal had scribbled on the manuscript. She couldn't read most of his notes, and the ones she could read didn't seem to have anything to do with the novel: "the bomb," "Peggy's dog," "blind." She spent the evening erasing them. By the time he read the book again, he wouldn't remember that he had written any notes.

When she went to bed in the quiet and peace, she lay watching the lights of passing cars reflected on the ceiling, and remembered the warm light of a long-ago London gas fire, laughter, a dusty rug under two bare bodies, the scent of hot chocolate.

NIGHT WOMAN

15

Randal could fly home to the States on schedule, Dr. Boone said. They could meet Jay and Beth in Luxembourg and use their December return tickets.

While Randal was at Fairlawn, Mary practiced getting to the airport: she would have luggage to watch, and she would have to lead Randal in and out of stations, up and down stairs and escalators. Randal had been suicidal, Jeanne said. Mary took the route there and back, taking notes, watching for dangers.

There was a farewell party on Randal's last morning at Fairlawn.

"Thanks for everything you've given me," Mary told Jeanne when she found her alone in the living room. "You've helped me so much. I can go on now."

Jeanne hugged her. "Live your own life," she said. "You are the strong one."

"I hope I'm strong enough," Mary said. "I hope I can get him home."

Rob and Jeanne and Peggy and Dr. Boone waved good-bye at the door of Fairlawn, wishing Randal success with his new novel, watching him go down the street with his shoulder bag. Mary carried a box of his extra clothes and books.

Mary told Randal about George Blumberg's call. "A movie?" Randal grinned. When had she last seen him smile?

She hugged him as they waited for the bus. "I didn't tell you while you were at Fairlawn—Dr. Boone would have doubled his fee the minute he heard the word 'movie.'"

Randal kept his arm around Mary all the way home. She admired a small glass vase in a shop window on Kensington Church Street, and he bought it for her. He said he couldn't wait to make love to his beautiful, smart, precious wife.

"We'll go to dinner," he said when she'd unpacked his clothes. "You deserve a good dinner out! Every day!"

But the manuscript lay on the table beside her typewriter. Randal stood looking at the title. His name was typed below it now. "I think I read it before, didn't I?" he said.

Randal began to read it. When it grew dark, Mary started supper.

"It's good!" he stopped reading to say.

"I'm glad," Mary said. She was cooking on the other side of the kitchen counter.

"I haven't lost my touch! It's better than *Net Worth!*"

When Mary took the typewriter off the table and put their supper plates down, he moved the manuscript over so he could eat and read.

Mary finished her supper quietly, seeing what he was reading, knowing every line on every page. He laughed at the right places. He grew serious when sadness crept into the book. He was the first one to see what she had created: the nine-month words that had come from her brain to the crisp page.

Now and then he penciled in the margins as he ate. "Just improving a little on 'the trance of the Muse,'" he said, grinning at Mary. "I write better than I know."

He told her how he loved her. He shaved his beard off because she didn't like it. He dried the dishes. She was such a good mother, he said, watching her rush to send a letter to Beth and Jay at their last Amex address.

He watched her clean the apartment. He watched her pack. One dark December morning he watched her look for a last time at the rooms on Kensington Church Street: golden lamplight on a table, a bedroom where they had made love. Then she turned off the lights, locked the door, and walked with him down a street as dark as the one Beth and Jay had taken, traveling away from her toward Greece and Italy.

Randal walked beside Mary, pleasant-faced, talkative. They appeared to be two happy, middle-aged tourists when they were seated in the plane at last. Mary buckled Randal's seat belt and hers, leaned back, shut her eyes.

"Tired?" Randal said. Mary said she was, and slept all the way to Luxembourg.

Mary found their Luxembourg hotel again. Standing at the hotel desk, she heard Beth and Jay's voices. There they were, excited, full of energy. When they hugged her, she felt light and safe. The three of them would get Randal home.

"A movie of your book!" Beth said to Randal.

Jay slapped Randal on the back. "You'll be famous!"

"If I can ever write another book," Randal said.

Someone knocked on their hotel door with a letter from Don. The letter said that he and Carla were fine, and had Christmas ready.

Randal was his old, depressed self again. "It scares me," he told Mary in their Luxembourg bed that night. "What if I can't write when I'm not sick?"

"You say that every time," Mary said, feeling how tense his body was beside her. "You've got your brand-new novel. George will have to sell it, and then it takes a year for it to come out. You've got plenty of time."

"But what if I can't write?" Randal said.

Randal asked that question over and over during long hours in airports . . . in customs . . . in the plane. When the four of them descended at last to snow-covered Nebraska, and Don and Carla brought them home to the old house,

Randal's face was grim. He didn't seem to see the Christmas tree or smell the spiced cider. He turned his back on them, hung up his coat, and sat down in his study chair. "What if I can't write?" he said to Mary when they lay in their own bed once more.

Snow fell. Icicles hung from the eaves of the old house. Christmas was almost upon them. Mary and the children baked cookies and carried plates of them to neighbors, and talked about Michael who could not come home. Randal sat with the manuscript beside him, reading it over and over.

"George said he wanted you to send the new book in as soon as possible," Mary said one afternoon.

"Shut up," Randal said. "Can't you see I'm still working on it? You've got nothing to do—it must be nice."

When Randal was taking a nap, Mary leafed through the manuscript. He hadn't put one mark on it.

The children were shopping. She sat down by the Christmas tree. The house was as quiet as the London flat where she had imagined freedom, a place for herself, hidden away, until her own best book, *The Host,* brought her fame and money and independence.

She went to look again at the neatly stacked manuscript. Randal had not even noticed that only the first page had his name on it.

He slept all afternoon until dinnertime, but when Mary stopped at his study door on the way to bed, he scowled at her. "Maybe *you* can go to bed, get some sleep, but I have to stay up late—somebody has to work in 'is house. You spen' all th'money I make, don' do any work—I'm one's got to lose sleep." He was beginning to drink too much wine again; his voice was groggy. "Leave me 'lone."

At last the magic of Christmas Eve entered the house with ritual after family ritual. Randal ate the oyster stew and strawberry shortcake on Christmas Eve. He watched them open presents by the fire. Mary had bought and wrapped all the children's gifts, as always.

"I'm not giving any presents this year," Randal said when

all the packages had been opened and he sat with a pile of new clothes and gadgets and books in his lap. "Our trip abroad was your Christmas present—it cost enough." But he didn't drink too much wine. He laid the fire and put on log after log, and sat in the middle of their Christmas joy as if it, too, kept him warm. Mary watched him and remembered the terrified hunt for the egg, the poppy pinned to his hand, the bomb that would fall in half an hour if he couldn't stop the world. Now firelight fell over him, at home and safe in his own house.

And she watched him go back to his new book, over and over again. He was never far from it. She woke in the night, still afraid for him, and crept down to find his study light on and Randal sitting in his pajamas, reading the book.

"Aren't you cold?" she asked him.

"Leave me 'lone," he said, his eyes bitter, his words slurred with wine. "I'm working—you know what that is? You got a 'dea what it takes to write serious book?" He got up to scowl down at her. "When you goin' write serious book?"

Before dawn his cold feet slid against her in bed, wandering up the backs of her legs to warm themselves.

Randal's doctor said he was well enough to drive the car and teach his classes in January. Randal slept through Christmas morning with its smells of turkey in the oven. Mary and the children sat around the dining-room table to plan their parts in Don and Carla's wedding in January. Beth would be a bridesmaid. Jay would be best man. A small family wedding, Don said—without Michael there. They talked of Michael, far away in Africa, while they stirred and tasted, filled plates, and carried the old rituals one year farther. Randal sat in his study turning the pages of the new book.

"Where's Dad?" Jay asked one dark evening before New Year's. The children had brought the Christmas tree down; the rug was strewn with its finery.

"He had an appointment with Dr. Parker," Mary said, wrapping tinsel icicles around a card.

Don held up a string of glowing stars. "Do we have any new light bulbs?"

"Here," Beth said.

"He's sure putting away the wine," Jay said.

"And we thought the trip would do him so much good," Beth said.

"At least he's got another book," Don said.

Beth sighed. "He won't send it to his agent. He just sits there turning the pages over, turning the pages over, snarling if we get near it."

"We have so much to be thankful for," Mary said. The living room sparkled with colored lights. "We've worried about how we were going to pay for graduate degrees and Don's start in business, and now maybe the books will do it."

"But if there's money, Dad won't let go of it, will he?" Beth said. "Isn't he like his father?"

"Not when it's education," Don said.

Mary began to wrap ornaments in tattered tissue—old ornaments from her parents' tree, from the Eliots' tree: a dimpled hexagonal gold one, tarnishing to bronze . . . a little blue teakettle—how had its spout and handle lasted all these years?

"What about Don?" Beth said.

"Randal will help him set up his western-wear shop," Mary said. "I think. If I can get him used to the idea."

"He tells me I'll go bankrupt," Don said, and laughed. The rest of them smiled at him, looking up from cardboard boxes and a pile of felt stockings Mary had embroidered for the children with the date of their first Christmases, their names, and Christmas symbols that stood for them.

The doorbell rang.

Their Chartres madonna roundel was still on the side window of the front door; Mary peered through an open space in the Christ child's halo to see dark blue, leather, and metal. She opened the door, and two policemen stood there, caps in hands, telling her their names, asking if she was Mrs. Randal Eliot, and could they come in?

Beth, Don, and Jay looked up from Christmas ornaments, then scrambled to their feet, asking what was going on, what—

"Are these your children, Mrs. Eliot?" one of the policemen said.

"Yes," Mary said. "Is there some—"

"You might want to sit down with your mother on the couch there, two of you," the policeman said in a kind voice. "Won't you sit down, ma'am, while we talk?"

Mary did as she was told. Beth and Don grabbed boxes and hanks of tinsel from the couch. The three of them sat down, and one of the officers came to kneel so that his face was level with Mary's. "There's been an accident," he said.

"Randal," Mary said in a soft voice.

"I'm afraid so, Mrs. Eliot. We're very sorry. He skidded off the highway. Hit a patch of ice. There was nothing anyone could do—we think he was gone instantly."

"Gone," Mary said.

"Oh, *Mom,*" Beth said, putting her arms around Mary. Don put his arms around her, too, and Jay came to sit on the couch arm.

"Just a little while ago?" Mary said through stiff lips.

"Less than an hour. He was alone in his car. He didn't have a seat belt on."

"Where is he?" Mary asked.

"At Crandall Hospital."

"I'll go . . ." Mary half rose from the couch.

The policeman said, "Ma'am, I wouldn't—"

"Don't, Mom," Beth said.

"You stay with us," Don said.

"Do you have any relatives in town? You have your children, I know, but is there some older relative, or perhaps a neighbor, or your priest or rabbi or minister we could notify?" the policeman asked.

"Randal's father lives in town with a sister, but he's in his nineties and not quite himself, and his sister is elderly, too, and quite frail," Mary said. "Our minister is Reverend Darnley at First Methodist here in town. Betty Jacobs lives next door—she's a good friend." Shouldn't she go where Randal was, lying by himself . . . shouldn't she be there . . .

"We'll give them a call," the policeman said, rising. "You folks just help each other out." He looked at Beth, who was staring straight ahead with tears running down her face. "Maybe you want to make your mother a cup of coffee. One of us will stay here for a while to make sure you have everything you need." Jay cleared ornaments off a chair, and the policeman sat down, turning his cap around in his hands, while the other policeman went out to his car.

Betty Jacobs hurried over at once. Reverend Darnley came too, and he prayed. Mary remembered that afterward. She remembered that Beth had cried, while Don had said, "Dad . . . Dad," over and over, and Jay kept asking about the accident as if some simple mistake had been made and Randal could still be alive. She remembered colored lights glowing on the rug, and the Christmas tree lying along the floor, its dried branches bare.

16

Nora Gilden and her maid came at once when Betty Jacobs called her. They cleared the remains of the Christmas tree, and took the plastic madonna and child stained glass from the window beside the front door. They organized the kitchen, and sent word to Michael in Africa, though that word wouldn't reach him for weeks. Food and flowers came to the front door with whispers and blasts of cold air, and Nora and Betty and women from the church put food on the table for Mary and her children, arranged flowers, and talked to the Eliots in soft voices.

Mary, Beth, Don, and Jay drove to the funeral home the next evening. Snow plastered the windshield almost too fast for the wipers to clear it.

The funeral home's door closed behind them and they were wrapped and muffled in subdued light, subdued voices, as if they were fragile glass, easily broken. The rugs in dim rooms were no particular color. The music playing in the background had no particular melody. The official who whispered to them and led the way seemed to have no particular dead person in mind, Mary thought: he called Randal "the deceased."

The deceased lay in the polished wood casket Mary had chosen. He wore the shirt and tie she had brought from Randal's closet, and Randal's best blue suit. His skin seemed as translucent as paraffin and was tinted pink.

They stood by the open casket, and Mary's mind was, as usual, alert to strangeness: they were a family of six, but one was too far away to know he should be there, and another lay flat on his back under half a lid, almost swallowed by quilted satin.

Four of them had sad faces and open, fixed eyes. The fifth one was asleep—so sunken and soaked in sleep that he seemed hardly there. His folded hands and eyes and mouth seemed clamped on a secret he knew and was not telling, even if they shut the lid of his box and buried him, which they would have to do.

Mary murmured words, held the children's hands, felt tears on her cheeks. After a while she thought they should turn and leave; wasn't that the next part of the ritual?

Just as they went out the door into wind and snow, Mary caught herself wondering where Randal was—he had stayed away again, missed something important to his family—

Bitter winds and sleet began the day of the funeral. The doorbell rang as friends brought more food and flowers and subdued voices.

Faculty members came to the service at the church, and there were town friends, and those who had heard about the writer Randal Eliot, but only the family went to the cemetery in wind and sleet to watch a casket and its heap of roses tip a little, right itself, and disappear into a dark hole.

Randal's father and Aunt Viola stayed in the car. When they brought the two of them back to Viola's house, Mary put her arms around him. "At least Randal had the second trip to Europe that he always dreamed of, D.L.," she said. "And you made us so happy when you gave us our honeymoon there. Remember?"

D.L.'s watery eyes wandered around Viola's living room. "And he changed his name to Brogan!" D.L. said.

D.L. was thinking of a cousin who had not wanted to be an Eliot, Viola explained, smoothing D.L.'s jacket sleeve. D.L. had never forgiven that cousin.

Sleet had turned to snow when the four Eliots came home from Viola's. Carla said good-bye, kissed them all, and left for home. Nora Gilden and a half dozen other close friends were waiting in the living room where there were bouquets and notes of condolence and newspapers on the couch that announced ACCIDENT KILLS FAMOUS LOCAL AUTHOR, and RANDAL ELIOT DEAD AT FIFTY-FOUR.

"We thought the four of you might want to be alone after a hard day," Nora said. "There's a hot supper ready in the kitchen."

Mary hugged Nora and Fran and Steve and Jean and Betty and Walter and watched them go into the snowy night. "I'll get into some jeans," she told the children.

"Should we eat by the fire?" Beth said.

"We'll build it," Don said. The boys took the stairs up two at a time and changed their clothes, then clattered the fireplace grate downstairs, getting rid of old ashes, building the fire as Randal had always built it.

Mary, dressing in the big bedroom at the front of the house, heard that familiar sound. When she came down the narrow, steep half-flight of stairs to the kitchen, Beth was already there, her long pale hair tied back. "You boys want the spaghetti?" she leaned around the door to the living room to ask.

"That's fine," Jay answered.

"Apple pie," Mary said, looking at the array of food. "Chocolate cake."

The fire cast a cheerful yellow glow on the four of them at the card table. They were used to eating without Randal; his empty study chair watched them from the next room.

"It seems good to be alone," Beth said after they had eaten in silence for a while. "People coming to the house, bringing things, calling up, shaking hands at the funeral . . . they're nice, but I'm glad they've left us alone tonight."

They smiled at each other, sharing pieces of pie and cake.

The fire leaped and snapped. "I missed Michael," Beth said. "All day long I've missed him."

"We all have," Don said.

After a while Mary said, "I want you children to know how our finances stand. I don't want you to worry. Randal and I had wills that left all we had to each other. We'll get quite a bit from the university annuity, and there's Randal's insurance. We'll be all right. Michael's getting good pay now from his university, and you don't have to change any plans for your educations, or Don's new store."

"Maybe Carla and I ought to wait to get married," Don said.

"Of course not," Mary said. "It's all planned."

She relaxed a little in the firelight that played over young faces and old furniture. The house rose around them, solid and safe against falling snow and a rising winter wind.

But after a while the constant, relentless voice of that wind seemed to bring darkness into the room. This was Randal's first night in his grave. The casket, then his clothes, then his body had lost, hour by hour, the last human warmth they would ever hold. Now he would be as cold as the winter ground.

She ought to cry, thinking of that. She ought to cry for anyone lost to air and light, a warm fire, young faces, the sounds of home.

The children were quiet, too, as if they were listening to the wind. Finally Don said, "I wondered . . . Dad didn't kill himself, did he? Run into that wall?"

"I don't know," Mary said. "We've all wondered about it, I suppose. There's no way of telling. He was going fast and hit the ice."

They sat watching the fire lick and quiver. "How about the new book?" Beth asked Mary. "You're going to send it in?"

"I don't know," Mary said.

"Everybody said he was such a good writer," Beth said. "I'd go by the bookshop on the Hill, and there his newest book would be in the window—even when I was just little. 'That's my dad's book!' I'd tell my friends."

"Not many people can write five good books," Jay said. He didn't look at his brother and sister; his eyes were on the fire.

Tears ran down Mary's cheeks then. The children noticed, and came to hug her.

Viola helped D.L. into bed and turned on the night-light by the door. "You just call me if you want me," she said, as she had said every night for years.

"And he changed his name to Brogan," D.L. said.

Don, Beth, and Jay went up to bed; Mary sat by the dying fire. When the house was still, she went to bring her journals from the high cupboard in the kitchen.

Three new novels, partly done, and two others slowly gaining shape in her mind . . . Mary put the journals on Randal's desk, turned on the lamp. Long habit and hard practice put her pen to the paper; she lost herself for hours in a world she had made from nothing.

At last she discovered she was shivering, and heard the keening wind. She got up, stiff, exhausted, and found a box in a drawer of Randal's desk. She lifted the lid to see the manuscript she had typed in London. Only the title page of *The Host* had Randal's name on it.

Mary went up to bed, moaning a little with tiredness, stretching her arms and legs out on smooth, clean sheets. Randal would come to bed late, his feet running up and down her legs to warm themselves . . .

No. Randal was in the ground.

Mary felt her heart beat, her blood pound in her veins, her warm body grow warmer yet. She sighed and curled into a ball, listening to the wind.

Her eyes grew accustomed to the dark. She peered at a

row of Randal Eliot's novels on the corner bookshelf. *You've got a new book! Don't you remember? You've just finished a new book while you've been sick! Don't you remember dictating all night to me?*

Mary lay awake for a long time, her pillow wet, staring into the dark. "I gave you my book," she whispered to nothing but the wind. "I gave you all my books. You were happy."

Sleet hit the window nearby. Half asleep, she saw two college men standing on a riverbank. "That's Randal Eliot with Bob Fitch!" a young woman named Gwen told young Mary Quinn. The two men called, "How about a double date?" and the women turned their canoe toward shore. "I'll introduce you," Gwen whispered to Mary. When Mary stepped from the canoe, her hand was in Randal Eliot's hand.

III

$$=== 17 ===$$

I KEEP THINKING: *When Randal comes home from the hospital,"* Mary said weeks later, looking through the front-door window at the snowy park. "It's habit, I guess, or a scar, like those Roman lines of march—remember? Centuries later, the farm fields grow less green where they were."

Jay squinted into the snow-light, his curly hair glistening. "There was always a certain feel to the house when Dad was gone."

"We listened for his steps on the porch," Beth said.

"When he came, everything changed," Jay said.

Beth sighed. Then she said, "At least Michael's letter came. We know he's following that tribe into places where there aren't any roads or maps. Or he was, anyway."

The three of them were silent for a moment, looking out at the park. Somewhere in Africa Michael was beyond their reach. He didn't know his father was gone. Randal was alive—for him.

They locked their door and left for Don and Carla's wedding, picking their way across the icy porch.

Snow squeaked under their boots. Mary's new car at the curb surrounded them with its new-car smell as the three of them settled in their seats. Turning the key, Mary frowned a little, then sighed.

"It'll be lonesome for you," Beth said, sitting beside her mother. "Going to the wedding without Dad."

"I feel a little like a tree must feel when the one growing next to it goes down," Mary said. She didn't say what that feeling was—she was ashamed to admit it, even to herself: *Now the sunshine is all yours. You're the Parent. You don't stand beside him in his shadow. You don't have to watch him, study him, guess what he's thinking, defer to him, eat what he likes to eat, stay awake to watch him . . .*

Snowy Nebraska cornfields, ridged with dark lines of stubble, stretched away on either side of the road. The conversations of the three in the car had a relaxed, guilty sound. Sometimes they laughed; there was a lilt in their voices . . . then they stopped, and looked faintly ashamed. But before long the jokes came back, the bantering, the companionable silences.

Carla's small hometown was a cluster of roofs among white fields. It had numbered streets on each side of Main Street and only one church. The church had once been a department store, and then a town hall. Now the building had a steeple, rows of pews, and drafts blowing across the sanctuary floor.

Jay was best man. Beth was maid of honor. Mary hardly recognized them in their finery and their public, socially correct expressions. She watched the bride and groom with tears in her eyes—they were such children. Her parents must have seen her as just such a round-cheeked, dressed-up child. When had she grown old enough to look at her own wedding pictures and see little-girl-Mary with little-boy-Randal, pacing down an aisle to leave childhood behind?

But when she was close to Don in the chattering line, she watched him meet strangers with poise. As a boy he had cried every night at the table, miserable under his father's shouts. Now he was a handsome young man whom people drew close to, feeling his warmth. She had thought he might fight with his father: she had seen the two of them, white-faced, coming close to blows. Now his arm was around his wife. They smiled at Mary, and she smiled back.

The church basement was much warmer than the sanctuary: there was steam from the kitchen, and the voices of people Carla had known all her life.

"How sad that Don's father can't be here," people told Mary, putting an arm around her or patting her shoulder.

The newlyweds flew away to Colorado: Don was opening his western-wear store. He was gone: Mary stood in the doorway of his room looking at his empty bed, and the place where Michael's bed had been.

When Beth drove to Texas with Waldo the cat to begin her graduate assistantship, she left her shadow box of china animals by her bedroom door, and posters of London above her bed.

Jay was the last to leave; classes were starting at Minnesota.

"That old house of ours," Mary said to Jay on the way to the airport. "The foundation's cracked, the basement's wet—"

"Move," Jay said. "Buy a new house. Buy just what you want. Sell the old one."

"Move? What would Mike and Don and Beth say?"

"They'd say you were smart. The house is old, and the neighborhood's getting worse every year. Buy yourself a new house. You don't even have to stay in Nebraska. Come to Minnesota. Go to Texas or Colorado. You've got children in all those places—not to mention Africa."

"I want to be here," Mary said.

"We'd all like to be here," Jay said. "But where are the jobs?" He sighed. "You can stay. Buy yourself your own house. Sell the old one."

Buy yourself your own house.

"Where would I get a down payment?" Mary said. "Randal's paperback money is gone, and we need the money from the university to live on—your tuition and Beth's tuition and D.L. and Aunt Viola, taxes, my day-to-day—"

"Use money from selling the old house for our graduate tuition. Beth and I both have part-time jobs, and we're paid up until next semester," Jay said. "By then you'll have money from the new book."

Mary stared at him and didn't say: *It's my money from my own books.* She kissed Jay good-bye, watched his plane nose upward into clouds, then crossed the airport's windy parking lot.

All four children were gone into their own lives now.

She started her own car: how new it was. How new it smelled.

She would be all alone now, she told herself. But the dashboard twinkled and shone. The motor hummed. Warm air from vents blew softly on her cheeks.

Buy yourself your own house. Jay's words sparkled at the back of her mind.

Mary drove home and stood in her heavy coat and boots where the Christmas tree had always stood. She looked through the living room and Randal's study to the dining-room windows and a row of cars parked beyond the back fence.

The house smelled musty and old. There were garbage cans overturned down the alley.

Net Worth might be a movie. Her own first novel, *The Host,* might bring a big advance.

"Buy yourself your own house," she said aloud to the still rooms. She said it the next day, and the next. The words seemed as magical as "you have three wishes" or "open sesame."

"I called a real-estate agent," she told Don when he telephoned at the end of the week.

"You what?" he said.

"I called her and she came over," Mary said.

"To sell the house?" Don asked in a startled voice.

"To buy a new one," Mary said. "I told her I'd like a fairly new house on a wooded lot, and I'd want a particular kind of house. I needed a large workroom and a bedroom for myself, and a room for each of my four children when they visit." Mary looked around her as she spoke. A box of scribbled-over envelopes lay on Randal's desk yet.

"A new house!"

"The houses she showed me were all exactly alike—magazine-picture places—I couldn't tell them apart!" Mary cried. "Vaulted living rooms, paneled television rooms, garden-level entertainment rooms with bars, kitchens with the newest push buttons! I kept thinking of Tolstoy's Ivan Ilych—remember? He thought his new house was unique, when actually it was only the house middle-class people built when they wanted to be exactly like each other."

"So you didn't find anything?"

"We looked at about a dozen. Finally we drove to one more ranch house in Cedar Ridge: a blue-green one across from woods on a winding road—it *looked* small . . . the usual thing, but not so new—the original part is twenty years old. It's got open stairs going up and down—split level. Downstairs is a big living room with a fireplace, and a half bath and kitchen, and a new family room and double garage. And it isn't as expensive as the others."

"You liked it?"

"It's got character: it was built in two parts, so it isn't what you expect—it's not small. It has a big bath and four bedrooms upstairs that belonged to the old house, and then the new rooms. The honeymoon suite." Mary laughed.

"Honeymoon!"

"Newlyweds built a big bedroom over the double garage. It's got a picture-window view of a wooded ravine, and a fieldstone fireplace across one corner, and a dressing room and bath behind a half wall—the bathroom's got a Jacuzzi!" Mary was giggling. "But across from the bedroom is my workroom, my tree house—a great big, new room with skylights, and twenty-nine built-in drawers, and a desk, and bookcases floor to ceiling, and a view for blocks over trees and gardens!"

"Uh-oh," Don said. "You bought it."

"I did! I did! I signed documents and then went back home and danced around yelling, 'My home! My very own home!' You can't imagine such a mother."

Don said yes, he could.

Mary called Jay. Jay told her "Well done!"

When she called Beth, Beth said, "A *new house?*"

"I'll have to sell the old house right away," Mary said. "I'll send you children the things you want to keep. The nicest things go with me: the Jacobean dining-room set—I've eaten my meals on that since I was ten! And my Jenny Lind bed and maple pieces, and D.L.'s cherry bedroom set and walnut bedroom set—all of them are solid wood. I'm having them refinished."

"Great!" Beth cried.

"When I watched them carried out of the house this week and realized they'll never be here again, I knew I was really moving out."

"How does it feel?"

"Like those daredevil sentences in books," Mary said. "'He plunged from the cliff,' or 'Her dress slithered to the floor.' And I'm buying a new stove, refrigerator, dryer, washer, and dishwasher—and your room is blue. Dark green carpeting downstairs. Curtains! Do you know what curtains cost? I'll make my own!"

Beth was laughing. "Mom! Mom!"

"I can't get used to the idea!" Mary cried. "I can't!"

But the moving van parked at her curb early one morning. By night Mary's familiar belongings stood in strange rooms. Furniture pieces she had known for years arrived refinished, as smooth and shining as new ones fresh from a store. "And yet they're familiar," Mary told Don when he called. "So they comfort me."

"You'll love it," Don said.

"Six months ago the five of us were in London! Six months ago all I thought I wanted was to bring Randal back safe. And now he's gone." There was a catch in Mary's voice. "And now I'm leaving."

"Tonight you'll sleep in your new house!" Don said. "No more nightmares, Mom. It's your turn to be happy."

Mary wandered her new home, turning the wrong way in the upstairs hall, forgetting where closets were. At last she left lights on, locked the door, and drove to the old house.

It stood with dark windows under its snowy roof. No room in it was the same: furniture was missing, and pictures gone from the walls. Mary walked through the half-empty, dark place. Snow fell beyond every window, and was falling, too, on Randal's grave.

"Good-bye," she whispered to Randal where their bed had stood. "Good-bye, my dear, my dear."

Old clothes still hung in the children's closets.

She had crept along the upstairs hall Easter after Easter to leave presents and rustling baskets inside the children's doors. "Time to get up!" she had called thousands of mornings. "Time for bed!" she had called thousands of nights.

How many times had she spanked one of the children in the rooms that stood empty now? She had not always been kind or patient or understanding—their noise and fights and dirt—she was so sorry. She hung her head, there in the narrow, dark hall, and was so sorry, too late, for times long gone.

Mary paused in her small study at the top of the stairs. All her novels had been typed there on an old desk her father had refinished. She had stared at the space above that desk for hours at a time, until the wall's random cracks and spots had become, in some odd way, her companions, her confidants.

Going downstairs, she imagined that there might be dust from all those years in floor cracks, or a baby's sticky fingerprint from long ago on some door.

The living room echoed in her ears with the welcoming cries of guests, birthday-party games, angry lectures, Christmas carols. She walked through Randal's study. Was there a trace of stale smoke still in the air?

She stood in the shadowy dining room to whisper "Good-bye" to her parents, to Randal's mother, to Randal himself. They had come to so many family dinners, until the last dinner. When had it been? Nobody knew it was the last; they had put down napkins and pushed back chairs, and not one of them guessed that they would never meet at that table again.

Her kitchen . . . she stood in darkness, but she knew every chip, door-creak, shadow, and scent of it. She had made her children do the dishes at that sink every night. When she was deep in her writing, she had heard them returning from school and wished sometimes—oh, yes— that they would not come home at all, but leave her, leave her . . .

"Good-bye," she said in that still place.

She looked through the round window of the big front door. Once it had framed a young Mary and Randal Eliot with two-year-old Michael, hunting for their first home. As she locked the door and crossed the porch, it seemed to her that she had shut away the Randal of long ago in that empty house, a second grave.

She couldn't help it . . . she couldn't help it. Bitter cold wind buffeted her as she ran down two flights of steps to her car. She drove to University Mall. She'd have dinner there, and then—

"Home!" Mary cried to herself. "Home!"

18

PAUL ANDERSON WATCHED MARY ELIOT SWING THROUGH the doors of University Mall. March snow dusted the shoulders of her coat and shone on her hair. Her boot heels clicked over polished floors as if she had somewhere to go, and was getting there.

Paul rose from a sandwich-shop table to stand between Mary and the mall. She stopped: he blocked her way.

"Hello," Paul said.

"Do I know you?" Mary said.

"I'm Paul Anderson—new professor in the English department at the university. My first year on campus."

Mary hesitated.

"Sit down, won't you?" Paul said, and pulled back a chair. "I've been trying to get up nerve to call you—then I saw you just now . . ." He seated her and said that her husband had been such a fine writer . . . he had read all Randal's books, studied them . . .

Mary sat and smiled. The mall lights above her lit silvery strands in her dark braids and the small sequins of snow caught there.

"Could I possibly talk with you about Dr. Eliot?" Paul said. "At your convenience, of course. Perhaps at dinner, if you'd like that? If you can bear to talk about him, that is."

Mary gave a short, rather dry laugh. "I've done nothing *but* talk about Randal, I'm afraid, since his death. Interviews. Articles . . ."

"Of course, of course," Paul said. He ran a hand through his thick hair. "You really can't stand any more of it. I can see how it would be."

Mary sat quietly before him.

"I don't want to intrude, or take your time," Paul said, "but you do have to eat anyway, don't you? Perhaps dinner on a weekend?" There was eagerness in his voice. "A week from Saturday night? I'll come for you, say, seven o'clock?"

"All right," Mary said. She looked a little surprised as she spoke. "I'll see you then. Do you have my new address?" Paul wrote it down. "I've just moved."

Paul got up when she said good-bye and watched her until she turned a corner of the mall. She'd moved out of Randal's house . . .

Paul went into the snowy parking lot to find his old Ford. How could she move out? . . .

The car heater didn't work. Paul was cold, but he drove away from the town center to a suburb of turn-of-the-century Nebraska houses nested in wide porches. When he reached one that stood in the middle of a block, he slowed down, then stopped. It was a brown-and-white house, tall and broad, under a huge tree.

Randal Eliot's house.

All the windows were dark. Mary Eliot had moved out—he could hardly believe it. Falling snow veiled the white pillars and brown clapboard walls. She had moved out of the home where Randal Eliot read his work to his family, perhaps . . . helped his children with their homework . . . put them to bed . . . wrote late at night in one of those rooms . . .

Paul watched the house fade in snow in his rearview

mirror. The old Ford slid at the bottom of the hill. Paul swung the wheel hard, got the car back into icy ruts, and drove home.

His apartment was near the campus among old houses crammed full of students. It was too close to a beer joint that spewed empty beer cans for blocks every weekend. Loud music pounded from windows. Cars ground the lawns to mud.

Paul parked on the mud and stamped snow off his shoes inside his apartment's back door.

Student papers lay in a ring around his kitchen table. He stepped over them to drop his coat on the couch in the stuffy living room.

Then he halted, put on his coat again, buttoned it, turned up the collar a little, and stood in front of his hall mirror. "I'm Paul Anderson," he said to his reflection, raising his chin, smiling just a little. "New professor in the English depart—"

His telephone rang.

"Hi." His sister Hannah had a soft, breathy voice, as if she were telling secrets. "Remember me? Takes me months, but I'm back in your town. Pick you up for dinner— eightish?" He imagined her sitting on a motel bed in the lotus posture, a cigarette dangling from her lip.

She came for him in her new red sports car. "Hard day," she said, and grinned with her big white teeth. "Stinkin' day."

"Me, too," Paul said, glancing over her thin, sharp profile and short skirt. "How's the Nebraska First Office?"

"I tell them, 'Build your factory in Nebraska,'" Hannah said. "'Film your movie in Nebraska.' That's what I say all day. And I smile-smile-smile."

"That bad?"

"Not bad-bad. Bad-boring. I've got to be in Sioux City tomorrow." Hannah was driving to their favorite restaurant, taking corners with one scarlet-tipped hand on the wheel.

Paul said, "I've finally met Mary Eliot, and she's having dinner with me a week from Saturday night."

"Kudos, kudos," Hannah said, slowing for a fat woman jaywalking. "How did she act?"

"She's pretty tired of the fuss about Randal," Paul said. "Big-gun critics haven't always been nice, even though he's dead. When the prizes come in, the writer had better duck, and Randal *has* ducked, so to speak."

"Middle-aged. I've seen her on TV. Could be pretty if she wore the right makeup and cut off all that hair," Hannah said. "She looked sort of scared, as if she were glad they weren't shooting at her."

"A biography of Eliot—my one big chance, before anybody else gets to be the official biographer." Paul's very blue eyes sparkled. "It would give me a job for life—I'd get tenure."

"She probably has all his money now. I suppose there's money, isn't there? Rich widow. Nothing to do but bask in his fame and cash in, and she's got a nice figure—she ought to buy some good clothes. How about marrying her and getting capital for my very own public-relations firm?"

Paul shrugged his overcoat collar high around his handsome head and gave his sister a sidewise glance.

Hannah made a face. "I don't have any such luck finding *men*. The rich ones haven't got brains, the brainy ones haven't got looks, and the handsome ones are either dumb or poor." She sighed. "But a rich widow's just the thing for you, if you don't drink and keep your temper."

"Mary's *forty-eight*."

Hannah, stopping for a red light, glanced at her brother. "You're forty." She hesitated, then went on in a flat, noncommittal tone: "You support Sandra—I know you do, and I know why you do—but you've got to forget all that, after all the years—"

"Don't talk about it," Paul said.

"That's what you always say," Hannah said in a dry voice. She pursed her thin lips in a grimace and was still for a while. Then she said, "You've mailed in that essay on Randal Eliot? It'll be published?"

"Haven't sent it yet."

Hannah shot him an exasperated glance.

"My Intro to Lit class is a joy," Paul said.

Hannah hit the wheel with the flat of her hand. "You're hopeless! If I learned anything working a year in a dean's office, it's that *nobody* teaches in universities any more. They write grants, and when they aren't writing grants, they write papers, and when they aren't writing papers, they review papers, and when they aren't reviewing papers, they go to conferences and deliver papers. And they publish and publish and publish. Teaching is what they do if they're failures."

"I'm a failure," Paul said. "That's what I do best: fail. 'I guess you could say I've a call.'"

"I guess I could say you're a strange one, if you weren't my brother." Hannah parked the car, and they ran through pelting snow.

Paul opened the restaurant door for Hannah and said, "Mary typed Eliot's manuscripts, and lived with him for twenty-nine years. Think of how much she knows about him. She's got his papers and drafts. But she's moved out of Randal's house! Moved out! He wrote all his books there, and she's moved out! If I could live there . . ."

"You're hopeless," Hannah said, letting him take her coat in the restaurant lobby. "You've got a terminal case of Randal Eliot."

They sat at a table and looked at menus, but Paul wasn't reading his. "I've got a case of hopelessness—that's what I've got." He rubbed his eyes as if he were tired. "If I don't get tenure here, then what? Who'll hire me—a high school? Or do I sell insurance? Maybe encyclopedias—'Ma'am, your children should read about the great people and places of the world, impress their teachers, improve their grades . . .'"

"The grilled fish," Hannah told the waitress. "And Chablis."

"Same," Paul said.

"Your luck is *turning!* Get some inside stuff from Mary Eliot! Write articles on Randal, get them printed, read them at conferences . . . there's your easy, tenured life." Hannah stared at him. "The department head called you in again? Said you had to get something published or out you go?"

"That's about it."

"Get busy! Write! Marry the famous author's widow! You'll be able to do your bit for Sandra, and wear nice clothes every day, and read the newspaper in your office. You get summers off—no cleaning out grain bins or pumping pig honey from under barns—"

"Sometimes I can't believe how far we've come," Paul said in a low voice. "Remember how we didn't have *anything?*"

They sat in silence, watching snow fall past restaurant windows. Lights of cars in the parking lot were dim with swarming flakes.

Snowplows began to clear the roads and shove snow across shopping-mall lots, piling it high at corners.

Mary Eliot finished her dinner, paid her check, and ran to her car to scrape windows while the heater ran. The car was warm when she drove along Golden Drive and saw her yard light gleaming far ahead along the narrow road.

As she entered her driveway, her double garage doors rose before her; she parked in the light while the doors descended behind her to shut out cold, night, and snow.

"Home," Mary whispered, putting her key in the door. "Home," she said to gleaming furniture she had lived with all her life. "I'm home."

She took off her coat and boots, poured herself a glass of wine from her new refrigerator, turned on her gas fire, and sat before its fake logs and licking flames. Then she thought of Paul Anderson, whose eyes sparkled when he spoke of Randal Eliot.

The telephone rang.

"Mom!" Beth said. "You're there. You're in your new house!"

"My first night," Mary said. "Lots of curtains to make yet, and the things I need most are at the bottom of some box, but I'm home. I've used up almost all the paperback money—let's hope I can sell the old house fast. And I've got a date a week from Saturday night."

"I don't know if I'm ready for this," Beth said.

"Paul Anderson, a professor in the English department," Mary said. "He just wants to talk about Randal."

"That's what they all say. Handsome?"

"Very. Blue eyes with long, dark lashes all around and thick white hair, but lots younger than I am. He must eat right and lift weights and live a moral life to look the way he looks."

"You deserve it."

"He's after Randal's life story, not me."

"Would-be biographer," Beth said.

Mary sighed. "I don't know much about men."

"You were married to one for *twenty-nine years.*"

"I got married before I had a chance to learn anything much. My mother used to say, 'Mary Quinn, all you do is think about men,' but I was hardly thinking about men at all. I was thinking about *me.* What about the little lines around my neck? How did my hair look in the back where I could never really see it? If lipstick was supposed to be shiny and wet-looking, what should I do if somebody wanted to kiss me and my lips were sticky from all that spit?"

Beth was laughing on the other end of the line.

"I've told you—it was very difficult: I was supposed to be pretty and popular and a virgin."

Beth made an indecent noise.

"I could have hobbies, of course." Mary stretched out on her new blue couch in the firelight. "I wrote poetry and won prizes. A nice hobby. But my business in life was to be a helpmate."

"And a virgin."

"I didn't know *anything*. Sex came as a great surprise. At first it struck me as so—peculiar. I remember wondering if Randal had made it up."

"Oh, Mom, Mom, Mom!" Beth wailed.

"My experience is *limited*," Mary said.

19

Every morning Mary woke in a bedroom that took her by surprise. Sun flooded through green plants; the room was bright with yellows and greens against the pale walls and cream-colored rug.

No chipped sinks. She turned on gold-metal faucets, and could take her choice of smooth, shining showers and tubs. New carpet was plush under her bare feet as she went downstairs to nothing old, nothing worn, and admired her new refrigerator, made coffee on her new, spotless stove. Her own morning paper waited on the doorstep, crisp, unread.

"Randal," she said aloud, "how do you like the house *my* money bought? *Wouldn't you like to get your hands on it?*" She was silent then, her face in her hands.

When Nora Gilden came to lunch, Mary gave her a glass of wine and said, "If Randal could have started all over in a house like this . . ." She looked out at her garden in the snow. "Left his old self in the old place . . ."

"You're lonely," Nora said. "You ought to think about meeting some men."

Mary laughed a little. "I've got a date Saturday night."

"Well!" Nora said. "About time!"

"Not really a date," Mary said. "Paul Anderson in the English department. He wants to talk about Randal, so he'll buy me dinner."

"He's *single*," Nora said with satisfaction. "He's *handsome*." She pulled up Paul Anderson's facts from her marvelous mental file that Mary had always admired. "Maybe forty. Hasn't been here long—came last fall. Taught at a couple of places in the East—got his doctorate real late at Wisconsin. American lit. Divorced. Don't know why or what for. No children. A sister here in Nebraska. Made marvelous chocolate cake for the department Christmas party. Lives in a dump over on Henrick Street. He's talked about doing critiques of Randal's novels, but he doesn't publish, so he's in for some bad news next year. That was his trouble at the other jobs, I gather. Doesn't like processed cheese or William Styron." Nora frowned in concentration. "Or polyester pants."

"You're an encyclopedia!" Mary cried.

"And I suppose he wants to do Randal's biography?"

Mary stared at her. "I suppose. And the children will have to see their father's whole sad life in print!"

"Not necessarily," Nora said. Mary was leading the way upstairs, and Nora followed, puffing a little. "Who says Paul's going to write it? He'll talk about it . . . he's been talking about what he's *going* to write for years. So you can listen for years—and enjoy the view."

Mary didn't answer; she opened her study door. "I've bought a trestle table for my typewriter, and a swivel office chair, and files."

Nora said she supposed Mary still had a lot to do for Randal—correspondence, the estate . . .

Mary smiled there in the tree-house room where she could write novels in daylight, and put her own name on them. She said, "I'm doing some writing of my own."

"Look at these." Nora peered at prize certificates framed on Mary's study wall: prizes for Mary's books, with

Randal's name on each one. "He was a *great writer*. Don't they make you proud?"

Mary spread her arms as if she could gather the whole world in. "Yes!" she said.

The middle of March dumped snow on the Midwest again. Hannah Anderson was delighted to be sent to California on business; she telephoned Paul. "Big brother, I'm in L.A.!" she crowed over the long-distance line. "It's *warm* and *sunny!* Describe every snowdrift! Tell me Nebraska's freezing! I love it!"

Paul scowled as he drove to Mary Eliot's house, fighting ridges of heaped snow that snowplows had left at crossings. His car bucked and skidded and was as cold inside as outside. He went back and forth on Golden Drive, waiting until he was exactly on time, then pulled his old Ford into Mary Eliot's driveway among snow-laden spruce trees.

As he rang Mary's bell, the heavy door knocker's brass face—was it a man's or a woman's?—stared at him from under its leafy crown.

Mary answered the bell at once. "Come in, have a glass of wine before we go," she said.

"That's a beautiful door," Paul said, touching its oak as he stood with her on a small, mirror-bright landing.

"The door knocker's Victorian. I found it at Portobello Market in London last year." Mary took his coat and shut the brass face out in the cold.

"Before your husband died," Paul said.

Her living room was down a half flight of open stairs. Firelight dappled a deep green carpet, gleamed on polished wood, and quivered through a wine bottle's deep red. There was a dim, snowy garden beyond the windows.

"Wine?" Mary said.

Paul took the glass she offered him. "A beautiful house," he said, and meant it. He sat down when she did and heard a first-rate stereo playing in another room. A wall of books on shelves showed through a doorway. "You're going to London again?"

"Every year or two, I hope," Mary said. Her dress was made of some glossy stuff, blues and greens. "I'll persuade one of my children to go too, if I can."

"Twist their arms," Paul said.

"Hard. Often. Show my teeth."

"I haven't traveled abroad," Paul said. Mary refilled his wineglass, rising and sitting down gracefully. She was "middle-aged," Hannah had said. It was the heavy crown of hair that made her look old: it seemed too much for someone so small and slim to carry. She had a charming way of looking sidewise, then flaring her dark eyes wider when they met his, as if she were surprised.

She had lived with Randal Eliot for almost thirty years.

He wouldn't mention Randal Eliot yet. While they drove to the restaurant, he asked Mary about herself, and wished he had a car with a heater that worked.

They ordered dinner. Paul was still asking polite questions. "Yes," Mary said, "my children are all far away. Michael's twenty-eight; he has his Ph.D. in anthropology and teaches at Yale, but just now he's in Africa on a grant. Beth's working on her M.A. in English in Texas—Austin."

Mary heard the pride in her voice, and didn't care. She sighed to herself there in the candlelight, wishing she were home by her own fire. A woman her age should be smart enough not to dress up and drag her half of a conversation through a long evening just because a man asked her to dinner. Her panty hose were tight and didn't keep her warm; her bra was tight and didn't let her breathe. The conversation was ordinary and left her brain numb. She was already tired of being watched so respectfully by handsome Paul Anderson because she was her husband's widow.

"And your other sons?" Paul asked. The restaurant lights were dim, but he saw that Mary was wearing no rings.

"Don's married and has his own western-wear store—he's in Dillon, Colorado," Mary said.

Not to wear Randal Eliot's ring . . . it seemed to Paul that any woman would wear such a ring until she died.

144

"And Jay's beginning graduate study at Minnesota," Mary told him. "Zoology."

When their dinner was served, Mary began to ask about Paul. No, he said, he wasn't married—he'd been divorced. No children. He told her where he had taught, and said he liked gardening and good music and cooking. No family but his unmarried sister living between Omaha and Lincoln. "I'm a devotee of your late husband's work, as you've probably guessed," he said at last.

"So am I," she said.

"Perhaps you don't want to talk about him just yet," Paul said. "How he wrote the novels, what he was like. I saw him once from a distance—that's all. I began teaching just before he took his unpaid leave and the five of you went abroad. I thought I had plenty of time to know him. I blame myself for that. But for more than ten years I've read and reread his books, written essays about him, saved every review of his work, given papers about him—my sister says I have a terminal case of Randal Eliot." Paul smiled his handsome smile. "I'm fascinated by his first novel, *In the Quarters*. I think I've caught references to *Alice In Wonderland* and *Through the Looking Glass* in it."

Mary took a quick breath; she leaned toward him, her dark eyes lit with the white of the tablecloth, her dark braids streaked with silver. "Not one reviewer has caught that," she said.

"The young bride comes to her husband's plantation the way Alice comes to Wonderland—isn't that it?" Paul said. "And everyone condescends to her, just as everyone condescends to Alice in Carroll's books."

For the first time Paul saw Mary's face grow almost young, glowing with excitement and pleasure. She said, "The old man is the Cheshire Cat—he tells the bride, 'We're all mad here.'"

"The White Queen is Louly—she can't cope, can't put her clothes on straight—she's hopeless." Paul laughed.

"And the Red Queen?"

The smiles left their faces. "Aunt Byrd," Paul said. "She knows how to handle slaves. You don't have to whip them or put them on the treadmill. But you have to run very fast to keep the slavery system in place."

"Randal's books have never found their devoted critic and scholar—someone who doesn't have to be told what their structure is, how they're *built,*" Mary said. "Reviewers nowadays seem to think you review a book by telling its plot—like schoolchildren giving a book report!"

Coffee was cooling in the cups before them, but Paul didn't see it, didn't taste it—Mary's animated face and voice held him. She spoke of characters in Randal Eliot's books, connected scene with scene, traced patterns—he struggled to remember all she said. His eyes never left her face.

After a while other tables in the dining room were empty. Their lonely lights flickered around Paul, but he only heard Mary's voice that was sending him home to write and write again.

A waitress watched the good-looking man and the middle-aged woman. They laughed, gestured, leaned toward each other, recited words together as if they had discovered something new, then laughed again.

She sighed and shifted her weight to her other tired foot. They were obviously lovers, blind to a restaurant closing, or a bill to be paid.

= 20 =

MARY WOKE THE NEXT MORNING CRAVING A TYPEWRITER and blank paper. She wrote all day, hardly eating. She wrote all week.

Beth called from Texas on Saturday.

"Paul's coming at seven," Mary told Beth. "He's bringing supper over." She didn't say: *He's the first person in my whole life who talks to me about Randal's books—my books. No one ever cared what I thought.*

"He *cooks?*" Beth said. "And he's good-looking? Go for it!"

"I'm forty-eight years old! I've *lived* with a man. I've *had* that," Mary said. "There are very hungry widows in this world, but I'm not one of them. Men have to be stroked, they have to be listened to, their feelings mustn't be hurt, their socks have to match—"

"Mom, you're *young*. Have fun!"

"What I'm going to do with him is *talk*. He's the first person I've ever met who knows what Randal was trying to do in his books *before* I tell him. You can't imagine what talking to him does to me! I've been so lonely. But don't worry," Mary said, "this isn't any candlelight-and-flowers rendezvous."

When Mary hung up, the doorbell rang. She pulled her satin bedspread straight and ran down to open the door. The first thing she saw was flowers.

"Hi," Paul said behind a bunch of nodding golden mums. Mary backed up and he came in loaded with sacks, giving off winter-night cold. First she caught the flowers' acrid scent; then she smelled something delicious to eat. She hoped he couldn't hear her stomach growl, sharp and hungry.

"Dinner delivery." Paul's smile was nervous. "And a centerpiece." He stood in her green-and-blue living room with his sacks and flowers while the snow on his boots melted. "I'm making a mess of the carpet," he said, craning his neck to see his feet.

"It's just snow," Mary said, leading the way to the kitchen. "I'm not used to being coddled like this!"

"Famous authors' wives should be treated famously," Paul said, letting a heavy sack down gingerly on the kitchen counter. "Casserole. And a salad. Wine. Decadent bit of chocolate mousse."

Mary's mouth watered. "I'm so hungry."

"You sit down," Paul said.

"But let me get—"

"Just tell me where the glasses are," Paul said. "Then relax and praise my taste in wine, and I will cheerfully find the china and the silverware and the right knobs on the stove."

"On the shelf over the sink. However, I'm afraid I'm not dressed for the Chez Plaza de Ritz this evening." Mary looked down at her shirt and long wool skirt and pushed her heavy coil of hair back from one ear.

"But the managers of the Chez Plaza de Ritz have noticed (haven't you noticed?) that they have an American Book Award winner's wife in their elegant midst, so they've turned away all other clientele, no matter how moneyed, and we are enjoying the Chez Plaza de Ritz ambience à deux." Paul brought her a glass of wine. "And the waiters are so well trained that they make themselves utterly invisible."

Mary sat down by the fireplace and sighed. "This is very nice." She stretched her tired back and took a sip of the wine. "And this is very good."

"Thought you might like it. It's from Iowa . . . the Amanas." Paul was in a half squat before her microwave, punching it in the face until it hummed. Then he went around the kitchen work space opening drawers, clattering silverware, hooking long fingers through cup handles.

"You must be tired—you had classes today," Mary said. She admired Paul's shape: no beer belly. And he was tall: he brought her black glass vase down from the highest cupboard with one swipe of his hand. A man and woman alone in a house: the electricity of that was playing around her like children's sparklers on the Fourth of July—silly woman. Silly forty-eight-year-old woman. She pretended she didn't notice the soft, busy little fountains of sparks.

"One," Paul said. "Plus committee meetings, which produce still more committee meetings, like those microscopic animals that break in two and then those two break in two. Our committees may be absolutely insignificant, with tiny, even microscopic agendas, but the one thing they are is *fertile*. Where do you keep your soft drinks?"

"Bottom of the fridge."

Paul ran water in the black glass vase, added some Seven-Up. "Flowers love it."

"They do?"

Paul put the mums in the vase and poked them a few times. He came to stand near Mary with his glass of wine. The living room's shaded lights left half his handsome face in shadow, but Mary could see those blue eyes intent upon her. "I've been talking so much because I'm nervous," he said. He took a sip of his wine. "Talking to the woman who knew Randal Eliot and worked with him on his books makes me a gibjabbering idiot."

Mary laughed. "Gibbering? Jabbering? A combination? Have a chair. I could use some new words this evening." She leaned back and closed her eyes.

She heard a chair creak a little as he sat down, and noticed that their talk had changed whatever was between them, brought them closer. Yet his boots weren't dry yet, and she hadn't finished her wine, and the sparklers were still fizzing. "Old words all day?" Paul asked.

"Old words. Begging. A professor from Yale came here wanting Randal's notes and papers and work sheets and correspondence—like the rest of them. A would-be biographer in search of a would-be primary source. He stayed all afternoon."

"Yale? You said he could have them?"

"Have what? Randal made notes on the backs of old envelopes—nobody could read them but me, and most of them have been thrown out. And he dictated a great deal. I've got work sheets—in my handwriting. The letters don't amount to much. He didn't correspond with other writers, or write anything more profound than 'How much money?' to his agent. Now every month or so somebody pleads to see me, flies from somewhere, tells me how much it would mean, on and on."

Mary sighed. Paul sipped his wine and said nothing. He was silent even when she opened her eyes to look at light glinting on his white hair. He was looking into his wineglass.

He had worn a suit. He hadn't unbuttoned his suit coat. He hadn't loosened his tie.

In a minute he got up. "Bet supper's ready," he said. "Sit still. I'll get it." He squatted near her to look at the fireplace.

"Turn the little black handle inside to the right," Mary said.

Paul opened the fireplace doors and turned the handle. Immediately flames appeared and began pretending to consume fake logs.

"That's a fiction-writer's fireplace," Mary said. "Only the flames are the real thing."

"I should write that down," Paul said, hesitating at the kitchen door. "You speak so well. After our dinner Saturday night, I had a half dozen new ideas about Randal's work."

"I'm only showing off. I'm drinking wine on an empty stomach."

Paul lifted a table and set it before the fire, then went in the kitchen to put plates and glasses on a tray.

Mary's big living room flickered with real flames. She stretched her feet before her, yawned a delicious yawn, and felt the wine glimmering along her tired nerves like light.

Paul passed her, taking care, not rattling silverware or dishes. When he seated her where there was candlelight and flowers, she laughed, thinking of Beth.

"Like it?" Paul said in a pleased tone, pouring her more wine. "You've been neglected by the department. Famous writers' wives shouldn't have to get meals when they're tired."

"What luxury," Mary said, and tasted the casserole. "Um. This is delicious, whatever it is." She meant everything the firelight touched, but Paul said, "Salmon."

The casserole had such beguiling flavors on the tongue. The salad was walnuts, oranges, lettuce, and some herb she couldn't separate from the total effect.

The fire seemed to warm the room, but Mary knew it was really the wine, and the man across the table who could cook, and could be silent, and watched her when he thought she didn't see.

They talked about Randal's *The Strange Girl* at the table. They talked about Randal's *For Better or Worse* by the fire. They talked before the hundred-year-old face of the French clock on the mantel, whose pendulum was a lion's head, swinging hour by hour. The sun face on the front watched their laughing faces; the women's heads on the side did not smile. The cupid on top was as golden as his gold hourglass. Black filigree hands moved from porcelain number to porcelain number. The clock struck.

"One o'clock!" Paul cried.

"One?" Mary echoed.

Paul gathered up his belongings, apologized, and was out the door and gone.

Mary sat by the fire again, alone with a bouquet of chrysanthemums and a clock whose hands moved very slowly now below the face of a golden sun.

21

MARY COULD WRITE IN BROAD DAYLIGHT, HER NEW BOOK spread out in her big tree-house study. No one was asleep in the rooms around her. She wasn't tired from a long day's work. She didn't need to hide what she was doing.

When she ran out of words, she unpacked boxes, filling the many cupboards somebody had been smart enough to build everywhere in her new house.

Beth called, wanting to talk about the letter that had come from Michael: at last he had heard his father was dead. "How sad," Mary said. "But the family seems complete to me now . . . isn't that strange? Because now we all know."

Beth sighed, then said, "I'm working awfully hard. How about you?"

"I'm full of energy!" Mary said. She didn't say: *When I can discuss my own work with someone who loves it! All the ideas that come!*

"No buyers for the old house?" Beth asked.

"Not one, after *months,*" Mary said.

"Is George Blumberg after you to send in Dad's last book?"

"He's left me alone so far, but I suppose he'll call before long," Mary said.

Beth chattered on, but Mary was thinking what she did not want Beth to hear: *We are running out of money.* When she said good-bye and hung up, Mary sat at her sewing machine again and imagined sending her own book to George Blumberg. She sewed past the drape's corner, thinking of "*The Host,* by Mary Quinn."

"Paul," she said aloud, ripping the seam. After a while she said, "Think of the money. Think of the advance I'll get—thousands and thousands."

She sewed the seam to the end, clipped it, then hid her face in its new-smelling folds. "No one," she said, "has ever talked to me about my books . . . loved them . . ."

She sang as she worked in her new house. On Saturday nights she sat on her bed watching the road and the ravine's sea of bare branches, waiting for Paul's old car to pull into her drive.

"Come in, come in." Dr. Butterfield motioned Paul Anderson to the chair on the other side of his desk. "As your department head, I'm naturally interested in your welfare."

Paul sat down.

"How is your projected biography of Randal Eliot progressing? That's what I called you in to discuss," Dr. Butterfield said. "I don't need to tell you that a book like that would bring you automatic tenure."

Paul said, "I hope to work with Mary Eliot—"

"Ah," Dr. Butterfield said, staring at Paul. "Harvard and Yale—Princeton, too—are after Eliot's papers. You've approached her? She's agreed to make you the official biographer? Allowed you access—"

"I have strong hopes in that direction," Paul said. "She's still mourning him, of course, and one doesn't intrude."

Dr. Butterfield was still staring at Paul. "But you certainly have gained something from talking with Mary?"

"I haven't felt I should publish my work until I've seen

Randal Eliot's papers, his work sheets, his correspondence . . ."

Dr. Butterfield rose. "I hope you'll take my comments this afternoon in the spirit in which they're intended." He went with Paul to the office door. "The Eliot biography is what you need. Write it. That's my advice."

Paul said "Yes" and "I understand" and "Thank you for your time," and drove home. He understood, all right: Butterfield was threatening him—publish or perish. He dumped a new batch of student papers by his kitchen chair. Some of them would begin, "The theme of this play is that . . ." He sighed. There might be one or two worth reading. There might be one that would teach him something.

But he didn't pick up a paper and begin; he stood looking down at a pile of scribbled notes by his typewriter: he had eaten dinner with Mary every Saturday night in March, then gone home to write down what she had said—it was brilliant; she saw the structure of every Eliot book. Now he could write essay after essay; he imagined them printed on slick paper in the best journals: "Eliot's Wonderland," "Colette's Worldly-wise Children on a Slave Plantation," "Faulkner's Bear Hunt As Eliot's Rite of Womanhood." *If* he got to work on them . . .

Paul sighed and looked out his kitchen window. His next-door neighbors were raking leaves in the warm spring sun.

Paul put on jeans and a sweatshirt that said *Randal Eliot* above a row of Eliot's books. He drove to Cedar Ridge under trees just beginning to cast shadow. The man/woman face on Mary's door watched him as he knocked.

"I'm going door-to-door, ma'am, raking gardens," he said when she answered.

Mary was wearing jeans, too. Her long hair was tied back with a scarf. "Come in," she said. "Where'd you get that shirt?"

"I had it printed at the shop downtown—would you like

one? Perhaps you've heard of Randal Eliot, the local celebrity?"

"Let's see . . . is he the one who wrote those novels?" Mary said.

"I think so."

"But you must have better things to do than rake gardens."

"Not a thing," Paul said.

"Then I'll help you," Mary said. "How about a beer?"

"After I've raked," Paul said. "Where do I begin?"

"With the top inch or two," Mary said, leading the way through her furnace room and garage to the shed. They unhooked rakes from nails there. "I don't know what's in the garden yet. The natural scientist of my family says I have to take the leaves off in layers." She leaned her rake against a tree and tied her head scarf tighter. "The first layer you rake off. The second one you lift off by hand."

Paul started on a fence bed where leaves had climbed the links two feet from the ground. "That's a first-rate metaphor —you're aware of that, I'm sure," he said over his shoulder.

"They grow in the spring, too," Mary said. "Metaphors."

"I've been thinking about a metaphor at the end of *A Strange Girl,*" Paul said as he raked. "Those three trees Randal used. They're shaped like women, and when Thorne's car passes them, the sunset on his windshield is 'carried before it as a man carries a lantern in daylight.' Randal says the trees 'bear the scrutiny of that light in turn; rejected, they stand green, darkening toward night.'"

"Yes," Mary said.

"Diogenes!" Paul cried. "Thorne is like Diogenes—'as a man carries a lantern in daylight'! But the trees are shaped like women, and his light rejects them, so they 'darken toward night.' Thorne has been looking for 'a woman' all his life—a real woman, not the American females we call that. He raised Catherine to be that real woman, but now she'll be rejected by him, and she knows it, so she runs away, hides in the night!"

Mary nodded, her dark eyes shining. "Most people travel

on the top layer of Randal's books like flies on cellophane—
they don't go deeper for the real thing. Randal got so many
letters asking him, 'Why did you end *A Strange Girl* like
that? You broke my heart!' But how else *could* it end?
Catherine has become an American woman, so she'll be
nothing in Thorne's eyes but a cripple." She turned her back
and went on raking.

A cardinal's shrill whistle pierced the garden air. Far
away, another one answered. After a while Paul said, "Gary
Cooper. Thorne's like him."

"How did you *know?*" Mary cried, straightening up, her
jeaned legs buried to the shins in leaves.

"I always thought of him when Randal described
Thorne."

"No one has *ever* seen that!" she cried. "And did you
know—I discovered that Gary Cooper played the White
Knight in an *Alice in Wonderland* film?"

They leaned on their rakes, talking and talking, oblivious
to the leaves they stood in, or the sun that went down after a
while, or the dusk falling.

At last it was too dark to see leaves or rakes, but the two of
them had built an analysis of Randal Eliot's *A Strange Girl*
that was as solid as a beautiful, finished object—Paul
shouted when he saw it, and threw his arms around Mary.
They hugged each other, there in the light of the moon rising
and the electric crackle and snap that played between them.

They stepped apart in the rustle of dry leaves. "We're
crazy!" Mary cried. "What would people think of two idiots
who'd stand in the cold talking about a novel for hours?
Come on in!"

They hung up jackets, kicked off their shoes, and went
stocking-footed through the kitchen to a warm living room.
"Don't mention the novels—we'll get started again!" Mary
turned on the gas fire in the fireplace. "We were supposed to
go out to dinner." She looked down at her old clothes. "I've
got stuff for a salad, and we'll order pizza, and I've got some
wine. You'll have to stay for supper. I've frozen you solid,
talking and talking. Can you stay?"

He could stay, Paul said, if he could buy the pizza and help with the salad.

"Have you submitted any of your essays to journals?" Mary asked, taking tomatoes and cucumbers out of her refrigerator.

"Not yet, I'm afraid," Paul said. "I'm working on them, though—I've been tracking down the phrase 'without a net' that runs through *A Strange Girl*," he said, finding a knife and the cutting board and another thought about Randal's work. Then he looked sheepish. "Sorry," he said. "I can't stop talking about the novels."

Mary called in their pizza order, then starting rinsing tomatoes and lettuce.

Paul said, "The first 'without a net' tells Jack that Thorne's cut him out and slept with Janet, right?"

"Right," Mary said.

"And then Thorne says the same thing, but this time he says that raising Catherine has been 'like a game of tennis without a net.'"

"Butterfly net, then tennis net." Mary dumped sliced tomatoes in a salad bowl.

"And the final one is 'old man like an acrobat on a high wire up there, without a net.'"

It was no use—off they went to roam Randal Eliot's novel as if it were a jungle full of rare flora and fauna. The pizza came, and they ate it without noticing, and never finished the salad, but sat very close on the couch, involved in what they were saying, interrupting each other, brushing hands as they gesticulated in a rush of words.

At midnight they finally stopped talking and sat together watching the gas flames dance on the hearth. Close to Mary, Paul watched the light run along the silver in her hair and deepen the lines around her mouth.

"I've got a favor to ask," Paul said. "I've got more than one." Mary turned to look at him. "Your old house that's vacant. Could I rent it from you?"

She looked back at the fire and didn't answer.

"I'd be a devoted tenant," Paul said. "After all the years

I've worshiped Randal's work—can't you imagine how I'd feel, actually living there! And I've got a confession to make—I used to be *angry* that you'd moved out of that house."

"But I have my own house—I love my own house!" Mary cried. "My first new stove and refrigerator and washer and dryer—Randal and I always had to buy used ones, old ones! No basement with mushrooms growing in the floors!"

She was so close that Paul could see the joy glittering in her eyes. "No attic where squirrels store nuts in your boxes of books in the fall, and roof nails collect frost all winter and drip on them in the spring!" She doubled up on the couch beside him, excited, hugging her knees. "Now I have *my* house. *My* garden. The children sleep in my own pretty rooms when they visit. I can stay out all night if I want, drive my own car anywhere! I've never had such things in my whole life!" She pushed a strand of silvered dark hair away from her happy eyes.

"Then you wouldn't mind if I lived in the old house?"

"If you want to. I wouldn't ask much rent." Mary frowned suddenly. "Except that I have a confession, too: I need money. The paperback of *Net Worth* made some, but Randal spent quite a bit on our trip abroad before he died, and the government took a big chunk of it, too. And if I want to get Beth and Jay through graduate school . . ."

"Then it's settled. And you'll get whatever rent you think is fair. It'll help both of us."

"If you want to rattle around in an old wreck," Mary said.

"I don't care about mushrooms or squirrels—to live in *Randal Eliot's* house!" Paul hunched his shoulders. "Guess you think I'm a fanatic."

"As long as you like the books, I think you're a very good friend of mine," Mary said.

They looked at each other, then looked away.

After a while he said, "While we're confessing."

Now she looked at him again.

"My intentions," he said. "You know what I want. I want to be Randal Eliot's official biographer. People are coming to see you—I know that. They want you to work with them, give them access to his work sheets and correspondence, tell them how he lived—"

"Yes," Mary said. "I've sent them all back empty-handed."

"And they can't believe how much you know—I've talked to a couple of them, the ones from Harvard and from Chicago anyway. I talked to Fairchild from Harvard. 'She knows every line Eliot ever wrote,' he said."

"I ought to," Mary said.

"But that isn't the main reason that I'm here—you know that. You give me *energy!* Ideas! I've written a half dozen essays on Randal's work now. I go home from talking to you, and the words pour onto the page—it's incredible, like being in Randal's 'trance.'"

Mary stared into the fire. She said, "I want his work to be analyzed *critically, intelligently,* from the inside out."

"I can try, if you'll let me. If you'll tell me about him—anything, everything—"

Paul saw the closed look on Mary's face. She was silent.

After a moment, Paul said he should go home. He told her he'd call and talk about moving into the old house.

When he said good night and opened the door, moonlight gleamed on Mary's spruce trees. He backed his car to the street. Mary, standing against the light, was a slim, dark shape in her open door.

Paul drove home, parked his car, took off his coat, and sat down at his typewriter. He sat there a long time and wrote nothing.

He went to bed, saying to himself: "In Randal Eliot's house!" He punched his pillow, laughed out loud. "In that house! I'm going to live in that house!"

He tried to imagine that place, those rooms, but what he saw was a woman in a doorway, framed in light.

22

MARY MUST HAVE THE PAPERS, THE WORK SHEETS—SHE *lived* with Randal!" Bill Rivers said, sitting on the edge of a table in the English-department mail room. "If you're having dinner with her nearly every night, which is what people say . . ."

Paul was silent, riffling through a handful of envelopes.

"We've had these Harvard and Yale and NYU profs sniffing around every month or two, wanting to see Mary Eliot."

"She won't talk about a biography. Not yet, she says." Paul didn't meet Bill's eyes.

"But you've been interviewing the whole department, asking us to remember every word he uttered!" Bill said. "I hear you've seen his father . . . psychiatrist . . . doctor . . . minister . . ."

"I've been doing some preliminary research," Paul said.

The mail-room door opened. "Hugh!" Bill said. "Back from the dusty libraries of Spain!"

"Just back," Hugh said. "Not even unpacked."

"Here's Paul Anderson," Bill said. "Hugh Bond. Paul

came last September after you left. Paul's a Randal Eliot scholar."

Hugh shook Paul's hand. "Going to write his biography, now that he's gone?"

"I've rented his house," Paul said.

"Oh-*ho,*" Bill said. Hugh asked, "Any ghosts?"

"Haven't moved in yet—I'll do it today." Paul stuffed mail in his briefcase.

"If you hear glass breaking, it's him," Hugh said. "Loved to smash glass. Kicked it out. Kicked out a plate-glass restaurant door, cut himself up. Threw stuff through windows."

"I've found that out," Paul said.

"The top boys won't want it talked about much, I suppose, now that's he's put the whole university and town on the map." Hugh was scowling. "But you go see his neighbors—they'll tell you."

Paul said, "I think Mary's reluctant to let his life—"

"Of course he *had* to be crazy to write that well," Hugh said. "Who ever saw an ordinary genius? Somebody who goes to his kids' parent-teacher meetings, rakes the yard . . ."

Paul said good-bye and drove home in the warm spring sunlight. He didn't need a jacket to go back and forth from his apartment to his car, loading boxes.

When he parked in front of Randal Eliot's house, Mary sat on the old porch swing waiting for him.

"The place certainly isn't fancy," she said. "I've had it cleaned for you, and there are rugs on the floors, and enough dishes still in the kitchen, and curtains at the windows." She opened the big, sagging front door with one practiced lift-and-push.

Paul hesitated as he crossed that threshold. *Randal Eliot's home.* "I don't want to change a thing," he said, standing in the living room. "Where did Randal work?"

"In that chair," Mary said, pointing into the next room. "He hardly ever used the desk." The chair was a fake leather recliner, cracked on the arms so that stuffing leaked out. It faced the front door and the living room.

"Center of the downstairs," Paul said. "Center of the house!" He ran a finger over the back. "I'll never have enough nerve to sit in it."

"Make yourself comfortable," Mary said.

"I imagine the six of you had years of good conversations in here." Paul looked at bookshelves that covered one wall, then at a bay window that showed a maple tree, the neighbor's house, and the park across the street. "Wish I could have been one of those books, listening in."

"He liked to be alone," Mary said. "We did most of our talking in the little room at the top of the stairs."

"He'd go up there, settle down with you and the children?"

"No. I meant that the children and I talked up there. It was my study. Pretty small, but I did a lot of typing in that room."

"Not down here?"

"No. My typewriter was upstairs."

Paul shook his head. "It's obvious how little I know about Randal's life."

"People talk about him, I'm sure," Mary said, pushing a cupboard door shut that wouldn't stay shut.

"They talk about his work. He's the greatest man this town has known in a long time—maybe ever."

Mary opened the door to the dining room, and went on into the kitchen. "The stove's an old one, but it bakes well," she said. "It was my mother-in-law's."

The stove gleamed before Paul. "When Randal lived at home with his parents?" he said.

"Yes. She had it for years and years," Mary said.

"He saw his mother use that when he was a child," Paul said, half to himself. "And then he had it in his own house." Mary was already out the kitchen door and taking the small, narrow steps to the second floor and the room at the top of the stairs.

"This was my study," she said.

The room was hardly ten feet square, and one corner was filled with a tall cupboard. An old-fashioned oak desk with battered drawer handles and a railing around the top took most of the space. "Not much room," Paul said. "For the five of you to talk." He had already turned away to look at the big front bedroom.

"It was cozy," Mary said. "And it was mine."

Paul followed Mary into the front room. It had a single bed in it. "The master bedroom?"

"Yes. I thought you might want to sleep where you can see the park," Mary said, and went to look out three tall windows, then started downstairs.

"I'm sure it's hard for you to come here, missing him as you do," Paul said, following her.

Mary said nothing, but looked into the blackened fireplace, then into Randal's study.

"I shouldn't make you stir up memories," Paul said.

Mary gathered the big collar of her jacket around her face, said she hoped he'd be comfortable, and good-bye. He watched her go down the steps of the pillared porch with her quick, energetic step. She never looked back.

Paul walked through room after room of Randal Eliot's house. The air smelled ancient and dusty: old wood, old cloth. He sat on the desk chair in Randal Eliot's study, looking at half-empty bookshelves and the recliner's stuffing leaking from cracks.

He began putting his books on Randal's shelves, his clothes in Randal's closet. He found himself tiptoeing sometimes, or stopping to listen.

Finally he locked Randal's house behind him. Spring sunlight still flooded Mary's garden when Paul went to find her at suppertime. She stood among softly moving masses of tulips. Jonquils starred the path edges. The heavy scent of hyacinths weighted the air.

"My new garden!" she cried to Paul, her arms spread wide to light and color and spring air.

"How about eating on the patio?" Paul said.

"'For winter's rains and ruins are over,'" Mary said, quoting Swinburne as she came along the curving garden walk.

"'And all the season of snows and sins.'"

"Yes," Mary said, her dark eyes very large and thoughtful as she passed him and went into the garage.

Paul closed the garden door behind him; daylight was only a few bright stripes and cracks in the garage's darkness that smelled of gasoline and peat moss. "'The days dividing lover and lover, the light that loses, the night that wins.'"

"'And time remembered is grief forgotten,'" Mary said in the dark, close to him by the furnace room door. In that small, blind moment or two she was near enough to touch, with the scent of her bouquet of hyacinths surrounding them, as dense and fresh as his pleasure.

"You're a poem-keeper, like me," he said.

He heard her light laugh. "I didn't think there was another one around," she said, still in the dark by the unopened door, as if she, too, felt the pleasure. Then she went in, trailing her hyacinth scent.

"I memorized poems by the yard when I was plowing or disking or harrowing," Paul said, reaching to bring down a vase for the hyacinths. "I'd stick a poem up by the tractor wheel and chant to myself by the hour. I was a loner."

They carried a table through the patio door.

"I didn't date in high school," Mary said. "Nobody ever asked me."

"I was shy," Paul said. "Just a farm boy. But I've always been close to my sister. When she comes to town, you'll meet her." He carried a chair to the patio.

Mary followed with another and stood beside Paul, looking at a drift of yellow jonquils.

"My dad planted flowers in rows," Paul said. "Farmer style. He saw it as a crop of flowers."

Mary said her father knew the Latin name of every flower. Paul said his father wouldn't have morning glories—he'd fought too much bindweed in his fields.

"He wasn't a big man," Paul said, "but when he laughed,

he sounded immense. He sang in the hog house: 'Don't you know, don't you know what a fellow ought to do when he's got a little family depending on him so . . .'"

"My mother knew long poems by heart. In her day, every child in the family had to have a 'piece' to say whenever guests came," Mary said. "Now *there's* a lost bit of Americana."

They brought a tablecloth, plates, silver, and wineglasses to the sunny patio. *We're talking like lovers,* Mary did not say aloud. *Sharing our pasts. But don't be silly.*

Paul saw Mary smile. Her heavy braid of hair was slipping over her ear; she stopped in the last sunlight to pin it in place, and the gesture was a pretty one.

Paul brought out the wine bottle. "There are poems that bring back every detail of my time on the farm," he said. " 'When the hounds of spring are on winter's traces'—I say that and I'm back in the field. I've just shut off my tractor, and all I can hear is the humming electric lines along the road . . . maybe wind in high grass . . . maybe I see a killdeer running down a row ahead of me, pretending it has a broken wing."

Mary sat down and watched him pour wine in her glass. "I saw an early version of that poem in Swinburne's handwriting at the British Museum last fall," she said.

Paul stopped pouring wine to look into her lifted face. "I can't imagine that," he said. "The paper, the pen strokes—that poem actually hovered there once between his pen and the page."

"And came to you in a Nebraska cornfield."

Paul raised his eyebrows and finished pouring the wine. "I was a very peculiar farmer's son. I'd finish work for the day with calluses on my hands and a new poem in my head."

The smell of the farrowing houses . . . the bang of the pig feeders . . . mud tracked in the back door . . . "That life's gone now," Paul said, putting salad on Mary's plate. "Gone. Like my parents."

"Nothing left?"

Paul shrugged. "There's a tenant farmer. The old house is empty, boarded up."

"You weren't happy."

"I went to school in town, and I was one of the 'farmies,'" Paul said. "We were the clods, the ones who couldn't be in plays or on the football team because there were chores after school, and work on weekends."

"Outsiders," Mary said. "We were both outsiders. I was one of the poor ones who wore the same clothes over and over, because I was saving for college. But I never got there."

"I saved, too," Paul said. "As long as I can remember, I saved. We saved. And my folks finally managed to send me to Wisconsin U., and then I put my sister through college."

The sun went down as they finished their supper, but they talked until it was too cold to stay outdoors. They hardly noticed the furniture they moved inside, the dishes they did, the fire they lit, the striking of the French clock. They started poems, finished poems, struggled to remember lines, traded memories and images. Paul loved Emily Dickinson: "'There's a certain Slant of light,/Winter Afternoons.'" They finished it together, there in the firelight—"'When it goes, 'tis like the distance/On the look of Death.'"

"Randal had that 'distance,'" Mary said. "In his casket."

They were quiet for a while, looking at the fire.

"My former wife didn't die," Paul said. "I can't imagine how it must be. But it seems to me as if I never had one."

"You never hear from her?"

"Not really. I still send her money every month—she's in a nursing home."

"An illness?"

"Brain damage from an accident."

"How awful!" Mary stared at him in horror.

"We met at the university. She was going to be a veterinarian. She quit school to work while I got my doctorate."

"And then she'd get her degree?"

"That's how we planned it—but we were so young! You think you can't fail, when you're young."

"And you loved her."

"Yes." Paul was watching the flames lick around fake logs. "But it was a hard life . . . she had a job, and she raised fancy dogs to sell. Until she fell down a flight of stairs. She can't remember doing it, can't think, can't talk, can't walk . . ."

"What a tragedy." Mary couldn't think of anything else to say. She repeated it: "What a tragedy."

Paul rubbed his hands together between his knees. "I support her. I can do that," he said. Firelight lit creases at the corners of his eyes and edged his thick lashes.

23

"THEY GO EVERYWHERE TOGETHER," MICHELE WILDNER SAID one hot night, sneaking looks at Mary and Paul. She was a new instructor in Paul's department; she balanced her plate on her lap in the courtyard of the university arts building. Paul and Mary had brought their own plates and glasses to a table nearby, and sat talking over their suppers.

"She looks so . . . ordinary," Deb Iverson said, and licked cream cheese from a celery stick.

"His car's always in her driveway," Susan Fink said.

Harriet Thorman laughed. "Maybe she wants somebody to take care of again."

"She's had enough of that, I bet. Randal went wild, even on campus—she had to get him to the hospital how many times?" Deb said.

"Paul's the one I like to look at." Michele drank half her iced tea in one thirsty gulp.

"Mary's got everything," Harriet said. "Doesn't have to work . . . her kids are out of town . . ."

"She's *old,*" Michele said. "Look at that hair."

"She must have something," Deb said.

"Randal's money," Susan said.

"That's not all she's got—Paul wants to write Randal's biography—that's what I hear," Harriet said. "Profs come from the East, West—she won't talk."

"So that's the attraction," Michele said.

"Paul's a lot younger than she," Harriet said. They watched Paul leave Mary at the table and go toward the buffet. His white hair was whiter still in the sunlight; his very blue eyes shone.

"Nice," Michele said, watching Paul with narrow eyes.

"You're thirty," Susan said. "Leave the old ones for us."

"He's not old," Michele said. "Besides—my Ph.D. thesis was on Hemingway, and I've got an article on Randal Eliot and Hemingway I'm writing."

"Since when?" Harriet said.

"Today."

Harriet, Susan, and Deb watched Michele's shapely progress toward the buffet table. Paul was talking to Bill Rivers, but Harriet caught Paul's single quick glance: he was aware of a woman in a summery green dress coming toward him. Michele stood on one foot and swung herself slightly before Paul as she talked, her bright brown hair moving on her bare shoulders.

Nora stopped at the table where Mary sat alone. "You look happy," she said.

"It's fun," Mary said.

Nora laughed. "Of course!"

"It's just that we have so much in common, because he's fascinated with Randal's work! We get started on some character or some scene, and the next thing we know, it's after midnight!" Mary's face was flushed as she spoke; Nora told her she looked pretty. Mary's eyes were on Michele Wildner talking to Paul at the buffet table.

The summer grew hotter and hotter. Paul sat on a redwood bench outside the old house, looking up at its gables and chimney and television aerial. Mary had told him that Randal had built the bench and laid the patio stones, and had looked out at that yard from his study window. A bird nested in an old grapevine on the side porch; Paul heard leaves rustling there. Children flew back and forth on park swings beyond Randal's picket fence and the quiet street.

A screen door slammed. Paul saw a fat woman carrying a box down the steps of the house next door.

Paul watched her put the box in a station wagon and go upstairs. When she came out again with two cardboard cartons, Paul was waiting by her front steps. "Let me help with those. I live next door." He smiled, taking the cartons from her. "Paul Anderson."

"Betty Jacobs," the woman said. "An old settler on this block." She opened the back of her station wagon; Paul put the cartons on top of others there.

"Anything more to go?" Paul said.

"Afraid so," Betty said.

"If you need help," Paul said.

"I'd love it. Come on in." Betty held the door wide for him. "What a mess."

Back and forth they went, propping the door open for each other, asking questions now and then. Betty was "between," she said. "Between jobs, marriages, a rock and a hard place," she said, keeping the screen door open for Paul with her substantial backside. Paul said he was between most of those himself, or had been.

She was renting the upstairs of her house to make ends meet. He was still new in town, Paul told her. "Have a drink," Betty said, when the station wagon was full. She handed him a cold beer. "And sit down, if there's any place *to* sit down."

They cooled off for a while in silence. "You knew the Eliots?" Paul asked.

"For about twenty years," Betty said, finishing her beer and crushing the can with a considerable grip. She looked about sixty, Paul thought. "Real well. Mary used to come over here and hide when she was scared of him."

"Scared?" Paul stared at Betty.

"Yelled at her from the yard—didn't care who heard. Threw things."

"When he was mentally unbalanced, I suppose."

"If he was mentally unbalanced all the time—yes. Come to think of it, he probably was. Mary was such a good mother—her kids'll take care of her now."

Paul glanced out Betty's dining-room window. "You can see Randal's study from here."

"He sat in his chair in there—just sat. Once in a while he got up, poured another glass of wine. Threw something and broke the window once, I remember."

"Mary typed for him, sometimes all night, I hear. While he dictated to her?" Paul said.

"He was up late, all right. I never saw her typing in there. Never saw her in there much at all. He wanted them all to *keep out*. Not that they'd want to come in. Would anybody?"

"It's just that I'm living there, and I wonder about Eliot. He's becoming so famous," Paul said.

"He's dead, that's the main thing," Betty said. "Maybe his books are great, but *I* know what his real masterpiece was."

"What?" Paul asked.

"Driving into that wall at sixty miles an hour."

Paul sat in Randal's study in the dark that night. Betty's uncurtained, streaked windows showed her walking back and forth next door. *Mary used to come over here and hide when she was scared.*

Randal's old house surrounded him, hot and dark, keeping all its secrets, like Randal's father in his wheelchair had kept his. Did he remember his son, Randal? Paul had asked the old man. But Donald Eliot, slumped in his chair at his sister's kitchen table, would only talk about the state Capitol across the street, and somebody who had changed his name to Brogan.

Paul walked back and forth in Randal Eliot's house. Randal had never put in air-conditioning; it was almost too hot to sleep. At last Paul started two big fans, one in the back bedroom window, one in front of his bedroom door. He lay listening to that steady pulsing as rivers of dark, hot air streamed through the hall.

He couldn't sleep. He went down the creaking stairs and then the narrow steps, his feet sidewise, hanging on to a dim balustrade that had one broken post wrapped with tape.

Moonlight shimmered in patches everywhere; Paul walked on carpets of moonlight in big rooms with high ceilings. A ray of moonlight, twinkling with the shadows of leaves, fell across Randal Eliot's study. Five downstairs doors stood open to singing insects and rustling trees.

Paul walked back and forth. His typewriter stood on Randal's desk now beside piles of interviews: the words of those who had known Randal Eliot.

He had hunted for the teachers of Randal Eliot's children. Most of them were dead or gone, but Miss Mildred Caldwell lived in town. He'd found her house, knocked at the door, and heard her call, "Come in!"

Paul had found her in a rocking chair among piles of newspapers. A large white cat blinked at Paul from her lap.

Paul had introduced himself. "I'm beginning a biography of Randal Eliot," he said. "I believe you had his second son, Don, in grade school?"

"Sit down," Miss Caldwell said. Paul had settled on a pile of papers; there seemed to be no other place.

"First grade," she said. "I dreamed about him nearly every night."

"Randal Eliot?"

Miss Caldwell had looked over her glasses at Paul. "Don. He was the saddest little boy I ever saw. That father of his—he was all the child talked about, and with that look in his eye. Bragged about how his father was born in *New York City.* Talked about his father's books and how famous he was, and all the time I saw that sad look in his eye. His father made him do the most peculiar, insane things. Don told me." She stroked her cat. "Other boys talk about going to a baseball game with their dads, or fishing."

"What kind of things?"

"Tearing up pictures of his grandfather! Can you imagine?"

"Randal's father?"

"It was night, Don said. His father made him tear up the pictures, and then he took him to the cemetery—at night! That little boy had to dig a hole on his grandmother's grave and bury all the pictures there!"

They sat looking at the cat; it had jumped to the floor and was rubbing against Paul's jeans.

"Sick," Miss Caldwell said. She rocked in the narrow space between newspapers. "Children are tough, thank heaven. Don's doing well with his business, I hear, and he got a B.A. He came to see me a few years ago. And his father's dead. If you're doing Randal Eliot's biography, you can put down that I said Randal Eliot might have been a writer, but he was no father." She snatched a newspaper from a pile, shook it, and began to read.

"Thanks so much," Paul said, getting up.

"Bring the paper off the porch, will you?" Miss Caldwell said. "It's hard for me to bend down."

Paul picked the newspaper from her door mat and brought it to her.

"Thanks," Miss Caldwell said, fitting it neatly on top of a pile beside her chair.

"Good-bye," Paul said.

"He was sick," Miss Caldwell said.

24

HANNAH SAID, "THERE'S A BREEZE," AS IT CAUGHT THE
blanket she spread in shade near the river. She watched her
brother unpack the picnic basket. "Look at that *food*. No
wonder she's in love with you."

"Who?" Paul stopped uncorking a bottle of wine.

"Mary, of course. You can *cook!"* She grinned at him.
There was a ripple and splash as canoes passed on the river.
"She ate as much of your dinner last night as I did. How'd
you like my PR work for you—telling her how hard you
worked on the farm to pay for my college—the whole
loving-sister bit? And you're in love with *her*. All you used to
talk about was Randal, Randal, Randal. Now it's Mary,
Mary, Mary."

"You're a soured romantic," Paul said, working on the
wine cork again.

"You watch her all the time," Hannah said. "And Mary,
well—it doesn't matter if *I'm* talking. If you so much as
scratch your ear, she looks at you, and I don't think she
hears a word I say."

Paul wasn't looking at Hannah. "The two of us like to

talk." He had the wine cork out now. "She made you laugh last night—isn't she clever? And she says profound things: a first-rate mind! I go home and take notes on what I can remember—she's amazing on Randal's work."

"See what I mean? Mary, Mary, Mary." Hannah laughed and licked salt from beneath one of her long red fingernails.

"Randal, Randal, Randal," Paul said. "I've talked to some of his neighbors. I've discussed him with members of the department."

Hannah was watching her brother closely. "You look as if you don't like what they say."

"I had no idea, that's all. I admired his novels more than any novels I'd ever read. I moved into his house."

"A real bastard?" Hannah watched Paul pour wine. "His psychiatrist wouldn't talk, I suppose."

"Not much. He did say that Randal was shut up in some kind of mental hospital in London just before he died. He got sick, and Mary had to find a place to put him."

"An insane man on her hands in a foreign country—great vacation," Hannah said.

"I suppose. But he wrote, even in London, Parker says. And here's the magnificent thing I found out: Randal told him he'd finished a new book called *The Host.*"

"A *new* book?" Hannah stared at her brother. "Where is it?"

"I don't know." Paul fiddled with a salad fork. "Maybe Mary's still typing it. She's always working up in her study."

"All the time?" Hannah said.

"She says she starts at six o'clock in the morning and doesn't quit until supper's ready," Paul said, stretching out on the blanket.

"And won't talk about him."

"And won't talk about him." Paul gazed at a sky full of picture-book clouds. "But she let me have his lecture notes for all his classes."

"Brilliant, I suppose," Hannah said.

"No," Paul said sharply. "Dull. Worse than that. It looks as if he got everything—even his examples—from a book

I've used. To look at his notes, you'd suppose he read out of that book, and assigned another one to his students."

"Hey," Hannah said, *"I* could do that!"

"Anybody could," Paul said. "But that's not the way he taught at all. His students tell me he was mesmerizing, and they let me see their class notes. Amazing stuff—he winged it—a spellbinder."

Hannah licked another fingernail. After a while she said, "If she's got another book of his, it'll make her money. That's probably why she's working so hard."

"I suppose." Paul squinted against sunlight flashing on the river.

"Reflected glory," Hannah said. "Handmaid to the famous novelist. You can see that she's perfect wife material —she gardens . . . talks over the back fence with the neighbors . . . showed us the photo albums she makes for the kids . . ."

Paul gave Hannah a sidewise look from his blue eyes. "Randal was the bizarre one. But Mary can take Randal's work apart, word by word. That's where she shines. She could have been the professor. She's smart enough."

"I like her, even if she can't even *see* me when you're there." Hannah stripped a drumstick of meat. "You like living in that old house?"

"Not as much as I did," Paul said. "I know a little about what went on there." He sat up and pulled grass blades at the blanket's edge.

"How about the would-be biographers who keep coming to see her?"

"She tells them Randal didn't leave any papers, and she doesn't want to talk about him."

"Marry her! She won't say no to you—she'll want you to be famous, like Randal. And then you might have a dollar or two to invest in your sister's public-relations business." Hannah laughed. "Just think—I wouldn't have to make my boss coffee, or get the teeny-tiny assignments to be in Swamp Center for a feed-store opening . . . or go to West Farm Gate to interview a prize pig."

Paul watched the river flowing past, flashing with sun. "Now she's being invited to speak in New York . . . L.A. . . . Boston. She could do it. She's amazing when she talks about Randal's work. But she won't go."

"I bet she knows she doesn't look good. She's got to cut that hair of hers—a really smart cut—and use mascara and eyeliner . . ."

Paul yanked at the grass.

Hannah dropped an empty carton in the picnic hamper. "I'm going to talk to her. She could look years younger. I watched her on TV last week. They asked her the same old questions about Randal being in that trance of his." She sighed, bit her lip and said softly, "I care about you, big brother. Maybe I sound tough, but I'm only joking about the money—I want you *happy.* I want you *settled."*

Hannah's tone was tender. Paul squeezed the grass in his fist, then threw it away. His hand smelled of it, rank and green.

Hannah was determined. She would be in town only a week, she said. She called Mary the next morning and took her to lunch and then to a beauty shop. After that, she said, they would go to a makeup consultant.

Mary laughed and went with Hannah, talking about old dogs and sows' ears. Her daughter Beth had tried to make her do this for a long time, she said. It was kind of Hannah to spend her time . . .

"You'll be beautiful!" Hannah told her. "You're a celebrity—going on television, being interviewed—you should look like one."

"Well," Mary said, sitting down in a pink-and-chrome chair without looking at Hannah, "perhaps . . ."

The hairstylist came in when his assistant had swathed Mary in pink linen. He circled Mary several times, then flourished his scissors and hacked at Mary's long hair as if he were killing a poisonous snake. Soon it lay dead on the floor in a black-and-silver skein.

What was left of Mary's hair was pasted flat to her skull,

then strung out to curl, then dried, then brushed violently, then coaxed and talked to until—at last—the stylist said, "Young is short, with a soft, sexy lift!" and handed Mary a mirror.

Mary looked at herself from all sides and said, "I'm either coming in for a landing or taking off."

"A bit too wide, we think?" The stylist patted Mary's head between his hands. "Less lift. A bit more soft and sexy."

"Whatever," Mary said, watching him in the mirror. "That's better." Then she was enveloped in a cloud of hair spray and came out on the other side to pay her bill and tip. She felt half naked and light-headed. "I've had that hair for half a lifetime," she told Hannah.

"You look *wonderful*," Hannah said. "Except for the makeup. That comes next."

"So much trouble," Mary said, looking at long trays of colors that a blond makeup specialist was dabbling in. The young woman's face looked like a very smooth white egg that had been dyed for Easter with watercolor pastels, especially her rainbow eyes. "How long does it take you to put all that on your face every morning?" Mary asked her.

"Only half an hour," the specialist said. She was, unobtrusively, chewing gum. While her businesslike glance roamed with various brushes and pads over Mary's face, Mary amused herself by watching for the furtive, slight rotation of the young woman's chin.

At last Mary was allowed to look at herself. All she recognized at first was the startled expression in the eyes. They peered from their thick fringe of lashes, amazed to find themselves in such surroundings. If the dark eyes were mysterious and half submerged, the mouth was soft pink and rather vulnerable, Mary thought. It seemed to have nothing to do with those eyes, or the swoop and bounce of the shining hair.

Mary had to take the makeup off. Mary had to put it on. There were tricks to it. Finally she was allowed to graduate with a fortune's worth of cosmetics in a fancy sack and a face that stared at her in amazement in every mirror she passed.

"You look about my age!" Hannah crowed.

"If you're forty-eight," Mary said. "And where do I keep this big sack of art supplies?" She thought a minute. "My mother-in-law had a vanity table—plenty of room for paints and powders, with a mirror lid and a bench to match. Let's stop by Paul's and see if it's still in the attic."

Paul opened the door for them. "Well," Hannah said to him, turning Mary around to face him. "What do you think?"

Paul didn't speak, but Mary laughed, sparkling at him with her great, secretive eyes, then said if he didn't mind, she'd poke around the attic for a minute. He heard her quick steps on the narrow stairs.

"Well?" Hannah said.

"Pretty," he said.

"Sexy," Hannah said.

"Hot," Mary said in a few moments, coming down again. "I found the table and bench, but it's a hundred and twenty degrees up under that roof."

"We'll help," Hannah said, and Paul went ahead of them to dust the table and bench off with an old sheet, then hand the two furniture pieces down steep attic stairs to two pairs of waiting hands.

"I can get them in my car, if you want them at your house right away," Paul said. Hannah and Mary followed his car through the hot afternoon streets, and the three of them carried table and bench into Mary's upstairs hall.

Paul and Hannah looked around them. "This house is bigger than it looks," Hannah said.

Mary's beautiful new eyes sparkled at them. "I've got a bedroom for each of my children, and a whole suite for me," she said. "And my study," she said. They caught a glimpse of a long room, great ivy plants hanging under skylights, and a typewriter flanked with stacks of papers.

"This part of the house was built later," she said, her short hair swinging against her cheek as she turned at the end of the hall. "This was the honeymoon suite—bedroom, dressing room, even a Jacuzzi."

Mary set her end of the table down in a dressing room that had a gold-and-cream-colored sink and walls of closets. "Right here," she said. "The table ought to go right here." It did. The wall between closets and a row of windows fit it exactly.

Paul slid the bench under it, then went to look out the row of five windows. The driveway lay below him among tall evergreens, and beyond the narrow road was the wooded ravine.

Paul turned to see a satin-covered bed, a wall of bookshelves, a desk, and a curve of fieldstone. "What a fireplace!" he said.

Mary said yes, she'd admired it the first time she'd seen it . . . there were stones from many parts of the country . . .

Mary's mouth went on talking, but all Mary saw was the look in Paul Anderson's eyes. He stood beside her bed, one hand dimpling its satin coverlet.

It was deep, hot summer now. Mary had cut half-moon flower beds before the windows of her sunken living room, and planted impatiens that seemed to grow while she watched: fountains of scarlet, pink, fuchsia, white. She had bought two Victorian benches for that round garden-within-a-garden, and a pair of stone shells for water, topped by a small, naked stone girl. Cardinals drank at her stone shells; at dusk the hawkmoths hovered.

Windows, floor to ceiling, opened onto the patio, and Paul set the glass-topped table for supper there. He was tired of words by the end of the day, he said. Cooking a meal relaxed him and saved time for her. "A nice arrangement," he said, stretching out on her couch in white shorts and shirt, smiling his handsome smile.

Mary, half caught in the world of her newest book, often came to supper with her dark eyes a bit withdrawn and apt to stare at a glass of wine, a flower, or Paul's bare brown legs as he came and went from the kitchen.

And Paul watched her. Mary felt it, coming slowly out of her long day's fight to say what she meant without saying it, tired of walking that hairline, following that almost invisible thread through the labyrinth in the dark.

Sometimes Paul read Mary a new essay he had written about Randal's novels.

Mary smiled as he read, recognizing her own analyses of her own work. Paul smiled back, glad that she liked what he had to say, happy to read his well-thought-out sentences in candlelight that flickered before a twilit garden.

But Mary was thinking how easy that kind of writing was—so easy, so secondhand. It was only writing about writing: it clung for support to the hard rock of her words, her novels, her art.

25

MARY SAT AT HER DRESSING TABLE, LOOKING IN ITS MIRROR at a woman who might be . . . forty-two? She turned her head a little, and the striking silver streak in her black hair shone. Her eyes gleamed under their long, dark lashes. Writer of the eighties. The voice of her generation. The next winner of the Pulitzer Prize. Someone young enough to write many more books.

She would wear the pale blue dress with its pale blue coat. Mary sprayed herself in new scent, put on her clothes, looked at Mary Quinn the famous novelist in the front hall mirror, and drove to Nora Gilden's house.

"My God!" Nora Gilden cried when she opened her door.

Mary stood there, smiling.

"Can't believe it—what happened?" Nora said. "Come in and tell me! No, come in and turn around!"

Mary turned around, then took off her coat and sat down. "Well!" Nora said.

"Do you like it?"

"I'm too speechless to say!"

"What was your first impression?" Mary asked.

Nora frowned, thinking. "That you looked apologetic for being so happy."

"I am," Mary said.

Just as she spoke a very small, very old lady came through a doorway dragging a rocking chair. "Greatgran!" Nora said, and went to help her.

The old lady flapped a dried-up hand to keep Nora away, settled her chair near Mary, and sat down. "Your face is sure painted," she said to Mary.

"Greatgran, this is Mary Eliot," Nora said. "Greatgran's come up from North Carolina for a visit," she told Mary. "You're so *pretty*. You look about ten years younger."

Mary said she was glad to meet "Greatgran." Greatgran smiled with very white false teeth and rocked.

"You remember Paul's sister?" Mary asked Nora. "Hannah Anderson? She said I had to look glamorous for television."

"She's right!" Nora said. "You're a celebrity."

"And she helped me buy some new clothes."

"Nice of her," Nora said, looked hard at Mary, and laughed. The maid came to announce lunch. Greatgran sat where she was; she seemed to have gone to sleep.

"Greatgran's so old she forgets how old, and she's lived her life in the no-running-water-in-the-house, chop-your-own-wood mountains," Nora said when they were out of earshot. "When I was back in North Carolina a few months ago—you remember—I asked the relatives to come visit sometime, the way you do in the South." She sighed. "Greatgran wanted to come, so I paid her airfare."

"Oh, look!" Mary cried. "Where did you get this?" One of Nora's dining-room walls was now an expanse of woven blue and white: blue wool, white cotton. The rich, thick texture came and went as Mary looked: wheels of blue cobwebs stood out, then receded as her eyes picked up delicate verticals, then diamonds . . . squares . . . blue plateaus . . . white roadways . . . ovals . . . snowflakes, and —always—the latticework and the circles, four by four.

"A real, made-to-be-used coverlet," Nora said. "That

pattern's hundreds of years old: Double Chariot Wheels. Greatgran brought it as a present—wove it herself. Told me she'd heard people up North liked such things. I said they certainly did."

Mary touched its sturdy, intricate surface. "Imagine planning that: keeping that harmony of the great pattern and the minor ones." Taking her place at Nora's table, she still kept her eyes on the coverlet.

"So," Nora said, settling herself in her chair, "Hannah decided you ought to look glamorous."

Mary smiled, spreading her napkin in her lap. "She wants her brother to marry me. That's what I think."

"And what does *he* think?"

"He thinks about a biography of Randal. Hannah probably tells him he should marry me and then he'll be biographer-in-residence, so to speak." Mary's long eyelashes hid her eyes.

"What about his first wife?"

"I've found out they were married young, and she supported them while he was doing his graduate work—raised fancy dogs for sale. He hated dogs all over the house. Then she had a terrible accident—fell downstairs, had such brain damage that she doesn't remember falling, doesn't talk . . . he pays for her keep at an institution outside Boston. She was very intelligent, he says. Pretty. Blond."

They were silent, thinking of a young woman shut away, damaged. Finally Nora said, "You want him?"

Twenty-nine years of lying beside Randal . . . the sunlit freedom of her house . . . her own money in her wallet . . . books with her name on them . . . an assistant professor in a minor university . . .

Mary said, "I haven't got time."

"For what?"

"For worrying about my underwear," Mary said. Nora laughed. "Thinking all day about what he said last night, or what he didn't say last night, and does my hair smell nice, and is the bed made up clean, and what will we have for breakfast, and when will he leave so I can work, and why does he fold my newspaper the wrong way, and why is he out of sorts this morning, and must I have his friends for dinner tonight, and can't he do the shopping for a change, and who will pay for this, and can I tell him when his writing stinks, now that we're—oh, I've *had* all that! And he's only forty. Too young for me. I've got *wrinkles.* I've got *stretch marks.* Everything about me is lower. If I marry somebody, I'll pick somebody *old* and *rich* who'll think I'm very young— somebody who reads stock reports all day and just wants my teenaged company at dinner." Mary stopped for breath and smiled at Nora and did not say the thing she pretended she did not even feel: *I am a writer of the first rank.*

"Well," Nora said. "You're a picture in that dress."

"I'm happy," Mary said. "Of course, it's *Randal* Paul's interested in. He wouldn't look at me twice if I weren't Randal's widow—and he doesn't really see me, as it is. He sees someone who lived with Randal." She leaned across the table. "But if I'm invisible, I'm happy! I wouldn't say this to anyone else in the world—I feel like I've got a wife."

"Perfect," Nora said.

"He makes a wonderful supper nearly every night at my place, or we go out. We talk and talk—I love it! He treats me with a certain . . . respect? Because I'm Randal's widow?"

"Ah," Nora said. "He's taking it slow. Smart man." She grinned. "Most of them leap on you by the second date, even if they're so old they creak. Stupid. The first days are the best days. Make them last, I say."

Make them last.
Mary sat beside Paul at plays or concerts. His shoulder touched hers in the dark; he leaned close to whisper in her ear.

He's taking it slow. Mary bought high-heeled sandals. She found a necklace to slip into the low-cut neckline of a blouse, and earrings for her newly pierced ears, and wished she had money for truly beautiful clothes.

Money. Money had to go to Randal's father and Aunt

Viola every month. Beth and Jay both had jobs, but it cost so much for university tuitions and books. Paul's rent helped to buy groceries, but she desperately needed to sell the old house, and no one came to look at it; no one wanted to buy it. And Randal had left debts she had not known about; they invaded her mailbox: envelopes with "Randal Eliot" in computer print behind their shiny windows.

The Host. It would be the first book with her name on it. She should send it to George Blumberg—his words hovered in her mind day by day: *Tell Randal to get a new book done as fast as he can. It will make him a fortune.*

But this book would be her first book, and it wasn't quite good enough. It had to be the best she had ever done: *The Host.*

So she worked at it, worked at it, worked at it, while Paul drew closer. He told her about his hard years alone on the farm after his parents were gone. She told him how her mother had died of cancer and how her father had not wanted to live, but most of the time she listened to Paul. She watched his handsome face grow tense and bitter as he described a farmer's life: the pressure of the seasons and weather. And he had had so little money, and came so late to graduate work.

"I wish I'd been kinder to Sandra," he said. "If I drink, I've got a quick temper." He shrugged. "But she's taken care of. I send the money."

"You don't see her much?"

"Hardly ever," Paul said.

Bit by bit they shared stories of their lives, talking in the light of the fire, or the sun of the garden, or the moon of soft nights on the river. Mary could tell him about her life, but when she talked about Randal, she saw the look in Paul's eyes sharpen with fascination. She was Randal Eliot's widow. The first time they kissed, Mary thought she felt that worship in the very pressure of his lips, in the way he held her.

She had forgotten how kissing a man changed everything.

You crossed those few last inches of space between your lips and his and were in another country, and there was no going back.

She shouldn't have kissed him. She called herself names in her empty house. When she saw him again, they tried to talk as they had before about the novels . . . Mary's novels . . . talk that was precious, rare, useful . . .

She tried to keep her head. She tried not to look at him much. She sat on the other end of her couch. She fidgeted, then tried to keep herself still and calm, as if she had been in the arms of many loving men, not two.

Paul was tall and warm and solid, and had an unnervingly intimate voice she heard for the first time. And all at once they were playing that oldest game of now and not yet and sometime and maybe that her instincts knew by heart; Mary stood to one side, astounded at what she had not forgotten. And her body was the worst of all, pounding and perspiring and revving itself up—

"Mary Quinn," she said to the wide, clear mirror in her bedroom. "Money . . . my own house. My own book."

But the mirror showed her a rumpled and melted woman who had run upstairs to stare at her smooth bed and listen to Paul Anderson drive away.

Make them last, Mary said to herself, putting on makeup at her vanity table. Then she said, *Money.*

"Sell your first book," she said to the woman in the glass. "What are you waiting for?"

The mascara wand slipped, hit her eye, and stung as sharply as the lack of money.

Her eyelashes had smeared below her eyes when she blinked—a mess. She had to clean it all off and start over.

She had to have money.

Her eyes were blurry with cold cream now: she couldn't see at all. Mary squinted at her nearly invisible face in the mirror. Where was the writer of the eighties, the voice of her generation . . .

"Here," Mary said aloud, scrubbing at her eyes. Her

name would be on the new books—let Paul write about the old ones.

Mary lifted her chin, looked at herself, began to make up her eyes again. "If you liked my *books* . . ." she said aloud, thinking of Paul, sweeping the mascara brush to the end of her lashes, "you'll love *me*."

Now her made-up face smiled at her from the mirror.

Mary heard Paul's knock on her door.

She came down her carpeted stairs to smile at Paul's compliments and kiss him, her eyes shut, her body feeling his through their summer clothes.

It was pleasant to think of kisses and caresses to come as she clicked in her high heels through restaurant doors.

It was pleasant to sit with Paul in candlelight and smile over the menu into his blue, blue eyes.

Paul poured another glass of wine for her, closed his menu before him on the table, and said, "Later on, I want to talk about my idea for an essay. I'll call it, 'The Manic-depressive South of Randal Eliot's *In the Quarters.*'"

Mary's wine had dulled memories of her day's struggle with words, lack of money, all of it. She was a woman in a soft pink dress, and when she moved she caught the scent of her perfume. The man across from her had a cleft in his chin, blue eyes, lips that she . . .

"What?" Mary said, her eyes wide and shocked in her candlelit face.

"'The Manic-depressive South of Randal Eliot's *In the Quarters,*'" Paul said again. "I haven't thought about this kind of essay before."

The waitress came for their orders, took the menus, and left, so that Mary couldn't hide behind glossy cardboard. She stared at Paul.

"I've talked to people who knew Randal—how could I help but meet them all over the place?" Paul said.

Mary didn't answer.

"I've been taking notes about his work. Now I feel I've got to consider his life."

Mary's eyes turned to the river flowing below the restaurant's windows. The candle on their table lit her pink dress so that it threw a faint, soft blush on her face and throat.

"He was a genius," Paul said. "And he was a deeply disturbed man." His voice was a little louder than he meant it to be. "I have to know it all in order to be honest about his work—to sum it up and not make major errors."

"It seems to me," Mary said, and stopped. Her hands were fists, pressed together before her on the tablecloth.

Mary began again: "You're able to judge his work in terms of the *work itself*—I've already seen that. The *work itself*—can't that be your major subject?"

"One of them, of course, but—"

She saw what he thought in his face. "Modern scholarship," she said in a flat, dead voice. *"Biography.* How many modern readers read biographies of famous writers and never look at the *books?* How many people will know that Randal Eliot was a manic-depressive who believed he wrote his novels 'in a trance'—and *that's all* they will ever know of his work? That's what his writing will come to."

"Oh, surely not!" Paul said as loudly as he could without drawing attention. "I'm simply providing a frame, a structure for enhancing Randal's work."

Mary looked at him, her face serious. "For centuries, nobody thought of reading a writer's work in the light of his life. People wrote 'lives' of kings and statesmen and generals, but a biography of a composer? A writer? A painter or sculptor or architect? What use would such biographies be? The paintings and writings and statues and symphonies and buildings spoke for themselves. They were enough—the true thing."

Paul said nothing.

Mary's eyes glittered at him across the candlelight.

They went to a film and talked afterward over coffee. They never mentioned Randal Eliot.

They kissed good night at Mary's door. She shut it. She went upstairs to open a copy of *In the Quarters* and turn page after page, lost for a few moments in her world of

South Carolina slave society that had taken so many boxes of notes, so many nights of work while the family slept.

"The Manic-depressive South of Randal Eliot."

Mary took a deep breath there in her study's lamplight, then opened a drawer to look at a manuscript: *The Host, a Novel by Mary Quinn.* Another novel with her name on it lay beside it: *Prayer Wheel.*

26

YOU KNOW RANDAL WAS INSANE AT TIMES—YOU LIVED WITH him," Paul said. Mary lay in his arms under a starry sky, and the fragrance of her garden was all about them. It seemed impossible that his new ideas about Randal had come between them like sheets of ice.

Mary wouldn't answer. "You won't tell me," Paul said. "You won't help me. Why can't we talk about Randal's illness? You have marvelous insights—you know what you've given me—"

"Pay attention to his *work*," Mary cried, and sat up, shaking herself loose from Paul's arms.

"You're trying to protect him, I know, and that's natural. You're as devoted to him as I am."

"Devoted to his *work!*" Mary cried.

"But you can't pretend he didn't have *wide* cracks in his personality. They show in his work—they're indispensable to an understanding of his work!"

"No!" Mary jumped up. Her body shut part of the starry sky away from Paul where he lay on the blanket. "We know almost nothing about the lives of great Greek writers—we

192

write about their *work!* Maybe Shakespeare's mother married his uncle—does that account for *Hamlet?"*

Paul rose to his feet, too. The blanket lay between them on the grass. He said, "You're the one who knew Randal—if you don't help me, how can I write about whole sections of Randal's work?" His voice went higher in exasperation. "You don't realize how modern scholarship works with the *facts.* I've got to have the *facts!"* His voice was loud with anger now; he advanced on her . . .

"Randal's work can stand alone! No matter who wrote it, it's *there!"* Mary turned and ran into her house, shut her doors. Paul was left to snatch up the blanket, throw it in his car, and drive home to Randal's dark house.

One September afternoon Paul stood in Randal's study with a letter trembling in his hand. His voice was jubilant over the long-distance line to Hannah. "Remember all those ideas I've had about Randal's work? I wrote to Matrix Press and told them I was working with Randal's widow, and I've got a contract! I've got a ten-thousand-dollar advance! They want me to do *the* biography of Randal!"

"You're off! You're launched!" Hannah yelled. "What mad, irresponsible, expensive things are you going to do with an advance like that?"

"I'll get tenure at the U—that's the first thing I'll do with it," Paul said. "Blessed tenure—you get it and you've got a paycheck for life—sure beats farming. I'll get Butterfield off my back, once I've got the contract and start work."

"A biography of Randal Eliot," Hannah said in a teasing voice. "Now, *how* will you ever persuade his widow to tell all?"

"You can laugh," Paul said. "It's not that easy." He played with a row of pens on Randal's desk. "I haven't seen much of her lately."

"You what?"

"Haven't gone out with her—not for weeks."

"What *happened?"* Hannah sounded shocked. "What did

you do? Your temper . . . you've been drinking? I bet you went into one of your—"

"Well," Paul said, "I did yell at her. She'll only talk about Randal's *work!* She won't discuss his life—not any of it! She hasn't been trained in scholarship. She doesn't understand how you hunt for the man in his writing, how you find the bends and kinks and breaks in his life that show up in the novels . . ."

"So you lost your temper, scared her—"

"Every one of Randal's books has manic-depressive written all over it!" Paul's voice was a snarl now. "And I can't even talk to her about it!"

"She's wearing her makeup? Getting her hair done?"

"How should I know?"

"Listen—go over to her house! Tell her you yelled at her because you love Randal's work so much. Tell her you've got a book advance—go on! Tell her it's going to be a biography of Randal, and wouldn't she rather have you do it than a stranger? *Somebody's* going to do it. Tell her that."

Paul was silent on his end of the line.

"Look at it this way," Hannah said. "She's always had a literary man to live with—somebody who writes books and needs her help, that kind of thing. You can be her new writer-in-the-house if you get her to help you, be your muse, your woman, your dark lady of the sonnets and so on. Otherwise you're going to be bookless, right?"

"Right."

"And we're not talking about that house of hers, or her money that's Randal's money, after all—and aren't you his biographer? We're not thinking about you *at last* getting your Ph.D. paid for. None of that!" Hannah laughed. *"You're* her man-who-writes now . . . let her see that. Tell her you need the kind of wife Randal had. And for God's sake don't lose control of yourself! The trouble is, you think you've got 'Randal Eliot the Great Writer' as your rival. You're crazy. He's dead—you're alive!"

"She's the most fascinating woman. I keep thinking about—"

"And you've got one more advantage over Randal Eliot," Hannah said. "You're in love with her."

"But she doesn't—"

"And the final advantage is . . ." Hannah laughed. "She's in love with you."

Paul said good-bye to Hannah and sat for a long time watching rain glaze the street before Randal's house and darken the trunks of trees in the park.

A few miles away, the rain streaked Mary's bedroom windows and dripped from the blue-green spruces beyond.

Mary, sitting on her bed, listened to George Blumberg calling from New York. One of her sweaty hands folded and unfolded the bedspread's edge. Rainy light struck stars from a silver-backed brush on her dressing table.

"I've read *The Host*. We've all read it here," George Blumberg said from his New York office. "It's a marvelous book." Mary said nothing; she folded and unfolded her bedspread's flowered satin.

"The question we have . . ." George paused. "It's your letter . . . and your name on the book, not Randal's."

"My letter is perfectly clear, I believe," Mary said. "My name is on the book because I wrote the book."

There was silence on the other end of the line. Finally George Blumberg said, "I'm sorry—I'm confused—this new book of Randal's—it's obviously *his*—"

"I wrote it," Mary said. "Randal is gone. Surely I can have my name on my own book now?"

"You're saying—"

"That I wrote *The Host*. It would have had Randal's name on it if he had lived, but he didn't. He doesn't have to be protected any more. Therefore I would like to have my name on my own books from now on, please, and if you will continue to represent me as my agent, that will be fine."

Again George Blumberg said nothing for a long moment, then blurted out, *"The Host* is *Randal Eliot,* through and through. It's the best thing he's done! His tone, his voice, his style—"

"I do think I've improved in this book. I'm glad you think so, too," Mary said.

"It's his *voice,*" George said. "It's his *tone.* None of us ever thought for a moment it wasn't an Eliot book—"

"Randal's gone," Mary said.

"But you can't just put your name on your husband's book." Now George's voice took on a soothing tone. "I know you're devoted to his work and his memory, and you've just lost him . . . we all understand how you must feel when it was so unexpected, so sudden."

"You don't quite understand," Mary said as calmly as she could. "I don't want to detract from Randal Eliot's memory. His four children are very proud of a man they think was an author. Let his first four books continue to be his—"

"Think was an author?" echoed George Blumberg. "My dear lady, I'm sure you're still suffering and grieving, and we really shouldn't discuss this yet. Perhaps in a little while . . ."

"No," Mary said. "Grieving has nothing to do with the fact that I wrote *The Host* and would like you to represent me as my agent. I'll be working on a new novel while you are selling *The Host*—the new book is called *Prayer Wheel.* Randal Eliot did not write *The Host,* or any other book. He talked about writing books for decades, but he never wrote one. I wrote *In the Quarters* and *A Strange Girl* and *For Better or Worse* and *Net Worth.* Now I have written *The Host.*"

Again there was no sound on the other end of the line.

"You know how this happened—you've heard Randal say he had to publish to save his job," Mary said. "It was even more crucial for *him* to publish because he was in and out of mental hospitals during most of our marriage. No university is going to keep a manic-depressive who never publishes, and no other university is going to hire him."

George Blumberg said nothing.

"I listened to him talk about *In the Quarters* for years. Finally I was so frustrated that I wrote it, just to prove it could be done, even at night, even if it were never published.

But when his job was at stake . . . when he had electroshock treatments and couldn't remember . . ."

"I am having *great difficulty . . ."*

"Of course you are," Mary said. "That's understandable. And I'm not asking that I be given credit for *In the Quarters* or the other three books. But now I am free to publish my own novels, I think. Certainly there have been couples in the past who were both authors. The Brownings—"

"But even if this is *so . . ."* George Blumberg's voice was hesitant; Mary could hear the wariness in spaces between his words, all the way from New York. "The style, the voice . . . you can see what you're asking. Editors, critics, reviewers, readers—they won't believe *The Host* isn't Randal's—not that I think you're making this up," he said quickly. "Not at all."

"I can't prove that I wrote all the books," Mary said. "All I have is *my* work sheets, and journals in *my* handwriting, not Randal's. There are no versions of any of the novels in his writing at all, except for a few boxes of old envelopes with scribbles over them no one can read." She twisted the bedspread's flowered satin. "I know what people might say: 'He dictated to her. She simply wrote and rewrote what he told her to put down.' Or: 'She destroyed all his papers, and now she claims it's her work.'"

"You see the problem," George said.

"I suppose they could say *I'm* crazy now."

There was silence on the phone line for a moment. Then Mary said, "You understand that I couldn't tell Randal. How could I? His happiness depended on those novels . . . awards . . . prizes . . ." Tears were in Mary's eyes now. "And I don't want to take the first four novels away from him—let them stand as his. My children are so proud of him. Don't tell anyone they're mine."

"Then can't we let him have one more?" George said. There was indulgence in his tone. *"The Host* can be rushed through and there'll be money-money-money! You've found out how little the IRS lets you keep. You need plenty of it to get kids through grad school, and for yourself—right? *The*

Host will *sell.* It's Randal's best yet, and he's hot. He got the American Book Award!"

"I got the American Book Award," Mary said.

There was silence on the other end of the line.

"You don't believe me," Mary said.

"The Host is going to make *money,"* George said. "But it'll only make money *if* it's the posthumous book from the man who wrote in a trance! *Everybody* knows that story! It sells books! It's pure gold, that 'dictating in a trance'!" George's voice had gained certainty; he was on firm, financial ground. "What's nicer than money? You've got your kids' educations to pay for, and you want to help Don in business—don't mess anything up, and we'll both be rich."

"You're saying that if I put my name on *The Host,* it won't make money."

"If I take it to an editor, what's an editor going to say? 'Who's this Mary Quinn?' So I tell the editor, 'She's the widow of Randal Eliot.' And what's he going to say? 'Who's she? What's she done?' And I tell him, 'Nothing. It's her first book.' And he says—well, you know what he says. You know the kind of advance Randal got for *his* first book."

"Five thousand," Mary said.

"Maybe I could get you ten."

"Ten thousand," Mary said.

"That's the princely sum. *If* I can find an editor to take it," George said. "First novels? They're hell to sell."

"If? But you've said it's the best thing I've ever written!"

"No. I said it's the best thing *Randal's* ever written. Wait until you see the reviews. And maybe *Net Worth* won't make it to a film, but this one will. Can't you just see—"

"No," Mary said. "I can't. I can't see Randal's name on a book I've written. I can't see that anymore."

"Picture your name on the *checks,* not on the *book,"* George said. "Think of all the hassles you dodge if you're not 'the author.' You were only beginning to see what Randal was in for. You're going to be drowned in requests to review books. If they know *you* won the American Book Award, every writer with a book coming out will ask you for a puff. 'Promising manuscripts' are going to start arriving with every mail. You get to be on television—Randal already had some of that—you're put on show between somebody who killed his grandmother and an interview with a talking dog, and nobody's read your book but you. They'll come to your house and film you walking through the woods or cornfields or hog lots—they always film writers in some landscape or other—who knows why? People will call you long distance and ask if they can have a bit part in the film of *The Host.* People will call you long distance to tell you they liked your book, or they didn't like it, or they're really talking about somebody else's book, or they're trying to write, and do you have some writing tips? And once a week somebody will telephone and tell you the whole plot of this great book that *really* happened to them or their favorite uncle, and all you need to do is write it and split the profits with them. And how about the promotional trips? An interview with the *London Times* where they take two hundred pictures and ask about that many questions, and then tell you that if you'll say you *really lived through* the horrible things that happened in your books, they'll give you half a page in the *Times,* but otherwise. . . . And how about sitting in a drafty store for hours, waiting to autograph books that nobody's buying that day?"

"It's not the fame I want—"

"Then what *is* it you want?" George asked.

Mary watched rain fall from leaf to leaf. "They are *my* novels," she said at last. "Randal doesn't need the credit for them any more. I want my name on my own books."

"Then it's fame you want," George said.

Mary didn't answer.

"You'll always get the money. You've got the life you want to live," George said. "You've got shelter from the weirdos and publicity hounds and nasty reviewers. You don't have to hire a secretary to answer your mail. You don't have to sign books or go on lecture tours. You're freer than any other author I ever heard of—you've got everything." George laughed a little. "Everything but fame."

Mary was silent.

"And let me tell you more," George said. "If you want to be 'the Author,' not 'the Widow,' then all the publicity stuff is just the beginning. When you're a 'Big Author,' you start working up a 'persona,' a public face—you know what I mean? The next thing Randal would have had to do—if he'd lived—would be to build on his writing-in-a-trance stuff. What kind of false face could Randal have . . . something everybody'd remember long enough to buy his books?"

"A middle-western college professor?"

George's laugh had relief in it. "You get the picture."

"He could have been the Master of Manic," Mary said in a bitter voice. "The Bipolar Genius. The Daredevil of Depression." She looked at herself in the mirror across the room. "And what would I be?"

"Who knows? What have you got?"

Mary looked at her mirrored self in the rain-streaked light of a Nebraska afternoon.

"If you're Randal Eliot's widow, you get it all," George said. "I know you're still grieving, and I don't want to make it worse, but I have to tell you the truth. You've lost him, so they're going to leave you pretty much alone. If you want to write, go on: you're hidden out there with all your time to yourself. His books make money? You get it. But how about nasty reviews of Randal's books? They'll never embarrass *you*. You can say, 'How sad that they don't appreciate Randal's work,' and go on enjoying life."

Mary watched rain blown by the wind against her bedroom windows. "I'm already being approached by writers and scholars who want to do Randal's biography."

"Just say no—tell them anything—tell them you can't bear to talk about him—tell them you'll do it down the road someday."

"They're writing articles interpreting Randal's books in the light of his mental illness! My books! They're hunting out facts about his life . . . his parents . . . our children . . . and then writing about how his life affected his work—*my* work!"

George sighed. "Look at it this way: they're not sniffing around to find out whether you were in love with your father, or if you're a closet alcoholic, or dye your hair, or enjoyed beating your children every Saturday night, or slept with every man on your block—"

"No," Mary said.

"You can put your name on *The Host* as Randal's *editor*," George said. "Which you are, after all. And listen: we're talking about *money* this time. Six figures, for a start. You'll be a *rich woman*."

Mary said nothing for a moment. Then she said, "That much?"

"That much. And that doesn't include book clubs or paperback bids or foreign translations or movie options."

"What about my new books?"

"Simple!" George Blumberg's voice was crisp, professional. "We'll say Randal kept dictating—dictated like mad! Kept going into his trances, maybe had a premonition—"

Mary broke the connection.

She looked for a long time at blue spruce trees in the rain.

Then she lay facedown where pale light shimmered on satin.

27

MARY LAY WHERE SHE WAS FOR HOURS. RAIN FELL.

At last she saw it was evening; she crawled off her bed and made it up neatly. She washed her face. She put on her makeup, perfume, a gauzy cotton blouse, slacks, sandals.

"Six figures," she told the woman in the mirror.

She went downstairs to open the refrigerator door listlessly. She poured a glass of milk, buttered a piece of bread, and curled up in a corner of her couch. "Thousands and thousands," she said aloud. "The children's educations."

The fireplace Paul had lit so often was black behind its glass. She had eaten on the table by the fire night after night, watching the light play on Paul's silvery hair and his blue eyes that watched her . . . watched her . . .

Her eyes were sore and dry from crying over a dream of her own books—a dream as fragile and senseless—she saw it now—as one egg carried across London. She paced her dark living room. *Fame,* she said once in a hard voice.

She remembered that Paul squared his shoulders when he smiled. His eyes had a look . . . when he and she had been quiet together for a moment . . .

Old, Mary said. After a few more circles around the living room, she said: *Paul.* And then: *A public persona.*

When she sat down on the couch again, the sense of her own home grew around her, substantial as its walls. *You want to write, go on—you're hidden out there with all your time to yourself.* The French clock on her mantel struck nine as if in answer.

She climbed the stairs and stood in the doorway of her writing room. Her new novel's chapters lay scattered over her big table and the expanse of work spaces under the windows. A sentence on her typewriter was half finished: she had left it when George Blumberg called.

Paul's warmth—when she came close to him, she could feel it: his aura. When he shrugged his shoulders, he ducked his head, too. He rubbed the back of his neck when he was thinking. His chuckle seemed to come from below his belt. He laughed—big ha-ha-ha's—then looked faintly surprised at his own joy. But when he was angry, he grew stiff and white.

Mary leaned against the door frame and shut her eyes. *Mary Quinn the novelist. Mary Quinn the prizewinner, voice of her generation, the writer of the eighties.*

Her doorbell rang.

She ran to brush her hair. She looked at herself in her vanity mirror, then cranked a bedroom window open to call, "Who is it?"

"Paul." His voice came from the roofed-over space before her front door.

"I'm coming!" she called, and put on lipstick. She'd had a bath that morning. Her hair was clean.

When she opened her door, Paul seemed to fill her house completely. He stepped inside, and she thought every room must be taking note of him. Paper rolled into her typewriter sensed he had come. Each dish in her cupboards, she imagined, must be aware of him.

"Just thought I'd see how you were," Paul said. The look in his eyes hadn't changed; he straightened his shoulders and smiled a little. He was wearing a good-looking shirt and blue pants that matched his eyes.

"I've been so busy," Mary said. "Come in. Sit down."

He sat beside her on the couch and held out a letter. "I wanted you to see this before I showed it to anyone else," he said.

Mary read the letter he gave her. She looked pale and tired in the lamplight, Paul thought, watching her eyes move down the page.

"That letter's my chance at tenure—the only chance I'll ever have to be a faculty member, a professor, with enough salary to pay the bills for my Ph.D. and have a decent life," Paul said, taking the piece of paper back. "I'm a poor farm boy. You know that. You know what this means."

Mary sat beside him and said nothing.

"You know I'm a fanatic about Randal—I've worshiped his work since I read the first word of it. I'd die before I'd see his reputation tarnished . . ." Paul's eyes were on her face. "And you know it's you I have to thank for this. My ideas about Randal's work brought this offer. You helped me with every one of them."

Rain streaked the living-room windows; lamplight turned it to flowing quicksilver. A dim garden hung heavy with leaves and rain. "I've been honest with you," Paul said. "You know this is what I've dreamed of for the last ten years—being Randal's biographer."

Mary was silent.

"You're melancholy—what's wrong?" Paul said.

"I've been writing."

"Poetry?" Paul said. "Is that what you do in that 'secret room' of yours upstairs?"

"I wrote a . . . story," Mary said.

"A story? You wrote it?"

"Just to try my hand." Mary's face was half hidden by the fall of her short hair. "Randal's agent doesn't think he can sell it. I talked to him today."

"A story? Oh, now, don't be so unhappy, don't worry!" Paul put his arm around her shoulders. "You're just starting!

None of us can expect to sell the first things we write!" She smiled a little at that. "What you need is a good shot of whiskey," he said.

"I don't drink hard stuff," Mary said, drying her eyes.

"You have some. You know where it is."

"Yes, you do. Think of mountain climbers. When they're feeling lost, a dog finds them, and what does he have around his neck? Tea?"

Mary smiled a little. Paul brought a bottle and two glasses.

"My story is 'derivative,' Randal's agent says." Mary's voice was bitter. "He told me my work sounds just like Randal Eliot's—everyone will think I'm putting my name on some new work of his."

"A small glass," Paul said, handing it to her as he turned off the bright lamp.

"Thanks." Mary didn't sound like herself; he hardly recognized her voice.

They sipped whiskey in the dim light from the kitchen. "It's just a story," she said.

"That's right," Paul said.

"I've worked on it for a long time," Mary said. "It's good. I ought to know."

"You're an excellent judge of fiction."

"I'm a good *writer,*" Mary said, looking into her empty glass. Paul filled it again.

"Of course you are! You worked with Randal." Paul's voice hushed a little. "He's the finest writer of the twentieth century—that's what they're saying about him."

Rain dripped from the eaves in the dark.

"I have to make some money," Mary said at last. "And I want to tell you what nobody knows yet." Paul thought he heard a catch in her voice. "I only decided today after I talked to Randal's agent one last time. After we'd discussed my . . . story."

Paul said nothing. She seemed to be struggling with her words. "There's a new book of Randal's," Mary said. "He dictated it to me before he died—dictated the way he always did, night after night, never sleeping—"

"A new book?" Paul cried. "A book by *Randal?*"

"I only decided today," Mary said. "It will sell if it's Randal's book. It will sell—"

"It will!" Paul jumped to his feet.

Mary stood up, too. "His agent said so. I need money for the children, and for me."

"Of *course* you're upset," Paul said, and put his arms around her. She put her head on his shoulder, and he held her close and murmured, "Never mind . . . it will be a wonderful book."

"I know!" Mary cried. "I know! I ought to know!" She was trembling; Paul held her tight. When she turned her face to him, he kissed her, and her arms tightened around his neck. Then she pushed herself away and ran upstairs.

He waited. He walked back and forth in the dark living room. Perhaps she was up there crying.

Paul listened for a little while longer, then climbed the carpeted stairs. Mary's study door at the end of the hall was shut, but her bedroom door stood open to the sound of soft sobbing. A dim glow from the front-yard light fell through rain-silvered windows.

"Mary?" Paul said, sitting near her on her satin bed-spread. "Mary?" He could feel the bed shake slightly with her sobs. He reached out and began to rub her back. "You're tired," he said.

"Yes," she said, her voice muffled. She stretched out on her stomach, her head under pillows, and Paul massaged her shoulders and the long column of her backbone. The shirt she wore got in his way; he pulled it up and stroked, kneaded, circled.

Paul pushed a pillow to one side and touched her cheek, brushed her tear-wet hair away, smelled her perfume. Bending over her in the dark, he whispered to that wet hair and cheek, "I love you—you know that. You've known it for a long time. Marry me."

She turned over then, warm and damp and fragrant in his arms. He kissed her wherever his hands bared her skin, pulling her clothes off, pulling his shirt and shoes and pants off to hold her wet face against his, her body against his. Nothing but Mary's wet face was cold—suddenly she gave off the same electric energy she had when they talked, touched, laughed—

Their breathing slowed at last. Their heartbeats slowed. Paul kissed her over and over, then reached across her to turn on the bedside lamp—

"No!" Mary cried.

Paul gave a low laugh, his face in the sweet scent of her hair. "The dark lady of the sonnets . . . woman of the dark? Marry me . . ."

Mary sat up to run her hands over his furry chest and through his thick hair, then bent to kiss him. "I can't marry you unless I tell you . . ." She stopped, then went on. "Randal didn't write his books—"

"Of course he didn't!" Paul said, his lips close to hers in the dark. *"You* wrote it all down, saved it—where would he have been without you?" Paul's words came out in a rush: "And I need you as much as he did—I'll keep this job because of you, and be the Randal Eliot scholar because of you!" He shook her gently by her bare shoulders, then pulled her down to lie in his arms again.

Mary lay very still; they heard rain drive against dark windows. "You'll be proud of me—just like you were proud of Randal," Paul said softly. "We can keep Randal from being forgotten. You'll see me taking his name all over the country, and you'll know you've made it possible—just the way you stood behind Randal." He kissed her again and again, until they fell asleep listening to the rain.

Before dawn the rain was over. Half awake, Mary found herself with a wide-awake man in a slippery satin nest; she giggled, teased him, said she didn't believe it, and made love to him as if she were twenty again . . . as if it hadn't been so many years . . .

They slept while dawn came. The fieldstone fireplace began to show its browns and red-browns, grays, sparkling bits of mica. The first birds sang in the rain-soaked trees.

Mary woke, came back to herself and her new, astonishing

body that was a woman's body again, like other women's bodies in still-dark houses, lying in a man's arms after love.

She opened her eyes to see Paul's thick white hair against her green pillows. Her satin sheet gave his bare brown body a green tinge wherever it lay against him.

Slowly, carefully, she slid from under his arms and hands. She stood beside him, looking for a long time at the man in her bed, then showered, put on a robe, and crept downstairs.

Her soft carpets shone in morning sunlight. Birds sang in the wet garden beyond her living-room windows. For a moment, far from Paul asleep in her bed, Mary threw off her robe and danced in her house. She ran to mirrored closet doors on the landing and turned around and around, peering at her bare body as if it were somebody else's.

Her refrigerator . . . the food in it . . . her patio room, the floor cool under her bare feet . . . and all the money coming. *Six figures. Another honeymoon in Europe* . . . Mary waited for the water to boil for her tea, covering her face with her hands for a moment, laughing to herself—a man . . . all night . . . Then she shivered, put on her robe, and carried her cup of hot tea upstairs.

She closed the door of her writing room behind her and put her newest manuscript at the bottom of a drawer—all but the page that had been in the typewriter when George Blumberg called.

She shut all her novels away, hidden.

Paul lay asleep in her bed across the hall.

Mary stood in her quiet workroom, looking around her as if she had never seen it before. If anyone prowled through her past, it would be Paul, not some strange scholar—and he saw what she was trying to do in her books—he saw it!

Tenderness flooded through her. He wouldn't write much. He wouldn't write fast. Maybe he wouldn't care about a university job at all when he saw what kind of money they'd have. He wouldn't need to write a word. He'd never owned nice things . . .

Mary sat before her typewriter. She'd left a sentence half finished when George Blumberg called. For a minute she did a small bit of arithmetic and found out how many dollars each one of the words on the page in her typewriter would bring, if they were Randal Eliot's.

Reading her last sentence again, she remembered the rest of the scene she had planned; she knew what came next.

The tapping of her typewriter keys was no louder than the ticking of a clock where Paul slept in her rumpled bed.

IV

28

"HOW COULD I BE ANY HAPPIER?" PAUL SAID MORE THAN once at his wedding. Mary was beautiful in her cream-colored dress. They stood together on her back lawn; a leaf fell on Mary's veil while the minister asked Paul if he took Mary as his wedded wife. Paul plucked the bright maple leaf from the tulle and said, "I do," and smiled down at Mary in the sunlight of her autumn garden.

"A honeymoon in New York," Beth said at the wedding luncheon.

"Plays," Don said.

"Concerts. Museums. Restaurants!" Jay said.

"And you didn't *tell* me . . . you didn't *really* tell me how beautiful you look now!" Beth whispered to her mother.

Hannah sat beside Paul. She wore a dress that matched Beth's bridesmaid dress. Paul looked around him and said in a low voice to Hannah: "Remember the folks' farm?"

"Dreadful," Hannah said. "Salvation Army furniture. Rugs with the nap worn off."

"Hot haylofts," Paul said. "Pitching those grain sacks in that dust. Plow points skidding on stones."

"Hand-me-downs," Hannah said. "Make-do." She could

213

read her brother's mind. "Now you've got everything—money from Randal's new book, and your house, job, biography . . ." She smiled at him.

Beth smiled at her mother. She whispered, "I wish Mike could come back from Africa to see how happy you are—that huge book advance! You're rich!—and Paul . . ."

"I need a man to take care of, I guess," Mary said in Beth's ear, looking embarrassed. "But Paul's nothing like your father."

"He depends on you, doesn't he?" Beth whispered, watching her mother closely.

"He does?"

"He watches you. I've seen him. You're important to him."

Mary whispered back, "He's writing Randal's biography, and I can help him with it." Her eyes met Beth's. "I love him, and it will change his life—writing that book. It's what he wants to do most in life. When I met him he was so . . ." She searched for a word. "Diminished."

Beth glanced at Paul at the other end of the table. "He'd better be good to you."

"He is," Mary whispered, and blushed a little. "I haven't been loved and cared for like this—not since I was young." Her eyes were level and dark under her silver-streaked hair. "I couldn't turn him away—not help him. He thinks I'm the perfect wife for a writer."

Beth's voice was dry. "Look how you helped Dad all those years."

New York basked in Indian summer. Sunlight still warmed the glassy face of the Plaza Hotel when Mr. and Mrs. Paul Anderson stood in a lobby that Mary remembered.

Paul had an appointment with his editor—how pleased Paul was to say those two words: "my editor."

"And you'll be there," Paul told Mary when they had unpacked in their suite. "He'll see why I married Randal

Eliot's widow—because she's *beautiful*"—he kissed Mary —"and incredibly smart. In incredibly smart clothes."

The next morning Rob Rosen at Matrix Press ushered the two of them into his office and treated Mary with all the deference due Randal Eliot's widow and the editor of Randal Eliot's new book: he found a comfortable chair for her and brought her a cup of coffee. Then he sat across from Paul and turned to the business at hand: arranging and rearranging the sequence of chapters in Randal Eliot's biography.

The two men at the table seldom glanced Mary's way. Once they had a question about Randal and remembered that Mary was there to answer it. "Marvelous to have our primary source instantly available!" Rob said.

The primary source drank her black coffee from a paper cup. The coffee was bitter, but she thought of the night coming, and their big bed in a Plaza suite, and Paul. Somewhere in the Plaza Hotel was the small room where Randal Eliot had yelled, "Take this down! An idea for another book!" and paced until dawn with New York's reflected light on his bald head.

Rob and Paul discussed "Randal's Early Life." Oh, yes, they agreed: his feelings about his father ought to be thoroughly discussed in the biography, and linked to father figures in his books. *"In the Quarters* has the slave owners," Rob said. "Thorne in *A Strange Girl . . ."*

Mary drank her coffee.

"Randal's manic-depressive episodes," Rob said.

"The insane husband in *For Better or Worse,* certainly," Paul said. "But images of insanity are everywhere in his work—you can see how his own illness affected his view of the world."

"You said you'd spoken to some of the teachers who taught Randal's children," Rob Rosen said, looking over his notes. "Certainly his attitude toward fatherhood is fertile ground for study—his attitude toward his father . . . his attitude toward his children . . ."

"One of my projected chapters for the book analyzes the images of parenthood in his novels," Paul said. He smiled at Mary then, but didn't quite meet her eyes.

Rob Rosen smiled at Mary too, as she sat so quietly there, a half cup of cold coffee in her hand. "Amazing, isn't it?" he said to her, bringing her into their conversation politely. "Amazing—the way a man's life illuminates his work."

"Yes," Mary said. Only Paul caught the irony in her voice. "Amazing."

When they took a taxi back to the Plaza after lunch, Paul shut the door of their bedroom, closed the heavy drapes, and said, "A long morning! What I need is a nap."

Mary laughed softly as he kissed her, kissed her again, slipped his hands under her blouse, pulling it off, pulling her clothes off and his clothes off.

He could make Mary gasp and moan and say his name in a choked voice in their dark bed—a Mary who couldn't believe her body remembered intimate pleasures, the play of two people intent on sharing joy.

At last Paul fell asleep. The dim, curtained room muffled the sound of New York's afternoon until it was only a murmur below the windows. Mary tiptoed into the suite's living room to dress, found the room keys, and went downstairs.

Love had made her hungry: she had tea and chocolate cake. Roaming past shop windows, she thought of the Plaza's big banquet room.

The door of the banquet room stood ajar down a broad hall; it was filled with bare tables and empty chairs. A cleaning woman polished silver urns, hidden behind a wall of folding screens.

"I heard footsteps," the cleaning woman told one of the porters that night. "High heels, you know, and here comes this short, skinny woman—nice clothes—maybe forty-five—dark hair turning gray—you seen her?"

The porter thought he had.

"She didn't know I was there, and she walked right up to

the head table—the one on the platform, you know? And just stood in front of it, halfway down. Just stood there."

"What for?"

"How do I know? And she started talking out loud, like she was making a speech."

"Practicing, maybe. Ahead of time."

"I guess. I watched, but she didn't take anything, or touch anything. Just stood there and talked, and then went away out the door."

"What'd she say?"

"Some kind of a speech about mooses. How she shouldn't forget to thank the moose that comes at night."

"There's a bunch of men called mooses," the porter said.

"Must be that then," the cleaning woman said.

November came with fires on the hearth and leaves to rake and burn. Christmas came with Beth and Jay, Don and Carla; Mary bought them tickets to fly home, and Hannah came, too. They sat by Mary and Paul's big tree to open presents, and teased the two pairs of newlyweds, and admired Paul's car that was his present from Mary.

When they had gone, the snow fell. Paul had Beth's large east bedroom to work in; Mary had turned the room into his study, though he often worked at the old house "for the ambience."

"It's magnificent," Paul said when his study was finished. Mary had bought him walls of solid oak bookcases, and an oak desk big enough for a president of a corporation. Padded leather chairs swiveled, or reclined flat if Paul wanted to recline. From a row of windows Paul could watch what Mary saw from her study: the drifted yards and roads and trees for black-and-white blocks—a winter etching.

Paul would teach through the spring, but in the fall he would have a year's unpaid leave to work on the biography of Randal Eliot. He had read Randal's new book, *The Host*, over and over. "It's the best thing Randal ever did," he told Mary after breakfast one Saturday morning. "We talk about it, hours on end—aren't you sick of it?"

"No," Mary said, hugged close to Paul in the light of the fire. "Talk about it. You can't bore me." She kissed Paul under his chin. "What would you do if Randal were here? Would you tell him what you think?"

Paul pulled away from Mary. "What? Randal? I'd be so much in awe, so . . . overcome . . ."

They sat for a while, their eyes on the fire. "I'm speaking for him," Paul said softly. "Writing the story of his life for him. I'd fight for him—fight for his reputation!" Fire sparkled in Paul's eyes. He shut them and said, "I can hardly stand to be in his house sometimes—and to think I never met him when he was alive, right in this town! His *genius!* Overpowering! I'd have a hard time if he were here— probably do something insane—bawl, maybe. Kiss his hand."

Mary said nothing, but her dark eyes widened a little in the firelight.

Paul kissed her and got to his feet. "Breakfast's over—off to work." He looked down at her. "Sometime I'd like to try dictating to you, Randal-style. Maybe there's magic in it. It certainly worked for him!"

"Yes," Mary said. "It certainly did."

"When I think that I'll have a *book* with my *name on it* next year!" Paul stopped halfway to the stairs. "Thanks to you." He climbed to the landing, then said, "And you'll get something published before long. You know you will."

How do you know? Mary thought, watching him disappear upstairs. *You've never been interested in my work, never once asked to read it.* Going to the kitchen, she dumped breakfast silverware in the sink and scowled, then laughed softly at herself and said softly, "Thank God."

Paul shut his study door, reclined in one of his new chairs, and rolled his head restlessly on the chair back. He wasn't getting any writing done. Mary wouldn't talk about Randal anymore—wouldn't even let him explain how important it was to understand the workings of Randal's mind . . . his illnesses . . . how Randal saw the world . . .

"Bitch," he said very softly to himself. He woke each

morning to the gas fire Mary turned on in the bedroom's stone fireplace. Sometimes he watched TV from the bed; sometimes he lay half asleep, hearing the tapping of her typewriter start, stop, start again across the hall. He hated that sound.

But when he leaned back in his new recliner, he smelled the leather, and yawned, and smiled. Every morning he went downstairs after his shower. Mary heard him, and went down to put breakfast on the table, and they read the paper together, until he went off to the campus to teach.

Paul got up to sit at his new desk and look over snowy fields. Mary was putting dishes in the dishwasher; he could hear water running. Sometimes she did a wash, sometimes she went shopping. Paul paced the floor, talked to himself, read books, went down to make himself some coffee. He was hungry by the time Mary had lunch ready.

NIGHT WOMAN

29

MARY'S HELPING YOU WITH THE BIOGRAPHY?" HANNAH asked when Paul called her in March from the old house.

"She's very good at critiquing the novels, and of course I haven't had to look up much about Randal—she knows it all, from his birth in New York to how he looked in his casket." Paul scowled through Randal's study window at bare trees and a white park.

"But what?" Hannah said.

"She's *impossible!* The same old thing—she doesn't want me to talk about the *facts*—that Randal was sometimes insane, wrote in a 'trance,' was a manic-depressive, made his family's life miserable. How can you write a biography without that?"

"She's loyal, right? Doesn't want any dirty laundry—"

"My God! It's as if she thinks the truth might hurt *me.* She hates the idea of the biography—a book of essays on his work is what she'd like."

"You haven't gotten . . . upset?" Hannah asked. "You're not knocking back any hard stuff?"

Paul gave a grunt.

"Don't!"

"Beginning next October, we'll have a few months on the Continent and in England—maybe stay until spring. Maybe she'll talk about Randal when we're over there."

"Seven months and then no classes to teach, trips abroad, a loving wife—lucky man!"

Paul's voice took on a cheerful tone. "The wife bit is great—Mary sends clothes to the cleaners, keeps the house in order, shops—that kind of thing." He played with some pens and pencils on Randal's desk. "And there's plenty of money—that tremendous advance for *The Host,* and a paperback offer already!"

"She lets you handle her *money?"*

"She says it belongs to both of us—joint accounts and all that."

Hannah made a disbelieving little noise on her end of the line.

"You should read some of the advance reviews." Paul was shuffling through papers on the desk. "Listen to this: *'The Host* by Randal Eliot almost breaks the barriers of language, qualifying him for the Pulitzer he so richly deserved.'"

"Mary must be happy."

"She is, I think, but she's hard to figure out."

"Doesn't like the housewife bit? But she's got you there to cook those meals of yours—"

"I can't take the time to cook," Paul said.

"You can't?"

"We settled that when I moved in. I simply told her I couldn't get suppers every night—I was teaching *and* I was *under contract.* I had a deadline—my job depended on that biography. She didn't say much—she's lived with a writer. And she's used to housework—she's done it all her life. A cleaning woman comes in once a week."

"Then what's the matter?"

"Nothing's the matter."

"Listen, big brother, I know you."

"She's so *driven* to get something of her own in print! She won't tell me *anything* about Randal that's really important. I wonder if she thinks I should work around the house so *she* can write! Sure, I've gotten mad—my writing is my *professional work*. Hers is just a hobby."

"Hobby?"

"Why should she bother trying to write when Randal's books keep the money rolling in? And she should be used to living with a serious writer—someone who's in national competition in his field. I'm on my way to the *top.*"

"If you're *careful,*" Hannah said in a dry voice. "I'm fond of you—don't do anything—"

Paul hung up. He put pens and pencils in a neat row on Randal's desk. The desk's finish was worn off in circles on the front corners; Randal had filled his wineglasses there, Mary said.

Paul wandered around the drafty rooms where Randal Eliot wrote books that "almost broke the barriers of language." The house smelled of old wood and dust.

His own house had a glowing oak door with a brass face on the knocker. When he closed it behind him, he could smell Mary's good cooking, and a fire burned on his hearth.

Nebraska winter melted at last and filled brooks and streams and rivers. Mary worked in the garden, and sometimes Paul went out to help her for a few hours when he wasn't busy with classwork or the biography. As summer came on, Mary had a series of parties on the patio, with tables on the green circle of the inner garden.

"I propose a toast to Paul's fine work in progress: *Tortured Life: A Biography of Randal Eliot.*" Dr. Butterfield raised a wineglass to the late afternoon sun and members of his Department of English Language and Literature.

Paul bowed to his department head and smiled.

"Paul's got everything," Harriet Thorman said to Michele Wildner and Susan Fink as they watched from a patio table.

"He's got that book contract, and they're going to England and the Continent this October. For *months,*" Susan said. "He's a fanatic about Randal Eliot. Works in Randal's wreck of a house even when he's got a big study at home.

Writes letters to any reviewer who *dares* criticize Eliot!" She laughed. "So Randal's going to step out of his grave and say thank you? If you ask me, Mary's the one who could write about a 'tortured life.'"

"Not now," Harriet said. "She's happy—look at her. She's back to playing the writer's devoted wife." Their eyes were on Mary. She stood by herself in front of the patio windows, smiling at Paul. Then Harriet and Susan looked at Michele and laughed.

Harriet said, "She's got Randal's money, but I know somebody who's got Paul."

The garden was full of color and conversation. Late at night when the champagne was gone at last and the moon went down, the final guest said good night and drove away.

"I'm *tired,*" Paul said, and went to bed.

Mary's cleaning woman had done the dishes. Mary dumped the overflowing ashtrays, picked up wadded napkins in the garden grass, carried chairs back to their places, folded tables, stacked trays.

At last she climbed stairs slowly to the open front door. The brass-faced knocker wreathed with grape leaves stared at her: Dionysus, Greek god of wine, drama, and writers. She locked the door.

Paul was almost asleep when she set the alarm for her usual early hour. He was naked in the satin sheets, and pulled the top sheet back, murmuring, "Come to bed . . ."

"I'll shower," Mary said. Paul's towel was thrown over the rod in the big bathroom, and his pants and shirt were on the floor. She carried his clothes to his study, put his towel in the laundry basket, and stepped under the hot water. It rushed over her tired eyes.

"Hidden," she whispered under the water-rush. "In a safe burrow." Then she said, *"Time to Burn."* That new book had been difficult to push past the magical point when a novel began to run downhill to the end. But at last she was having to dig her heels in, hold the book back with all her strength, afraid she might miss some richness and power as the novel brought in its great load to the last page. She soaped herself and tried to rinse away her worry in the milky water.

But Paul would love travel. He'd be happy roaming France and England.

Fragrant with bath soap, Mary rubbed her hair almost dry. When she stood in the bedroom doorway, the hall light fell over her satin sheets and Paul; he was lean, and brown with the summer sun. She snapped off lights and slid into bed.

Paul felt her bare skin against his and sighed; his breath quickened. He turned over then, kissed her, his hands in her soft, damp hair, and she gave herself up to pleasures she had only read about for all the years before Paul . . . she hadn't dreamed . . .

Every month of the summer Mary had lunch at Nora Gilden's house, where Greatgran's coverlet hung in state beside the dining-room table.

"I've tried to make her comfortable," Nora said. "I got her out of her black dress and into some designer pants and Italian knit tops that she likes because they're warm."

Mary smiled at the picture of stylish Greatgran.

"It's her hair!" Nora said, and sighed. "I bought her a wig, but she comes to meet my friends with the wig on backwards or sideways and those little black eyes of hers looking out from under."

Mary laughed in delight.

"And she's so flat in front that her clothes don't fit, so I bought her padded bras," Nora said. "But she sits and sews in a corner at my parties, and she sticks her pins in that foam rubber." Nora grinned at Mary, who was howling with laughter. "Sure spoils the effect."

"Where is she?"

"Come take a look," Nora said. "You won't believe what she's doing."

Mary followed Nora to her back patio. There was Greatgran in her designer pants and top and an apron with lace on it, down on her knees in a chrysanthemum bed. Every now and then she straightened up and grunted, then went at her trowel hacking again, pitching weeds over her shoulder into a growing heap on the grass.

"Weeds!" she said when she saw Nora and Mary.

"Your hands are bleeding!" Nora said.

"Bother," Greatgran said. "Lost my calluses, that's all. Set in a parlor and you lose 'em—should have known better than set in a parlor at my age."

Her black eyes sparkled at Mary. "Yes," Mary said. "At any age."

"I can't get her to stop working," Nora said helplessly.

"Nothing in this world like work," Greatgran said. "Good old God-made, mind-resting, callus-raising, sweat-popping work—better than all the sunshine in parlors."

"Come in and cool off—we're having our lunch," Nora said to Greatgran, and took Mary into the dining room. The maid poured wine while they talked, and in a little while a washed-up Greatgran came in and sat down.

"I want to tell Mary about your coverlets," Nora said.

"Them coverlets and me," Greatgran said, "we're 'antiques.' I can't help it if some fools in this town'll pay enough for them coverlets to buy me years' worth of work for Mary Louella and her William."

"Who's Mary Louella?" Nora asked.

"She's got a baby and a busted-up husband," Greatgran said. "They're starving over at Nuncie's Landing. You don't know. You ain't seen."

"Charter's Home Shop is going to pay her three hundred dollars for every one of her coverlets," Nora said to Mary. "But it takes so long to make one—she's so particular."

"That's *my work* that's going to be on fancy folks' beds," Greatgran said. Again her bright black eyes met Mary's and stayed there. "I never could make trash, and I'm too old to mend my ways for money." She shut her eyes.

"Tell me your news," Nora said to Mary. "You look tired. Working with Paul on the biography?"

Mary folded and unfolded her napkin in her lap. "I haven't helped Paul much. Not for months."

"Why?" Nora's eyebrows went up.

"He . . . knows I don't really like the idea," Mary said. "Don't tell anybody that."

Greatgran's eyes were on them now. "She's got a husband who's making her some trouble," Nora explained to her.

"Never heard of any other kind," Greatgran said.

"He's using Randal's mental illness to explain Randal's novels," Mary said. "So I haven't even seen the book. He goes into a rage if I criticize."

"Well," Nora said. She sighed. "I'm sorry."

"I get up early and stay up late writing for myself," Mary said.

"Randal's correspondence, appeals from writers, that kind of thing?"

"My own writing," Mary said. She was looking at the coverlet's strong, intricate patterns. "Work," she said to Greatgran. "Good old God-made, mind-resting, callus-raising, sweat-popping work!"

"That's *grand*," Nora said. "Do I get to read it? Is it romance? Science fiction? Maybe crime? I love mysteries."

"Yes," Mary said. "I know you do."

"Don't tell me!" Nora cried. "I know I should be buying the new novels! I know I should reread the classics—who'll keep literature alive if even literature teachers don't read it?" She laughed. "But I've told you and told you: lots of the English department goes home and reads *mysteries. Horribly written* mysteries, full of plodding description and clichés. That's what they do."

The maid put a shrimp salad in front of Mary. "I'm not writing mysteries," Mary said. "Sorry."

"Never mind," Nora said. "What does Paul think of your writing?"

"He can't imagine what I do in my room upstairs for hours on end."

"He doesn't work that hard? But at least you have good meals."

Mary didn't look up; she was buttering a roll. "If I make them."

"I thought he was such a cook."

"He was," Mary said. "But then he said he was a professional writer—had to meet his deadline. At least he comes to meals—that's more than Randal did."

"You could find a housekeeper."

"Such a loss of privacy," Mary said. "I'd rather do the work myself."

"If you're doing all the housework *and* your writing, I hope there are compensations," Nora said.

Mary looked at her, batted her long, dark eyelashes, and said, "Lots."

Nora leaned back in her seat. "That's all right then." But Mary didn't smile.

Greatgran's eyes had closed and they thought she was asleep, but suddenly she said, "They're good at *that*. But then you've got 'em for life. If they traveled around like crop pickers, they could hire themselves out and then get out. It'd save a world of trouble."

30

Wʜᴇɴ ᴛʜᴇ ᴘʟᴀɴᴇ ʀᴏsᴇ ғʀᴏᴍ ᴀ Cʜɪᴄᴀɢᴏ ʀᴜɴᴡᴀʏ ɪɴ
October, banked over Chicago, and turned east toward
Paris, Mary felt her unhappiness leave her, like the lights of
Chicago dimming below. Two years before she had not
touched the man beside her. Now she smiled at Paul as the
earth disappeared in clouds, and they held hands.

Paul said, "Paris!" softly to himself as they left the airport
and caught a taxi to their big Paris hotel. He wanted Mary to
tell him everything about Randal in France—everything
from the very beginning: "How he suffered over here
. . . how he dictated *The Host*."

Mary was watching the Paris streets go by. "We got in the
wrong train compartment on the way to Paris," she said.
"Randal had to pay thirty dollars more, and he was angry.
Our trip worried him from the beginning. He thought we
were spending too much—we'd have to go home early."

"That was the family trip."

"Yes." Mary helped Paul count francs to give the taxi
driver. "When we were here on our honeymoon, the hotel
was cheap and the ceiling leaked on our bed, and we made
love most of the night, and the maid came in without

228

knocking the next morning . . ." The taxi pulled to the curb and she laughed a little, climbing out.

No shoulder bags to carry on this trip abroad: the doormen carried their matched luggage to their room. No black pantsuit and sensible oxfords for Mary—Randal's new book had bought her soft wool suits and coats, silk blouses, silk nightgowns, silk slips and petticoats. Showered and freshly dressed, she stood at their wide window to watch traffic on the street far below and heard Randal say, *The children will get lost. I told them to stay with us.*

"What did Randal think of Paris?" Paul asked, coming to put his arms around Mary; they watched the street together.

"He was lost from the minute we stepped on foreign ground."

"Lost?"

"Scared. Like a little child. How would we eat? The children would never find their way back to the hotel. Wouldn't we run out of money?"

"Randal scared?"

Mary turned in Paul's arms to meet his eyes and smile. "You've written so much about Randal's mental problems —but you haven't asked very often: what was it like for me?"

"I'll want to write about that, of course," Paul said, stroking Mary's cheek.

"The novels," Mary said, turning away from his caressing hand. "All in a row, all strung on the string of his insanity."

Paul opened his mouth, then closed it. He shrugged, and followed her downstairs. The dining room had soft lights on masses of flowers, and the wine and food were as artfully arranged as the bouquets.

When they had eaten too much and were relaxed and sleepy, they walked hand in hand down Paris streets. As twilight fell and lights began to glow, Mary stood in Paul's arms at the center of that long vista from the Louvre through the gardens, across the Place de la Concorde, up the avenue des Champs-Elysées to the far-off, misty Arc de Triomphe. Paul's eyes traveled over her face; his solid body shielded her from the twilight wind. She kissed him there at the heart of Paris, keeping her eyes open to see it all.

"Randal stood here," Paul said. "Two years ago."

Mary's short, shining hair blew around her face, and her coat clung to her in the wind. "Yes," she said, and looked away so Paul couldn't see her shining eyes. *The Triumphal Way*.

The Louvre, Notre Dame, the Pompidou, the Cluny, Chartres—Paul saw it all. Having enough money softened travel's sharp edges for Mary: she stepped in and out of taxis while Paul paid, and she was never too tired to wake for creamy coffee and croissants in bed, or eat *poulet au porto*—juicy chicken steeped with mushrooms, port wine, and cream, roasted and flamed with cognac. "I'm going to get fat," she told Paul. "You're making me too happy." She blushed then, thinking of the nights.

In Paris there were inscrutable stone faces, worn by the rain, and French faces that passed on the street, and Paul's face against Mary's as he whispered in the dark. There were paintings at the Pompidou, raw and startling, and Mary's own raw, startling desire. She was hungry for Paul night after day; she was hungry, too, for sponge cake and custard melting together in a crème with caramelized almonds and crushed macaroons . . . lobsters in butter sauce sprinkled with cheese . . . goose stuffed with chestnuts and sausage . . . apple crepes with dark rum . . .

They stayed in Paris for Christmas, and walked there in new-fallen snow. They ate in small nooks and sidewalk cafés and restaurants gleaming with crystal and silver. Paul murmured wonderfully embarrassing things in Mary's ear, until her body felt bare even in her beautiful clothes. *Worth it,* she said to herself sometimes, shutting her eyes, Paul's kisses warm on her skin.

Their last night in Paris was clear and starry, and they strolled on the avenue des Champs-Elysées.

Paul's arm was around Mary. They passed the same shop windows that were full of new cars, boats, and clothes.

Floodlights shone on the Arc de Triomphe's great door that stood open to nothing but the darkness and January wind.

Once, that last night in France, Mary looked over her shoulder, but she never heard a shuffling behind her, or saw any dark, dogged shape following her against the brilliance of Paris.

When their taxi left the London airport, row houses of England lined the highway for miles into London. Each one had its high-walled garden, its small windows, its chimney pots. "London!" Paul kept saying. "London!"

Paul had insisted that they must stay at the flat on Kensington Church Street. "I want to live where Randal spent his last autumn," he said. "That's what matters."

When their taxi turned onto Kensington Church Street, there was the house with the old stuffed toys in the window —Mary caught a swift glimpse—they were still crammed behind the glass. "Remember I warned you this is no luxury flat," Mary said.

There was the shop where Randal had bought her a glass vase . . . another where he had bought her roses . . .

The liquor store.

"Wait," Paul said after he had paid the taxi driver at the curb on quiet Haverford Gardens. Mary hardly heard him; she was a stranger where nothing had changed. She was back with Randal in London before dawn, leaving for home through that apartment house door.

"Tell me exactly how it was. What do you see?" Paul put his arm around her at the wrought-iron gate. She told him exactly what she saw.

They unlocked the flat. The door swung in on familiar dark red carpeting. Beth's small bed stood in the hall, and Jay and Don's cots were still pushed under the living-room shelves. There was the kitchenette beyond its counter.

Furnished in Early Battered. Mary looked into the small bathroom while Paul brought their luggage in. There was the window Randal had broken with his razor.

"A double bed," Paul said from the bedroom.

"There were twin beds then, but we've probably still got nice, short, slippery, fuzz-ball nylon sheets and cases, no bed pads, and granite pillows," Mary said, and heard Beth wail, *"No,"* from the hall.

The empty apartment swarmed with the three children and Randal. *You're going to have to stop smoking in here. . . . You can put your elbows on the table.* The table was the same one, standing beside the same lamp.

Mary stood at the bedroom window and had no heavy braid of hair to unravel there. Just beyond the apartment's walls Kensington traffic still rumbled and whined and ground gears. The passengers of a red double-deck bus watched Mary as they sped by.

Mary unpacked again in those rooms, telling Paul how it had been, living in two worlds at once. Randal smoked his pipe in the bedroom armchair, the children read maps at the table, and Paul stood at the door to the little patio, asking about meals.

"We don't need to cook much," Mary said. "Lots of restaurants around here to choose from."

Cold wind made them turn up their collars as they hurried to Notting Hill Gate. "I watched Beth and Jay walk away down this street to fly to Greece," Mary said. "I thought I'd die if I couldn't leave Randal and go, too."

Paul asked question after question: he never tired of talking about Randal. And Mary . . . what was she not telling? Hour after hour he followed the cadences of Mary's voice. Over and over he heard her choose the exact word, so that a single image of hers held a scene in it the way a bubble could mirror a view.

"I want to take you to all the places I loved last time—the museums, Leicester Square—all the theaters and the London Coliseum and Covent Garden, Johnson's house and Sir John Soane's house—we've got months to see it all. But remember . . ." Mary's eyes met Paul's. "Randal didn't see any of those things."

"He didn't see any of them?" Paul stared at her.

"No."

"What *did* he see, all that time?"

"Some of the libraries. Hyde Park Corner." Mary frowned, trying to remember. "Greenwich."

"That's *all?*"

"And the liquor store across the street. And the house Dr. Boone put him in when he was sick, out in Dollis Green."

"But what did he do for—how long was it—nearly three months?"

"He was in this flat," Mary said, looking around her. "He stayed here. And then went to Fairlawn."

"He wrote here?"

"Yes," Mary said. "He left quite a pile of papers."

"And I haven't seen them?" Paul stared at her. "You said there weren't any."

"I have them at home," Mary said, not meeting his eyes. "You won't find that they're much help."

Day by day, Paul listened for facts about Randal Eliot. Mary took him to her favorite places and clasped her hands and laughed like a girl when she enjoyed a play. She hushed and held her breath at Portobello Market when Paul bought her an Italian silver filigree necklace a century old, delicate as cobwebs, and fastened it around her neck.

"A fly on the locket," Mary said, fingering the small, perfect silver insect.

"'Call her one, mee another flye . . .'" Paul began, quoting Donne, and Mary said, "Yes!" and put a snapshot of Paul in the locket. She bought him handsome tweeds and a winter coat. Paul found a white wool sweater for her in a Chinese shop: it was bordered with crystal beads in the palest pink, green, and blue; they gave off sparks of light.

At Stratford Mary paused at the theater railing on the way to their seats in the front row. "The five of us stood here," she told Paul.

At Greenwich she walked again down the rows of ship figureheads. *We go to the Tate and the National Gallery and*

Albert Hall for concerts, and to plays, and Covent Garden, and on those walking tours, see the Abbey—Dad just sits and scribbles.

Mary stood before the *Gravesend* figurehead and watched Paul coming toward her. A woman was watching Paul. Women often did.

"What did Randal think of the ship and the figureheads?" Paul asked.

"By that time he was living in some kind of dream," Mary said. "He didn't seem to notice where we were."

"And you had to send Jay and Beth off alone to Greece and Italy," Paul said, emerging with Mary on the *Cutty Sark's* deck. The blue March sky above was crisscrossed by a web-work of old rigging.

"Randal hardly noticed," Mary said. "But I sat in the apartment for hours just hanging on, trying not to leave him and run after the children—use my ticket—go!"

Paul listened to the anguish in Mary's voice. She did not tell him that Randal had watched the traffic all night, sure that an atomic bomb would fall . . . and lost the money she needed for taxis—had thrown it in a mailbox—and had dropped his underground ticket in a guitar case . . . had gone from store to store, hunting for a single egg.

I can't tell him what really happened, Mary said to herself sometimes. *And I can't tell myself I'm being noble: protecting Randal's memory. No. It's that I can't bear to see my own novels explained by the fact that Randal's mother threw herself in front of a train once, or that Randal rushed from a subway car and left me behind, or would not come through a turnstile, and pinned a paper poppy on the back of his hand.*

Paul took notes on what Mary said. "No other biographer will ever know so much about Randal Eliot's final days," he told Mary, and she gave him a glance from her beautiful dark eyes and said he was right.

They went to Covent Garden to see *Sleeping Beauty*. At intermission, Mary sat in her fashionable clothes, smiling now and then at her handsome husband, answering some harmless questions about Randal. The ballet put her in a fairy-tale mood—her sentences were rich and strange, she supposed: Paul took notes on the back of his program until the lights dimmed.

They watched the Prince find the huge and thorny thicket that enclosed Sleeping Beauty; her lilting theme called to him through the tangled brambles. Mary felt a little dizzy with the wine they had drunk at intermission; she looked at Paul beside her, and at his program covered with notes: her words.

Mary watched the Prince cut through the brambles and enter Sleeping Beauty's hidden castle. He bent over the princess on her gilded bed.

The theater was dark, but Mary took the pen from Paul and wrote on the edge of his program: *You can find me. Listen for me beyond the tangle of words.*

Mary handed Paul his program and smiled. He smiled back, lit by the brilliance of the stage. Later, when he had read what she'd written, he whispered, "Wait until tonight in bed . . . I'll find you . . ."

"Tell me about Randal at Fairlawn," Paul said. "I want to know everything he did, everything he said."

It was cold and raw when they took a taxi to Fairlawn. The usual pint milk bottles stood beside the door.

A middle-aged woman in an apron answered the bell. "Aw, no," she said to their questions. Fairlawn had been there, but it was gone. It was moved. They could come in.

Paul and Mary stepped into the hall, looked into the living room. *We try to give people here their freedom.* None of the furnishings were the same, and yet the angles of the walls brought back Fairlawn—the smells of it, the big couch where Jeanne had curled up in one corner to say: *You've done what women have done from the beginning.* The torn-up book had been scattered on that floor. *Will you autograph your book for me?* A naked man had run through that room . . . set fire to curtains . . .

They thanked the woman and took their taxi back to Notting Hill Gate and Haverford Gardens. Mary told Paul the facts about Fairlawn: how long Randal had stayed, that he had roamed the neighborhood, that the weather had been cold.

Standing in their flat again, she said, "Gone. All gone. That house was real. I was the ghost."

Paul poured wine. Mary took her glass. The skin on the back of her hand had patches of brown, and was beginning to loosen over muscle and bone.

Mary saw his glance. "They're 'grave spots'!" she said, looking down at her hand. "That's what the British call them—ugh!" He saw her swift glance in a mirror nearby. In harsh light, her face was like her hands: loosening. She had learned to be clever at camouflage, and when she spoke her eyes shone; she looked almost young. But when she read a book, or listened to a concert . . .

Paul held her close, kissed her, told her she was beautiful, and knew she wasn't telling him what had really happened. She was shielding Randal. He felt like shaking her until the truth fell out—the sick Randal, the suicidal Randal, the cruel father, the insane husband. He watched her leaning toward a dresser mirror, putting on lipstick, humming in her happiness. She shopped for first editions along Charing Cross Road, excited by the musty smells, the dusty treasures. She laughed in delight at Westminster Abbey: someone had left a feather duster on Queen Elizabeth's tomb, and the coil of a vacuum cleaner snaked along its worn stones.

April wind whistled through London streets. Paul and Mary sat crammed together at small, sticky pub tables, talking, talking of Randal Eliot's novels. Paul worked late on his notes while Mary slept in their dark bedroom and Kensington traffic shook the walls.

On their last night in London, George Blumberg called from New York. "I never call unless I have good news," he said. "And this is magnificent news! You've got an option from Paramount—they're making *The Host* into a major motion picture. How about that?"

"A film," Mary said softly. She turned to Paul. "Paramount's optioned *The Host* for a film!"

George talked about the money . . . so much money . . . and the national promotion, the new edition of the paperback with the movie stars on the cover . . .

When Mary put down the telephone receiver, she imagined for a moment that she could say, "It's *my* book. He's talking about *my book.*"

Paul saw how Mary's eyes sparkled with the news. "You're so proud of him!" he said. "You're so proud of *The Host!*"

"Yes." Mary glanced for a moment into his shining eyes, then looked at a red-carpeted room growing dim with dusk. Its kitchenette caught faint light on a glass, a spoon, a chrome handle. The boys' beds were pushed under their shelves. Once she had put a print of Monet's *Antibes* on the wall. Once she had finished *The Host* in this room, free at last to work in the open, her manuscript spread around her.

Paul was talking. Mary hardly heard him—she was listening to blind Randal in that living room: The Host? *I don't remember writing it.*

"You stayed here in the flat alone," Paul said. "And *The Host* was dictated here."

"Alone," Mary said, hearing Randal's voice: *I'll never write again. And who am I if I'm not a writer?*

Mary got up and turned on the lamp. "I have something exciting to tell you," she said. "You like surprises. I saved it for our last night in England. I have another book Randal wrote. It's called *Prayer Wheel.* I'll give it to you to read when we're settled at home again."

"A new book!" Paul cried. His wine slopped out of the glass; he mopped at his pants with his handkerchief. "Another novel by Randal! My God! You never told me!"

"You can use it in the second part of the biography," Mary said.

"You never told me!" Paul stared at her. "You've been working on it? That's what you were doing in your room for months—working on it?"

"I wanted to be true to my memories of it—Randal dictated it when he was so upset that I could hardly keep up with his dictation—"

"I can't believe it!" Paul walked around and around the room, repeating that he couldn't believe it . . . she'd been typing it in their house and he hadn't dreamed . . .

"We'd better get some sleep," Mary said.

Their packed suitcases stood near the door. Mary crawled into the double bed in a room where she had been so happy . . . the same room where she had clung to a battered headboard through the night, until Beth and Jay had flown away too far for her to follow.

Paul lay beside her, smoothing her hair. "Tomorrow we'll be home. You'll be glad to be out of this flat. All those weeks you spent alone!"

Mary hesitated for a moment, her mysterious, dark eyes on him. Then she laughed, almost as if she were laughing at him. "No," she said.

"You didn't mind?" Paul propped himself on an elbow to look at her.

"I loved it!" Mary leaned toward him. *"Never* in my whole life had I been left alone to go where I wanted, stay as long as I liked, spend my own money, lie in bed until noon or not go to bed at all—I was in heaven!"

Paul stared at her. Mary sobered. "You don't know me very well," she said.

"Don't I?" Paul murmured. "Don't I?" He snatched her to him and made her cling to him and cry out and gasp for breath and moan.

When Paul had fallen asleep, Mary watched light from the street brighten and dim as cars went by.

How many books would have to come out before critics

began to say, "Something's not right. A dead man can't turn out this many books"? And then Paul would know. He would know, and look at her, and remember . . .

Beyond the sound of traffic was the dense, dim roar of miles of London in all directions, moving, murmuring, breathing, surrounding that small cell where Mary lay remembering a burning coal, a shape sitting in shadow.

31

THIS IS RANDAL ELIOT'S FAMILY HOME," PAUL SAID ON A HOT Nebraska afternoon, speaking slowly and patiently as if Mary only needed a little time to understand. "If we don't preserve it now, who'll ever do it right? You remember exactly how it was."

Mary looked around Beth's old bedroom, empty and still in late May light. "I slept in my Jenny Lind bed my whole childhood. Beth slept in it for years, too."

"I know you're fond of the furniture," Paul said in the same forbearing tone. "Of course you are. But it's for such a cause—can't we think ahead? Randal Eliot is this town's Shakespeare, or Milton, or Keats. What have they done with those writers' houses? Preserved them. Filled them with the authentic pieces."

"I hate to give my family furniture up," Mary said.

"Whatever color this house was painted when he wrote most of his books—we'll reproduce it," Paul said. "The carpets are still the same, but we might want to put down new ones like them, paint the interior walls and woodwork, get the leaky basement waterproofed—don't you see? You own this house! We can do it exactly right, and then donate

240

it to the city! We've got the money. *Nobody* cares as much about preserving Randal's family home as we do."

Paul was watching Mary; her reluctance made his voice go higher in faint exasperation. "And someday people will tour this house! There'll be my biography for sale here, with the stories about you in it—how you helped him, encouraged him, took dictation—this house will be your monument too."

Mary said nothing. Again she was setting herself against what he wanted so badly to do—Paul's blue eyes blazed at her. "For months you haven't helped me—not in Paris or London, not here! Randal was *insane!* He was *unhappy!* But all you'll tell me is what Randal thought about fellow writers, or what books he read over and over—nothing *vital!* You're deliberately keeping it all from me! How can I write this book, get tenure, make something of myself?"

Paul's face was white. Mary started into the upstairs hall, but Paul leaped to block her way. He grabbed her arms and shook her until her short, shining hair flew back and forth. "You're supposed to *help* me!" he snarled. "I'm trying to write a *scholarly book.* You get to live on Randal's money, have lunch with friends—and you won't *help!*"

His hands hurt her arms. Mary tried to pull away, but he jerked her almost off the floor until her face was inches from his furious eyes. She wouldn't look at him; she pushed against his chest trying to break his hold. "Randal was *insane!*" Paul yelled.

So close to him, Mary kept her voice low. "He wasn't insane when he wrote. It's the *writer* and the *writing*—"

"He was insane! He had a warped view of the world! You can't change that! I used to think you were protecting him—you're not!" He let her go so abruptly that she almost fell, then crowded her against a wall. "You're jealous of me! That's what it is!"

Mary, watching him, realized that he wanted to hit her—might hit her—she grew as cold and careful as she had been with Randal.

"You envy me!" Paul snarled. *"I've* got a book coming

out, and you can't get anything in print! That's it, isn't it? You won't help!"

"I think you should write about his *work,* not *him,"* Mary said. Her words were a challenge, but she spoke in a low, soothing voice, as if she were talking to a dog with bared teeth.

"Stop it!" he shouted. "Who do you think you are? You only took *dictation* from Randal Eliot!"

Mary pushed him away, ran down the hall, down the stairs. She stood by the front door rubbing her bruised arms and heard a man's yells like an echo: "You've got nothing to do! It must be nice! I'm working—I'm writing—you know what that is?" Paul's voice came with the pounding of his feet downstairs: "You have any idea what it takes to write a scholarly book?"

Mary ran down tear-blurred steps to her car and drove home.

Tulips, jonquils, daffodils, and hyacinths swayed with the wind in Mary's garden. The bruises on her arms turned from red to dark blue to green and brown and yellow. Paul kissed them and said he was sorry, and she made love to him as if she believed him, as if their nights were too short for all of love's pleasures.

"You've been back from England for an age, and I haven't even seen you!" Nora Gilden said when Mary came to lunch. It was cool in Nora's big house; Mary gave a sigh as she left the outdoor heat. "You stayed long enough to be British citizens."

"We were waiting for weather like this," Mary said. "In May! Imagine." Mary wore a pretty rose-red summer dress and smiled a little at Nora.

"Have fun?" Nora asked.

"Honeymoon."

"Uh-hm," Nora said. "Good?"

"Nice," Mary said.

"I saw Paul on campus—his handsome self. Said his book's coming along well."

"That's what he tells me."

"How's your own writing going?"

"Mine?" Mary shrugged. "Haven't had time—I've been buying furniture. You've heard about Paul's Randal Eliot museum?"

"Amazing."

"He's determined to put all the furniture back—even my childhood maple spool bed in Beth's room—everything. The movers are taking it to the old house this afternoon. I have to be on hand to tell where everything was when Randal lived there."

"A bit creepy?" Nora said.

"One foot in the past," Mary said. "And the new furniture we bought isn't the same . . . it's nice, but it's just—furniture. He wants to put everything back the way Randal knew it, replace the carpets, rebuild the cellar . . ."

"I suppose he'll charge admission?"

Mary made a face. "Do you know—there's hardly one first-rate woman writer who owned a home you can visit now? There's Sir Walter Scott's castle at Abbottsford and Henry James's house at Rye—*two* Dickens homes, houses belonging to Kipling, Shaw, Shakespeare, Keats, Milton, Wordsworth, Coleridge—but the great women? You can see Jane Austen's *table*. You can see the Brontë sisters' *writing boxes.*"

Nora shook her head. Mary sighed, looking up at Greatgran's coverlet on Nora's wall. "Tell me what's really been going on while I've been away."

They started lunch and Nora opened her mind's huge file of news. Mary settled down for the enjoyment of it. Sometimes Nora only gave headlines. Sometimes she sketched in a cartoon. A few important affairs were covered in depth, and others carried Nora's editorial comment.

"Wonderful!" Mary cried every now and then. "Wonderful!" While they ate their apple pie, Greatgran came in, dragging her rocking chair behind her.

"Greatgran sent for the coverlets she's woven," Nora said. "But I can't get her to stay past tomorrow, because Charter's Home Shop want her to be on TV to show her coverlets. I don't know why she doesn't want to be on TV."

"Who would?" Greatgran said to Nora. "Think about it. You tell me something you got that you set store by."

"I don't know . . ." Nora said. "My new Buick?"

"Well," Greatgran said, her black eyes snapping at Nora. "Someday they'll be wanting you on TV to show off your old Buick—if you're lucky and got it yet, and if your brains ain't scrambled by then. And that Buick will maybe be as good as new, but you won't. So there you'll stand, looking funny and old, explaining your funny old Buick on whatever they *got* for TV then. I hope you will, since you're my kin and you've been awful nice to me."

The three of them sat for a moment, their eyes on the intricate blue-and-white cobwebs of Greatgran's coverlet: delicate shadings of blue wool on white cotton, and white on blue—shapes of wings and ovals and leaves and winding roads, coming and going as they looked at the white or blue.

"Double Chariot Wheels," Mary said.

"And I got the Wheel of Time, too," Greatgran said. "My greatgran gave me that draft. I got Snail's Trail, and Lace and Compass . . . Pine Burr . . . Bonaparte's March . . ." her old voice trailed off.

"And you'll help Mary Louella?" Mary asked.

"Help?" Greatgran's eyes were little black coals in her old face. "They're mountain folk. You can bury them. They'll let you help bury them."

"When they starve to death," Mary said.

Greatgran plucked a threaded needle from the front of her Italian knit top, knotted the end of the thread, and put it back with a jab that made Mary wince. "Except they won't. They'll get a weak little old Greatgran they can move in with and take care of. And I'm going to have to set in the parlor and teach them about beaming-in and tying and sleying and harnesses and heddles, and the scouring and dyeing, too." She scowled at her quilt on the wall. "So they can make coverlets fools will pay you a fortune for and not even put on their beds."

Mary said good-bye to Greatgran and left Nora's. She drove to meet Paul. A hot May afternoon had brought people to the park in shorts and shirts and sandals, and a moving van was already in front of the old house. Mary parked down the block and sat in her car a moment to watch men carry the head and foot of her maple Jenny Lind bed up the porch stairs. Two years before, that bed had gone the other way. Now the gleaming maple spindles vanished as she watched; they disappeared into the past like an image in a film run backwards.

She followed the maple bed in. "Mary?" Paul cried from upstairs. "Tell us where the bed goes!"

"There," Mary said when she reached Beth's room. "In the corner. No—turned the other way." She heard the sharpness in her voice.

It was an old room. Beth had painted it yellow. Cracks in the walls still showed, and the ceiling was netted with wrinkles like old skin. But the bed and highboy had been refinished; they were beautiful furniture in a shabby room. Paul's blue eyes glowed. "Now this room is just the way it was when Randal lived here!"

Mary ran her hand over her bed's warm maple.

The movers had gone downstairs. Paul put his arms around Mary and whispered, "We'll have a double bed in this house now, won't we?"

Mary turned in his arms to hold him tight, run her hands through his soft, thick hair, kiss him . . .

"Now the dining room!" Paul said. "Just exactly the way Randal knew it!"

Paul wanted the original living-room curtains put back; Mary found them in the attic, faded and half rotted by years of sun. They'd have them relined, Paul said.

"That old cloth? It'll fall off the hooks!" Mary said. "I can find some new material just like it, I think."

She hunted through fabric stores for a week, coming from

their cold aisles to the furnace blast of summer days. At last she found what she wanted.

Mary put the rolls of cloth in her car, picked up some lemonade and ice cream, and drove to the old house. Paul would be working there "to feel closer to Randal."

As she drove along the park, the past crowded close, heavy as the heavy-leaved trees above her. She imagined her children as babies, toddling beside her on those streets. She remembered them shouting on the park swings, raking leaves to make leaf houses, sledding down the snow of Walnut Street hill.

Mary sighed, then smiled, thinking of the double bed in the old house now . . . on a summer afternoon . . . she climbed the front stairs to open the screen door without a sound, sidestepping porch floorboards that creaked.

Paul liked surprises. His office furniture had been a surprise, and the European trip, and his new car.

The rooms were hot; they smelled musty and old and familiar. Mary listened, but heard nothing. Paul wasn't in Randal's study. Papers were spread on the floor around Randal's chair.

And there was Randal's new book, *Prayer Wheel,* on the desk. She had given Paul the neatly typed manuscript the evening before. "I promised the book to you in England—remember?"

"Prayer Wheel." Paul's voice had been full of awe. *"Prayer Wheel."* He repeated the title as if it were, indeed, a prayer.

"I'd rather not talk about it until you've read it," Mary had said. "Until you've made up your mind about it. It's a new kind of writing—not quite like the others."

Her book. Mary sighed and went through the study door. The dining-room table, gone from her new house, was back in its old spot and stacked with library books. She touched the back of a dining-room chair. The set had belonged to her parents. She missed the old furniture, solid and familiar. Now Paul called this place "Randal Eliot's Family Home."

There were dirty dishes in the kitchen sink, and two

empty whiskey bottles. *I wish I'd been kinder to Sandra. If I drink, I've got a quick temper.* The memory of those words of Paul's in the warm sun of her garden, in the first days . . .

Mary turned away from the whiskey bottles on the counter. *Almost three years.* Almost three years since Randal's first big check had come. He had stood in that kitchen doorway and yelled, *We're going overseas, stupid ass!*

Frozen lemonade cans were cold against Mary's ribs, and the ice cream would melt before long. She put them in the refrigerator's small freezer. Its door still had a broken spring; she wedged the door shut with the same old wad of cardboard.

Mary tiptoed through the study, skirting piles of papers. Paul must be upstairs . . . maybe taking a nap. She smiled a small, wicked smile, thinking of that, and began to unbutton her shirt as she went through the living room . . .

But she stopped at the foot of the stairs.

There was a woman's T-shirt on the landing. Shorts and a bra lay on the next step. Skimpy bikini panties crowned one of the banisters with a rakish cap of pink lace.

In the moment or two before Mary turned to leave without a sound, she heard Paul's laugh along the upstairs hall from Beth's room, and then a woman's answering giggle. "In that old double bed?" It was Michele Wildner's voice. "The floor's cooler than *that.*"

Late afternoon came and went without a breeze. New leaves blocked the glow of the streetlights when night fell, and the scent of lilacs hung over yards and alleys.

Randal Eliot's old house was cool downstairs, but the back bedroom was warm and close.

Paul left Michele on the double bed there and turned on fans in the upstairs windows.

An old shack of a house—Michele looked around her at what must have been a kid's room: posters of Europe on the walls . . . a shadow box of china animals by the door . . .

Rivers of hot summer air moved through the dark hall now. "This room belonged to one of Randal's kids?"

Michele asked when Paul came back. She ran her fingers along the top of the maple spool bed.

"It was Beth's room," Paul said. "We put the furniture back in it—Mary's childhood bed—it's just as it was when Randal lived here. 'Randal Eliot's Family Home.'"

"You know everything about Randal Eliot," Michele said, pulling Paul on top of her, bare skin to bare skin. "World authority."

"I ought to be," Paul murmured, sliding his hands over Michele's smooth young face, smooth young body, hearing the faint cries of children playing in the park.

"Got to leave," Michele said, kissing Paul.

"Come back tomorrow? About three?" Paul said, stretching himself lazily on Beth's dim bed.

"See you." Michele got into her clothes as she went downstairs, stopping at the front door to tie her sneakers.

A storm was coming: heat lightning pulsed beyond the park trees. Michele heard thunder. Three children in swimsuits ran under a streetlight; they had left the city pool to get home before the rain.

Thunder cracked overhead.

Mary heard it where she sat doubled up on her blue couch in the dark. The lightning had come first, a hard glare brighter than day, showing her where she was. Tears ran down her face.

Lightning turned the park trees white against black sky.

Michele ran through the first heavy drops, and was safe in her apartment as rain drummed on the windows. "Missed me!" she yelled at the thunder that rumbled overhead.

"Did Paul?" Teresa said, and lapped with her tongue at a pizza's dangling cheese.

"What?"

"Miss you?"

"Well, I'd been away from him for twelve whole hours," Michele said. "Practically a century." She threw herself on the couch, shut her eyes, and said, "Give me some of that." Teresa passed her the pizza box. "What a house."

"Old," Teresa said.

"Abandoned," Michele said. "Kids' junk in their rooms. Kids' clothes still in the closets. Smells musty. It's got a side front porch that's falling off. The stove and refrigerator are *ancient*—and Paul loves every dent and chip and crack, because 'Randal Eliot lived there.'"

"What's Mary Eliot like?"

"Old. Paul says she's fifty."

"Her side porch's falling off? Dents and cracks and chips . . ."

"She has money, honey." Michele licked her fingers.

"That you ain't got."

"Money can't be enough, or he wouldn't be after me. Pass the pizza."

Teresa put the box on the couch. "I'm off to shower. Harley's taking me to dinner."

"So why are you eating pizza?"

"One piece. Have the rest on me," Teresa said. "What if Mary decides to visit her old haunts and finds a bed occupied?"

"She never comes, Paul says—she loves her new place. And she's married to Paul, so she's happy, and Paul's the Randal Eliot biographer, so *he's* happy, and I've got the fun!" Michele smiled and snapped at cheese stringing from her pizza. "Everybody's happy."

The hard-driving rain softened, then stopped.

Paul went downstairs when Michele had gone.

Now he was alone with Randal's manuscript.

He looked at it, touched it once, then began to roam Randal Eliot's house.

Night came early on a cloudy night, making the house an island, cut off from the neighbors, the street, the park, the town. Paul stood in the upstairs bedroom where Randal had slept, and looked for a while at the park. *Prayer Wheel* had been written in this place.

Paul slid his hand along the banister, going downstairs: Randal had touched that wood how many times? He dropped heavily into Randal's shabby recliner and lay back, the manuscript beside him on a table. After a while he cried, *"I speak for you now! We'll be famous—both of us!"*

Paul leapt out of Randal's chair to open a whiskey bottle in the kitchen. He poured himself a drink, and stood in the center of Randal's study. "To your new novel!" he cried to Randal, and held the glass of whiskey up to the shimmer of light from the park. "And to me!"

Paul finished the glass. "And to *fame!*" he yelled, and thought the dark house gave back a faint echo: *Fame*.

In an hour or so he stopped pacing and dreaming and picked up the first few chapters of *Prayer Wheel*. He was too drunk to read it. He was too drunk to go home. He called Mary to say he'd stay over to finish the novel, then went to bed.

32

I'M GOING TO READ THIS NEW BOOK VERY SLOWLY," PAUL told Mary when he telephoned her the next morning. "I'll stay here in his house so I can feel Randal's ambience, his spirit . . ."

"Yes," Mary said, her voice rather flat. "I imagine that's what you're doing there: feeling Randal's ambience."

"It's wonderful," Paul said cheerfully.

Mary said nothing.

"And then I'll want to take a look at the notes of Randal's. The ones you told me about in London."

"They're in marked boxes in my workroom closet," Mary said. "Don't forget we've invited department people over for supper next Monday night."

"I'll be through by then," Paul said. "Plenty of time. I'm in heaven. You know how I love every word Randal wrote. Can you imagine how I feel, having a whole new book?"

Mary said yes, she could, and said good-bye. She curled up under satin sheets again with the echo of Paul's voice full of his rights and duties as Randal's biographer, Mary Quinn's husband, a university scholar.

The house lay still around her until she heard the garbage

truck come down her road. It stopped, and men leapt off to clang lids and cans together. She'd put out the trash; Paul had stopped doing it long ago.

Morning sun lit the room. She hid from it, covered her face and remembered talking about the novels—her own novels—while she lay in Paul's arms . . .

Tears filled her eyes. She couldn't lie there any longer: she had to plan Monday night's department party. Michele Wildner would come, and smile at Paul Anderson's wife as Paul entertained his guests by explaining how Randal's mental illness was the key to Randal Eliot's great work . . .

Mary rubbed her wet eyes. She would need to borrow Nora's folding chairs again. She hadn't called the florist . . .

"My work!" Mary whispered into her wet pillow. "My books." For a moment she remembered a woman's clothes scattered on steps, but then she sat upright to cry, "An assistant professor!"

She sprang naked from the bed to look at herself in sunlight.

Now her voice was quiet and furious. "You are Mary Quinn," she said, and Mary Quinn in the mirror across the room looked back at her with cold and narrow eyes.

Her new word processor could print a whole novel in a few hours. Mary went naked across the hall to stand before the machine. She hunted disks, put the first one in the slot, stocked the printer with paper, and watched the double-spaced pages begin to fill the hopper.

Hannah was in Omaha that week, pursuing clients for her new firm, Hannah Anderson, Inc. She worked until late; it was two in the morning when she finally crawled into bed and fell asleep.

Her phone rang.

"Hannah!" her brother said.

"It's three o'clock in the morning! Where are you?" Hannah's voice was foggy.

"At Randal's house. I've got to talk to you about the book—Randal's new book—"

"You call me at three A.M. to talk about a *book?*"

"It's all there!" Paul cried.

"What's all there? Wait a minute—let me put on a light and get a drink."

"The manuscript collection at the British Museum—we read those letters!—the beheading of Mary Queen of Scots! And London theaters, Covent Garden—it's all in this novel!"

"Here I am again," Hannah said. "What were you saying?"

"I've just finished that new book of Randal's! Mary gave it to me last Thursday. I've read it carefully for days, and my God—I'm sure Mary's been *rewriting Randal's work!* She's put in the things we saw together in London—everything—"

"But Randal was in London."

"He never went to those places—Mary told me that herself! So she's added all kinds of stuff to Randal's novel! Who knows what parts of it are *his? That's* what she's been doing up there at her typewriter all the time. Of course she didn't want me to see—"

"Maybe she did that from the beginning," Hannah said. "What?"

"Helped him write."

"She typed what he dictated . . . she knows every word of every book! But what about this new one? If she's fooled with it—"

"Is it good?"

"It's *superb!* I can tell her that, but then what? And how can I write Randal's biography if I don't even know how much she changed his books?"

"Ask her."

"She said I'd understand what she'd been doing when I read *Prayer Wheel.*"

"Whatever she did, she must not have made the novels worse."

"Who knows?"

Hannah laughed. "Maybe she has a genius for wrecking good novels until they're masterpieces?"

"But there's one thing I can do," Paul said. "She told me in London that she had Randal's notes for some of the novels, and I could see them. I'll go tomorrow and take a look."

"That sounds good . . . you can't go home and accuse her all over the place. And be sure you don't drink. Don't let yourself start—"

"I'll look at them. I'll see how they correspond to the final novel."

"And call me back. Keep thinking about the wonderful life you've got with Mary: the beautiful home, money, travel, your book to write . . . just what I've always wanted for you. Call me back the minute you find out anything—promise?"

Paul promised and said good-bye. He had a couple more drinks and paced the house. Fans brought cooler, rainy air to the upstairs. At dawn he crawled into the maple bed's damp sheets.

Rain began at dawn. It fell all morning. At noon there was thunder and lightning, but Paul only grunted and turned over in bed. It was three in the afternoon by the time he sat up and tried to focus his eyes. After a while he didn't feel so sick, and went down the hall for a shower. By five o'clock he was a little hungry. Mary would have supper ready.

It was still raining when he drove to Cedar Ridge, pulled into the garage, and saw that Mary's car was gone. She was shopping, probably.

There was nothing ready to eat—the kitchen was tidy, the dishwasher stood open and empty. He had some bread and butter and coffee, then went up to Mary's workroom.

It was neat, as always. Her great ivy plants hung in the skylights, looking like trees without trunks; the wall of curtains was striped pink and lavender and blue. A new word processor waited on a trestle table—waited for what? For more "work" on Randal Eliot's books? Paul swore.

Four cardboard boxes on the closet's top shelf were marked "Randal's Notes" in Mary's handwriting. Paul took them down, furious to think he had slept for more than a year within a few dozen feet of a primary source . . .

He opened the first box carefully, reverently. Randal's handwriting had been rounded and sprawling; his lines sagged downhill.

The box was full of used envelopes; Paul saw that at once. They stood on end, layer by layer, held by rubber bands, and there was writing on their backs.

The first bundle he looked at seemed to have been put in by mistake. Each envelope was covered with nothing but the kind of scribbles a toddler would make with a sharp pencil.

The second pack was no different, except that some pencil strokes had dug through the whole envelope, as if the pencil had jabbed.

Paul took out pack after pack, until at last the box was empty. He had flipped through them all, and they were all the same.

Mary was playing some kind of joke? He shoved the box aside and opened another, and then another. He looked through every banded pack. The last box was filled with the longer, narrower size of paper used in Britain, each sheet covered with scribbling that went downhill, line by line, and had only a few recognizable letters or words on each page: "atomic," "St. David's," "Crayons for Peggy" in Randal's handwriting, sprawling but recognizable.

"A joke!" Paul yelled. "Nothing but a joke! She's trying to make a fool of me?"

Then the doorbell rang.

Mary had forgotten her key, probably. He hurried to look out their bedroom window at the drive, then backed up at the sight of his department head's car . . . and Bill Rivers and Hugh Bond pulling in behind Butterfield . . .

My God.

The party.

The Monday supper for the department.

Nothing to eat in the kitchen . . . nothing ready . . . Mary's car was gone . . .

The doorbell rang again.

Paul sat on the satin bedspread. He wasn't here. He was gone, too. Somebody had made a mistake. The doors were locked. He pulled a pillow over his head and lay absolutely still.

People joined other people in the drive below, calling, chattering. The doorbell rang again and again.

After a while Paul sat up on the bed and heard nothing but rain dripping from the roof. He crept downstairs to look through a chink in the furnace room curtains: empty doorstep, empty drive.

"Damn!" he cried. "I'll be a joke to the whole department! Nobody home!"

Rain drove against the windows again. "Bitch!" he yelled at the empty rooms.

Finally he got in his car and went first to the nearest supermarket where Mary shopped, walked down every aisle.

No Mary. No Mary at other places she might go—the special produce store, the mall—

It was growing dark. Paul went back to the house, slamming every door behind him.

It was eight-thirty by the time he thought to look and see what she'd taken. He ran to the closet where the luggage was kept. Two cases were gone.

He drove to the airport, a small place with only a few dozen cars in the long-term parking lot. One of them was Mary's.

He drove home, swearing, slamming his fist on the wheel. The telephone was ringing when he unlocked the door.

"You're there." It was Mary's voice. "I called the other house first."

"I'm here—where are *you?"* Paul shouted. "The whole department came for the party, and there was *no party!* What'll they think? Where did you go? You made fools—"

Mary's voice was cool. "Don't worry about me. I'll come

back when I've had a rest. And Michael's flying home from Africa tomorrow. The letter came while you were gone."

"A *rest?*" Paul yelled. He heard a click. A hum. "Mary?" he cried to no one.

Mary put the receiver down.

She began to cry.

She sobbed in her suite at the Plaza, weeping until the view of New York from the windows wobbled and ran before her eyes.

When she stopped at last, Mary stared at the hotel dressing table: it was spread with the beautiful leather traveling set Paul had given her. There was a cosmetic case with a brass lion's-head clasp, and matching stationery case, standing mirror, clock, and double picture frame. The frame held a portrait of her smiling children on one side; the other showed Paul in shorts and T-shirt, feet apart, tennis racket in his hand.

He played tennis with Michele Wildner every week. Who was Paul smiling at in that photo? Mary had never stopped to think; Paul had seemed to be looking straight at her. But now she saw there was a third person in that picture: the photographer hidden behind the lens who was meeting Paul's smile with her own.

Paul walked back and forth in the living room. At last he called Butterfield, his voice apologetic and concerned: he was sorry he had inconvenienced everyone, but Mary had flown off to Texas because Beth was sick. They'd raced to get Mary on the next flight, forgotten the party . . . he was sorry . . .

At last he had called everyone in the department but Michele. Then his phone rang.

"Wasn't at your party." It was Michele.

"Yeah," Paul grunted.

"I didn't come because I thought your lascivious eyes might roam over my compliant body—to quote any current best-seller—and everybody would know our guilty secret. But Nora Gilden just told me there wasn't any party and Mary's gone and Beth's sick. How is she? Have you heard?"

"Not yet."

"We-e-ll," Michele said. "Maybe I should come over and comfort you in your adversity?"

"Something like that," Paul said.

"Be over," Michele said.

She parked a block away and sneaked in. Nobody saw her, she said. She was damp with rain, warm and fragrant in Paul's arms.

Michele was asleep soon, but Paul's eyes wouldn't close. He eased out of bed and sat across the hall in Mary's workroom. Randal's scribbled envelopes were dumped on the rug. They bore Randal's name and address, and their dated postmarks showed they were years old.

He went back to bed, but he couldn't sleep. Rain fell all night. Morning came to light rivers and streams that were over their banks.

Michele woke to hear the constant beat of rain on the roof. Paul's eyes were open; she kissed him. "Nice," she said, sitting up, wrapped in a satin sheet. She looked around the big bedroom. "Sure beats an old double bed and china animals and posters."

Paul went downstairs to get breakfast.

"Damn!" he said in a low, furious voice, breaking eggs into a pan. Mary hadn't done a wash for a week. He didn't have one clean shirt left.

=== 33 ===

MARY TOOK A TAXI TO THE ENGEL AGENCY ON THE AVENUE of the Americas the next afternoon. "I have an appointment with Justine Engel," Mary told the receptionist at the immense brass-trimmed desk. "Mary Quinn."

"Ms. Quinn!" the fashionable young woman said. "Ms. Engel will be down in a moment."

Mary glanced around the room. Everything was sleek and new and seemed to glitter, including Justine Engel's smile as she came to take Mary's hand, escort Mary upstairs, ceremoniously introduce Mary to various people who had imposing titles, then install Mary in a huge office with china cups of hot coffee, and windows full of the New York skyline.

Mary sat down and was not "a primary source." She was the object of Justine Engel's intense interest.

"Of course you can imagine we're in a state of shock here," Justine said, her pretty brown eyes on Mary's good-looking linen suit. Justine's accent was nasal New York; the rings on her fingers twinkled as she spread her hands on the manuscripts before her.

"Yes," Mary said.

"Three new Randal Eliot novels? We can't believe it. Has anyone else seen these?"

"No."

"We've sat up two nights reading them—not much time before you were coming—and they're absolutely stunning —his best work yet! Of course we'll represent you with these, but . . ." Justine waved her ringed hands over the manuscripts, then laughed a little.

"Four novels coming out after the author is gone?" Mary said.

The twang in Justine's voice softened. "Randal was such a loss—to you and to everybody. A first-rate talent, even if he wasn't one of ours."

Mary looked over the rooftops of New York. "Then these three new novels will sell?"

"Sell? Like you've never seen—we can bring one out every year. This is vintage Randal Eliot—we're struck with the magnificent imagery in *Prayer Wheel.* And *Life Thief* is a book that you can't help but finish at one sitting. *Time to Burn* is a Randal Eliot first, something new for him. Deeply affecting." Justine saw how rigidly Mary sat in her chair. "You have a particular publisher you want us to approach?"

"As you know, the contract with George Blumberg has run out," Mary said. "But a few years ago he told me I'd get a ten-thousand-dollar advance on the first of these novels."

"What?" Justine stared at Mary.

"Ten thousand."

Justine gave a startled laugh. "He's joking! Ten times that . . ."

"No," Mary said. "And he's right. After all . . ." Her eyes met Justine's. "Randal Eliot's gone, but his novels will continue to appear. These are only the next three. And you'll have to sell them with my name on them, not Randal Eliot's. So ten thousand is all I can hope for, as a beginning author—unless you and I are very clever. That's why I've come to you—you have a reputation for cleverness."

Traffic on the Avenue of the Americas flowed beneath the Engel Agency's windows, and for a moment it was the only sound in the room. Then Justine said, "You're Randal Eliot."

Mary and Justine sat looking at each other.

"What can I do?" Mary said.

"Tell me the whole story," Justine said, "then give me a day or two—we'll think of something."

That night was rainy in New York; traffic crawled along streets that were clogged with playgoers bound for home. Justine and Bob Klein were among them; they ran through midnight rain to find Justine's limo and climb in.

Bob had a one-room place, but Justine's apartment was large and full of the stark curves of art deco. When she unlocked the door, a fire her housekeeper had lighted warmed the big living room.

Like an old married couple, the two of them hung up wet clothes, slipped into loose, soft wraps, and sprawled together on a fur rug before the fire. Justine rubbed Bob's bare brown back; he grunted with pleasure every now and then.

"So what about Mary Quinn's problem?" Justine asked him.

"Her husband's playing around a bit?" Bob asked.

"That's what I suspect. She's eight years older than he is."

"So why's she so upset?"

"What?" Justine stopped rubbing and pummeling.

"A bit Victorian, isn't it?"

Justine stared at him for a minute, then fell back on the fur rug. "Behind the times in the Midwest, you mean?"

"Even if she is Randal Eliot." Bob shrugged.

Justine picked up their wineglasses and said, "Come to bed. I've got a hard day tomorrow."

Bob followed her, and they slid under her pink-and-gray sheets. Justine poured a little more wine into their glasses and lay down in Bob's arms to rub her cheek against the soft hair on his chest.

"This husband's a zero, I think, except in bed," Justine said. "Looks like he never wrote anything until she helped him, and still hasn't published a word. Teaches in some little unknown U in Nebraska and won't keep his job unless he gets out this bio of Randal Eliot."

"And there's no Randal Eliot." Bob laughed.

Justine took a gulp of wine. "He'll write *her* biography now, and get rich, rich, rich. And he's a fanatic about her novels. That's in his favor."

"So now he'll love her for her writing?"

"Something like that, except maybe she doesn't care anymore."

"Why didn't she tell him in the beginning?" Bob yawned, turned off his bedside lamp, and pulled up the sheet.

"Randal's agent wouldn't sell her books under her name, and she was out of money."

"Write in secret, love and kisses, help him write," Bob said in a sleepy, slow voice.

"Right. Except he cheats on her. Except he flies into rages and gives her bruises." For a while Justine studied the high, ornate plaster ceiling where their two bedside lamps had merged their circles of light. "She says he scares her . . . and what will he do when he finds out?"

Bob didn't answer. He was asleep.

Justine's lamp lit her sleek bedroom and sent a single shaft of yellow into the big rooms beyond. The apartment's monthly rent was more than Bob made in a month.

"It's not easy to be Ms. Big Name," Justine said softly to nothing but the far-off sound of New York traffic and the lonely circle of light on the ceiling's plaster roses. "It isn't so sexy."

She turned off her light and slid down next to Bob. "It isn't much fun."

The next evening Justine took Mary to a restaurant; then they talked in the lobby of the Plaza.

"You have to trust me," Justine said in her crisp voice.

"We're in this together—we really are. What you earn I get ten percent of, and I like money." She smiled at Mary.

Playgoers and barhoppers were coming back to the Plaza in couples or small groups; Justine watched a giggling pair of lovers go by and said, "The Writer Who Lied for Love."

"What?" Mary put down her empty wineglass.

"That's what we'll call you. You lied about who wrote those novels, but you lied because you loved Randal and your family. It wraps it all up: the lying, the devotion, the fact that you're Randal Eliot. And it tells everybody why you did it—for love. Who can't identify with that? And who's going to blame you? And it will sell *books!* Your whole story will sell books—George Blumberg let a gold mine fall right out of his pocket. Imagine what's going to happen when the publishing world finds out who Randal Eliot has been—all these years!"

"If they believe it," Mary said. "I have no proof at all. Randal could have dictated every one of my novels before he died."

"Who needs proof? Who's going to sue? Your children? They'll inherit a fortune from their *mother's* writing. We'll use Randal's publishing house, so the publishers will rake in money from the minute your story hits—*they're* not going to run to the lawyers. Everybody's going to make money— you, me, everybody. But suppose a Big Somebody at the *Times* attacks your story? They can't find any real evidence, so it's *publicity.* It's *free.* You can't *pay* enough to get that kind of notice."

"Yes," Mary said in a faint voice.

"The unbelievers have to prove you *didn't* write the books. How do they do that if there's nothing in Randal's handwriting? And new novels of his will keep appearing, every one in Randal Eliot's unique style and voice—every year there'll be a new one. How many books can a dead man write? Sooner or later everybody's going to ask that."

"I've had parts of these novels done for years. I hurried to finish them, and I'll have more."

"You don't need to change Randal's name to yours on the first five books," Justine said. "Everyone's going to know they're yours, and that's part of your persona—that you put his name on them because of love."

Mary sat looking at her empty wineglass. Justine said, "You realize you're going to get awards! Eight books out. You can think about the big prizes."

"Yes," Mary said in a flat voice. "The writer of the eighties. The voice of my generation. The next winner of the Pulitzer Prize."

Justine looked surprised and laughed. "Of course!"

"That's what they said about Randal," Mary said. "Here at the Plaza almost three years ago. And Randal told them in his speech, 'I mustn't forget to thank the Muse, that fickle woman who visits writers by night, by luck, in secret. One must not offend the Muse.'"

"One certainly must *not*," Justine said. "Especially if one's resident muse writes one's *novels* while one *sleeps*."

Justine would come to the Plaza the next afternoon, she said. She needed to think through problems and get advice from her lawyers and accountants. Mary slept late, had breakfast in her suite and lunch in the restaurant.

"It's all settled," Justine said when she came at two. "Everyone thinks we've got the right angle—can't see any holes in it." She watched Mary, who stood at a window looking at New York streets below. "You seem worried."

"I am."

"About Paul?" Justine shrugged. "He doesn't like successful women?"

"He thinks he's working on his life work," Mary said. "What will he do when he finds out he has to begin again and write about his *wife?*" They sat in silence for a moment. "I thought we could be happy for the rest of our time together, and then he could find out . . ."

"But you're scared of him."

"Maybe I shouldn't be." Mary turned her rings around on

her finger. "Maybe I've lived with a violent man so long that I . . ." her voice trailed off. Then she said, "George Blumberg told me that I'd be happier hiding away, pretending Randal wrote the books, dodging publicity, enjoying my days with Paul. Being 'the Author' would mean having a public mask—a persona."

"You've got your persona!" Justine cried. "You'll be 'The Writer Who Lied for Love.' That's a hell of a lot better than writing in a trance! And you'll get used to being famous. It's not so hard to take. Lots of people who aren't as smart as you are seem to manage it. You'll find out this whole 'Love Liar' thing is gilt-edged dynamite. Believe me."

Mary was silent. Justine gave her a sharp glance and said, "And as far as Paul goes—it's not so bad being the *husband* of a famous writer, you know. All the money, all the fame. And you've forgotten one thing. The most important thing, for him."

"What?"

"From now on he won't be just the biographer of a dead writer—he'll be married to a live one and living with her! Of course he'll pretend he knew you were the writer all the time—you can just bet he will."

Mary stared at her. "Yes."

"He hasn't published his book yet—he can make his publisher *very happy indeed* by making it the story of the amazing secret novelist who lied for love—*his own wife!* What a read!" Justine's eyes gleamed. "Won't that sell! He'll probably get a movie out of it. People buy biographies. They *love* biographies. Never mind the writer's *work*. *Biographies* are the huge best-sellers." She leaned forward, her long, ringed fingers interlocked. "Would Paul consider letting us represent him? Tell him he can make a fortune with the 'Lied for Love Bio'—who's his publisher?"

"Matrix."

Justine grinned. "They're a hole-in-the-wall publisher! We'll get him to the top."

"Yes," Mary said.

"You don't need to worry about Paul," Justine said. "He'll be happy for years with his money, and he can spend his time tracking down every detail of your life to match some passage or other in one of your novels, if he wants to be the famous scholar."

"He does," Mary said.

"But I have a suggestion. Get out of the country for a while," Justine said. "Until the excitement dies down. Take Paul with you. He can get used to the idea of his own fame and fortune, and the sharks won't get at the two of you."

"Leave right away?"

"Why not? I have to tell your publisher who Randal Eliot is—if you want more than that ten-thousand-dollar advance."

"All four of my children will be here tomorrow for the weekend—we'll be together after years—Michael's back from Africa!" Mary's eyes shone. "Then perhaps Paul and I can go somewhere . . ."

"Go to Italy. The Villa Christa on Lake Como. It's for writers and scholars, and it's peaches and cream, and I can get you in. You and Paul will have nothing to do but eat breakfast, have tea in your room at ten, then lunch. Coffee at your door at four, cocktails on the terrace at six, marvelous dinner at seven . . . A second honeymoon! There'll be international writers and scholars—groups of them come and go at the villa all the time. They'll make Paul feel important even when he finds out about you—they'll realize he's *your* biographer now. The two of you will have your own suite. Balconies over the lake . . ."

"I go as the 'Liar for Love'?"

"No," Justine said. "The idea is to get you away before the news breaks." She got up, looking at her watch. "Let me arrange all this for you—I'll come here tomorrow morning —say eleven? Meanwhile—enjoy! Buy yourself a whole new wardrobe for a month on Lake Como!"

* * *

Mary supposed she should buy clothes. She supposed she should enjoy going from store to glittering store. But when Justine came the next morning to ask if Mary hadn't had a wonderful time, Mary sat down and sighed.

"You didn't have fun?" Justine said, looking at the fine new luggage that had just been delivered to Mary's suite.

"They're full," Mary said, looking at the suitcases. "All packed for Italy—even underwear and panty hose. And that stuff cost a fortune."

"Of course! You deserve it. What's the problem?"

"The problem is that I *feel* twenty years old," Mary said. "Have for years. But when I went in those fancy stores and looked in all those fancy mirrors, I wondered what old lady the fancy clerks were draping things on."

"You're not old!" Justine cried.

"And those clerks meet you at the door!" Mary said. "And all at once you know they see your purse isn't quite top grain, and your jacket's got machine-made button-holes, and your shoes are so old they've been polished." She groaned. "I began to be homesick for a nice, private, department-store dressing room—'Limit Six Garments'—with pins on the floor and gum wrappers on the shelf and cozy conversations going on in the next cubicle."

Justine was laughing now, her brown eyes sparkling.

"*I* can remember an old-fashioned 'dime store,'" Mary said. "That's how old I am. Nobody ever met you at the dime-store door, but shopping there was *serious shopping*. Dime stores had everything to make a house a home—your children could grow up happy with sheets made into curtains, and towels sewed together to upholster chairs—yes! And there were glass jars for terrariums and crepe paper for May baskets . . . egg dyes for Easter . . . bandages for cuts . . . perfume for Mother's Day—"

"Paradise," Justine said.

"And at Christmas you could buy notepaper for your

teacher, and tinsel . . . and for birthdays there were those inedible, colored-rock "Happy Birthday" letters for birthday cakes! And you sat at a counter and had big, thick milk shakes and hot dogs in shiny buns—I can taste that mustard!" Justine laughed, but Mary's mouth watered, there in her suite at the Plaza.

=== 34 ===

THE NEXT AFTERNOON MARY LOOKED AT HERSELF FOR A long time in her hotel-room mirror. Perhaps she had cried enough—what good did crying do, once it melted the hard rock in your chest, and you didn't wring your hands or sigh any more? Paul was with Michele, no doubt, but she was here and she was Mary Quinn, and she would see Michael today, after more than three years!

She began to put on makeup. The woman she saw in the mirror, deep in reflection, had dark, shining hair; her eyes gleamed under their thick lashes.

As she put on lipstick, Mary's imagination—that gift, joy, misfortune—suddenly showed her a woman in armor. Where had she seen her?

Once . . . at the beginning of *A Midsummer Night's Dream*. The play had begun with a startling, vicious battle between two armored knights. Their heavy swords flashed, metal clanged—then they slid from their crowned helmets and chain mail like moths from chrysalids. One was a handsome king. The other was a woman—the beautiful queen Hippolyta, all in white with flowing hair, the marks of her armor still upon her . . .

Mary got up and went to a window to watch New York traffic far below. The cars and trucks and vans followed each other like docile sheep, but now and then sunlight struck one and spun stars from it.

Soon she would have to meet her children at the airport.

How brilliant they had always thought their father was—not just another professor of English in a state university, teaching his classes, earning his money, going to his grave.

And she, for those long years, had been a liar.

All afternoon her children flew in from Texas and Minnesota and Colorado, and they threw their arms around each other. Michael drove from Connecticut, sun-brown and strange—yet there were his eyes they knew so well, and his smile. None of them asked why they were there . . . what was so important that she had paid their way for a weekend in New York.

They unpacked in her big suite, and ate supper in the hotel restaurant, telling Michael about Randal's funeral, Mary's house, Don's wedding, Mary's wedding, and listening to Michael's tales of Africa. Once more they saw him throw his head back, laughing, or slap his booted foot on his knee. Even though Mary was tense—they could see that—she relaxed a little, because all her children were around her at last.

Don described his thriving business; Beth told about a womanizing professor. Jay had stepped on a rattlesnake in the desert, he said, but it was at dawn and cold, so the snake hadn't struck. All four watched Mary.

Back in her suite, they pulled drapes shut and sat in the plump chairs.

Mary looked at them, started to speak, hesitated, then said, "I wanted you all together. I have important things to tell you before anyone else tells you."

"Is it Paul?" Beth said, pushing her long, light hair behind her ears. "You and Paul aren't happy?"

"We're not," Mary said, "but the most important

thing . . ." They waited in the lamplight, their eyes on her. "I don't know how to begin," Mary said. "Another novel, *Prayer Wheel,* is coming out, and then two more."

"With Dad's name on them?" Don said. His eyes were green, like his father's. The look in those eyes, the slight note of banter, kept Mary silent. Or had she heard scorn?

"Mom," Beth said, and this time Mary caught a note of loving exasperation.

Jay said, "The minute I saw you at the airport—"

"It's about *time,"* Beth said. She looked at her brothers. "We've talked about this together, the four of us," she said to Mary.

"For years," Michael said.

"About *The Host,"* Beth said. "And the other books, too."

Mary stared at them. "I wanted you to think, all your lives . . ." Her voice faltered a little. "That your father was a famous writer." She had grown pale with what she saw in their faces. "He believed me," Mary said. "He had to."

"I like *Prayer Wheel,"* Beth said. "It's not like anything else you've done."

"But that snowstorm at the beginning of it!" Don said. "I had nightmares about getting caught out in the fields in a blizzard!"

"I've forgotten some of it—I read it years ago," Jay said. "And I can't remember plots."

"The woman in *Life Thief!"* Beth said. "I've always wanted to ask you—is she Grandma Eliot?"

Michael began to laugh, watching his mother. "The writer is lost for words!"

"Nothing to say?" Beth teased her mother, and came to hug her. The five of them sat close together on one long couch now, relief and pleasure in all their voices, especially Mary's. "It saved your father's job—it saved all of us—he was so happy!" she cried.

"Mom—you had to," Michael said. "We figured that out awfully fast."

"We found your journals in the kitchen," Jay said.

"*I* found the journals in the kitchen," Don said.

"Way up in that old cupboard," Beth said. "When was it? Long before we went to Europe, anyway."

"So of course we read them," Jay said.

"Sneaks that we are," Michael said.

Tears stood in Mary's eyes. "Liar that I've been."

"You *had* to, Mom," Don said.

"The voice of her generation," Beth said.

"Why didn't you *tell* me?" Mary cried.

"The next winner of the Pulitzer Prize!" Don said. "And we thought you'd tell us someday."

"You put my ant farms in *A Strange Girl,*" Jay said. "Dad didn't know anything about ants—or the monarch butterflies, either."

"Our glass bumblebee houses in *Net Worth!*" Michael cried.

"And Dad used to write all his book notes on the backs of old envelopes, remember?" Don asked.

"Stacks and stacks," Jay said.

"I sneaked looks at them sometimes," Beth said. "Scribbles."

"You said you could read them," Michael told Mary.

"I used to hate Dad when he went after you," Don said to Mary. "So I'd steal a whole pile of those envelope notes and hide them under my bed—I even threw them in neighbors' trash cans—and Dad never missed one note. Neither did you."

"You helped us with homework," Beth said. "Made us clothes, visited school, bought our Christmas presents, listened to our troubles—you were always there, and when I found out you were the writer, too . . ." She faltered to a stop, at a loss for words, and looked at her brothers. They nodded.

Mary stood up with the force of the feeling that, once more, she was shedding something heavy. "I thought I'd never have to tell you. I thought I could let Randal have the first books, and then I'd start writing under my own name."

"You can't?" Michael said.

"Randal's agent told me I couldn't," Mary said.

"They think Dad wrote them," Jay said.

"Why?" Beth cried. "He's gone—he can't write book after book after book . . . *The Host,* and now *Prayer Wheel* and *Life Thief* and another, too."

Mary heard Beth name the books as if she had known them for years. She had.

"But Mom writes like he did," Jay said. "Because she always did. That's the trouble."

They looked at each other, deep in thought.

"I tried to change my style, but it's *my* way of writing," Mary said. "I told George Blumberg almost two years ago that all the books were mine. He didn't believe me; he thought I was crazy, but he didn't say so. He told me I was just beside myself with grief. Then he put it in financial terms: he could make money on Randal's novels, even if Randal were dead." Mary felt so light, as if she were getting rid of an armful of heavy stones. "But he didn't even know whether he could *sell* a first novel by unknown 'Mary Quinn.' If he could sell it at all, he'd only get a ten-thousand-dollar advance. We all needed money. 'Don't mess us up here in New York,' he told me, 'and we'll both be rich.'"

"So what did you say?"

"What could I say? He went ahead, and *The Host* came out." Mary raised her head; her mouth was a grim line. "But there was one thing I could do, and I've done it."

"What?" Michael asked.

"Write," Mary said.

"More books and more books," Beth said.

"You're going to make them say, 'These can't be Randal Eliot's books. How could he write so many?'" Jay said.

"In a week or two the publicity will start," Mary said. "I've got a new agent. She's going to call me 'The Writer Who Lied for Love.' I guess that's part of what I did, anyway."

The five looked at each other.

"What about Paul?" Beth said.

"Randal is all he can see. And all he can see in *my* work is *Randal's* illness."

"Oh, *Mom!*" Beth groaned.

"So we don't talk. We live like enemies. I won't help him make a fool of himself, and he can't imagine that the books aren't Randal's. He flies into a rage if I suggest he write *only* about the work itself—he scares me."

"Wait till he finds out," Don said. "He's making a shrine of that old house—"

"But Paul's going to make *money,*" Mary said. "If he ever writes anything. He's going to be famous. He's married to the author of those novels." Again she had the sensation of emerging from armor. Her voice softened. "The four of you ought to be proud of Randal yet. He had so much courage. He supported us all his life. He kept going as long as he could."

The children said nothing.

"Well. That's enough for tonight," Mary said. "More than enough. Let's go to bed and have a good time tomorrow— I've got play tickets. We'll forget all this for a day or two." They watched her cross the thick carpet to her bedroom door.

"Where's Paul?" Beth said.

Mary stopped and turned. "I gave him *Prayer Wheel* to read. He'll probably think Randal wrote it, even though he knows Randal never saw the London in that book."

"You want him to figure it out by himself," Don said.

"And he doesn't know you're here?" Michael said.

"No. I called to tell him I wanted a rest for a while, and didn't tell him where," Mary said. "But the two of us will be invited to a villa on Lake Como in Italy next week, supposedly as Randal's editor and biographer. A gorgeous villa, a suite with all the luxuries."

"You'll see Italy!" Jay cried. "You couldn't go with Beth and me—now you'll see it!"

"We'll be out of the country when the publicity breaks."

"And then you'll be the famous one," Don said. "And Paul will be just the famous writer's husband."

They turned off the lamps, scattered to their rooms, and began to get ready for bed. In a while Beth knocked at her mother's half-open door. "Mom?"

"Come on in," Mary said. She was taking off her makeup at the dressing table.

"It's Paul," Beth said. "I'm worried about him—can't you go to Italy alone?"

Mary looked at a red-smeared tissue in her hand. "I think if I can keep him from drinking . . . he's so mad at himself, really: he hasn't written a thing."

"But he's rich now, and he'll be richer."

Mary was looking at herself in the dressing-table mirror. "He's *crazy* about Randal's work—and of course it's *my* work, so that's what drew us together from the beginning . . . even more than love . . . even stronger." Mary's eyes wandered to the red glow of New York's neon on sheer curtains. "The good talk . . . and the love . . ."

Mary fell silent, staring into her mirror. Beth came to put her arms around her mother. Cheek to cheek, they looked at their reflections. "Don't go home," Beth said. "Go straight to Italy."

"I have to go back," Mary said. "I have to shut up the house and make plans."

"Maybe one of us should go with you—"

"He'll be happy!" Mary said. "He's going to be invited to the Villa Christa in Italy as a resident scholar!" She smiled at Beth.

Beth, after a moment, smiled back, kissed her, and said to her mother's reflection in the mirror, "Good night—*Mary Quinn!*"

35

MARY FLEW HOME FROM NEW YORK. IT WAS NIGHT WHEN her plane descended; she couldn't see flooded Nebraska roads, or trees on the riverbanks of town, sunk to their branches in swift-flowing water after a week of rain.

She had called Paul to say she was coming, and he opened the door before she reached for the brass-faced knocker.

She asked how he was.

He said he was fine.

She asked if he had had supper.

He said no, and carried her luggage upstairs.

It was late; Mary was tired and hungry. She changed clothes, then came down again to look in the refrigerator. She cooked some spaghetti and sauce and found enough vegetables for a salad. When Paul came into the kitchen, she stood at the stove with an apron over her white summer dress. "Supper's about ready," she told him.

He blocked her way in the middle of the kitchen floor. "What's going on?" he said in a hard-edged voice. "You run off and we don't have the department party . . ."

"I'm sorry," Mary said. "I forgot about it."

"Forgot?" Paul cried. "Forgot they're my *colleagues?* That

I have to work with them? I don't sit around home all day, or go flying off for a rest somewhere—I have to *work*. I have to *teach*. I'm a *scholar* with a book coming out!"

Mary said nothing.

"The next day I had to call a couple dozen people, make up a story that Beth was sick and you'd flown off at the last minute—that we didn't have time to let anyone know the party was off."

Mary wouldn't look at him.

"And what about those boxes of Randal's notes?" Paul said. "You told me where they were and I found them. You're playing some kind of joke?"

"There's nothing much there."

"Nothing! Where are his *notes?*" Paul cried.

"Those envelopes with scribbles on them are all I've ever had," Mary said.

"Scribbles? You're saying he dictated *everything* to you?"

"You can see what his notes look like," Mary said.

"So how much of this new book is *his?*"

"Randal's name will be on it—I'll be the editor—"

"Editor! This book's got dozens of London details in it—details *Randal never saw!* You told me yourself he never went to museums, theaters—Johnson's house, Soane's house—"

"He never did," Mary said quietly. She was looking at him as if she expected something.

"Then *you* put them in the book!" Paul yelled. "You've been typing away up there, changing Randal Eliot's wonderful novels to suit yourself—and he's *dead!* He can't fight back!"

For a second Mary and Paul glared at each other— suddenly Paul's hands were around her throat, hot and hard. "Eat your dinner yourself!" he yelled; she shut her eyes, breathing his whiskey breath. "Live in your fancy house yourself! I'm living in *Randal Eliot's* house!" He let her go, and she almost fell. "The real Randal Eliot, not some secretary who thinks she can write like him!"

Paul slammed Mary's front door until the brass-faced

knocker clapped behind him, gunned his new car down Mary's driveway, and went to Randal's house to sit on the redwood bench in the dark garden.

Children on park swings kept up a constantly varied back-and-forth creaking. Now and then a car went by. The house next door was dark. "Rewriting *Randal Eliot!*" Paul said to nothing but a park light striking through the maple tree. "She dares to think I'll let her touch *his work!*"

A bird rustled in the grapevine on the side porch. When Paul looked up, the house that was Randal Eliot's stood against stars: dim gables, dark windows.

Mosquitoes were out after the rain; they drew blood from Paul, but he hardly felt the bites.

Mary had probably been with Beth—had Beth seen how crazy she was?

Should he call Beth and her brothers? Say: "Your father's death has affected your mother more than we . . ."

Damn mosquitoes. Paul slapped a couple. His empty stomach growled.

He went in. Halfway through the garage door, he stopped, staring at the faint shapes of a lawn mower and bushel baskets. "Nobody but me," he yelled in the dark. "No one can stop her but me."

"My God! There's nobody else!" Paul cried, going into the kitchen. The kitchen echoed his voice. "My God!"

"Swearing this evening?" Michele said, filling the kitchen doorway with her low-cut tank top and very short shorts. "I saw your car."

Paul sighed. "I'm hungry."

"Let's hope so."

"For food," Paul said. "First." He tried to smile.

"There's always pizza," Michele said. She looked in the old refrigerator. "And ice cream. And we could have a nice glass of iced tea?"

Paul didn't notice when she called for pizza. He ate it without tasting it, and tried to keep up with Michele's brittle repartee. He made love to her a time or two in Beth's unmade bed, but late at night when Michele was gone, he couldn't remember a thing about the evening except that the iced tea had tasted good. He went downstairs in the hot, still house and opened the freezer.

Michele had used all the ice.

Randal Eliot's old refrigerator took days to make ice cubes. Randal Eliot's fake leather chair stuck to Paul's back when he sat in the study. Randal Eliot's desk stood before him: a cheap, scarred oak box, its front corners stained and bare of varnish where Randal had poured his wine.

Tortured Life: A Biography of Randal Eliot by Paul Anderson.

Paul clenched his hands and beat them on the arms of Randal's fake leather chair. He went upstairs again and paced the upstairs hall.

Hannah picked up her phone, then held it farther away from her ear. "Take it *easy*," she said. "Paul!"

"What's the problem?"

"Butterfield called me in, gave me the old publish-or-perish ultimatum again—'You have taught at the university three years, and your publication record does not meet our standards'—when he *knows* I'm working hard on the book! So I waited awhile and then told him I'd been invited to Italy as a resident scholar. That certainly shut him up! Nobody in the department has ever had such a—"

"So what's the problem?"

"It's Mary! She's the problem!"

"She can't go with you?"

"She flew out of here last week—no warning—went somewhere—she won't say where, but I suppose she was with one of her children—left me with the whole damn English department coming to a party at our house and nothing ready—"

"She left you? What for?"

"You're not going to believe any of this. Mary came back last night, and she's gone absolutely crazy! She as much as admitted that she's changed Randal's new book he dictated to her—put stuff of her own in it! How do I know how much *she* wrote! And what if she goes around telling people? They'll start asking whether she's right, and how much of Randal's work is hers."

"Then you couldn't bring out your biography?"

"Right!"

Hannah was quiet for a moment, then she said, "Did she write part of his stuff?"

"What?"

"Is she telling the truth, maybe?"

"She's crazy! Randal Eliot's neuroses are in every line of his books! My whole biography is based on a very close textual study—"

"But could you be wrong?"

"Wrong? How could I be wrong? Do you think some little midwestern, middle-class woman with no college degree who raises her children and tends her garden and chitchats with her neighbors and does her housekeeping could write those novels? Randal was a genius!"

"Then where's she getting the new books, now that Randal's dead? First there was *The Host.* Now it's this *Prayer Wheel* you've been reading."

"God knows! She calls herself Randal's 'editor.'"

"Does the new one sound like Randal?"

"It's *magnificent.* The best thing he's done yet."

"What if she says she wrote part of it?"

"People will say she's crazy! But they'll *laugh* at my biography!"

"Can't you keep her from bringing out *Prayer Wheel* until your biography—"

"They'll say if she's insane, then everything she's told me about Randal might be *wrong!* Maybe my press won't even publish my book! Even if they do, it'll be a joke! I'm supposed to go to Italy and be the Big Joke Biographer on Lake Como? And my university *tenure's* based on my book!"

"M-m-m-m," Hannah said.

"My *book,* my *job,* my *home,* my *life*—crazy bitch! The crazy—"

"Paul—"

"Everything! She'll take everything!"

"Paul!"

"Dead!"

"Paul! Listen to—"

"She ought to be dead!"

"Listen! Now you just listen to me! I'm coming there just as soon as I can get away!"

"My whole life gone! Years of work! And what about Randal? She's trying to ruin *Randal!*"

"Wait! Don't you do a thing!"

"I'll do something!"

"Paul! You do what I *say!* Don't you *move* until I can get there! You do what I say. Don't you even *think*—"

Paul slammed the phone in its cradle.

36

Paul paced back and forth in Randal Eliot's house. He
hadn't slept much for most of a week. He hadn't even tried
to lie down after Michele left.

He got in his car and drove to the river.

Morning light gilded the thick brown currents running
high. Paul parked his car and walked to the middle of the
Main Street bridge.

The river in flood had smashed debris against the bridge
pilings; it rushed beneath him, carrying mud and leaves and
broken branches.

He got back in his car. There was a lonely road running
close to the river. He'd picnicked there with Mary once,
made love to her in a little grass-carpeted room fenced by
trees in spring darkness . . .

The river road was posted with a DANGER sign. Paul's car
pitched and tossed along ruts until, quite suddenly, the road
disappeared: it was lost, drowned in the river.

Paul sat for a while looking around him, watching the
dirty water carry a log past, turning it as it would turn a
body over and over.

Bark had been stripped from the log: it was as pale as

water-soaked flesh. The remains of a crooked branch jutted
from it like a bony arm. "Bitch," Paul said to no one. Then
he murmured, "No one but me."

Paul watched the log until it was out of sight.

He took the rutted road back to Main Street. The sun hurt
his eyes; he drove to Cedar Ridge, and knocked with the
brass-faced knocker—he'd run off without his house key.

"Come in," Mary said when she answered the door, her
words and voice so formal that—for a moment—he was the
English professor who had followed her that first evening
down a half flight of open stairs, looking at a deep-green
carpet and polished wood. The stereo was playing again in
the patio room; the garden was bright with flowers beyond
the windows.

"I'm making coffee," Mary said.

Paul was wearing a new shirt that matched his eyes. Blue
and earnest, they looked into her dark ones. "I came to say
I'm so sorry. I've said awful things I didn't mean. You were
hurt—I hope you can forgive me," he said. "And I came to
tell you some wonderful news—wonderful news for both of
us."

"I can't talk long," Mary said, turning away from him to
measure out coffee at the kitchen sink. "I'm going to Nora's
for lunch at eleven."

She didn't see his cold eyes. He kissed the nape of her
neck and said, "You look tired."

They sat at the patio table and said nothing about
Randal's books, or secretaries who thought they had written
those books. They talked about new chrysanthemums in the
oval flower bed. They admired birches they had planted and
named "the Three Graces": the slim trees swayed in sunshine on the lawn.

Paul poured the coffee and brought it on a tray. "I've just
had a telephone call from New York, and I came here—
wanted you to be the first to know. There's a place called the
Villa Christa on Lake Como in Italy, and they've invited me
there for a month, all expenses paid. I'll be one of the
resident scholars."

Mary glanced into his eyes, then watched cream swirling, a spiral in her cup. "Not for wives, I suppose."

"Yes. You'll be going, too. Spouses are included. And we leave day after tomorrow!"

"Wednesday!"

"Early. We fly to London, then to Milan Thursday morning. I know it's terribly short notice—probably I was second choice . . . maybe even third or fourth." Paul's voice had a humble tone. "All kinds of scholars are invited to live there, and other groups come and go for a few days—conferences, that kind of thing. I'll make important contacts."

"Yes," Mary said.

"And it's all due to Randal and you," Paul said. Mary didn't answer, so he went on: "Hannah may be driving over before we go, maybe tomorrow. She called and invited herself, and I told her we'd be busy—"

"She won't be a bother," Mary said.

"But there's the packing to do, and getting the house ready to leave . . ." Paul bent over Mary and kissed her cheek. "Another honeymoon for us." Mary closed her eyes and sat very still. "In Italy," Paul whispered into her dark hair. "You've always wanted to see Italy." He pulled her up to stand in his arms, and kissed her. "A honeymoon for us," he murmured.

"Yes," Mary said against his cheek. She slipped out of his arms and sighed. "I'll be late meeting Nora for lunch. I'd better go up and dress."

Paul listened to her footsteps go up the stairs and down the hall. He slammed his fist on the table and swore.

When Mary's car pulled out of the drive, Paul shut himself in her workroom to ransack it, closet shelf by closet shelf, file by file. In the bottom desk drawers, hidden under newspapers, he found heavy, black-bound journals.

He opened the top one. *In the Quarters* was written on the first page in Mary's neat handwriting. The next was *A Strange Girl.*

For Better Or Worse. Net Worth. The Host.

Black book after book, the first five novels were there—
Randal's novels in Mary's handwriting: books where the
story had been worked and reworked. He leafed through
every one.

"Shit!" Paul cried, and threw a heavy dictionary across
the workroom; it slammed against a wall and fell to the
carpet. "Shit!" Paul glared at the thick books. Randal's
name was nowhere on them.

August sun striped Nora's dining-room table and ran up
the wall to the Chariot Wheel coverlet. Nora's plump,
thoughtful face was lit from below, and both her arms were
around Mary. Mary had stopped crying. "Don't worry,"
Nora said. "I'll keep an eye on your house . . . send you
important mail . . ."

"You always have. And listened to my tales of woe, too."

"I keep thinking: poor Randal," Nora said. "He could
certainly *talk.*"

"And I could certainly *lie,*" Mary said. "Hiding and
lying—I've spent my life doing both. The children heard me
lie for years. I think that's the worst thing about it, for me."

"When I think of some of the foolish things I've said to
you . . ."

"It changes so much," Mary said. "Even after all these
years."

"Yes," Nora said, and was quiet for a while, thinking.
"You're still my old friend, but there's this world-class Mary
Quinn here at my table . . ."

"That's why I never told Paul."

"He likes his wives wifely?" Nora said.

"Every time I began to tell him, I saw myself as he would
see me: the competition, the one in the limelight." Mary
turned her rings around on her finger. "And now . . . there's
Michele. Of course there's Michele! Why wouldn't he want
someone young and pretty?"

"Just wait until he knows *you're* the writer he's worshiped
for years!"

"And he frightens me—that's the worst," Mary said. "When he's drunk, he's another man. I wonder now about his first wife."

Nora's face was somber. "Then why take him to Italy?"

"I want him to find out who I am in a place where he'll see the pleasures he'll have—the invitations and prizes, all the money he'll get for my biography . . . when he's happy, he's . . ." Mary's eyes were on her rings. "I suppose everyone—even you—thought I married him because he was younger and so handsome? Of course I did. But he loved my *writing*, my *work!* Can you imagine how that could be the greatest attraction of all . . . his love of my heart: my books?"

The two women sat silent for a moment or two in the sunny dining room.

"Well," Nora said, "you're already traveling first class in life—it's beginning. The rich and smart and influential will want *you*. They'll invite you and show you off!"

"'The knife is in the meat, and the drink is in the horn . . .'" The words of the ancient *Mabinogion* made Mary's dark eyes flash. "'And there is revelry in Arthur's hall.'"

"Revelry, indeed!" Nora cried, grinning. "On Lake Como!"

"'And none may enter but the son of a privileged country.'" Mary was smiling too, then her eyes narrowed. "'Or a craftsman with his craft.'"

"And you are *that*," Nora said. "'The craftsman with his craft.'"

"And if Paul finds out, and *understands* . . .'"

"I suppose the place will be full of people," Nora said. "But I wish you'd go alone."

"The place will be full of people," Mary said.

Nora shook her head. "I wish you'd go alone."

Paul paced Mary's study, picking his way through black-bound journals on the floor. He kicked one as he passed. It fell open to a page with half its lines crossed out and rewritten, and notes on plot and character in the margins . . . had Randal dictated all those changes? And who would ever know? He piled the journals in the drawers and covered them with newspapers again.

She'd tell everyone she'd written how much of those books? A quarter? Half? Randal was dead—he couldn't fight—and she was off yapping to Nora Gilden.

He paced the big room. If he had at least some of his close analysis ready to publish, maybe he could prove . . .

He swore. Mary was insane. He could tell everybody that—put her in some mental hospital, keep her quiet.

No time. No time. She'd be talking to everybody, going to Italy Thursday and talking—

There was a bottle of sleeping pills in a drawer under his winter shirts. He ground a dozen of them up with a spoon, mixed them with some instant coffee and water, and put them on a kitchen shelf Mary couldn't reach.

He'd been drinking most of the day. When he lay down on their bed for a moment, the fieldstone fireplace and green plants and white walls seemed to be circling him slowly, so he shut his eyes. She liked coffee for supper, and he usually made it. She'd be light to carry to her car . . .

Lying half drunk, he told himself not to have any more whiskey. He had one night and one chance—Hannah would come tomorrow. He saw the dark, lonely road running into the river, Mary's car half drowned, Mary turning over and over in swift-flowing water . . . the swollen river and a swollen body revolved in his head as the room revolved around him . . .

When Mary came home, Paul was drinking black coffee. He kissed her, and she smelled coffee mixed with whiskey. He sat with her in the living room and smiled, crossing his long legs, his eyes on the darkening garden. "In a couple of days we'll be in Italy! To celebrate, I'll get supper," he said.

"That would be nice." Mary looked tired. She went

upstairs to change her clothes and begin to fill Paul's suitcases. He left the kitchen every now and then to tell her what he wanted for the trip.

They ate in the patio room. Darkness beyond the windows was a black mirror for their candle flames. Paul smiled over his wineglass and asked if she remembered their first meal together in front of the fire. "The night when I brought flowers and Amana wine and stayed until one in the morning?"

Mary said she did. She wasn't eating much.

"Coffee?" he said.

"Maybe I shouldn't have any," she said. "I need sleep."

"Decaffeinated," Paul said.

"Thanks." Mary watched the reflection of candle flames as she stretched her arms and legs in the quiet room. *Italy*, she thought to herself, and smiled.

The doorbell rang. Mary started at the sound, and Paul swore in the kitchen. Something smashed on the floor.

Mary went to answer the bell, passing Paul as he reached for pieces of a broken cup.

"Hi!" Hannah said when she saw Mary. "Didn't want you two flying off without a good-bye and a bon voyage present!" She had two wine bottles under her arm. "Hi, big brother," she said to Paul, but he gave her no answer but a look as he went to get her suitcase from her car.

They made a quick supper for Hannah, and drank some of her wine. They talked about Italy. They talked about her public-relations clients. They talked about the town's flooded roads.

"I'm so tired," Mary said after a while. "You two will enjoy a private chat—I'll go to bed, if you don't mind. Your bed is ready," she said to Hannah. "Sleep as long as you like in the morning. Get a good rest."

They watched her climb the steps and go down the hall. The big bedroom's door clicked shut.

"I don't like *any* of this," Hannah said.

"Nothing's happened."

"Good."

"She's never trusted me," Paul hissed. "Never. Do you know what I found upstairs in her study? The first five Randal Eliot novels in *her writing* . . . words crossed out, paragraphs moved, plot notes in the margins—could he dictate all those changes in the few weeks she says it took before he went into the hospital? And those books have been there since we married! I never saw them. She never trusted me because I wanted to write about his mental illness—had to."

"You look awful," Hannah said. "You've been drinking."

"I haven't slept much," Paul said, rubbing his face.

"She's talking to friends? Saying she wrote part of the books?"

"How do I know?" Paul's voice was cold. He didn't meet Hannah's eyes.

"I suppose it's like living with a bomb?"

Paul pounded a fist on his knee. "She'll be out of the country for a month. At least she won't be talking to people here like some gibjabbering idiot."

"Gibbering?" Hannah said.

"Whatever," Paul said. "But she'll talk in Italy."

Hannah looked around her. "The last time I was here you were lovebirds."

"She changed to an enemy right before my eyes."

"Another woman?" Hannah said.

"What?" Paul said.

"Did she find out there was another woman, dear brother? You were always one for a little fun on the side."

Paul gave Hannah a sharp glance.

"I came here scared to death," she said. "I still am."

"Mary and I are as friendly as most married couples," Paul said. "Aren't we?"

"No. You're planning something." Hannah stared at Paul. Paul was silent.

"For God's sake," Hannah said in a low voice. "Do you think I don't know you? You think I don't remember Sandra?"

Paul got up and turned his back on her.

"I'm your sister. I owe you a lot, but I know you, and I'm the only one who can tell you, and I'm telling you—watch out. You drink. You lose your head. You can't count on another wife—"

"You're as crazy as Mary," Paul said. He didn't turn around.

"You can have it *all,"* Hannah said. "Money, this house—and if you don't want to teach, so what? If she says she's written part of those books, so what? You don't need a job—not for the rest of your life."

Paul swung around fast. "Be a gigolo? A crazy old lady's escort? A sort of . . . decoration?"

"Women are escorts and decorations—they do that all the time."

"Women can do it." Paul's voice was low and bitter. "I'm not going to do it. I'm a scholar. I've studied Randal Eliot's work for years—"

"You're a *fanatic.* So what are you going to do?"

Paul didn't answer.

"For God's sake." Hannah glared at him. His eyes were blue ice. "Let Mary do whatever she wants to . . . you can have it all. Don't ever forget that. You can have it *all."*

"Of course I won't forget," Paul said. "Don't I tell myself that all the time?"

Paul left Hannah at her door, undressed in the dark where Mary lay, and crept into bed. He held her tight, kissing her until at last she kissed him back. Her pillow was wet with tears.

37

THE PLANE TAXIED UNDER THE BLUE SKIES OF MILAN. ITALY!
Mary said to herself. Her face was flushed; her eyes sparkled.

Inside the airport a uniformed driver waited with a "Villa
Christa" sign. He didn't speak English; the only thing he
could say, it seemed, was "Mary Quinn."

"Paul Anderson. Resident scholar at the Villa Christa,"
Paul said, but the man said, "Mary Quinn."

"Mary Quinn. That *is* my name," Mary said; she glanced
at Paul and shrugged her shoulders. The man smiled and
bowed and wheeled their luggage to a limousine.

They drove for miles through Milan. At last the city
disappeared in slopes of oleander among olive and chestnut
trees. Villas faced a larkspur-blue lake. The mirrored snow
of the Alps, thousands of feet above, glimmered in that blue.

The limousine took narrow tunnels and honked around
blind curves. Watching the miles of Lombardy pass, Paul
said nothing to Mary, but his eyes gleamed with what he
saw. Then Lake Como lay before them. Mountains surrounded it, and a point of land thrust itself into it like a

boat's prow. Above the cream-white walls and red-tile roofs of the town, the Villa Christa crowned that point.

The driver signaled and private gates opened; he drove away from the town along a stone-walled road. High above them were terraced gardens, and then the villa's golden walls.

Mary had read about the Villa Christa. It stood on bloody ground. Twenty-five centuries of fighters—Celts, Romans, Guelphs and Ghibellines, German mercenaries, Sforzas, the French—had taken and retaken that point. When the limousine came to a stop before the door, Mary glanced at Paul and felt one more battle run a shiver down her back.

"Welcome to Italy!" A plump young man opened the limousine door and introduced himself as Hud Brewster, villa director. "I hope your flight from London was pleasant?"

Paul said it was very pleasant.

Mary stepped from the limousine to look at the villa's four-hundred-year-old facade. It was pale gold under its red roof. The same red ran up pilasters, divided the first and second stories, and warmed the windows above with rows of red shutters.

"Quite a drive from Milan," Paul said, following Mary and Hud through white French doors. "Must have been thirty miles." Mary glanced at him: he looked drawn and weary.

"Forty-seven," Hud said. His eyes had been on Mary since she arrived; now he walked the long, curving hall with her. Paul walked behind.

Tapestries, marble tables, gilded leather chairs, mirrors, and sconces looked tiny under the high ceiling of that hall. At the top of a wide flight of stairs was another corridor almost as large and long as the first. Hud opened a door to the glow of sunlight. "This is your suite," he said. "We've combined two scholars' rooms for you."

Each of the large rooms had its adjoining bath, a desk and typewriter, vases of flowers, chairs, and a large bed, but in one of them double doors stood open, and Mary gasped at the view: first the roofs of the town, then miles of rumpled blue lake, then slopes rising toward great mountains. When she stepped out on the balcony, she hung above that immense scene like a flying bird.

Hud and Paul had gone into the second room, but Mary stayed on the balcony to watch, far, far below, a black-and-white toy ferry leave its slip in a toy town. It spread a widening fan of ripples on the lake's silky blue.

I haven't inherited this, she said to herself, and felt her happiness spread like the ripples. *I haven't married it.* For a minute she was perfectly happy. *I've earned it for myself. It's mine.*

A man brought their luggage in. Another appeared with a tray of coffee and small cakes, a bouquet of roses nodding beside them.

"Make yourselves comfortable," Hud said, coming from the other room with Paul. "We'll see you at luncheon. Drinks on the terrace at twelve-thirty." He started to shut the door behind him, then put his head in again to say, "Tonight's quiet here, but tomorrow we've got about fifty U.S. literary agents and editors arriving for a weekend conference. They'll no doubt be interested in talking to you both."

"Agents and editors?" Paul said, but Hud was gone.

"Some coffee?" Mary asked Paul, and poured him a cup. Cream and sugar were in small silver urns; the cakes were scented with anise.

Mary carried her coffee into the second room. Paul's suitcases stood on racks there, and his coat was on the big bed. She began to hang his clothes in the closet, stopping for sips of coffee. The room had no balcony. When she looked out a window at the same beautiful view, she realized they inhabited an inside villa corner: she could see the balcony of their other room on its right-angled wall, clinging to the villa's yellow face like a barnacle on a ship.

As she looked, Paul came out on the balcony. She heard him say to himself, "Agents. Editors," and then: "My God."

Paul left the balcony to sit in a chair and rub his tired eyes.

She dares to think I'll let her touch his work . . . nobody can stop her but me. He wished he could sleep. A clock ticked on a table by the bed. He heard Mary unlatch one of his suitcases in the next room.

He got up to look through the "Information for Scholars-in-Residence" brochure on a dresser: "Health Problems . . . Library . . . Mail . . . Laundry and Pressing . . . Hairdresser . . . Keys to Villa Gates . . . Ringing for a *Cameriere* if Coffee or Tea Is Desired . . . Photocopying . . . Church Services . . ."

The brochure gave "suggested activities for spouses who would not be doing research or writing during their stay." The brochure said Mary could go on walking tours, shop, use the library, and there were short boat trips . . .

Paul squinted at Lake Como's expanse of late-morning blue, then went to the balcony again. He leaned out to look at a gravel road far beneath, winding below a wall that shored up the steep hill.

He opened the brochure again. A list of current resident scholars was enclosed. He tried to memorize the names—all men, all trailing their considerable credentials from around the world. University of Berlin . . . Imperial College, London . . . Yale . . . he paced the room, memorizing their names and universities, finding himself on the balcony again, looking at the hard road far below.

Mary came to the balcony door to tell him she'd unpacked his clothes, then started on her own suitcases in the room behind him. Paul sat on the balcony and looked at the brochure again: each resident scholar's wife was listed after the scholar's "Projected Work While at the Villa." Professor Crabbe was preparing a review of the role and future of the modern family. His wife was Ursula. Professor Dorn would work on "The Ancient Roots of Modern French Drama." His wife was Edith. Professor Albrecht was completing a novel about medieval France. His wife was Lucie. There was no Professor Paul Anderson on the list, with his wife Mary and his biography of Randal Eliot.

"I'm not on the villa list of resident scholars," Paul said, coming to watch Mary shake out clothes. The big bed lay between them. They seldom looked into each other's eyes, but their glances were often on that bed that shone with light from lake, mountains and sky.

"I was obviously a last-minute choice," Paul said.

"Perhaps," Mary said. She lifted an armful of clothes. "I'm going to find the ironing room Hud mentioned."

When the door clicked shut behind her, Paul went to the balcony again to look at the gravel road below: hard stone.

Dressed for luncheon, Paul and Mary went down the broad stairs and walked through parlors toward the sound of voices.

The large drawing room had painted panels, and so did the bar. A small group of people stood by the bar near an open French door. One of them, a distinguished-looking man with gray in his dark beard, came toward them with a smile. "I believe you're Paul and Mary Anderson?" he said. "I'm Dunne Faraday. Hud Brewster asked me to introduce you to the others here."

"Dunne Faraday." That famous name echoed in Paul's head as he shook hands with men and smiled at women. Dunne brought Mary a glass of red wine, and a martini for Paul.

Mary and Dunne were talking together now; Paul couldn't hear what they were saying in the hubbub of conversation—something about a Roman wedding. He waited on the group's edge for a while, then went out on a wide terrace to sip his drink alone. The cypresses, gardens, lake, and islands before him were glazed by hot sun that made his dull headache worse. Tables and chairs stood on expanses of gravel. Trees on a hill above stirred in the wind.

Paul went back inside. People were leaving the room now, so he followed them, glass in hand. His headache pounded. He was aware of every clock he passed.

In the ornate dining room there were cards at each place.

Paul saw that Hud Brewster had already seated Mary at the upper end of the table between himself and Faraday; they talked as they unfolded napkins.

Paul found his place card nearby and sat down.

"Hello," a middle-aged woman said. "I'm Edith Dorn." She leaned across Paul to the woman on his other side. "You haven't met Paul Henderson," she told her. "Ursula Crabbe," she said to Paul.

"Anderson," Paul said.

"Pardon?" said Ursula. She looked about forty, and was a plump brunette.

"Paul *Anderson*," Paul said.

"Oh—sorry!" Edith said.

Everyone was seated now. Mary talked to Dunne Faraday on one side of her, then Hud Brewster on the other. Her face was flushed and pretty under her short hair. What was she' saying? Paul strained to hear, but Edith was introducing him to blond, well-preserved Lucie Albrecht, who said, "You're from Nebraska?"

Paul said he was. Mary was talking about politics. Paul hardly noticed what he ate, or heard what the women were saying around him. When the meal was over, he tried to, catch Mary in the villa hall, but she walked away with Dunne Faraday.

Hud Brewster stopped beside Paul. They watched Mary and Dunne climb the stairs.

"I didn't know he'd be here," Paul said.

"He's the speaker for the conference," Hud said. "Last time he was here he brought his wife, but she died just after his last novel came out and he won the Pulitzer."

Paul followed Mary and Faraday when he could, and heard their voices in the upstairs library. He thought of joining them under the library's beamed and painted ceiling, but they were intent upon what sounded like a discussion of Dunne's latest book. They never saw him pass.

Paul went downstairs again.

Edith Dorn met him in the hall beside a red marble table. "Have you walked to the top of the hill yet?" she asked him.

"A thousand-year-old ruined fortress, and what a view from the top! Hundreds of feet straight down to the lake!"

Paul looked exhausted, she thought: he answered her as if he were in a dream. She watched through the French doors to see him take the road away from the villa, uphill through trees.

38

WHEN PAUL CAME BACK FROM THE FORTRESS, MARY WAS
asleep; the balcony's light was closed away with heavy
curtains and the room was dim.

Paul lay down on the bed in the other room.

Mary had put his little traveling clock on the table nearby;
he listened to it tick. The sound was as sharp as a bird's
beak, chipping away the little time he had left, second by
second.

He couldn't lie still. He couldn't rest. Both large rooms
had doors to the hall; he let himself out softly and explored
the villa library. He walked through gardens, terrace by
terrace, then wandered in the greenhouses, or listened to
water in a stone grotto drip like the ticking of a clock.

At last summer dusk began to close away views of
mountains and lake. Servants lit lamps in the villa's parlors,
where curio cabinets glowed. Lake Como changed from
deep blue to lavender to purple.

Mary woke and found herself alone. She bathed drowsily,
dreamily, then stood on the balcony for a while, watching
the mountains change as night came on. *Lovely,* she said to

herself, *lovely,* and thought of Paris nights with Paul . . . London nights . . . lost and gone, perhaps, like the "beautiful angels" the man had mourned at Chartres.

She sighed, roaming the red-and-gold rooms, then stopped before her leather traveling set on the dressing table. The brass lion's head on the cosmetic case showed its sharp, shining teeth. Michael, Beth, Don, and Jay smiled from one picture frame, and now their happy eyes seemed different. How many years had they smiled at her and known they were looking at the novelist Mary Quinn? Across from their picture was a photograph of her Cedar Ridge house.

Soft rugs. Sunset light. Expensive scent, a red silk dress. When Mary was ready for dinner, she stood a long time on the balcony, wind blowing her rustling skirt. She was so high that clouds drifted past her in flattened shreds almost within reach.

Lights had begun to string a chain of stars along the shore. Mary gripped the balcony rail and took a deep breath of that air. Her rings caught the last light and flashed. *You'll get used to being famous.* Mary laughed and leaned far out from her balcony, so that Paul, coming into the room, held his breath, walked softly toward her, then looked down at cars passing along the stony road beneath.

The villa's great parlors, gold and white, held a grand piano, carved wood, shining cushions, softly glowing lamps. Sunset light flooded through the drawing room's terrace doors. "I see you already have your glass of wine," Dunne Faraday said, coming to Mary. Paul was talking to Ray Dorn.

Mary and Dunne walked into the golden light of the terrace. "How long will you be here?" Mary asked him.

"Two weeks," Dunne said. He smiled at Lucie Albrecht and she smiled back: he looked distinguished in his well-cut tuxedo, his black beard streaked with gray.

They stood alone at the end of the terrace. "It's an honor

to meet a Pulitzer Prize winner," Mary said. She smiled, then looked away over black fingers of cypress trees to a misty lake.

"You'll soon be one yourself, I suspect," Dunne said.

Mary turned to stare at him.

"Hud Brewster told me—no one else," Dunne said in a low voice. "I'm here alone, so it's easy for me to . . . what? Be your guardian angel?" He smiled. "Hud can't do it, of course. Your agent called—she said she was worried about you."

Mary's eyes were still on his face; suddenly they looked beyond him, and he turned. Paul was coming from the drawing room.

"Would you like another glass of wine?" Paul asked Mary.

Mary said she didn't, thanks. Dunne smiled at Paul. "I don't believe I know what your field is," he said to him.

"I teach American literature. I have a biography of Randal Eliot coming out next year."

There was only the smallest lapse of time before Dunne said, "Ah. Of course."

Paul said, "I'm afraid they don't have my name on the villa's list yet."

Mary took Paul's arm. "I believe they're going in to dinner," she said.

The three of them walked to the dining room. Long and narrow, it was lit by crystal chandeliers and filled with the scent of the roses massed on the table. The place cards put Mary and Paul together.

Mary sat down, unfolded her napkin, and watched thick vegetable soup being ladled into her gold-rimmed soup plate. "Minestrone, of course," Hud told Mary from across the roses. "Known all over the world now, but it came from Lombardy."

For a moment Mary saw canned minestrone soup, the kitchen where she had dished it up so many times: six bowls on her parents' dining-room table, Michael and Beth and Don and Jay passing sandwiches . . . scraping plates into the garbage, bringing in wash from the clothesline . . .

Roses were reflected in the polished table. When Mary put down her soup spoon, a waiter set a plate of butter-glazed fish before her. "There you have *filetti di pesce persico,*" Hud told Mary. "Fresh caught. Our cook's from Milan."

Dunne said, "The conference is checking in."

"They may not all be down to breakfast," Hud said. "But you'll see most of them at lunch."

Paul ate hardly anything. He said he wasn't hungry.

After dinner Paul met Wilhelm Albrecht and Walter Crabbe. Crabbe, balding and fat, began to describe the failure of the nuclear family. Ursula Crabbe and Lucie Albrecht sat beside their husbands and smiled at Paul.

Paul could see Mary in the warm light of the drawing room, talking with Dunne Faraday. Her silk dress glowed against a white wall, a gold chair. Paul watched until he saw Dunne cross the room, then went in.

"I'm going to bed," Paul said to Mary. His blue eyes were expressionless; he looked like a handsome mannequin displaying a tuxedo, Mary thought. "How about an early-morning walk to the top of the hill?" he said. "You won't believe the view."

Mary hesitated. "If you feel well enough," she said. "You look tired."

Paul turned away as Dunne came back, and disappeared into the shadowy hallway. "Paul's exhausted, and he's going to bed," Mary told Dunne.

"Are *you* tired?" Dunne asked Mary. "Or would you like a short walk straight downhill to see the town at night? We could have a drink in one of the little outdoor cafés."

"I'd like a short walk straight downhill," Mary said.

39

Y OU'D BETTER TAKE MY ARM," DUNNE SAID TO MARY. "I'VE
got a flashlight, but these steps are so old they've almost
forgotten their way down." The beam of light showed stone
steps that turned corners and stopped at landings; lake water
twinkled with moonlight below. Then the stairs grew narrow and steep, like a tunnel lined with trees. Mary felt the
dark touch of their leaves as she held her long red skirt out
of the way with one hand. Dunne held her other hand, her
bare arm through his warm one.

At last the town appeared around a last corner; they
descended its broad stairs that were hollowed by centuries
of footsteps. Lanterns shone overhead among shaggy,
flower-banked balconies; the dark doors of shops stood at
right angles to the stairs. Far ahead there were cafés brightly
lit, and people strolling under stars.

When they came to a sidewalk café, Dunne found a table
and pulled out a chair for Mary. Mary sat down in the
murmur of conversation from other tables. A soft night
wind smelled of sun-warmed stone and food.

"Do you like rosé?" Dunne asked. "There's a nice local
wine: Chiaretto, from Lake Garda."

Mary said she did, and when it came, they raised their glasses to each other and smiled. "To writers," Dunne said.

"All of us," Mary said; wind from the lake ruffled her hair.

"I admire the end of your *For Better or Worse*," Dunne said. "The wife escapes her husband and dreams of being independent, and yet her new lover's sure he's going to own her. Did you plan that, or did it just happen?"

Mary caught her breath and stared at him.

"A stupid question?" Dunne said.

"No," Mary said. "But it's the first question I've ever been asked about *my* work: why did *I* end the book that way."

Dunne looked startled. "I keep forgetting you're a 'new author.'" He stared at her. "It's hard to imagine—I can't imagine—having your books read and reviewed and admired for years, yet never being able to say: *those books are mine.*"

"For more than twenty years," Mary said.

Both were silent a minute or two, sipping their wine.

"That last scene *was* a surprise to me," Mary said. "But you know how it is: the hard work and the great pleasure you get, now and then, if you can make your readers feel exactly what you want them to feel, and nothing else."

"You did."

"Isn't it the 'nothing else' that's the hard work?" Mary said. "Pleasures take care of themselves."

Dunne laughed, and they looked around them at narrow streets half-roofed with balconies, shutters open against stucco walls, and—here and there through gaps—the sparkle of stars and water.

A couple passed by, looking at the woman in the long red dress drinking wine, and the man across from her, splendid in his tuxedo. "Pleasures," Dunne said, raising his glass, and they drank to that.

Paul hung up his tuxedo, paced the two big rooms, then set his clock for four in the morning and went to bed in the balcony room.

The moon climbed through the rectangles of the balcony's French door and rose slowly through his fretting mind that remembered his father's farm, baked and cracked with heat, and the old frame house he'd lived in with Sandra and her yapping dogs. When she sold a puppy they could buy food . . . the smell of that house! It had been in his food and his clothes, and he had stayed up all night trying to finish his thesis, drinking, drinking, until Sandra had nagged him that last time, and he hit her—she had gone sprawling downstairs, making such heavy sounds, shaking the house—he had wondered, living it over and over again in his head, how a small woman could make those sounds, falling. She was quiet after that, and never spoke a word of blame, or any word at all. Year after year she sat in her neat room along a hall of neat rooms in a big building near Boston.

Paul cried out and sat up in bed. Far aloft now, the moon glowed above mountains and lake.

Midnight. Paul put on jeans and a shirt and sneakers. He paced back and forth, back and forth. Where was Mary? Most of the scholars must be in bed. She had napped all afternoon . . . she hadn't talked to anybody . . .

Paul swore. He wanted a drink. One drink. He shouldn't drink more than one. He went down to the bar.

A few lamps glowed in the big, empty drawing room. There were no servants in sight. Finally a man came through a swinging door, and seemed to understand when Paul said, "American whiskey." The man brought a bottle, set a glass beside it on the bar, bowed, and disappeared.

Paul went through French doors to the terrace. Alone under stars, he drank whiskey and whispered to Randal Eliot: "To the fame you deserve—and I'll see you have it. By God, I will." Randal's greatness had made his job safe, given him a book, brought him to Paris and London and a moonlit terrace on Lake Como. Paul raised his glass to the geniuses of the world, and their friends who had fought for them. Alone in the scented air of the villa gardens, Paul laughed aloud.

* * *

Dunne and Mary left the café when lights were turned off and a waiter began to stack chairs. They strolled along the waterfront while Dunne described his problems with his first novel, *Canterbury*. Silver-edged waves slapped boats at anchor. Mary answered questions about her books—her books! *"I* read for months about the World War Two years for *my* second book . . . and *I* rewrote Faulkner's bear hunt . . ."

"Yes," Dunne said, "I've done that, too—taken a scene from somebody else's book, broken it down, used the meat of it, the feel of it."

Mary's eyes shone. "Like the Navaho weavers—did you know that when they got blankets from the white man, they unraveled them to use the thread on their own looms?"

"Wonderful," Dunne said. "That's it. Somebody else's thread in your own pattern."

The town grew still as they walked its stone streets. Mary hardly saw moonlight that spread shadows of iron grillwork before them—for the first time in twenty years she was a writer; Dunne had read her books, and she had read his.

A cat licking its silvery paws in a doorway watched them go by, so intent on what they were sharing that they seldom looked at anything but each other. Hour after hour they sat on a stone wall or bench, then rose to walk again, asking, comparing, quoting, arguing.

The moon disappeared. Fog came like smoke from the lake, rising from the wharves to the streets to the steps uphill to the villa, the woods, the fortress in ruins. At last it snuffed out pale lamps and beaded Dunne's tuxedo and Mary's dress with pearl.

"Fog," Dunne said.

"Yes," Mary said, laughing. "We've been in it for half an hour."

Dunne's voice was sheepish. "Didn't notice," he said, and turned on his flashlight to look at his watch. "It's almost dawn."

"I slept so much yesterday that I'm not tired, but you must be," Mary said.

"We'll find our way back and sleep until noon," Dunne said. "Hang the Do Not Disturb sign on your door, and they won't." He took his jacket off and put it around Mary; the black wool was damp with mist. "You have a telephone—it's in the room with the balcony."

Fog climbed the stairs with them, swirling in their flashlight's thin beam.

Mist shrouded the road below the villa and blotted out gardens, terrace by terrace. Wisps of it snaked through privet and water-beaded fern to breathe cold wetness on the back of Paul's neck. He sat with his head on his arms at a terrace table; when he woke and looked up, he thought he was in another clammy, clinging dream.

But the terrace was solid under his feet. He could see lamplight almost drowned in mist, and walked unsteadily toward it. One of the drawing room's French doors had been left open; he went in.

Silence of great rooms, empty chairs, and high ceilings met him—rooms where editors and agents would question Mary tomorrow: "Will you be editing any more of Randal's books?" And she would say . . .

Rage and whiskey made him dizzy for a moment.

A few dim wall sconces lit his way to the stairs.

Mary would be asleep where a balcony waited, high above a gravel road's hard stone.

She wouldn't hear his key in the lock. He went down the hall past the door to the balcony room and softly let himself into the other.

The room was dark. So was the room next door. Now there was no traffic on the road below: how still it was. He could hear the night noises of insects in the gardens below his window. Softly, softly he went through the connecting door.

He could barely see a typewriter, a desk, chairs. The bathroom off that room was dark. He crept to the bed, thinking of nothing but her in his arms, small, light, hurled over the balcony rail—

His hands, exploring the bed, found an empty expanse of sheets, neatly turned down by the maids.

Not there! She wasn't there—he swore and gritted his teeth, then whirled—there was a man in the room with him—no. The man was only himself, reflected in a mirror.

Whiskey made his head spin. Paul stood swaying by the bed, one hand dimpling its sheets, and listened to the night that had a thousand insect voices. None of them told him anything.

Dunne and Mary had reached the villa road now. Gravel crunched beneath their feet in the courtyard.

"Good night," Dunne whispered in the dimly lit front hall. "We'll meet at lunch. Sleep well."

"Good night." Mary gave his jacket back and turned away as he started down the hall to his suite in another wing.

Mary was too wide awake to sleep; she went outdoors again and never saw Dunne look back, duck out of sight into a parlor, and watch Paul coming softly down the carpeted stairs to follow her.

Mary crossed the courtyard. Dawn light had begun to shine through mist. Her expensive dress clung to her with the dampness—shouldn't she change it? Then she laughed to herself, finding her way to the terrace. *Her money. Her dress. Her novels—every one.* She stood at a railing where immense trees, rooted deep in the terrace, leaned through space to disappear in white air.

Mary walked along the massive rock base of the villa. Cold stone breath oozed from grottoes cut into it. Paul would be asleep in the villa above, lying there tanned and warm . . .

She shivered, alone in the fog, and stepped into a stone room. Under the grotto ceiling the statue of a faun stared at nothing through the steady, idle sound of water falling.

Mary sighed and turned back to the villa, her head bowed, her damp dress dragging on stones.

Then she stopped to listen: there were footsteps coming

along the gravel. It was one of the many gardeners, probably, starting his work early.

But it was Paul who stepped out of the white air to face her. He wore a shirt and jeans and looked haggard, like a man walking in his sleep.

"Paul?" she said, as if she were waking him.

"I saw you from the stairs, going out the villa door."

"I couldn't sleep," Mary said.

"Then we'll take the walk I mentioned last night—go see the fortress up there," Paul said.

"So early?" Mary asked. She had smelled whiskey on him; she hesitated and half turned back to the villa.

"Come on," Paul said impatiently. Mary lifted her long skirts a little to follow him up the stairway to the road.

The gardens that surrounded them were lost in mist. Now and then the faint gray spire of a cypress rose against a wall of cloud.

Suddenly Paul said, "You'll ruin my life." His face seemed gray, like the fog.

Mary said, "I thought I could write in secret, help you—"

"Help me?" Paul cried.

"I helped you criticize the novels—didn't those ideas win you your book contract? We talked for hours in those days." Mary had tears in her eyes. "I'd never been able to talk about the novels with—"

"They'll all say you're insane! What'll that do to my biography? I won't get tenure! Where will I get another job? I worked to get off that farm and get my degree and help Hannah—"

"I was in love with you, and I thought you loved me," Mary said softly.

"Why can't you shut up!" Paul cried. "You want them to say you're crazy?"

They faced each other on the misty road before a statue of a dog and a stag. The stone hound had buried his teeth in the stag's haunch, but both had weathered to shapeless, writhing shapes and mossy hollows.

Paul turned his back to her, walked on. The road was lined with trees in silhouette: gray cutouts against white air. Mary watched Paul's bent head, his clenched fists. Then he turned on her. "My whole career will be a joke! They've invited me here to the villa because I'm writing the definitive biography of Randal Eliot!"

"No," Mary said. "You're here because you're my husband. You've lived with me for years and never found me in my books!"

Paul stared at her. *"Your* books!"

Mary said nothing.

"Your books! My God! Every word of every one of those books is *Randal*—his sickness, his genius, his magnificent—"

"Every word of those novels is mine."

Behind Mary a stone man sat under a roadside arch. Pliny the Younger's bearded face was tipped slightly, and one hand gripped the front of his stone toga as if, disturbed, he would rise in a moment and step from his niche.

Mary walked on with Paul behind her. In a few minutes the misty road led them to a flight of stairs and an arched opening. "You want to run all over telling everybody you've written parts of Randal's books!" Paul shouted. "Keep this up and you'll be in some institution—is that what you want? You want to ruin my *whole career*—make my biography of Randal a *joke?"*

When Mary stepped through the arched opening, she was in a room of broken walls and fog where her voice seemed smothered: "Your biography won't come out."

"Won't come out!" Paul's face was contorted. *"Won't come out!"*

"You can be glad it won't," Mary said calmly. "Your publisher will cancel the contract in a day or two when the newspapers carry stories about me."

"About *you?"* Paul cried. "A middle-aged midwestern *housewife*—four kids and fifty years old—a small-town, ordinary—who'll believe you? You're an *author?* You're a *genius?"* Paul flung his arms out, his face red with anger and scorn. "All you are is *crazy!"* His words were slurred, and when he yelled, spit hit her face.

An opening in the broken walls was filled with the faint light of coming dawn. Mary paused there, trailing the hem of her dress over the mossy threshold. "You can write my biography, I suppose," she said. "My agent says she can place it with a major press and make you a great deal of money—"

"Lies!" Paul's wild voice echoed among ruined walls. "You're telling them lies! They can't believe you're actually —don't they know—"

"They know," Mary said.

"I'm a resident scholar here! I've got Randal's biography coming out!"

"No," Mary said.

Suddenly the night mist on the hilltop was gone, blown away like a curtain. Early sunlight showed Mary the black, gaping fortress ruin behind her, and the low wall ahead. She didn't look at Paul; she was aware that he followed her as she walked across the grass. When she glanced over the wall, she looked down a sheer rock face to where, far below, lake water broke on the shore.

"I've decided not to come home for a while after I leave the villa," Mary said. "It will be better for you if I stay away. The publicity will die down, ultimately."

"You're going to run all over telling everybody this story? You won't listen to me? You're going to ruin my life and you don't even *care?"*

Mary looked far below, watching waves break. Their fingers of froth groped among the rocks, drew back. "I won't come back to Nebraska for a while. You'll be free to invite anyone you like to sleep with you, as you're in the habit of doing."

For a long moment there was no sound but the first scattered calls of birds. Then Mary heard the rising anger in Paul's drunken voice behind her: "So that's it. *That's* the reason you're trying to ruin my book and my job and my life—"

"I'm old." Mary's voice had a catch in it. "That's the reason. It's my fault—how could you love me?"

She swung around, tears in her eyes, moving too quickly for him to hide the look on his face.

She saw it. She saw his hands begin to lift . . .

She felt the distance below her to rocks hundreds of feet down.

40

IT HAPPENED SO FAST AND TOOK SO LONG—PAUL'S HANDS
rose so slowly. Instinct widened Mary's eyes, opened her
mouth and drove her—minutes seemed to pass—sidewise.

She watched the slow progress of Paul's hands upward
against green grass and ruined fortress walls. She seemed to
have all the time in the world to see the hate in Paul's face,
the sun on his thick, silvery hair, his blue eyes glazed with
light from the clearing sky, and she felt the heavy warmth of
him upon her in bed, the sweet kisses. She had time to think
how old she was, how handsome he was: "I'm Paul Anderson, new professor . . ."

She remembered firelight on their laughing faces under a
French clock even as she slowly, slowly moved sidewise
away from those rising hands, her silk dress caught and
snagged for a second on the wall behind her . . .

Paul's lips were drawn back from his teeth as his face
turned slowly and she saw Randal's face instead: *Leave me
'lone. You got a 'dea what it takes to write serious book?* She
opened a high kitchen cupboard and brought a journal
down to a still house . . . and her voice screamed all by
itself. Stone walls sent her scream back, a lonely, drawn-out

wail as she wrenched herself away from Paul with the force
of her heel against stone. Four young faces stared at her in a
New York hotel room. *And then you'll be the famous one.*

Her novels, her novels—they were all there as she fell
sidewise to the lawn, only grazed by Paul's hands as he
jerked them back. Then time returned, and she leapt to her
feet, yanked her long skirt out of her way, and ran—took the
fortress steps down two at a time—rounded the first bend in
the misty road—

A stone man in a niche seemed to half rise from his seat,
turning his face to Mary as she ran by. Dawn tinted the fog
pink at the next bend in the road; Mary listened for
footsteps on the gravel behind her, but heard only a plane
going over, and the first songs of birds. No one was behind
her when she looked back.

A pale woman in a red dress ran through mist that
thickened as she descended. Beside the road a stone hound
and a stone deer sparkled with water drops.

Then the villa lay below her, a shadow of itself. Mary kept
to the lawn, then tiptoed across the walk to a white French
door and crept in.

No one was there. Not a sound came to her through the
dim parlors and hall. She took the broad stairs to the suite,
ran into the balcony room, and shut—locked—bolted both
doors.

She stood with her back to one of them, panting and
weeping. A wild woman in the mirror on the opposite wall
had a face streaked with tears and hair plastered to her
forehead; Mary didn't recognize her. She was remembering
lake water that sent foaming fingers among rocks two
hundred feet down . . .

She held her breath, listening for any sound. The objects
around her seemed white as plaster, bleached by a horror
that had barely missed her to give her the sight of death far
below.

While she stood staring at nothing, time went on without
her; suddenly she was amazed to see sunlight on the rug. She
crept to look out a French door, but the sheer drop beyond

the balcony rail made her dizzy. Then she startled: the phone by the bed rang.

Was it Paul? Her hand reached for the phone, then drew back, as if his voice alone might kill her. But at last she answered it: "Hello?"

"Are you all right?" The voice was Dunne's.

"Yes." Mary's voice was only a whisper.

"Are you locked in?"

"Yes . . . I am. And the doors have bolts," she said. Dunne's voice was like a lifeline to the normal world; she felt as if she were inching along the sound of it, trembling.

"I saw you both at the fortress. I followed Paul. Do you want me to alert Hud?"

I saw you both at the fortress. Mary's hand shook, holding the telephone.

"I was too far away. I couldn't have . . ." Dunne's voice faltered and trailed away.

"Don't bother Hud," Mary said. "I'm all right."

"We could move you to another room. Or we could get you out of here completely."

"No." Mary's voice was stronger now. "I'm locked and bolted in, and there are people all around us."

"I'm sure you're exhausted. Can you sleep?"

"I . . . don't know."

"Your breakfast will come in a few minutes. I've been watching: Paul hasn't come back to the villa yet. You try to rest."

"Thank you," Mary whispered into the phone.

She stayed where she was, hardly breathing. Before long there were footsteps in the hall, along with a faint chink like the sound of silver on china, and a knock on her door.

"Breakfast," Mary said aloud. The commonplace word brought back a world of ordinary hunger, ordinary sunlight, the ordinary sound of a car going by on the gravel road below. There were ordinary people in the rooms around her, drinking their morning coffee. She took her tray from the man in the hall, then locked and bolted the door again, shut her eyes and took a deep breath.

She could rest. She could take a hot bath.

She stripped off her damp clothes. Her safe, familiar body was marvelous to her under hot water and soap. Numbness spread through her with the soothing heat. She was not thinking at all.

She washed her hair, blew it dry, shaped it. She sat down to her good breakfast. She was hungry. She was alive.

Paul had not followed Mary. He stood by the wall, his heart leaping in his chest, and watched her run from him, her red dress fading through the fortress door into mist.

Paul looked around him as if he had never seen the trees and grass and ruined walls before.

After a while he walked downhill toward town. Fog burned away with the morning sun. He passed chickens in a yard and stopped to stare at them.

Mary was insane. He watched the chickens and thought that Beth could put Mary somewhere—some mental hospital. A chicken came to peck at fence links and watch Paul, its stupid head on one side.

Suddenly Paul cried, "I'm a fool!" and turned to run back the way he had come, panting and sweating uphill—Mary would be talking to everyone at breakfast—he hurried to the dining room of the villa.

Mary wasn't there. No one looked at Paul in a strange way, or seemed to have talked to Mary. He stayed until everyone had eaten, and tried to eat a little himself. He couldn't swallow it. Hud Brewster stopped beside Paul. "More coffee?" Hud said.

Paul said no, and thanks, and went upstairs to the suite. Both the hall door and the connecting door to the balcony room were locked.

She was in there all right. She'd locked herself in. Paul lay down in the other room, covered his face with his hands, and saw her falling, smashed among rocks, a smear of red dress, dark hair . . . *My God,* he moaned. He'd been drunk. His crazy mind went on by itself to show him standing at the villa door, his face drawn with grief, telling a crowd: "She was discouraged—she couldn't find a publisher for her work, you know . . . a fine mind . . . devoted to Randal . . ." *My God.*

He hadn't hurt her. Paul got up to listen at Mary's door. Suddenly he began to throw his clothes into suitcases.

"Mary?" he called at the connecting door when he was packed. There was no answer. "Mary?"

He looked out his open window, and there she stood in a white robe by a balcony railing, her face turned away from him. "Mary!" he said sharply.

She stayed as she was, but she heard him, for her body stiffened.

"Are you all right?" Paul said. "I didn't know what I was doing—it's like a bad dream. I'd had too much to drink."

Mary said nothing.

"You're all right," Paul said. "That's all that matters. But we can't stay here. I'm going to talk to Hud—make plans. We'll go back to the States, have a good rest, you'll see. We can go visit Beth. I didn't mean to hurt you—you know that—I'd had too much to drink. We've been so upset, and it's my fault, I know. I promise—"

"I wouldn't talk to Hud if I were you," Mary said. "I'm tired. I'm going to sleep until dinner tonight." She had not turned her face to him. Now she disappeared.

Paul was left to look at the empty balcony, the sweep of garden slopes and cypress trees, and the blue lake.

Until dinner tonight, Paul said to himself. He had some time to plan. He went down to the villa office and asked for Hud. Mr. Brewster was gone but he would be back for luncheon, the secretary told Paul. Could she be of any help?

How could he arrange for the limousine to take them to the airport? Paul asked. They might have to return home— he wasn't sure. And did she have a schedule of flights? He listened to her explanations, wrote down information, and took the schedules away, keeping his manner and voice as calm as he could.

But once in his room, he threw himself on his bed and cried, "Christ!" They couldn't get out of the place until tomorrow—not unless he could make Mary hide with him at a hotel in town for the night, then leave . . . but she wouldn't go anywhere with him.

Paul swore. He lay and looked at the ceiling, but he saw Mary's eyes when she swung around at the wall, then ducked away from him . . . he groaned and shut his eyes. Exhaustion washed over him like waves over rocks.

Before luncheon was served, editors and agents gathered on the villa terrace with newspapers in their hands. "I suppose we'll be overrun with reporters?" one of them asked Hud Brewster.

"The villa doesn't allow reporters," Hud said. "This place is a fortress." He grinned. "Hasn't been taken often in the last thousand years."

"Mary Quinn arrived yesterday?" a Gerard editor asked.

"With her husband," Hud said. "They're resting. They'll probably be down for dinner tonight."

Editors and agents filled the terrace, glasses in their hands, talking of Mary Quinn, reading papers with headlines about "Liar for Love." They ate luncheon with discussions of the novels of Randal Eliot, and went to their afternoon meetings trying to guess what kind of advance Mary Quinn had been given for her new book.

On the hill above the villa, late-afternoon light threw the shadow of the ruined fortress almost as far as a low rock wall. The statue of Pliny the Younger watched a woods blurring with blue twilight haze. Bees still hovered in terraced flower beds, but the sound of the gardeners' hoes and shovels died away.

"What a place!" an editor said to an agent as they gathered on the terrace for drinks before dinner. "Paradise." The group of men turned to look at the view of gardens, cypresses, town, lake, and mountains.

Mary was not watching the lake or gardens; she had dressed for the evening, and stood before her mirror. Footsteps and voices went by her door. The villa was full;

someone laughed in the hall outside. She waited at her door a long time, listening.

When she stepped into the hall at last and turned her key in her lock, an elderly man came along. "Can you direct me to the library?" he asked her.

Mary walked with him down the long hall and around the corner. "I've just arrived," he told her. "William Lazaro, from the Philippines." They stopped by the open library door. "Your husband is a resident scholar?" He thought the woman looked a little dazed, as if she had recently awakened.

The woman hesitated a moment, her dark eyes thoughtful. "I'm a resident scholar. Mary Quinn."

Taken aback, he watched her turn away. "Thank you very much," he called after her.

Mary descended the stairs in her long, plain, white dress, her face so expressionless that she looked a bit bored, like a woman thinking of nothing more than a drink on the terrace, perhaps, or the evening meal.

The hall below had people in it—Mary saw that first. Then she was aware that all of them had seen her, and were coming toward her in a crowd.

Before they reached her, Hud Brewster stopped them with outstretched arms. He came alone to Mary and said, "The news of you is out, I'm afraid. In all the papers. I didn't want to disturb you—I knew you were tired."

Mary turned a blank face to him. "News?"

"That you're the author of Randal Eliot's books," Hud said. "Oh, and by the way, a telegram's come for your husband—"

"Mary Quinn!" a portly man said over Hud's shoulder. "This is such an honor!" He beamed. "I wonder if I might trouble you—" Now voices surrounded Mary. Talk of Randal Eliot and new novels and Mary Quinn filled the hall, entered the softly lit parlors, and was a subdued sound in the drawing room.

Lucie Albrecht leaned against the bar, surrounded by men

in tuxedos who wanted to talk about Mary Quinn. Then Lucie looked over their shoulders and said, "In fact, here she is."

Mary stood in the drawing-room doorway; she looked as if she were in a dream, Lucie thought. Men encircled her; she listened to them, her eyes moving from one animated face to another.

Tom Hocker didn't ask any questions. He stood at the edge of the group around Mary Quinn and looked at a four-hundred-year-old palace where dukes and cardinals and emperors had, no doubt, waited for dinner, too.

Tom got a glimpse of Mary over the shoulders of the crowd. She was short and very pale—she looked like she was sleepwalking, he thought: big black eyes staring at everybody. Maybe she wrote in a trance, if she were Randal Eliot—they said she was—it was a great publicity stunt.

Tom went for another drink, and came back to get closer to Mary Quinn. She was nice looking for fifty. Now and then she blinked, as if the lights were too bright; her long white dress had something shining at the neck of it, and rings sparkled when she twisted her hands together.

A housewife, the papers said. Never even held a job, just raised some children. Small town in Nebraska. What a story. What a con, if it weren't true. Mary's face was blank. Tom watched her closely, but never saw her lips move. Nobody, he thought, was asking about Mary Quinn's husband—an English professor, the newspapers said. A picture in one paper showed the two of them. He was good-looking—lots of light hair.

Tom looked around him for a good-looking man with light hair. A biography from Mary Quinn's husband—that's what the public would want. The Life of a Liar for Love. But where was the husband? He realized that the villa's resident scholars were easy to spot—they weren't clustered around Mary. Tom joined a group of them near the bar.

"I'm Tom Hocker of Doubletree Publishers," he said to a

bald man with a drink in his hand. "I believe you're a resident scholar? I'm interested in talking to Mary Quinn's husband. Can you point him out to me?"

"Walter Crabbe," Walter said, shaking Tom's hand. "I don't see Paul. He wasn't at lunch. Perhaps he went on some tour?"

Tom thanked him and left.

"Who was that?" Edith Dorn asked Walter.

"A Doubletree editor, wanting to talk to Paul."

"Paul looked rather sick at dinner last night," Edith said. "We all noticed it."

"Mary looks pale," Ursula said.

"Do you know what Paul told me at lunch yesterday?" Lucie asked. "He said he's writing a biography of *Randal Eliot.*"

"He what?" Edith said, her mouth open.

"He *did,*" Lucie said.

Edith and Lucie looked at each other for a moment. Then Edith said, "Maybe he was just protecting her. Until the news came out."

"Or maybe . . ." Lucie was watching Mary in the group of editors and agents. "Maybe he didn't *know?*"

They saw Dunne Faraday rescue Mary and take her out on the terrace.

"I'm afraid you're the news story of the month," Dunne said to Mary.

"Yes." Mary's voice was faint and low.

"They're being fairly civilized about it," he said. "When you go back home . . ." He shook his head.

Mary's dark eyes met his for an instant.

"You should stay over here a while," Dunne said. "If you would care to join a group of my friends and me, we'll be on a yacht in the Greek islands . . ." Hud Brewster interrupted him with a hand on his shoulder.

"We're so sorry about this!" Hud said to Mary. "I'm afraid you're the center of attention with this particular conference! If we'd scheduled the conference on Exchange Rate Theory and Practice, for instance, or the Leprosy

Research Symposium, or the group discussing Nitrogen-Fixing Tree Germ Plasm Resources, they'd have left you alone." He shrugged and went into the villa again.

People were standing in groups on the terrace. The bright colors of the women's dresses were comforting to Mary, and so was the ordinary conversation around her. She was vaguely aware that faces turned to her constantly; eyes sought hers. She heard her name.

"It's bound to be hard on you—like being born already grown up: a famous author, a new person," Dunne said. "I hope you slept well."

Mary looked up at him as they stood on the gravel. Her eyes were very dark, almost expressionless. "Yes," she said, "but I'm afraid you didn't."

"When I knew you were safe, I slept, too."

"I can't thank you enough. Knowing you were there . . ."

"I was worried," Dunne said. "I saw him follow you after we said good night, so I followed him, but . . ." He shrugged. "I wasn't close enough—didn't expect him to try—" He didn't finish the sentence; his face was somber. "You saved yourself, thank God."

"I ran."

"Both of you passed me, going down. I kept out of sight."

A soft breeze brought them the scent of the villa gardens. "I can't stay here," Mary said. "If I keep my doors locked, I'm safe, and there are always people nearby, but . . ." She shivered a little.

"It's simple," Dunne said. "Come to Greece."

41

PAUL HAD WAKED AN HOUR BEFORE DINNER, SWALLOWING,
blinking—then he leapt from bed and stared at a wall.

The clock ticked.

He'd had some sleep. He looked at himself in a mirror
and swore. He took a shower.

He unpacked his tuxedo again, and dressed carefully, then
looked for a while at his reflection in the mirror. He raised
his chin and said softly, compassionately, "I'm so sorry for
her. She's mourning Randal yet, and doesn't know what
she's saying . . ."

When he heard Mary's door open and shut, he waited a
while before he followed her down the wide stairs.

A man stepped forward as Paul descended. "Paul Anderson? How do you do? I'm Tom Hocker, executive editor of
Doubletree Publisher."

"I'm glad to meet you," Paul said, shaking his hand.

"Glad to be here with all the excitement," Tom said,
grinning at Paul. "Imagine it's a pleasure for you, seeing all
the press people coming into town—publicity never hurt a
book."

"Absolutely not," Paul said.

"And that's what I'd like to talk to you about. We're very interested in that biography of yours. I understand that you signed with Matrix Press for the initial one, but that should be no problem." Tom smiled.

"Doubletree has a fine reputation," Paul said.

"And there's no doubt you'll have a paperback, too—I'd say you'll make . . . six figures?"

"Yes," Paul said, staring at Tom. "At least."

"That's a conservative estimate. I hope we can talk more at dinner?"

"Of course," Paul said. *Six figures.* Thousands and thousands . . . he caught a glimpse of himself in one of the hall mirrors: Paul Anderson, biographer of Randal Eliot, walking in the Villa Christa with the executive editor of Doubletree.

Then he saw Mary. Dressed in white, she was with Dunne Faraday, and they were surrounded by men in tuxedos. What was she saying? She wasn't smiling. She didn't seem to be talking: she was listening to this man, then that. Paul knew she had seen him now—she gave him one glance, that was all.

So much money. "Six figures" became a pile of thousand-dollar bills in Paul's imagination as he went with Tom Hocker to the dining room. "Hope you don't mind sitting with us temporary folk tonight," Tom said, as they took their seats with other agents and editors. Mary came in late with Faraday, and they sat at the head table.

Paul watched Mary. She'd probably been telling the crowd her crazy story; that was the reason they hung around her. By now they'd have begun to see Paul Anderson's problem—perhaps Tom Hocker already knew it? The thought made Paul turn to him.

"Always wonderful food at the villa," Tom said. He wasn't looking at Paul with pity in his eyes; he was hungrily watching soup stream into his bowl from a silver ladle. He introduced Paul to others at the table: Paul tried to remember their agencies, their publishing companies, their names. "You and your wife are a couple of clever ones," a Kline and Bowditch editor told Paul, and Paul smiled and shrugged.

Tom Hocker spoke in a lowered voice about the fact that Paul's book would go into translations, of course. "And we have to think about possible movie options."

Paul nodded and smiled. He glanced now and then at important people surrounding him, watching him—he could see that. During dessert, Tom Hocker discussed signing contracts—if Paul might consider having Double-tree Publisher bring out the biography?

"Of course," Paul said. "I'm interested. That goes without saying. I've worked on the books for years—I've idolized Randal Eliot for years!"

Paul's words fell into a lull at the table, and an agent who had only joined them for dessert laughed. "You did better than that, Mr. Quinn! You married him!"

Every man around the table was smiling or laughing. Other tables looked their way. But someone at the head table began striking a goblet with a spoon. The room hushed.

An older man was on his feet, smiling over the wineglasses and coffee cups. "Since I have served you as the presiding officer of this conference, I'm entitled to the pleasure of introducing the 'new' author in our midst tonight." He paused and smiled at Mary beside him. She was looking at Paul.

"I doubt if there's a person here who hasn't read the newspapers this morning and said, 'How can it be?'" the older man went on. "'How can the magnificent voice we thought was a man's . . . the writer whom we thought was stilled forever by a sad and early death . . . be among us yet?'"

A roomful of people, comfortable after a good meal, sat nodding in agreement. To Paul, they looked like dolls—dolls wound up, heads stupidly bobbing.

"There are no television cameras or reporters here tonight, I'm glad to say," the man went on. "They'll descend soon enough. But tonight *we* are here: all of us who are connected in some way with the making of books. We can salute the author we thought we had lost forever, the author of *In the Quarters, A Strange Girl, For Better or Worse, Net Worth, The Host, Prayer Wheel, Life Thief,* and *Time to Burn*—Mary Quinn!"

Paul stared around him, his head ringing with the parade of book titles—the clapping hands—

Mary rose from her place.

"Thank you," Mary said in a faint voice. Her face was white, her eyes very wide and dark. Then, suddenly, she smiled. "And I mustn't forget to thank the Muse, that fickle woman who visits writers by night, by luck, in secret. One must not offend the Muse."

Again clapping filled the room.

"Now," the speaker said, "I would like to introduce Mary Quinn's husband, her biographer, the man behind the great writer we honor tonight!"

Paul came to his feet to face Mary, his napkin clutched before him. Clapping filled the room. If Paul's lips were moving, no one could hear what he said.

Hud Brewster tapped Paul on the shoulder as Paul walked into the drawing room with Tom Hocker. The crowd of agents and editors was gathered around Mary on the terrace: Paul could see them through the French doors.

"Pardon me," Hud said. "Sorry to interrupt you and Mr. Hocker, but I've been carrying around a telegram for you all afternoon." He handed the envelope to Paul. "And I should tell you," he said to Paul in a confidential tone, tapping a newspaper on a table nearby, "we were ready for this publicity coming out, naturally. There won't be reporters running you down here. Absolute privacy. We've been screening all the calls coming in—and they have been *coming in!*" He nodded to Tom and left.

"We can sit here," Tom said, waving at a couch.

Paul sat down, his eyes on the newspaper. It was an international edition in English. Mary's picture was on the front page, labeled "A Liar for Love."

Tom Hocker looked at it. "Nice phrase: 'A Liar for Love,'" he said. "Had you thought of it for your biography title?"

"Just let me interrupt for a minute . . ." a young man said, standing before them. "What a marvelous story! Back from the dead! Congratulations!" He shook Paul's hand.

"Now . . ." Tom said when they were alone again. "Perhaps we can come to an agreement while you're here—save time—get this biography out while Mary is in the news. You've got the manuscript well along?"

"Somewhat," Paul said.

"A kind of smokescreen until this news broke, right? Matrix Press won't bring it out—not now—and we can outbid them for the new book." He smiled. "How long will you need to turn it around?"

"Around?" Paul said, his voice sounding like a croak to him.

"You were making Randal Eliot the focus, obviously."

"I've . . ." Paul hesitated. "Yes. Of course."

"Interpreting the novels in terms of his life . . . his being insane at times . . . writing in a trance . . . dictating everything to Mary . . . that kind of thing?" Tom chuckled. "We won't need that."

Paul's eyes were on the newspaper picture of Mary.

"But what you've written so far *does* analyze Mary's writing *as* writing, doesn't it—close textual analysis—never mind what Randal's life was?" Tom asked. "I've been struck by Mary's *Alice in Wonderland* structures, for instance— I'm sure you've analyzed them. All through *In the Quarters,* for instance, and in her second novel, *A Strange Girl . . .*"

Paul remembered Mary's face glowing with excitement and pleasure as she said, *The old man is the Cheshire Cat—he tells the bride, "We're all mad here."*

Tom said, "Now, that's the kind of thing we need in the new biography."

"The new biography," Paul said.

"Mary Quinn's the hottest thing in the literary world right now, and everybody'll read your book if we hit the market right—the story's got *appeal!* The wife who saved her husband and his livelihood! The mother who educated her children and kept the roof over their heads and built up her husband's reputation! Three of her new novels coming out! The next winner of whatever prizes she fancies! *And . . ."*—he clapped Paul on the back—"who knows her better than you?"

"Yes," Paul said. "But if you'll excuse me now, I'm very tired. I think I'll turn in early."

"I'll be in Rome tomorrow," Tom said. "Shall we meet at breakfast the next morning?"

"Fine," Paul said. He shook Tom's hand and carried the newspaper away with him. When he reached the door, he looked back to see Mary sitting on a couch with a crowd of men around her. *We're all mad here.*

No one stopped him as he went to his room. Hunched in a chair, he read the newspaper account of Mary's life in a midwestern town, her children, her novels written to save the university position of her husband, Randal Eliot, who could never finish a book . . .

Paul didn't know how long he sat there. The villa grew still around him. At last he heard Mary's door open, close, and lock.

Paul crept downstairs then. The crowd was gone to bed. He went from room to half-lit room, finding newspapers on tables and couches. Some were American, some were in foreign languages, and Mary's picture looked up at him from them all. It was a picture he had taken: Mary against the wall of her house. The papers used only her head and shoulders; the dirt on her knees didn't show, or the trowel in her hand.

When he leaned on a table, he caught a soft crackle in his tuxedo pocket: the telegram. It was from Matrix Press: "Want contract immediately for bio of Mary Quinn. Letter follows."

Paul went upstairs again feeling nothing except that his collar was too tight and his tuxedo jacket was heavy.

He looked out his window.

The moon was coming up; its cold light bathed the balcony where a woman in a white dress stood. The moon struck sparks from her earrings and her necklace and his rings on her hand. Wind blew her skirts back and stirred her short hair, but she turned her face to it and to the moon. So close to him, she was set against the immense view: her averted face above the far-off mountains, her skirts blowing across half the town below.

Paul backed away from his window and sat on the bed, his eyes on his room's moonlit wall. He had stared so long at Mary that his eyes had recorded her all white against the black night. Now his eyes cast, for a moment, a sharp, reversed figure on white plaster: the dark shape of a woman silhouetted against brilliance.

He went to look at Mary again. She smoothed her hair with one sparkling hand, and he recognized that gesture: she had worn braids when he first saw her, braids wound around her head and sequined with snowflakes. Now, absent-mindedly, she felt for the heavy weight that was gone.

42

MARY WOKE TO BIRDSONG, AND THEN A TAPPING ON HER door. "Who is it?" she asked, and heard a strange voice. She took her breakfast tray from the man in the hall, and locked and bolted her door again, then telephoned the office to ask if she could have lunch in her room as well.

For a while she was aware of sounds in Paul's room. When he knocked softly at their connecting door, she sat still, sipping her coffee. She heard his hall door close and lock.

Mary put the manuscript of her new book on her desk. There was a soft tapping at her hall door. She sat where she was.

Soft breeze blew from a balcony. She forced herself to take her coffee there, sit down, look at the great distances below her slippered foot on the rail. She would not think of water among rocks. Trees, gardens, town roofs, lake, and mountains glowed in morning sunshine below Mary Quinn. Across the inner corner of the villa wing, Paul's window was shut and blank in the sun.

Paul heard the click of her typewriter when he came back to his room. Mary ate her breakfast without tasting it. When her luncheon tray came, she put it beside her and ate while she typed.

Hours passed, and she wasn't Mary Eliot or Mary Anderson or Mary Quinn, wife or mother, young or old, male or female. She was only tentacles of imagination that gathered details she did not know she knew. Where had she kept them, those useful things as sharp and clear as the glimpse of a queen shedding her armor?

Only when the light began to fade did she gaze around her and remember water foaming over rock, Paul's eyes full of hate, and the fact that she would have to go down to dinner.

"She's well, is she?" Edith asked Paul. They stood halfway down the villa's hall with before-dinner drinks in their hands.

"The publicity's difficult," Paul said. "She tries to avoid it, of course." He was watching Dunne Faraday at the foot of the stairs.

Then Mary appeared in a clinging, rose-scattered dress. She smiled as she saw Dunne, and they walked toward Paul and Edith. Mary gave Paul a single, brief look.

"Let me bring you a drink, Mary—red wine?" Dunne said.

"Please," Mary said.

Before Dunne could return with her glass, Mary and Paul were the center of a growing crowd.

"You're the husband?" a man said at Paul's elbow.

"Paul Anderson," Paul said, turning to face a thin man with sharp eyes.

"Mary's husband?" the man persisted.

"He's doing her biography," another man said, as if Paul weren't there.

Mary, standing beside Paul, smiled and took her glass of wine from Dunne. "A small-town, middle-aged midwestern housewife with four children—I'm too ordinary for a biography."

"Ah," one of the men said, "that's what makes you extraordinary! The great artist in disguise!"

Another man was looking at a newspaper in his hand. "You've taken years to write each book, I see. Justine Engel will be after you for a book a year from now on."

"She'll have to wait," Mary said crisply. "I'm too old to change my ways for money."

"Mr. Quinn?" A plump, cheerful man said to Paul.

"Anderson. Paul Anderson."

"Beg pardon—I'm Anthony Brampton, World One Publishers—saw your picture with her in the papers and it didn't say . . . glad to meet you." The man held out his hand and Paul shook it. "Quite a surprise you've given us—wonderful surprise. How did you keep it quiet so long?"

"It wasn't easy," Paul said.

Lucie Albrecht and Edith Dorn looked out at the terrace and the crowd. Lucie was watching Paul. "It can't be easy," she said to Edith Dorn.

"He wanders around the place alone—I saw him at the fortress after lunch," Edith said. "I like to go up there and read, but I didn't want to bother him; he stood at the wall a long time, looking down at the water."

"Imagine how it would be if *you* started to get all the attention, instead of Ray," Lucie said.

Edith raised her eyes to heaven for a moment, then turned to look at Paul and Mary. Sunset light shone on the handsome couple, one white-haired, one dark, surrounded by a chattering crowd.

Paul sat with Mary at the dinner table among the resident scholars. Walter Crabbe, his bald head gleaming, was at Paul's left; he held his knife in one hand, fork in the other, and said to Paul, "You teach?"

"English," Paul said.

"Mary teaches?" Crabbe asked, his eyes on the waiter deftly depositing broiled fish on his plate.

"She hasn't a college degree," Paul said.

Walter grunted.

Paul turned to Mary beside him and said softly, "Let me talk to you after dinner."

She didn't answer for a moment or two. He watched her hands pick up a knife, slice fish on her plate. They were small hands, wearing his rings. He had watched them work in kitchen and garden. They had given him pleasure in the dark . . . they had written . . .

She looked at him suddenly and saw his eyes on her hands. She put her hands in her lap then, and tugged at a finger. She dropped something in his tuxedo pocket. No one saw that small movement. She began cutting her fish again. Her left hand was bare.

Ursula Crabbe leaned across her husband to smile at Paul. "Will you be teaching next year?"

Paul said he would be. He slid his fingers into his pocket and felt the rings in it.

Paul turned to Mary. "I want you to tell me everything," he said in a low voice. "I was drunk. You know that."

"I told you everything," Mary said in a low voice.

"Let me read what you have of the new book," Paul whispered.

Mary didn't answer. Her arm touched Paul's now and then. He stole glances at her now and then.

Lucie had her eye on Paul. She said to Edith Dorn, "He must have felt like everybody was talking in a foreign language." She picked her fish apart, flake by flake. "Like one of those photographs where everybody's in color except one person in black and white."

"You think he really didn't know she wrote the books?" Edith said. "I can't figure it out."

Lucie said, "It's fascinating."

A waiter put a steak before Paul; it had a thin veil of hot vapor still rising from it, and glistened in its faintly pink juice.

Paul felt Mary's eyes on him. He turned to her.

"I'm going for a walk tonight," Mary said.

"You're inviting me?" Paul asked.

"No," Mary said, watching the waiter put steak before her.

Before she could turn away, Paul whispered, "I'll wait for you."

Mary was so close to Paul that he could see every hair in the white streak at her temple, and the quiver of her eyelashes. She never looked at him; she cut fat from her steak, her ringless left hand pressing her fork down.

Paul escaped the after-dinner conversations to walk the winding road to the fortress. He stayed by the low stone wall. Foaming water hundreds of feet below surged through great rocks, then retreated.

Darkness fell. After a while a shifting water-gleam along the shore was all Paul could see.

Mary's rings were in his pocket; he took them out and put them on his little finger. The diamond winked with starlight.

Night deepened around him where he sat on a stone bench. An animal or bird called from the forest below.

At last he groped his way back through the fortress door and along the weed-grown walls to the archway. The moon was rising, and it showed him the steps and dim road. A stone man in a niche wore silvery light on his knees. A stone dog and stag struggled together in their dark grove.

Conversation came from the villa's parlors, but Paul went upstairs without being seen and closed his door behind him. His bed had been turned down by the maids, but a notebook lay on his pillows.

Paul snatched it up. The new book! There were about a hundred pages, and the first two-thirds had been written on Mary's word processor; he knew her printer. But the last quarter had been typed—here at the villa? Where else would she have used a typewriter? He had heard that sound all day: the click of keys that started, stopped, then started again.

Paul turned on a lamp, sat down, and was lost at once in Randal Eliot's prose. No one ever seemed to be telling Randal Eliot's stories: they existed by themselves, like many-branched trees full of living things.

As he read, he heard a voice by a fire, in a garden . . . whispering love words in the dark. *Listen for me beyond the tangle of words.*

My God, Paul murmured now and then. He rocked back and forth a little, there on the edge of the bed, but never noticed his rocking, or the words he was murmuring over the words on the page.

43

Α FEW LAMPS WERE LIT IN THE LIBRARY AT THE VILLA Christa; their light glowed on the intricately carved beams above.

Paul could see the stairs from where he sat at a library table. He hadn't changed from his tuxedo. His eyes were on the door and the stairs.

The moon rode high in the sky now. He had stayed out of sight in the library since he'd finished reading her book, watching for Mary. Now, as Mary came upstairs, Paul caught, for a moment, a glimpse of her short, dark hair and rose-scattered dress.

He made no sound, following her on thick carpet.

"Mary," he said, and caught her arm, wincing as she gave a low cry and tried to pull away. "Don't," he whispered, "don't," and put his arms around her, held her close against his ruffled shirt. "Come into the library a moment." He took her hand, drew her along. "Come talk to me."

They passed shelves whose books, multicolored and rich, stood waiting in long rows. "I've read your new novel," Paul said to Mary. She sat at a table where the bust of a

Renaissance woman regarded the library with calm eyes. Paul stood across from her, a lamp edging his ruffles, his black broadcloth, his white hair.

Your new novel. Mary felt those words hang in the air. The book lay on the table between them.

"I haven't been working on it long," she said.

Your new novel. "Why didn't you tell me?" Paul said. "When we married. When I wanted to write the biography of *Randal Eliot.*"

Randal Eliot. Mary looked up at that name, at the sound of it as Paul said it. The tone and the words put Randal Eliot behind them, dead in his grave.

"You wouldn't have believed me," Mary said. "And when I tried to tell you, over and over again, you—" She didn't finish. Paul thought he saw her shiver. She ran her ringless hands up and down her bare arms.

"I was drunk," Paul said in a low, ashamed voice. "I was crazy with worry. I thought you were ruining my life—you were."

"I'd told you the truth."

"The truth? How am I supposed to know what the truth is when it comes from you?"

Mary's eyes sparkled suddenly, as if there were tears in them.

"I *know* I played around, cheated on you, but it wasn't *you,*" Paul said. "I thought you were somebody else. You lied to me—lied for years. I don't know the woman I married. Who are you?"

Mary said nothing.

Paul picked up the book before him. "You wrote part of this here at the villa." His tone was flat: it was a statement of fact. "Every page has Randal's tone, Randal's voice." He dropped it on the table, a sharp sound.

"No one would have believed me," she said. "I had to help Randal, but when he was gone and I tried to sell *my own books . . .*"

"Why didn't you tell me?" Paul said.

"You?" Mary's voice startled him: it was low and bitter and carried the whole freight of their years together—Paul saw them in one long, unwinding reel. "You loved *Randal*," she said. "As you say, you didn't put your rings on *my* finger."

Paul started around the table toward her; she rose at once and turned toward the door, then stopped. "You only saw *Randal* in every one of the books. You married *him*," she said, then gave a low laugh. "And you weren't faithful to him."

Paul was behind her as she turned to go; he stopped her and pulled her into his arms. "Yes," he said. "I married Randal, even if I didn't know it. I wanted to get as close to him as I could."

Mary, jammed against Paul's ruffled shirt, kept her head down and her hands against his chest. "And I did," Paul said, whispering into her hair. "By God, I did! I'm a fanatic. I told you long ago—*I* didn't lie. I worship the writer of those books."

He knew what his words had done: Italy was gone. Both of them had traveled back to firelight, to talk of Randal, Randal, Randal . . .

And Mary sighed. Then she gave a small laugh. "I asked you once: *What would you do if Randal were here?*"

Paul was quiet for a moment, holding her. Then he let her go and stood with his back to a shelf of books.

"What did I say?" Paul's voice was quiet and thoughtful. "I think I said I'd be in awe."

Mary made a small movement, but he went on: "I think I said I'd write the story of his life for him, and fight for him—for his reputation."

Mary stood very still now, her dark eyes on him.

Paul's voice was quiet, even matter-of-fact. "I think I said his genius was overpowering." He came close to Mary, snatched up her hands and put them against his face. She felt his warm lips on her palms; he murmured against them: "I said that if I ever met him, I'd be overcome."

He kissed her, a long kiss. Her eyes were closed. When she opened them, she looked dazed, then stepped out of his arms, snatched her book from the library table, and ran through the library door.

Paul followed her to the top of the steps, then stopped. The great hall below was full of people. They stood in groups watching Mary Quinn as she came down the villa's wide stair.

Paul went back to the library. Wasn't Mary's favorite perfume still in the room? He smiled a little, thinking of her kiss. *She loves me.*

Walking back and forth, he murmured, "Randal . . . Randal." The name brought Randal's house with it: Paul saw Randal's scarred desk, his battered recliner—

Paul stopped, grabbing a library-table edge, and heard Mary say: *This was my study* . . . remembered her standing in the doorway of the little room at the top of the stairs— a room he'd used for years as a storeroom filled with boxes and trash bags. *It was cozy,* Mary had said. *And it was mine.*

Paul sat down at the table. Of course! *Two* houses should be kept as author's houses now! *I love my own house!* Mary had said. For years he'd heard the faint tap-tap of Mary's typewriter across the hall, starting and stopping while he dozed in a big bed . . .

Paul smiled at the thought of that bed. She was angry, of course, but that bed waited for her with its satin sheets and its aura of a thousand nights with no light burning because she loved the dark. Let her write, book after book, then come to bed—

Paul began to pace the library again. There would be all the publicity. Talk-show hosts would ask: "When did you discover that your wife was Randal Eliot? . . . Is the lover in her latest book you?" Passing a glass-fronted bookcase, Paul stopped to look at his reflection there and straighten his tie.

He'd take care of the house and the correspondence:

there'd be requests to review books, go on television, do documentaries. And the money, for both of them!

Happiness made Paul's eyes gleam. "How could I be any happier?" he murmured to himself, and went downstairs to find Mary.

She wasn't in any of the rooms, or on the dimly lit terrace. He was conscious of glances as he passed small groups of people; they were curious about the husband of Mary Quinn, of course: her biographer.

Tom Hocker came downstairs as Paul entered the hall again. Paul said, "You're back from Rome."

"Ah," Tom Hocker said. "Paul. I'm glad to see you before I leave."

"You're leaving?" Paul said.

"I've got to get back to New York," Tom said.

Paul stared at him. "Do you plan to discuss the contract . . ."

"We can correspond about that later, perhaps," Tom said, taking a step away from Paul as if urgent business had a claim on him. "I'm told you haven't actually *written* anything, is that correct? And there's also the problem of an *unauthorized* biography. If Mary Quinn allows you access to her papers and so on . . ."

Paul was still staring at Tom, a confused look on his face. "She *is* my wife."

"Yes," Tom said. His eyes were on the big front doors, not on Paul. "You must discuss all this with her. I gather there may be difficulties—excuse me. I must catch Hud before he leaves—" Tom Hocker hurried away from Paul down the curving hallway.

People were watching. Paul forced himself to put a pleasant expression on his face, and went to the drawing-room bar. He told himself that if a Doubletree Publisher contract fell through, plenty of other publishing houses would be interested—there were editors all around him, having after-dinner drinks.

As if on cue, Anthony Brampton of World One Publishers

sat down with him on the terrace and said, "So you're going to be the biographer of Mary Quinn?"

Yellow glow from the drawing room fell on the terrace table where Paul had sat the first night, drinking whiskey and toasting Randal Eliot.

"That's right," Paul said.

The Kline and Bowditch editor joined them, and other agents and editors came up by ones and twos. Paul drank and laughed, a handsome figure on the half-lighted terrace, with the fortress hidden in massed trees above. "Of course, I've *lived* in both houses where Mary Quinn wrote her books," he said. He finished one drink and started on another. "I have a very good sense of her principal themes; we've discussed them for years. Mary's personality is very complex, of course. In the biography I deal with her years with Eliot, her children—I have voluminous notes. We stayed in the London flat where she had to stay alone, commit Randal to a mental ward—she's suffered so much . . . no one has any idea . . ."

The view from the terrace was lovely. Paul drank and talked, and the men in tuxedos listened to him, there in the summer night on Lake Como.

"I have known for years, of course, that she wrote the books," Paul said, feeling so expansive with the liquor and his joy that he thought he could sit there until dawn. "But she was loyal to Eliot's memory, so we have waited until now."

Paul lost track of the time. He spoke brilliantly, it seemed to him. And Mary had held him, kissed him . . . he watched for her throughout the evening.

At last only a few people were left on the terrace and in the lighted rooms.

Paul went upstairs, light-headed with whiskey. He found his keys in his pocket, along with the jingle of Mary's rings.

"Mary," he said softly to himself, letting himself into his

room. Then he tried his key in the connecting door to Mary's room.

The door opened.

She hadn't bolted it.

Ah, Paul breathed to himself. It was all right. She'd unbolted her door. He laughed softly. It was all right. He'd talk to her about the biography . . . talk to her . . . he felt dizzy, but he took a warm shower, and put Mary's rings on his finger. He'd have to go home and *write*—that was what he'd have to do . . . she'd unbolted her door . . .

He shut off his lights and went naked into her dark room, still feeling dizzy. Balcony doors were open, but the moon wasn't up, and he could hardly see Mary's bed. He groped carefully for it, found the foot of it, found the bedspread, found a smooth expanse of bedspread, found nothing at all but smooth, cool cloth.

He reached for a lamp, knocked it off, righted it, turned it on, and stood feeling naked and foolish by an empty bed.

She'd gone off for the evening somewhere, wasn't back yet.

Paul swore to himself. He'd wait for her, he told himself groggily, got in bed, and turned off the light.

She hadn't bolted her door. Lying there, Paul smiled and caught the faint scent of Mary's perfume in the sheets, ghostly because she wasn't there in the dark.

Half drunk and sleepy, he said aloud: "Money." So much money. A full professorship, with tenure—unless he didn't want to teach. He wouldn't need to work at all . . . but the faces of department people when they knew Randal Eliot was alive and he was her biographer!

"Mary," he murmured. Only half awake, he thought that he was back in the satin sheets of their bed at home, hearing the click of Mary's typewriter before dawn, a soft, steady sound across the hall.

He fell into a half dream where he held Mary, heard her voice . . .

* * *

Knuckles pounding on wood woke Paul. Moonlight fell through a balcony's French doors into the room. He struggled from the bed to the hall door, but the knocking came from somewhere else.

When he entered the other room, he heard only a faint rustle of paper at the door, and footsteps walking quickly away down the hall.

Foggy-headed, he fumbled for the light and reached for the piece of paper, but Mary's rings slid off his finger and rolled away; he crept after them across the rug.

It was an envelope that was stuck under the door; Paul ripped it open. A note in Mary's writing—Paul focused his eyes with an effort, seeing the word "good-bye," reading that Mary wouldn't be home for months . . . wouldn't authorize his biography of her or give him interviews . . . was arranging for a divorce . . .

The words were too black, too clear for a dream.

If he asked for money, the note said, or made the divorce difficult, or didn't leave her alone . . . Paul's hands were wet with sweat now, holding the letter . . . Dunne Faraday would go with her to court to describe what he had seen at the fortress one morning.

The last paragraph quivered before his eyes until he could hardly read it:

> The locks of my home have been changed.
>
> I have telephoned Nora Gilden and others, and they will supervise your removal to Randal's house. I imagine you will not live at Randal's house long, for you will need to begin your search for a new teaching position.
>
> I hope that you will be successful in your new life.
>
> Mary Quinn

Paul stood naked at the door, Mary's note trembling in his hand. Then he ran into Mary's room—turned on the lights—

There was nothing of hers left in that place, except her faint scent rising from tumbled sheets.

He threw open her closet doors and found nothing. Nothing of hers in the bath. Nothing at all.

The suite was only a suite in the Villa Christa, empty and still.

Far beyond the balcony a boat, pulling away from shore in the moonlight, spread a widening glitter over the face of the black water.